SEP - 2 2009

The Middle Ages Come W9-BWM-275

3 1170 00803 7883

The Dame Frevisse Medieval Mystery Novels
By Two-time Edgar® Award Nominee Margaret Frazer

"An exceptionally strong series . . . full of the richness of the fifteenth century, handled with the care it deserves."
—*Minneapolis Star Tribune*

THE SEMPSTER'S TALE

"What Frazer, a meticulous researcher, gets absolutely right in *The Sempster's Tale* are the attitudes of the characters."
—*Detroit Free Press*

"The daily historical details are well-done, the characters sharply drawn, and the reality of a Jew's precarious existence in an anti-Semitic world is sympathetically portrayed without easy resolution. Recommended."
—*Library Journal*

"As always, the author excels in historical detail . . . [She] takes the time to completely build the characters before delving into the mystery . . . this makes for a more complete novel. Highly recommended."
—*The Romance Reader's Connection*

"Highly recommended . . . A wonderful mystery that is abundantly enriched with fifteenth-century details. Medieval English society, culture, and politics come to life in Margaret Frazer's skillful application of vivid imagery, complex characterizations, and an intriguing plot."
—*BookLoons*

Also in the series

THE WIDOW'S TALE

A threat to king and country forces Dame Frevisse to choose where her loyalties lie . . .

"Action-packed . . . A terrific protagonist."
—*Midwest Book Review*

continued . . .

SEP - 9 200
the Benedic...   ...ing Us Murder.

THE HUNTER'S TALE

Dame Frevisse finds that the evil that men do sometimes lives after them . . .

"The book's charm lies in the author's meticulous research . . . The plot moves at a stately pace appropriate to its time and setting."   —*Publishers Weekly*

THE BASTARD'S TALE

Even in the charmed circle of medieval England's lavish royal court, no one is immune from murder . . .

"Frazer executes her . . . dramatic episode in fifteenth-century history with audacity and ingenuity."   —*Kirkus Reviews*

THE CLERK'S TALE

Dame Frevisse must find justice for the murder of an unjust man . . .

"As usual, Frazer vividly recreates the medieval world through meticulous historical detail [and] remarkable scholarship . . . A dramatic and surprising conclusion."   —*Publishers Weekly*

THE SQUIRE'S TALE

Dame Frevisse learns that even love can spawn anger, greed, and murder . . .

"Meticulous detail that speaks of trustworthy scholarship and a sympathetic imagination."   —*The New York Times*

THE REEVE'S TALE

Acting as village steward, Frevisse must tend to the sick—and track down a killer . . .

"A brilliantly realized vision of a typical medieval English village . . . Suspenseful from start to surprising conclusion . . . Another gem."   —*Publishers Weekly* (starred review)

THE MAIDEN'S TALE

In London for a visit, Frevisse finds that her wealthy cousin may have a deadly secret . . .

"Great fun for all lovers of history with their mystery."
—*Minneapolis Star Tribune*

THE PRIORESS' TALE

When the prioress lets her family stay at St. Frideswide's, the consequences are deadly . . .

"Will delight history buffs and mystery fans alike."
—*Murder Ink*

THE MURDERER'S TALE

Dame Frevisse's respite at Minster Lovell turns deadly when murder drops in . . .

"The period detail is lavish, and the characters are full-blooded."
—*Minneapolis Star Tribune*

THE BOY'S TALE

Two young boys seek refuge at St. Frideswide's—but there is no sanctuary from murder . . .

"Fast-paced . . . a surprise ending."
—*Affaire de Coeur*

THE BISHOP'S TALE

The murder of a mourner means another funeral, and possibly more . . .

"Some truly shocking scenes and psychological twists."
—*Mystery Loves Company*

THE OUTLAW'S TALE

Dame Frevisse meets a long-lost blood relative—but the blood may be on his hands . . .

"A tale well told, filled with intrigue and spiced with romance and rogues."
—*School Library Journal*

THE SERVANT'S TALE

*A troupe of actors at a nunnery is a harbinger of merriment—
or murder . . .*

"Excellently drawn . . . Very authentic . . . The essence of a truly
historical story is that the people should feel and believe according to their times. Margaret Frazer has accomplished this extra-
ordinarily well."
—Anne Perry

THE NOVICE'S TALE

*Among the nuns at St. Frideswide's were piety, peace, and a lit-
tle vial of poison . . .*

"Frazer uses her extensive knowledge of the period to create an
unusual plot . . . appealing characters and crisp writing."
—Los Angeles Times

Don't miss Margaret Frazer's mysteries featuring Joliffe:

A PLAY OF ISAAC
A PLAY OF DUX MORAUD
A PLAY OF KNAVES

The Dempster's Tale

Margaret Frazer

GLENVIEW PUBLIC LIBRARY
1930 Glenview Road
Glenview, IL 60025

BERKLEY PRIME CRIME, NEW YORK

THE BERKLEY PUBLISHING GROUP
Published by the Penguin Group
Penguin Group (USA) Inc.
375 Hudson Street, New York, New York 10014, USA
Penguin Group (Canada), 90 Eglinton Avenue East, Suite 700, Toronto, Ontario M4P 2Y3, Canada
(a division of Pearson Penguin Canada Inc.)
Penguin Group Ltd., 80 Strand, London WC2R 0RL, England
Penguin Group Ireland, 25 St. Stephen's Green, Dublin 2, Ireland (a division of Penguin Books Ltd.)
Penguin Group (Australia), 250 Camberwell Road, Camberwell, Victoria 3124, Australia
(a division of Pearson Australia Group Pty. Ltd.)
Penguin Books India Pvt. Ltd., 11 Community Centre, Panchsheel Park, New Delhi—110 017, India
Penguin Group (NZ), 67 Apollo Drive, Mairangi Bay, Auckland 1311, New Zealand
(a division of Pearson New Zealand Ltd.)
Penguin Books (South Africa) (Pty.) Ltd., 24 Sturdee Avenue, Rosebank, Johannesburg 2196,
South Africa

Penguin Books Ltd., Registered Offices: 80 Strand, London WC2R 0RL, England

This is a work of fiction. Names, characters, places, and incidents either are the product of the author's imagination or are used fictitiously, and any resemblance to actual persons, living or dead, business establishments, events, or locales is entirely coincidental. The publisher does not have any control over and does not assume any responsibility for author or third-party websites or their content.

THE SEMPSTER'S TALE

A Berkley Prime Crime Book / published by arrangement with the author

PRINTING HISTORY
Berkley Prime Crime hardcover edition / January 2006
Berkley Prime Crime mass-market edition / January 2007

Copyright © 2006 by Margaret Frazer.
The Edgar® name is a registered service mark of the Mystery Writers of America, Inc.
Cover art by Teresa Fasolino.
Cover design by Monica Benalcazar.

All rights reserved.
No part of this book may be reproduced, scanned, or distributed in any printed or electronic form without permission. Please do not participate in or encourage piracy of copyrighted materials in violation of the author's rights. Purchase only authorized editions.
For information, address: The Berkley Publishing Group,
a division of Penguin Group (USA) Inc.,
375 Hudson Street, New York, New York 10014.

ISBN: 978-0-425-21049-9

BERKLEY® PRIME CRIME
Berkley Prime Crime Books are published by The Berkley Publishing Group,
a division of Penguin Group (USA) Inc.,
375 Hudson Street, New York, New York 10014.
The name BERKLEY PRIME CRIME and the BERKLEY PRIME CRIME design
are trademarks belonging to Penguin Group (USA) Inc.

PRINTED IN THE UNITED STATES OF AMERICA

11 10 9 8 7 6 5 4 3 2

If you purchased this book without a cover, you should be aware that this book is stolen property. It was reported as "unsold and destroyed" to the publisher, and neither the author nor the publisher has received any payment for this "stripped book."

For Susan,
who suggested a story with someone like Daved in it
—and then reminded me until I did it.

Mordre wol out, certeyn, it wol nat faille . . .
The blood out crieth on youre cursed dede.

—GEOFFREY CHAUCER,
The Prioress' Tale

Chapter 1

The day was warm midsummer. At both front and back of the long chamber running the length of the narrow house on narrow Kerie Lane in London's heart the windows stood open, letting in the blackbird's bright singing from the small garden at the rear, while at the front were the talk and hurry of folk coming and going below the streetward window where the house thrust out above its lower floor and overhung the paved lane there.

It was a house much like the houses around it, with a shop in its narrow front toward the street and its kitchen at the back opening to the garden, with between kitchen and shop a steep wooden stair up to the first floor's parlor bedchamber, and an even steeper stair from there to the top floor under the bare-raftered slope of the roof, where children would have slept if there had been children, or the servants if there had been more than old Bette, whose arthritics kept her mostly to the kitchen from where, this afternoon, came a most promising smell of baking tansy cakes.

Breathing in the spicy smell of them, Anne smiled to herself over her embroidery frame beside the parlor's garden-ward window but did not pause in carefully setting the slightly twisted yellow silk thread in small, encroaching flat stitches along the outstretched wing of the St. John's eagle centered in a roundel that would, when done, be sewn to the green silk chasuble ordered by Lady Hungerford for a church in her patronage. The roundels with St. Luke's ox and St. Matthew's man were already done, and Anne was doing the eagle's last careful shading by way of small stitches laid over larger, couched ones, but there was still St. Mark's lion to do to complete the Apostles and then the chasuble itself to make, and it was wanted by St. Mary Magdalene's day. With just less than a month until then, Anne sewed steadily but even so kept an eye on Lucie on one side of her, embroidering a pillowbere's edge with a double-running stitch of red-dyed linen thread, and Jenet on her other side, plain-hemming a white towel, while Mary, having yesterday finished the belt she had been embroidering since Eastertide, read to them all from Hoccleve's *Regiment of Princes*. The three girls were as much her duty as Lady Hungerford's chasuble, their parents paying good pence for her to teach them reading, writing, plain reckoning, and skilled sewing. The reading, writing, and reckoning would be needed when they were London merchant's wives, and there was never harm in knowing how to sew; and if any of them proved well-handed at it, she could go on to teach them fine needlework by which they could earn their own living, should life come to that, as it had with her.

She put out a hand to stop Jenet's impatient tugging at yet another unwanted knot in her thread. Jenet put knots in thread more often than Anne had ever thought possible, but the girl's sigh as she let her sewing fall into her lap was so heavily discouraged that Anne took the sewing to herself, gently teased the knot loose with the needle's point, and took a few stitches along the hem before giving the work back with, "Just a few more inches and it's done." Jenet sighed again, without hope, and went on.

Today was the last of lessons before summer's two blessed months of break, and Anne meant that towel to go home, finished, with Jenet. She meant, too, to tell Jenet's mother that Jenet was skilled enough now at her reading and reckoning, that her writing was never likely to be better than it was, and that she should be set to learning some large-handed skill. Like ale-brewing. Anything except fine needle-work.

Anne took up her own needle again but paused to watch Lucie, who—unlike Jenet—was happy in her sewing, her stitches even, her counting of threads sure. The fine linen pillowbere was meant for her wedding bed, and with young ambition, she intended to embroider another after that and then bed-hangings. Anne's inward, smiling thought was that it was just as well she would be only fourteen come the autumn and not likely for marriage any time soon.

Mary read steadily, "Avarice is love immoderate Worldly riches for to have," in her clear voice, but Anne, beginning to sew again, listened past her to the blackbird in the garden. There had been a blackbird, though surely not this same one, in the garden all the years since she had moved here as Matthew's bride. Twelve years. Eight mostly happy ones as Matthew's wife. Four now as his childless widow, learning by broken fits and starts to be happy again. Her needlework and the blackbird had seen her through those first grief-blinded months after his death, just as her needlework had seen her into her marriage and the blackbird been part of her happy years. She had not been unduly surprised, aged twenty and a tailor's daughter, when her father had told her that he and Matthew Blakhall had agreed together on her marriage. She had only somewhat known Master Blakhall, ten years older than herself, a well-formed, well-spoken man, and a tailor like her father, but she was willing to her father's choice, had only asked for chance to talk with him before she accepted, wanting to know something of Matthew's mind, and was pleased when he told her that he wanted a wife who would partner with him in his work—that he had seen her needlework and thought that together they could move from his plain tailoring to the richer business of church vestments. Presently he had to hire out the embroidery that enriched the garments; if all the work stayed in his hands, the profit would be the greater.

Anne had liked the thought of that, had liked Matthew, too. They had married, and he had set to teaching her like an apprentice. It helped that she already knew how to make the plain chemises and shirts and veils that any woman could do, but Matthew had taught her the making of the deep-pleated tunics, close-fitted doublets, many-yarded gowns with trailing skirts, and the difficult hanging sleeves now well into fashion. He had lessoned her in judging all the sorts of cloth there were, including which were best used for what and what could be used almost as well if a customer could not afford the best; and, not least, how to deal with the drapers and mercers from whom both cloth and thread were bought, and with the silkwomen who could provide her directly with the best silk thread to be used for her embroidery.

Besides all that, he had hired Mistress Shaw, an older woman of the Broiderers' Guild, to teach her the embroidery skills of gold and silver thread that required such a delicacy and certainty of eye and hand that, "In not less than five years will you have it right, no," Mistress Shaw had assured her—and been right.

Their marriage had been six years old and they were comfortable with each other when Matthew had stood here in their parlor one afternoon silently studying her almost-finished work on a priest's stole—a pattern of vines and grapes in greens and purple and gold on tartaire silk, for the first time all her own work—then looked up from it to ask quite simply, as if asking her what she thought of the weather, "Would you care to become a femme sole?"

Anne had stared at him. To be a femme sole was to be a woman legally able to act in her own right in all her business dealings, with herself rather than her husband answerable under the law for all she did; and her answer had come slowly and as a question. "Why?"

Matthew had smiled at her. He had had a wonderful smile. "Because you are good enough at your embroidery that it would be shame, should aught happen to me, for you to have to work for someone else."

Such was the love that had grown between them since their marriage that she had felt ill at even thought of something happening to him, but she had been neither so young nor so foolish as not to know that things happened to people, no matter how loved, and she had taken hold of his hand, to feel him warm and there while she found her way through her thoughts before she said, "Mistress Shaw has said she'll see me into the Broiderers' Guild. Then, as femme sole, I could work in my own name." And had smiled at him with sudden mischief and asked, "What if then someone offers to pay me more for my work than you do?"

Matthew had thrown back his head with laughter and caught her into his arms and said, "Then I shall become a man of ease and live off your earnings instead of mine."

It had never come to that, but when Matthew did die, she had been left with not only the house but the right and ability to continue on her own their work of church vestments, altar cloths, and embroidered banners and hangings, with a widow's right to the business and her place as a femme sole in the Broiderers Guild to back her. For all of that and from her love for him, Anne still blessed Matthew every day in her prayers and on Sundays lighted a candle for his soul in St. Vedast's, where he was buried in the church-yard.

Prospering London widows commonly remarried, but she had not. There were offers, yes, including from two tai-lors of the Tailors Guild interested in joining Matthew's business to theirs, but in the first months after Matthew's death her grief had been too raw for her to think about mar-rying again, and by the time the rawest edge of her grief was gone to ache instead of agony, she had found she enjoyed running her life entirely to suit herself.

And then Daved had returned.

"Please, Mistress Blakhall," Jenet said despairingly, this time with a triple knot in her thread. With patience born of certainty that this would be the last time, Anne worked the knot loose and handed the bedraggled towel back to her. In-stead of taking it, Jenet looked at her hopefully, but Anne said, "Four more stitches, and you'll have it done," and watched while Jenet labored through the last stitches and fastened the thread. That safely done, Anne handed her the scissors, and Mary stopped reading and Lucie ceased stitch-ing to watch Jenet snip the thread, and then both clapped with goodwill for her survival of trial by thread and needle. Jenet heaved the great sigh of someone finished with heavy labor, and smiling on her with no less relief, Anne said, "There then. Do you and Mary go down and see if the cakes are done."

Both girls went readily, but Lucie, returning her heed to her embroidery, said despairingly, "I'm not going to finish today."

"Not today," Anne agreed. "But you may take it home to work on if you will."

That was a thing Anne never allowed, and Lucie looked up at her with shining eyes to ask, "May I?" She was still all long-legged, half-grown girl, with fair hair that sprang every which way from its braid and childish freckles patterning her nose—nothing like her brother Hal's thick spattering, thank goodness, her mother often said—but her hands had almost a woman's deftness at her sewing and would only grow more deft, Anne judged and smilingly assured her, "You may. Let's ready it to go with you."

They did, finishing as Mary and Jenet returned with the tansy cakes and a honey-drink and much merriment at being done with school. For the week to be ending so simply, so quietly, was a blessing of which Anne was silently aware and very grateful. Through much of this month of June in God's year of grace 1450, London had been fraught with fears and wild-running talk about a rebellion rising in the countryside south and east of the city. The leader of it, a man called Jack Cade, had gone so far as to send demands to King Henry that he reform his government and rid himself of false councilors and favorites. That was well enough, and there had been much talk in the rebels' favor, it being nobody's secret how badly the royal government was befouled with corruption. But rebels sending demands from a safe distance were one thing, and word that thousands of them were massed and closing on London was another.

The whole year had been a boiling of trouble, beginning with the bishop of Chichester's murder, followed by the Commons in Parliament demanding they be allowed to try the all-powerful duke of Suffolk for treason for his greed-ridden mishandling of matters in England and abroad. That had brought on Suffolk's exile by the king to save him and then Suffolk's murder at sea on his way into that exile; and through it all there had been seemingly constant reports of one small rebellion after another breaking out across the south of England and in other places.

Most had faded away to nothing or been easily put down, but Cade's had not. Instead it had built until there were said to be forty thousand rebels barely ten miles from London, encamped on Black Heath and sending demands to the king against the others in his government hated even now that Suffolk was gone. King Henry had finally ridden against them with a force of lords and knights and their armed retinues, and Anne had gone with most of London to watch and cheer them through the city and across London bridge in a clatter of armor and horses, with banners brave in the sunlight, certain that Jack Cade and his rebels were finished. But after days of rumors and reports flying back and forth and all around, nothing had come of it. King Henry had kept safe at Greenwich, only sending his lords to talk with Cade until the rebels had begun a sudden retreat into Kent from where they had come. The earl of Northumberland and some lesser lords had ridden in pursuit, been ambushed, and some of the king's own knights had been killed in the harsh skirmish.

London's rush of alarm at that news had been kept in check by the plain fact that there was still the wide Thames and London bridge's heavy gates and drawbridge between the city and Cade, and that surely now King Henry would move in full force against the rebels and make an end to the whole business. But he had not. Had only had two of his own men, the greatly hated Lord Saye and his son-in-law Thomas Crowmer, the equally hated sheriff of Kent, arrested and put into the Tower of London, maybe because he feared that London, in its loud and growing anger, would close against him.

One of Anne's neighbors had grumbled, "Half a ladle-full of traitors out of a bucketful of them," nor had he been the only one who saw it that way. And when, soon after that, King Henry and his lords and all had ridden back through

London on their way toward Westminster, still splendid in armor and with their banners and high-stepping horses, they were not cheered. The best they got was silence; though maybe they heard the dark, growling anger under it, because afterward, safely away in Westminster, King Henry sent for the mayor and aldermen, to order them to their faces to keep the rebels out of London, come what may.

"Taxes!" Master Upton two houses away from Anne along Kerie Lane had sworn. "We pay taxes to keep the king and his lords in ermine robes, and what do we get in return? 'Look to yourselves.' Like we wouldn't do that anyway, without his fool orders, God damn the lot of them, nobles and rebels and all."

He wasn't alone in his anger, but talk was only talk, and these past few days both that and London's anger had eased. The rebels had not come back and, "Saye and Crowmer are still in the Tower," Mistress Upton had said two days ago when she and Anne met in the street on their way home from marketing. "That's something to the good out of it all."

It was, and save for some heavy talk still going on among some folk, the general thought was the troubles would wear themselves out away in the countryside where it didn't matter, Cade's rebels were gone and everything was settling back to ordinary ways.

And Daved would be here tonight.

Three months ago, when he had last left her, he had not known when he would return. "It all depends on the angers between your king and the duke of Burgundy over the French war, and what happens to the trade out of Flanders because of it," he had warned her. Then he had gone and she had settled to the waiting that made up so much of her life now, so that she had been nearly unable to believe the quick-written message brought yesterday by a boy, telling her his ship was anchored below London bridge and asking if he might come to her tomorrow in the late afternoon. She had told the boy, "Tell him yes," and ever since had lived with her heart singing for gladness like the blackbird in the garden.

Neither the day nor even her thoughts were fully her own yet, though. She made the end-of-school as merry and brief as might be, waved Mary and Jenet good-bye from her front door, kept Lucie only while finding a small pipe of red thread in one of the shop's baskets, and was just giving it to her to take home with her sewing when the open doorway darkened with someone coming in. Anne turned to say the shop was closed but instead said happily, "Raulyn!" as Lucie said, "Father!"

Raulyn made a gallant bow to them both, like a hero in a noble tale. "Fair ladies! May I enter, Mistress Blakhall?"

"Enter, good sir, and be assured your welcome," Anne returned in kind, laughing at him. She had known Raulyn all her life; had once upon a long-gone time pined for him with a girl's hope that their fathers, being both tailors and friends, might marry them to one another. But Raulyn's father first apprenticed him to a mercer, then arranged his marriage to the mercer's daughter. Anne, having never been so foolish-young that she could not tell the difference between disappointment and despair, had never imagined her heart was broken and her easy friendship with Raulyn had gone on through the years, while he became a mercer himself and married the mercer's daughter much about the time she married Matthew.

Lucie wasn't his own daughter, though. When the mercer's daughter had died childless five years ago, Raulyn had married sweet Pernell, widow of another mercer, and become an indulgent stepfather to Lucie and her brother Hal. And returning Lucie's smile, he said, "I was this end of town for other reason and thought to give this young lady company on her way home. Her dimples permitting, of course."

Lucie fought and lost against the smile that mention of her dimples always brought and giggled as Raulyn poked a friendly finger at the nearest one. Smiling, too, Anne said, "Lucie, ask Bette if there's any cake left for Master Grene and perhaps something to drink. If you wish?" she added with feigned innocence to Raulyn, knowing his long tooth for anything sweet.

"I do," Raulyn granted with an equally feigned sigh, "if only for courtesy's sake." But when Lucie was gone into the kitchen, he cocked his head and said at Anne, "Mind you, there's something sweeter than cake I'd rather have."

"What a pity you will have to settle for cake," Anne said back at him firmly. His pretended lust for her was an old jest between them, started after Matthew's death and maybe meant just a little more seriously on his side than Anne ever chose to take it. He never pressed past jesting with it, though, and abruptly let the jest go now, asking seriously instead, with a glance to be sure Lucie was not already returning, "What I've truly come for is to ask if you've seen Hal today."

"Hal? No." Apprenticed to another mercer, Raulyn's stepson lived in his master's household in Rother Lane, well away across London. "Should I have?"

"The trouble is that no one has. He went out last night and isn't back. Master Yarford is fit to chew his ear off. Only one, mind you. He says he wants the other to shout in when Hal comes back." Raulyn bent forward and said low in her own ear, "My thought is that Hal went womaning south of the river." He meant Southwark, at the far end of London bridge, where the whores gathered—those that didn't defy the law that forbade them to work in London itself. "I think he went to try his luck but stayed too late, found the bridge gates locked against him when he would have come back, and decided he might as well be hung for a sheep as a lamb, as the saying goes. My guess is that he'll show up the worse for wear, but none the worse for that."

"Surely not," Anne protested. "Not Hal."

"He's of an age for it."

Which Hal was, being almost sixteen; but he'd been ever young for his years, with still a boy's round face and ways. "Does Pernell know?" Anne asked.

"She doesn't, yet. Nor Lucie." Raulyn made a warning gesture just before Lucie came in, carrying a generous piece of cake and an over-full bowl of ale. Raulyn thanked her with a grave courtesy that made her giggle again. While he ate and drank he tried to persuade Anne that she wanted to buy a length of rose-colored Luye linen from him, urging, "It would make a beautiful ground for a wall-hanging. Pearls against it would show to perfection."

"Where would I get pearls?" Anne asked.

"From me!"

Anne laughed. "You're not a merchant for nothing, are you?"

"I couldn't afford to be a merchant for nothing. I'd be out on the street in poverty."

"So would I be if I took to buying pearls for a wall-hanging nobody has yet bought," Anne returned.

"Come then, chickling," he said to Lucie. "Your mother will be wondering where we are." But with Lucie out the door ahead of him, he turned back to say low-voiced for only Anne to hear, "I suppose we'll be one less at dinner tonight, with our Master Daved here with you, yes?"

A blush sweeping up her face, Anne hissed at him, "Yes!" and closed the door rudely close on his heels as he went away laughing. By law, foreign merchants like Daved and his uncle Master Bocking were supposed to stay with London merchants (and be watched by them) while about their London business. Master Bocking's place had been with Raulyn's late father-in-law and now—and Daved with him—was with

Raulyn. It had been that way Anne had met Daved, but it was one thing for Raulyn to know about them and another for him to say it out so boldly. A little angry at both Raulyn and her betraying blush and at the same time silently laughing at herself, Anne barred the door and went past the stairs and into the kitchen.

There being only herself and Bette to the household, their meals were mostly lesser things, so Bette was humming over her cooking this afternoon, happy to have more to do; had rejoiced this morning that there were garden greens enough to make a goodly salad and talked at length about which herbs she should use on the pike she would bake for Anne and Daved's supper. Just now as Anne came into the kitchen, she had the lid lifted from the thick earthenware pot at the back of the fire and was poking a judicious fork into the slowly cooking fish. Anne sighed at the rich smell, and Bette said, "Aye, though I say it myself, there's not king nor duke will dine better than you and Master Weir tonight."

Among the blessings Anne counted in her life was Bette. She had been a servant to Matthew's parents and then to him and now was Anne's, and they were comfortable together. Nor had she ever given sign she minded Daved in Anne's life. All she had ever said was, "If there's to be a man in your life, Master Weir is a good one, and all the better for not being around and in the way all the time."

Nor did she seem to want Anne in her way, either, at present, saying briskly as she re-lidded the pot, "All's in hand here. You'll want to be ready for this man of yours, so take yourself upstairs. You might take that bread with you, to save carrying it up later. I still say it's odd looking." And had been saying so since Anne made the two loaves this morning.

Anne made no answer, only took the cloth-covered bread on its platter and went upstairs, glad at finally being able to turn whole-heartedly toward Daved and tonight. Having set the platter on the short-legged wooden chest against the wall beside the door, she closed the shutters across the front window so near the house across the way, then half-closed the gardenward window's shutters past anyone's seeing in, making the room into a place for her and Daved alone. Next she covered the small table in the room's middle with her best linen tablecloth, set the cloth-covered bread on its platter in the middle, and from the chest brought out her two silver spoons and the pairs of polished pewter plates and pewter goblets and set a place either side of the table; then from the chest again brought out two new silver candlesticks, the best things she had ever bought for herself, and two slender, never-lighted beeswax candles to go with them. Carefully, hoping she had it right, she set them either side of the bread's platter.

She had put fresh sheets smelling of lavender on the bed this morning, and then the green coverlet embroidered with summer flowers, so that was ready. She had also brought up a bucket of water to warm in the warm day, and having slipped out of her headrail and wimple and workaday gown and undergown and long chemise, she washed all over, using not her usual plain homemade soap but the dear-bought rose-scented castilian. Washcloth and water and soap slid pleasurably over her body, and she found herself thinking of Daved, wishing his merchant-journeys brought him to England in the winter, when nights were longer . . .

She took hold on her thoughts, finished washing and put on her new chemise she had close-embroidered with blue forget-me-nots around the neckline's low curve and then a deep green summer gown laced up the front. She did not bother to cover her hair again, and when Bette called up the stairs that everything was ready if she wanted to fetch it, she went down barefoot, taking with her a candlestub in the battered candlestick that usually served to light her evenings. Bette lighted it for her at the kitchen fire and put it on the tray full of covered dishes that Anne picked up from the table.

Upstairs again, she had only just set the tray on the chest beside the door when the knock came at the front door and her heart seemed to go still. Her breath short and uneven, she faced the stairs, stood frozen, listening to Bette shuffle from the kitchen to the door. There was the small thud of the wooden bar being set aside, the smaller snick of the latch being lifted . . . and Daved's voice lightly saying something to which Bette laughed. Anne pressed her hands over her heart with gladness and relief. He was here. He was safe.

Was on the stairs. Was in the room. Was come to a stop to look at her as she was looking at him, for them to see that all was well with them both and well between them. And at the same moment they moved toward each other, came into each others' arms with the fierceness of matching need, their kiss and their embrace full of remembrance of passions past and promise of passions to come. All too plainly, they had not forgotten each other's bodies, and when they drew apart, still holding to one another, Daved said, gazing down into her face, "Your loveliness never wanes, my Anne of delights. Days, weeks, months come and go, but always you are lovely."

"You planned those words ahead," Anne mock-chided him. "You'd say them no matter what, so you might have your way with me."

"I never plan ahead what I'll say to you," Daved protested with vast innocence. "I'm ever too worried you'll have changed toward me."

Anne took his face between her hands—his beautiful face, more perfect in line and bone and flesh than any carved

saint she had ever seen, framed by his dark, curling hair and
enriched by his dark, brown eyes—and pressed her body to
his, giving him to understand with another lingering kiss
that she had not changed toward him.

But though achingly aware of how near the bed was and
how long since they had lain there together, Anne also saw
how quickly daylight was slipping from the room, and she
stepped back from him, saying while she tried to steady
her voice and check her lust to have him, "I have something
for you."

He reached to draw her back to him, murmuring, "I
hope so."

She laughed and slipped away from him toward the table.
Laughing, too, he followed her. They were neither of them
heedless with greed, having found before this what pleasure
there was in putting off their final pleasure, how the ache of
longing refined into ever-deepening passion over supper and
wine and talk. But suddenly, too late, worried at what she
had done, Anne hesitated, her hand hovering over the cloth
still covering the two loaves of waiting bread. Daved, curious, reached past her and lifted the cloth. His stillness then
and his silence made her look up at him, afraid she had done
it wrongly. Or should not have done it at all. And she said
quickly, "It's challah bread. Or I meant it to be. I made it for
you. Two loaves, the way you told me about it. I remembered
what you told me, and today is a Friday, and I thought . . ."

She faded to a stop as his gaze shifted from the bread to
her, and she saw he was not angry as he said gently, "Just
challah. Challah is challah, complete in itself. No more need
to call it 'challah bread' than there is to call you 'Anne
woman.' Though woman you most surely are." He put his
hands on her waist and drew her back against him, adding—
and now she heard the sadness under his voice, "The candles,
too. You remembered them." He looked aside to where she

had left a basin of clear water, a cup, and a clean towel sitting on the chest beside the door. "And that. Anne, my love, it isn't safe. If someone should see . . ."

"No one will see," Anne said, aching for his sadness. She had done all this to make him happy, not sad. "Even if someone did see, they wouldn't understand. No one here knows any more what it means. They can't."

"They do not know, no," Daved agreed. "Because Jews were banished from England four lifetimes ago." And if it were found out that he was here and a Jew, he would answer for it with his life.

That Anne knew his secret and might well share his fate were they found out was measure of the love and trust between them, and she started to turn toward him, to reassure him and herself that here in her chamber where no one else would come they were safe; but he was looking past her to the fading light at the window that told the sun was slipped below London's housetops; and on sudden laughter he cast aside any worry over danger and said, "The candles have to be lighted before the sun sets. If we're not to waste your effort, we must do it now."

Anne immediately brought the lighted candlestub from the tray and made to hand it to him, but he shook his head, saying, "It's for the woman of the house to do."

Except for the one time he had told her, before they became lovers, that he was a Jew, he had said very little about his life. He sometimes told her bits and pieces, of his travels and his merchant-work—stories gathered and brought to her half as gift and half in reparation, she thought, for telling her so little else about himself. She did not even know where he lived, only that it was not France and seemed to be somewhere farther off than Flanders or Holland.

Because there was no use, she simply tried never to think of his . . . home. Even the word came hard to her.

His home, where he could drop pretense of being Christian. Where he had a wife. Where he might even have children. She didn't know. He had never told her more, until his last night with her here, when they were lying in each other's arms after love, taking pleasure simply in being near each other and knowing he would soon leave both her and England. Then he had talked about his . . . Shabbat. And she had lain quiet in his arms and listened. It was what he missed most in the months he spent seeming to be a Christian merchant, he said; and hearing the longing in his voice, Anne had drawn from him with soft questions everything she could about it, even to how to make challah. Her thought had been that if Shabbat was so dear to him that it was what he remembered most when he was away from . . . home, then she would give him Shabbat here, too—make it part of their memories together. It wasn't Christian, but nothing about it had seemed something that would damn her soul for doing it. And after all it was something Christ must have done all of his life, so how *could* there be ill in it?

Or so she had told herself until now—until this moment when, with candle in hand to light the Shabbat candles in their silver holders, she stopped and looked up at Daved beside her, hoping he would see only her uncertainty, not her fear.

"You light them," he said encouragingly. "Then I'll say the blessing over them, since you cannot."

Her trust in him had brought her to this, and she would go on trusting him. She lit the candles, and Daved stretched out his arms, drew his hands over the flames and toward himself three times, then covered his face with his hands and began, *"Baruch atah Adonai, Eloheinu melech haolam . . ."*

Anne shuddered. His voice was gone strange on the sounds that must be words but were like no words she had ever heard. They were a strangeness she had not known was in him.

He finished, lowered his hands, smiled at her, and was simply Daved again. "Now it's begun," he said, his voice his own. "And now I sing . . ."

Anne stiffened, afraid of hearing more of those sounds coming from him.

Daved saw and asked gently, "Or I do not?"

She had meant this as a gift to him. If she failed to trust him . . . so much of what was between them depended on their trust of one another; and she smiled at him and whispered, "Go on."

Afterward she would be beyond bounds glad her trust had been stronger than her fear then. He faced the candles again, began to sing, his voice so soft it barely carried beyond the table, and while she listened her fear went from her. The words and even their sound were still strange—"*. . . Bo'achem le-shalom malachei ha-shalom malachei elyon . . .*"—but there was beauty in them, and when Daved put out a hand to her, she took it, and he went on singing while the evening's soft summer shadows deepened around them, and she found herself wishing she could sing with him, there was such peace and longing in whatever the words were.

He finished and looked at her. In the increasingly shadowed room, there was now only the candlelight by which to see each other, with Daved's face half in shadow, half in warm candle-glow as he said quietly, "The song asks for God to bless this home with peace and, more deeply, that we find peace within ourselves, both on this Shabbat and afterwards. *Shalom aleichem.* May peace be upon you."

Faintly, trying to say it rightly, Anne echoed, "*Shalom aleichem.* My love."

He touched her cheek with his fingertips, and all her longing to have him returned in a rush. But he drew back a step and said, "The next part is to you, my *eishet chayil*—my woman of valor."

Anne moved her head in a slight nod, willing for him to go on, but he already was, still holding her hands, still gazing at her as he sang, *"Eishet chayil mi yimtza ve-rachok . . ."*

Chapter 2

The thick sunlight of the midsummer's early afternoon poured warmly into the square garth enclosed by the paved cloister walk and crowded buildings of St. Helen's nunnery, leaving the roofed cloister walk pleasantly in warm shadow, with the quiet of Sunday rest between the day's longer Offices of prayer lying over everything. If Dame Frevisse was displeased with it all—and she was—she knew the fault lay in herself, not in St. Helen's. Used as she was to her own St. Frideswide's priory set small among the fields of northern Oxfordshire, the change of place should—if nothing else—have pleasurably diverted her because St. Helen's was neither small nor in the countryside but in London, with all London's busyness of people and churches spread around the priory's own gathering of church, chapter house, hall, refectory, library, dormitory, kitchen, workrooms, parlors, and the prioress' private rooms, with the cloister walk and its garth in their midst, a high-walled garden at the back and, toward the street, the foreyard, guesthall, and the wide double gateway opening to broad, busy Bishopsgate Street running down toward London bridge and the Thames. And if that very busyness and crowding were what she disliked, here was the peace of the cloister walk, familiar to her from every nunnery she had ever been in, from her childhood times as a sometimes boarder in French nunneries to all her years in St. Frideswide's.

No matter if a nunnery were large or small, rich or poor, a nun's life was lived around the cloister walk. She passed along it to the church for the Offices and to all her other duties elsewhere inside the nunnery, sometimes worked there and often took her recreation, as Frevisse was now, walking around it. The very familiarity should have been a comfort to her but it was not, and for once she would have welcomed the chance to distract herself in talk with someone else; but while the Benedictine Rule of silence had grown slack in nunneries since she had become a nun, here the nuns still kept to silence on Sundays at least, denying her even the diversion of talk. Nor could she sit still and read as usually she would have gladly done and as other nuns were doing, including Dame Juliana who had accompanied her here from St. Frideswide's.

Seated in the shade on the low wall between walk and garth with a book of saints' lives open on her lap, she was probably more dozing over it than anything, Frevisse thought sharply, not in the humour for charitable thoughts toward anyone, however blameless. In truth just now she was ready to blame everyone, including herself, for everything; nor did knowing that was unjust and made no sense change her humour in the slightest. Which only served to irk her the worse as she continued to walk, her pace measured, her hands tucked quietly into the opposite sleeves of her black Benedictine gown, her head a little bowed, around the walk and around and around again, wishing she could settle, knowing it would be better not only for herself but for the seeming that she was come to London for only the plain reason given to everyone, including Dame Juliana.

The plain reason but a false one.

For the world and all to know, she was here on the matter of funeral vestments her cousin Lady Alice meant to give to St. Frideswide's in memory of Lady Alice's late husband, to go with provision of special prayers for his soul. That Lady Alice's late husband had been the powerful duke of Suffolk and murdered not two months ago on his way into exile made the gift less ordinary than it might have been but still straightforward enough: Frevisse was to meet with the vestment-maker to agree on the patterns to be embroidered and the cloth to be used and then confirm the commission on Lady Alice's behalf. Prevented as Lady Alice was by her present mourning from making the London journey herself, it was reasonable she had asked Frevisse be allowed to go in her stead, a measure of her favor and trust toward her cousin, with no reason for anyone to think the business over vestments hid another matter altogether.

But it did, and it was that other matter that had Frevisse restlessly pacing, angry to be here, as inwardly a-seethe as England presently was outwardly. With Suffolk's years of misgovernment for the king and this past year's headlong losses in the French war—with most of the late King Henry V's great conquests in France now gone—there was such a continuing rumble of angers and rebellions that this was no time to be traveling, which Lady Alice had acknowledged in her letter to St. Frideswide's prioress Domina Elisabeth when telling her of the intended gift and requesting Frevisse's part in it as well as promising the use of her own rowed barge so that Frevisse and her escort could travel by river rather than road from Oxford to London.

Domina Elisabeth, more than willing to oblige so wealthy a patron as Lady Alice, had agreed without apparent second thought. Frevisse, under a nun's vow of obedience, had had no choice but to accept and obey. She had been uneasy, though. She and Alice had not last parted pleased with each other, that Alice should be asking this of her now; and her unease had only increased at finding the barge stripped of any sign it belonged to the duke or duchess of Suffolk. From bow to stern the Suffolk colors of blue and gold were painted over to a plain brown, and the canvas tilt no longer bore the ducal heraldic arms.

Worse had come when the barge's master had taken secret chance to give her a sealed letter, saying with a wary look around them, "My lady ordered it was for only you to know of."

Frevisse had slipped the folded and sealed paper into her sleeve with a sinking certainty she was not going to like whatever it said. She had learned to be wary of Alice's secrets, and her wariness had not lessened when she finally had chance to read the letter, such as it was. The two sentences told her nearly nothing: "When my agent in London meets you about the vestments, he will have another matter for you that none else must know of. However much I have lost your friendship of late, I pray you, in mercy, to aid me in this." That was all; and just as the wax seal had been plain, there was no signed name to betray who had written it.

The writing had seemed Alice's, though, and Frevisse was left with nothing but to pretend all was as it outwardly was supposed to be while keeping to herself her low-held anger and ill-graced curiosity at what Alice wanted of her. And now, after scarcely a day in London, her waiting might be at an end. Across the cloister garth a nun had stopped beside Dame Juliana and, mindful of the Sunday silence, was moving her hands in quick signs, to which Dame Juliana shook her head and pointed toward Frevisse. The nun started around the walk toward her, and Frevisse walked on to meet her, trying to curb any outward show of impatience. When they met, the nun signed with her hands that Frevisse was wanted somewhere, and Frevisse nodded silently that she understood and followed the woman out of the cloister walk and away through several rooms to the parlor near the cloister's outer door where nuns met with such guests as they were allowed.

At St. Frideswide's the guest parlor was little used, friends and relatives only sometimes coming so out of the way to visit, but the nuns in St. Helen's were mostly of London families, with much come and go of visiting, and their parlor was comfortable with cushioned chairs, cloth-covered table, rush matting underfoot, and tapestried walls. As Frevisse entered, the man there turned from considering the tapestry showing the Foolish Virgins with their burned-out lamps, and the St. Helen's nun murmured, "Master Raulyn Grene," before sinking onto the chair just inside the door as if all the walking to and fro had worn her out. Since no nun should meet alone with a man, she would stay there, but Frevisse supposed that must be a difficulty this Master Grene had considered aforetime. Supposing he was Alice's agent. But who else in London was likely to seek her out?

At any rate, Raulyn Grene was a comely man in his early middle years and undoubtedly a prospering merchant of some sort, confident of bearing and his dark blue, three-quarter-length over-gown soberly cut but of a silken-finished worsted with the standing collar lined with green velvet, his black hosen close-fitted, his low-cut shoes of fine leather, and a pearl hung from the silver brooch on the rolled brim of his round-crowned hat that he removed as he bowed to her. He would have less by which to judge her, she knew, gowned as she was to her feet in the several layers and full skirts of black Benedictine habit, with her face encircled by a white wimple under a black veil, so that all of her that showed were her hands folded together at her waist and her face, which she was fairly sure betrayed nothing of her thoughts as Master Grene said, "My lady, it's my pleasure to meet you. Her grace of Suffolk has asked I be her agent and of service to you in this matter of vestments."

"It's equally my pleasure, Master Grene," Frevisse said as graciously back to him. "Although I hope you know more of the business than I do."

"I have my lady's commission in full. If you would care to sit?" He gestured to two chairs well away from the door, set either side of a small table where two goblets and a small plate of crisp cakes awaited them. As he led Frevisse to one of the chairs, Master Grene asked, "I hope your journey went quietly?"

"Quite quietly, save that we heard about the Kentish rebels only after we were on our way. Master Naylor kept us a day more in Oxford, until we heard they had drawn off."

"Master Naylor?"

"Our nunnery's steward." Frevisse sat and gestured for Master Grene to do the same. "He and his son saw Dame Juliana and me to London."

"He did well to be careful." Master Grene handed her one of the goblets, sat himself, and took up the other. "But London itself was always safe enough. The bridge can be kept against them easily enough."

It was courteous, shallow talk, the sort made between two people before setting to business. Here it was probably as much for the nun across the room as for themselves, and Frevisse kept it going with, "There's some wondering, I gather, that the king did not do more against the rebels."

What she had truly heard was outright anger at King Henry, but Master Grene said moderately enough, "He's a man of peace, our king."

Frevisse held back from saying tartly that if he were truly a man of peace, he would have seen to the truce with France being kept last year rather than letting it be stupidly broken and the French war flare out again. But about that she knew too much, held silent, and took a drink of the wine while Master Grene went on, "It does seem that he's going to have to deal with them after all, though. There's report that they're moving this way again."

"True report?" She felt no particular alarm. As Master Grene said, London bridge could be easily held against them. But Master Naylor would be unhappy at the news. Even more unhappy that he had been in Oxford at her insistence they go onward to London when he would rather have waited longer.

"Who knows, these days?" Master Grene said lightly. "Even if it is true, they'll still be on the wrong side of the Thames. Or, rather, on the right side for us. With the bridge shut against them, there's nothing they can do."

Except to Southwark at the bridge's other end and unprotected, Frevisse thought but did not say.

"But to business, shall we?" Master Grene shifted aside his goblet and the plate of untouched cakes, brought out several pages of paper from the finely worked leather pouch at his belt, unfolded them, and laid them on the table. "Here is somewhat what Lady Alice has in mind."

The top paper did indeed have the shapes of various priestly vestments sketched on it, and Master Grene shifted his chair around the table, putting him nearer to Frevisse as if the better to point out whatever was on the papers but also putting his back mostly toward the door and the nun beside it while he said, "I'm a mercer, you see. I've served her grace of Suffolk before this, and when she expressed her desire about these vestments in memory of her husband, God keep his soul, I could promise her not only a choice of fine cloths to her need, but recommend a woman for the work. One Mistress Anne Blakhall." He dropped his voice a little, making it less easy for the other nun to hear him without seeming to be hiding his words. "A widow, she's taken over her late husband's craft of tailoring and is in her own right a skilled embroiderer. Thus, she can both make the actual vestments and embroider them as well."

While Master Grene provided the undoubtedly very expensive cloth. If that had been all there was to the business, Frevisse would have resolved to make very sure of this Mistress Blakhall's skills and the quality of the cloth Master Grene offered. But the vestments were only a part of it, it seemed, and keeping her eyes to the paper, she asked in a voice too low to be heard by the nun, "And the other matter?"

Equally low-voiced and without pause, Master Grene answered, "It has to do with a sum of gold that must be taken to her grace of Suffolk without anyone knowing or even suspecting it's come into England at all." He turned over the first paper in front of them to a second scrawled with vague drawings of figures probably meant for saints. Randomly pointing at them as if they were intended designs, he went on, "When you visit Mistress Blakhall about the outward business, she will give you this gold in coins. You will keep them concealed and take them with you when you leave London, returning up the Thames as you came. No one will think it odd if you pause on the way to visit your cousin at her manor of Ewelme, so near the Thames, to report about the vestments."

"Why?"

Her question stopped Master Grene. "Why?" he echoed, as if he had expected no question from her, only acceptance.

But simple acceptance had never come easily to her. That had made her early years as a nun difficult, and although she had bettered at it after all this while, she was by no means perfect at it and saw no reason to be so in such things as this, and she asked, "Why must it be done in secrecy? Isn't it my cousin's money?"

"Of course it is," Master Grene said. In his surprise he was forgetful to be fully careful of his voice and added for the other nun to overhear, "You'll not find better samite for your purpose in London, I promise you." He dropped his voice again. "Of course it's hers, come to her from her husband. But there are those who were against him who might lay false claims if they knew of it."

Given what she knew of Suffolk, Frevisse had doubt about how false their claims might be. Those rights and wrongs were out of her knowing, though, and she only said, "I want to understand more about it."

She saw Master Grene want to say she only had to do what she was told, not understand it. She also saw him think better of it; but he gained time over his answer by taking a long drink from one of the goblets and setting it down before he answered, "Yes. Well. When the king exiled my lord of Suffolk, my lord of Suffolk saw fit to provide for his safety and comfort in exile by delivering a large sum of money here in London to the commissioner of a money-dealer in . . . of a city overseas. It doesn't matter where."

Nor did Frevisse care and said, to show she was not completely ignorant in such matters, "Suffolk had to do that because he'd not have been allowed to take a great deal of gold with him out of England." Because to do so was illegal. No ruler anywhere in Europe willingly let large sums of gold or silver or jewels leave his country if it could be helped. Wealth was power, and governments did all they could to keep power from sliding from their country to someone else's. So, no, Suffolk could not have openly taken his wealth with him and, "Therefore he bought a bill to exchange the money," Frevisse said.

"You understand how such an exchange works?" Master Grene asked, surprised.

Frevisse accepted his surprise. He knew nothing about her except she was a nun, and bills for the foreign exchange of money were hardly something for which a nun had use. "I know a little," she said quietly. "For such a bill, he gave up a sum of gold to someone here in exchange for a paper that confirmed he'd done so."

"Just so. Then, abroad, he would have given that bill to the money-dealer, who would have given him gold in return. A suitable fee for the service being paid in the course of it all, of course."

"And a chance for Suffolk to make money on the exchange if the sum of gold paid here is worth more in the place of exchange when the time comes to exchange it—" A thing she had never understood and did not try to grasp now. "—than what he paid for it here, yes?"

"You have it. As it happens his grace would have done well. The exchange was very much to his favor then."

"But he never lived to make the exchange. He never reached France. Wasn't the bill lost when he was seized?"

"He had sent it by messenger out of the country ahead of him, to someone in his service abroad. He thought to overtake it when safely into exile."

"But he did not, and now it's been sent back."

Perhaps glad to find a point of ignorance between them, Master Grene said quickly, "It couldn't be. Such a bill can only to be exchanged at a certain place, by a certain time. Suffolk's bill was changed to gold coins in . . . where it had to be."

"Then another bill could have been bought with that money, and the new bill returned to England, to Lady Alice, for another exchange into gold," Frevisse said with a wry certainty that she would not be here if it were that simple.

"That could have been done," Master Grene agreed. "And if it had, she would have seen some small profit on the return, given how gold presently stands here against its worth abroad. But . . ."

They had been talking rather long without feigning to consult the paper. Master Grene looked sidewise toward the other nun, and so did Frevisse. The warm afternoon and waiting had taken their toll: her head was nodded forward into what looked to be sleep, and Master Grene went on, "But the value of it in exchange abroad is presently very high. Suffolk's agent made the exchange as he was supposed to, yes, but the gold that he got, if used to buy another bill of exchange to send back into England . . ."

"Which would be legal," Frevisse said.

Master Grene gave her a swift glance while pointing at something on the paper at which neither of them were looking. ". . . would pay back only a little more than the original amount my lord of Suffolk paid. With all that's gone wrong for her this year, my lady of Suffolk is in need of the greater sum, not the lesser. Therefore choice was made not to make another exchange but to send the gold itself."

"Meaning," Frevisse said coldly, "that the gold has been conveyed illegally." Out of wherever the exchange had taken place—probably in France or Flanders or Holland.

With a small movement of one hand, Master Grene acknowledged she was right, then waited to see if she would go on from there. The next step not being difficult, Frevisse took it, saying, "Since my help is wanted, I must presume the gold is safely here, but since I'm wanted to take it secretly to Lady Alice, rather than her agent deliver it himself, there must be some trouble about it. Such as someone else wants it?" Which was not unlikely, given how much Suffolk had probably stolen in his years of ill-governing.

"Several someones, if reports are true," Master Grene said. "Who?"

"That's more than I know. Or you need to."

He was not warning her, simply saying the truth. And since, in truth, she did not want to know even as much as she did—there being small likelihood she would ever learn enough to make wise choice of what to do—she did not push the matter.

"What matters," Master Grene went on, "is that the gold is your cousin's, she is in need of it, and trusts you to take it to her, no one the wiser."

Frevisse bent her head in silent acceptance of that, then asked, "Why didn't Suffolk's own man, having brought it, simply take it onward to her?"

"It wasn't Suffolk's own man who brought it. He would have been too known to those watching." Master Grene hesitated, probably considering how little he need say to satisfy her, before going on, "The matter isn't as secret as it might be. It's known Suffolk had wealth and that now Lady Alice doesn't. Not ready-to-hand wealth that makes things possible."

Master Grene seemed someone who knew well the things that wealth-to-hand made possible. But of course to have Alice's patronage, he must be a successful mercer, and successful mercers were wealthy, with Alice's patronage and trust likely to make him all the wealthier. Thus his interest in serving her well in this matter.

Frevisse, still set on understanding more, said, "So there are those who know Suffolk's wealth is gone somewhere and are on the watch for it. Therefore, it's been brought into England by someone who conveys goods against the law."

"By merchants, my lady," Master Grene said quickly. "Plain merchants, who sometimes trade in deeper matters than the makers of simple laws allow for."

Meaning they were not "plain merchants," Frevisse thought sharply but held back from saying as Master Grene went on, "That they're bringing this gold *out* of France is to the good, of course. No one in England, even the law, objects to gold coming *into* the country."

That, Frevisse had to grant, was true enough; but still it had been perilous, and these merchants who had done it must be bold as well as well-witted. But, "Why can't these merchants, having brought it this far, take the gold on to Lady Alice themselves?"

Master Grene hesitated, giving another look toward the napping nun, then turned the first paper over again and leaned closer to it as if pointing out something there and said, "They can't go that far from London."

Which told Frevisse they were not English merchants but foreign ones, allowed into England for only a set while, with limits as to where they were allowed to go.

"I'd gladly undertake the business myself," Master Grene went on, "but my own leaving London would be out of my usual ways and maybe noted. That's why her grace of Suffolk asked your help and hopes you'll be good enough to give it."

He did not quite make that a question, but he looked at her, waiting for her answer. She went on looking at the paper, not really seeing it. She did not like what she was being asked to do, nor was it fair of Alice to have asked it; but given how Alice and she had last parted, the asking must have been hard, telling Frevisse something of how desperate her cousin's need must be. And since she had no hope of sorting out the layered rights and wrongs behind it all, she settled for simply accepting Alice's need and said, "For my cousin's sake, yes, I'll help."

And God forgive her for whatever wrong she did by doing so.

Chapter 3

cross the room the St. Helen's nun awakened with an upward jerk of her head, and
Frevisse, willing to be done with Master
Grene, said in a usual voice, as if having made a usual agreement, "I'll go to Mistress Blakhall tomorrow, then."

"Tomorrow won't serve, I fear," said Master Grene,
matching her. He began gathering his papers, using the
busy rustle to cover him softly adding, "Better there be a
pause while we make certain no one is heeding us out of
the ordinary," before he went on, his voice raised again,
"Tuesday is when she hopes you'll come. Her place is in
Kerie Lane off Gutheron's, just north of St. Paul's from
Cheapside. Someone here will be able to show you the way,
surely."

He stood up. Frevisse, standing up with him, said mildly, "I look forward to seeing her work."

"You'll find it more than satisfactory, I'm certain. She'll be able to well-advise you, too, about the cloth, though I think you'll find what I offer the best of anyone's." With the pointless papers folded and in his belt-pouch again, he bowed to her. Frevisse bent her head to him in return, while the St. Helen's nun bustled to her feet and opened the door ahead of him as he left. Because she would see him out the nearby cloister door and lock it behind him, Frevisse was left free to escape to the church with the hope that time alone and in prayer between now and Vespers would quiet her mind and give her assurance she had chosen rightly.

Unfortunately, neither quieted mind nor assurance came, either while she prayed alone or through Vespers' prayers and psalms with the other nuns. Supper followed and after that, in the usual way of things, would have been simply an hour's recreation until time for the day's final Office of Compline, with bed afterward. Today, though, was the eve of the feast of Saints Peter and Paul; tonight the Mayor's Watch would be kept throughout the city, with bonfires in the streets, tables with free food and drink for passersby set up by richer folk outside their houses, and after nightfall a torch-lit procession through the streets with drums and trumpets and the mayor and his attendants on horseback in their richest array, followed by the Sheriffs' Watch and all the standing watches of every ward and street in the city. They did not come by way of Bishopsgate Street, nor should the nuns be up at that hour to see them—the more especially because nightfall came so late this time of year, making the hours short from bedtime to the Offices of Matins and Lauds at midnight. But St. Helen's prioress indulged her nuns enough that after Compline, instead of to bed they and Dame Juliana and Frevisse were allowed to the nunnery gatehouse's parapeted roof to look out at Bishopsgate Street with all the lanterns lighted and torches flaring beside doorways bedecked with greenery and flowers and people wandering up and down in talk and laughter, with here a juggler fountaining balls, there three tumblers stacking themselves one a-top the other, farther along someone walking on stilts, and almost under the nunnery gateway a minstrel singing a song that nuns might have been better not to hear.

All of London would be the same, festive with light and food and sports and people making merry. The nuns even heard, not so very distantly, the drums and trumpets and cheering of the mayor's procession as it crossed Bishopsgate, passing from Cornhill into Leadenhall and on toward Aldgate. And when the nuns finally came down and returned into the cloister, there were spiced ale and ginger cakes waiting for them, for their own small celebration.

There was much head-nodding over prayer books at Matins and Lauds and a hurried shuffling back to bed at their end, and morning with its Office of Prime came too soon, but sustained by memories of last night's pleasures Dame Juliana was cheerfully ready for the day of seeing London, where she had never been before now. Frevisse, for whom it was not new and with other things on her mind, was less eager, but their own prioress had seen a journey to London paid for by Lady Alice as a chance for priory business to be done there, and she had given them a list of wants—things to be purchased in London if they could be found more cheaply there than in Oxfordshire. Spices were principal. Salt came from enough places around England to cost much the same everywhere, but such things as pepper, cinnamon, ginger, cloves, and sugar were another matter, of high expense because brought from abroad and their expense only the greater the farther from London they were sold.

And then there was cloth. "A good black linen for our summer undergowns would be welcome," Domina Elisabeth had said. "Our present ones are over-worn almost past bearing. If you should find a good black wool, too, not too dear, there are some of our winter gowns . . ." She had trailed off with a sigh that Frevisse understood better after this short while in St. Helen's. Domina Elisabeth had been a nun here before being made prioress of St. Frideswide's, and although St. Frideswide's was prospering under her, it would never have the prosperity of St. Helen's, where London merchants and craftsmen gifted the house while they lived and left it bequests at their deaths for the sake of their daughters' comforts as well as the comfort of their own souls.

Frevisse knew that beside St. Helen's nuns she and Dame Juliana in their well-worn habits looked like the poor country cousins they were, and though there was no shame in holy poverty, she had seen Dame Juliana quietly turning under the frayed edges of her sleeves. Worse, she admitted to the urge to do as much herself and had to grant that Domina Elisabeth was right: it was time for a large purchase of black cloth for new gowns.

So quickly did desire for worldly things take hold, she noted with an inward sigh.

And immediately admitted with wry, silent laughter, how glad she was that her even stronger urge to a worldly thing—more books for St. Frideswide's—was to be satisfied by another of Domina Elisabeth's behests. The priory's small scrivening business was thriving, making enough difference to the priory's income, that, "If there are some new-written books to be had," Domina Elisabeth had directed, "something we have likelihood of selling and not so long they will take us forever to copy or so costly we'll never make back our money, get them."

The promise of visiting stationers' shops on that search was the one great brightness in Frevisse's thought as she and Dame Juliana readied to go out at mid-morning. For Dame Juliana, though, all was delight. She was in a burst of excitement as she and Frevisse left the cloister to meet Master

Naylor and his son Dickon near St. Helen's gateway, with
young Dickon as near to bursting as she was, though he tried
to hide it. Near to twenty-one years old and nearly ready to
be a man in his own right, he was lean-bodied and lean-
faced, looking much as his father must have looked at that
age, Frevisse thought; but Master Naylor's face had creased
with years and duty into lines that looked like permanent
displeasure whatever his humour. Though presently displeasure was probably the truth with him. Frevisse had
never found him overly given to cheerfulness at the best of
times, but he was very unpleased with this London journey,
nor did it help he was under Domina Elisabeth's order to do
whatever Frevisse required of him in Lady Alice's service.

Dickon, on the other hand, seemed not cast down at all by
his father's demeanor. He was as ready as Dame Juliana for
whatever the day might bring, and as the four of them set
out along wide Bishopsgate—Frevisse walking beside Dame
Juliana, Master Naylor and Dickon following a few paces behind them—Dame Juliana's and Dickon's plain gladness in
the day began to take hold on Frevisse, too. That London was
at its most welcoming surely helped. With midsummer not
long past, an early morning overcast was burning off to the
perfect sunshine of a late June day, the high-riding sun filling the street with sunlight gay on the bright-painted
housefronts and sparkling on the glass of upper windows.
The first flourish of housewives' morning shopping was over
but there were still people enough—and carts and occasion-
ally a full wagon lumbering its way along toward London's
heart—to bewilder someone only just come from Oxfordshire. Dame Juliana for certain stared around, trying to see
all at once into the innyards they passed and the street-facing
shops with their shopboards out, displaying goods for sale,
and at the same time upward at the narrow, tall, out-thrusting
housefronts above the street and still not lose anything of all

the crowding folk among whom they were making their way.

Rain in the night had washed what refuse there had been into the runnel down the middle of the street, and housewives or their servants had been out to sweep the paving in front of their houses and make sure the waste piled beside their door was ready for the official scavengers to collect on their rounds. City law required, too, that householders keep the paving in front of their houses in repair, and on such a main way as Bishopsgate that was well-seen to. So except for the fresh annoyances of this morning's passing horses, there was nothing underfoot of which to be wary; but after Dame Juliana, because she was staring the other way, nearly collided with a woman carrying a wide basket of bread for sale on her head, Frevisse took hold on her arm and guided her along, leaving her to stare freely. She was a little older than Frevisse, a steady, good-humoured woman who had taken to the troubles of travel with the same merry interest she was giving now to London, and it was just as well they had been excused the rest of the day's offices until Vespers because trying to hurry her looked to be a cause lost from the start. They were past where Bishopsgate became Gracechurch Street, to where at Gracechurch was met by Lombard Street from the west and Fenchurch Street from the east, when Dame Juliana, looking one way, then the other, stopped short, drew and let go a long, quavering breath, and said, "It goes on forever, doesn't it? London. Everything in the world must be for sale here." She looked back to the Naylors still close behind and said, honestly a little worried, "You won't lose us in the crowds, will you?"

"I'll not," said Master Naylor. "You're in my charge, and I'll keep it." He fixed a brief, flat stare at Frevisse that told her he held it her fault they were here at all, and added, "Though it's maybe best you have your business done, and we go back as soon as may be."

Frevisse suspected he did not mean merely to St. Helen's but right away back to St. Frideswide's, but she only said evenly and to Dame Juliana, "We'll look at goods today but probably not buy. If I remember rightly, there are a great many drapers shops on Lombard Street. My thought is to see what they have on offer and then go on to the stationer shops in Paternoster Row where they'll have whatever's new in the way of books. Coming back through Cornhill into Bishopsgate, we can look in on more drapers if we're not too tired by then."

Dame Juliana was willing to all that, and they turned right into Lombard Street. Frevisse had last been here years ago but it was still mostly a street of drapers, their shops' wide fronts open to the street, their half-timbered homes rising over them as much as four storeys tall, with timbers deeply carved into patterns of vines and fantastical animals and galloping knights, and the housefronts painted most colors that could be thought of, ranging from deep cream to cheerful scarlet. It made a brave show, and the busyness of people all along and back and forth across it only added to the pleasure of going from shop to shop, where cloths of every common kind and color were laid out on the forward shopboards, while inside on tables or else draped over wallpoles were the more costly kinds—the silks and velvets and damasks—while those drapers who dealt in the most costly cloths—the camelines, tartaires, marbrinus, and cloths of gold—would have them safe-kept in rear rooms, to be shown only to those able to buy them.

Even so, there were cloths displayed that would make a lady's single gown worth more than all the gowns a nun might wear in her lifetime, and though Frevisse and Dame Juliana looked from outside, Dame Juliana making soft exclaims of pleasure, neither of them went in for nearer looks but were content with looking at and judging what was offered at the front of the shops. But even looking only at black cloth left them too much to see, too many choices to consider. Coarse-woven, fine-woven, deep-dyed or not. And could enough yards be supplied by one draper? Would there be advantage offered for buying in such quantity? Did the draper pack purchased cloth for travel, or would that be Master Naylor's problem?

Dame Juliana soon understood that London merchants were hardly different from those of Banbury she often dealt with on the nunnery's behalf, and she happily took over the questioning and judging and bargaining. Frevisse as happily let her, knowing herself not so skilled that way, but after half a dozen shops, even Dame Juliana was tiring and said, "Thank St. Frideswide we don't have to make up our minds today. Shall we go look at books a while?"

Frevisse was willing to that but said, "The stationers are mostly gathered into Paternoster Row beside St. Paul's and that's somewhat of a walk from here."

"I'd not mind seeing the cathedral," Dame Juliana answered, and onward they went, crossing the Stocks Market into wide Cheapside. Here were a great many goldsmiths, and Dame Juliana's staring at the gleaming displays of jewelry and plate slowed their going. Halfway along the street, standing in the middle of the way, was the narrow stone tower of the Standard, the grandest of London's public conduits for water piped into the city free for the taking by anyone. Farther along was the high Eleanor Cross, likewise in the middle of the street, rich with carved stonework and painted statues; but by then St. Paul cathedral's tower and spire—last seen clearly as they came down the Thames—were reared into view, unbelievable against the sky, drawing the eye from any lesser thing, and the four of them went aside, into the lee of a housefront, to stare their fill, Frevisse and Master Naylor, who had seen it this close before now, no

less than Dame Juliana and Dickon. "More than five hundred feet tall, not counting the golden cockerel at its top,"
Master Naylor said.

"But we'll save going inside for another day," said Frevisse. "After we've tended to our other purposes."

"So that we can spend a whole day in it if we want," Dame
Juliana agreed, but went on staring as they curved along the
long north side of St. Paul's churchyard toward Paternoster
Row. From that near, the cathedral was like a great stone cliff,
fretted with buttresses and pinnacles and stone-traceried windows, towering over even the towers and spires of the very
many London churches everywhere thrusting up above lesser
rooftops.

Once into narrow Paternoster Row, though, it was the
stationers' shops that took Frevisse's and Dame Juliana's heed.
Here was the heart of London's book-trade. Paper-sellers,
scriveners, illuminators, bookbinders, and booksellers all
existed together in mutual use to one another and their customers. Books of every sort were to be had, from theology in dark, dense lines of careful script—Frevisse spared a
moment's pity for the scribes who had to copy out those
works—to any of Chaucer's lightsome tales, either together
or singly, depending on the buyer's preference or purse, because books could be bought bound—in full, hardboarded,
leather-wrapped covers or simply stitched into parchment or
heavier paper—or unbound, if that should be the buyer's
pleasure.

To St. Frideswide's need, that latter would be the best.
Books were less costly that way and would save Dame Perpetua the work of unstitching from any cover. But that was
the simplest choice Frevisse and Dame Perpetua had to
make. By various borrowings from their prioress' brother, an
abbot, the priory had a sufficiency of devout works from
which to copy. "Something lesser and lighter," Domina Elisabeth had said. "But not too profane," she had added, and

after a happy time in one shop and another, their choice was come down to a small abece of children's learning-rhymes for certain and an uncertainty between a *Siege of Troy* newly translated from the French, a collection of Aesop's fables, and a lengthy Life of St. Katherine. "By that very learned Augustinian canon John Capgrave," Master Colop the bookseller at the sign of the Gilded Quill was telling Dame Juliana in one part of the shop while Frevisse lingered at the front over a copy of Thomas Hoccleve's *Regiment of Princes*. There was a directness and clarity of thought to Hoccleve's verse that drew her, and under her breath she read:

> *"That gift of peace, that precious jewel,*
> *If men it keep and throw it not away,*
> *Sons of Christ they may be named full well . . .*
> *There is no doubt that ambition*
> *And greed fire all this debate . . .*
> *Though a man be great, yet higher would he go;*
> *And these are causes of our strife and woe."*

But it was a long work and beyond the priory's purse and purpose, she feared and moved regretfully away from it.

"A holy story by a well-respected man," Master Colop was saying, still extolling Capgrave's St. Katherine.

A holy story, Frevisse thought wryly, of a girl defying in usually very rude terms her parents, an emperor, and several score of philosophers before going, still scornful but triumphant, to her martyrdom. It was a goodly blend of piety and daring ever widely loved and, she thought, reading some of Dom Capgrave's prose past Dame Juliana's shoulder, well-told here.

The Gilded Quill had choice enough, and Master Colop's prices were none so bad, that they told him they would consider and decide and probably be back. Then, with nothing purchased but much learned, they rejoined Master Naylor and Dickon, who had been waiting in the street with at least outward patience, and started back toward St. Helen's. Passing St. Paul's yard again, they saw a crowd was gathered into the corner made by the meeting of the cathedral's transept and choir, and Frevisse said, "There must be someone preaching."

"Preaching?" Dame Juliana asked.

"At St. Paul's Cross there," Frevisse said. "Anyone with words to say to Londoners at large can speak or preach from there."

"So long as what he has to say is not treasonous, heretical, or likely to rouse the crowd to riot," said Master Naylor, sounding as if he expected all of them at once and immediately.

The man there now, standing in the pulpit at the top of ten stone steps that put him well over the heads of the gathering of perhaps two dozen people, looked to be a Franciscan friar, which would be usual enough. The grey-robed Franciscans were given to public preaching, and their great London house of Grey Friars was not far beyond St. Paul's, toward Newgate. Although this man's voice carried over even London's street noise, Frevisse—following Dame Juliana toward him—could not make out his words for certain until nearly to the rear edge of the crowd, and by then Master Naylor could hear them, too, and said, like giving a curse, "Lollards. He's talking about Lollards." Heretics who claimed that by reading the Bible for themselves they were as able as long-studying churchly scholars to determine the meaning of God's word, and that therefore the Bible should be allowed to them in English. More than once they had brought their disagreement against the Church and royal government to such a pitch they had risen in armed revolt, attempting to force their will and ways upon everyone, so that they were a peril to men's bodies as well as to their souls.

". . . damned to Hell's eternal fires," the friar's voice rang out, "unless they can be brought to repent of their sins, but for most of them that will come only under the weight of the Church's hand pressing down on their heretical hearts!"

"Oh," said Dame Juliana, drawing back a step in disappointment. "I don't want to hear about Lollards and damnation today."

Besides that, she looked beginning to droop with a weariness that Frevisse would soon share, and they left the friar to his preaching and took the first chance that came, on a bench under a beech tree in a churchyard not much farther along Cheapside, to sit down out of the hurry of the street. Hungry now that she took time to think about it, Frevisse gave Master Naylor coins, and he and Dickon went away to a nearby food stall and soon came back with savory-smelling pork pies and a leather bottle of ale that Master Naylor poured into pottery cups, complaining as he did, "I had to give the man a ha'penny more as promise I'd bring back the bottle and cups. I warrant I'll get no more than a farthing in return when I do."

His voice was stiff with something beyond ordinary complaint, though, and Frevisse—having already found that the pie tasted as savoury as it smelled—saw his face was creased with more than its usual share of worry. Even Dickon was gone intent, and she asked, "What is it?"

"Those Kentish rebels," Master Naylor said grimly. "There was a man at the stall saying he's heard they've come back to Black Heath. That's the other side of the Thames and about ten miles away, so that's no worry." Which would have been to the good if Master Naylor had not, nonetheless, sounded worried. "Still, we're maybe best to have you back into St. Helen's quick as might be. To leave me free to find out better what I can about what's happening and being said. I don't like that they've come back even that far off."

Nor did Frevisse. For rebels to turn in their tracks and come back argued a lack of fear of king and nobles that was not comfortable to think on.

Master Naylor turned his head. "Listen. Word's spreading."

There were indeed voices rising in the street beyond the low churchyard wall, and the flow and come and go of folk in the street was changing into clots and gatherings of men and women talking hard together with gestures and alarm. Frevisse brushed crumbs from her skirts and took the filled cup Dickon was holding out to her. "I think you're right, Master Naylor," she said. "We'll do well to go back to St. Helen's as quickly as may be."

Chapter 4

Because Bette's bad hip was playing up, this Monday's buying fell to Anne, who did not go out to it until late morning, intent until then on laying the ground for St. Mark's lion with a brick-stitch in green silk. "Bread," Bette said, handing her the deep, tightly woven market basket. "If that fellow of yours is going to be here, a chicken, too, maybe? Plucked, mind you. The day is gone far enough, I won't have time for plucking a chicken if you want it for your supper. Or eels if you happen on any that look good. I could do an eel pie, if you think he'd favor that. And apples if you see any. I could do an apple tart."

Anne went out smiling at Bette's willingness to cook for Daved. A tailor who had come courting Anne soon after Matthew's death had been given not-quite-stale biscuits on

his visits, and Anne had not chided her for it, as willing as
Bette to discourage the man's interest. Now, even without
the hope of Daved's visits, she would have been loathe to
give up her single life; but she did have Daved's visits, and
he had promised when he left her Saturday before dawn that
he would come again on Monday.

"I'm not certain when, my love," he had said and kissed
her. "But sometime."

And now Monday was come, and all the morning she had
found herself smiling to herself over her sewing until now as
she stood with her full market basket over her arm at
the edge of the crowd gathered in St. Paul's yard around the
preaching cross, listening to a Franciscan friar declaring
against Lollards in a clear, carrying voice from the pulpit's
stone height.

His strong voice had turned her from the street as she
passed by on her way home from the butchers' stalls along
Newgate, and though she had neither seen nor heard him
before this, he had to be the Brother Michael she had heard
Mistress Upton praising of late with, "He's English, but
he's been in France a long while and come back very learned,
it's said. He's supposed to be a mighty hunter-out of heretics
there and, St. Paul be praised, he's been sent back here to
hunt out Lollards. You have to hear him. Truly, he's worth
the listening to."

He was, Anne silently agreed.

He was a young man—younger than Daved by a few years,
anyway—not overly tall and looking slightly built, even with
the thick, grey friar's robe rope-belted around him, with a
raw-boned, high-cheeked face, and his fair hair short-cropped
to above his ears. In any gathering of men, he would look only
ordinary, but his voice was otherwise. Sweeping his arm above
the upturned faces of his gathered listeners, pointing beyond
them to all of London, he was declaring, "They're there!

Heretics. Lollards. Satan's fools. Satan's tools. Set to trap others into their errors. Into their folly." His voice dropped without losing its force. "Into damnation. Utter and eternal." But even as he railed against all Christ's enemies, against all heretic-traitors to God, his voice was warm, as full of possibilities as richly spiced wine, winning his listeners to hear him, to heed him as he declared, "Understand well that Lollards are *your* foes as well as God's! Like these rebels out of Kent, Lollards, too, in their arrogance and heresy have in their time risen in revolt against God and man. Left to go their heretical ways, they will rise again! They are a pollution here among you. A pollution that must be found out, so that either their souls may be cleansed of their sin or England cleansed of their corrupting presence!"

He made that the challenge of a commander rousing men to battle, and there was much nodding of heads and a ready rumble of agreement from his listeners, men and women both, and Anne nodded with the rest because there was no denying what he said. It was almost twenty years since the Lollards' last open, armed revolt, but every now and again a Lollard was too bold and was found out, a reminder that the threat of them was not gone.

"Their stubbornness of heart," Brother Michael declared, "has set them against Church and King and *you*. For the safety of all those souls they seek to corrupt *and* for their own sake, too, they must be found out. You—*you* as good Christians—must keep watch for them and give them over to the Church's mercy, because they are damned to Hell's eternal fires unless brought to repent of their sins, and for most of them that will come only under the weight of the Church's hand pressing down on their pride-filled, heretical hearts!"

Out of seeming-nowhere, Anne felt a coldness of fear close on her own heart. Daved had once said, when she had let a little of her fear for him show, "Remember, love, the friars hunt heretics. By rights I cannot be a heretic, having never been Christian." Had said it lightly, the darkness under his words showing only a little as he added, "Save that of late the learned friars of the Inquisition have determined that Jews may after all be heretics despite never being Christian, and that therefore they can hunt us at their will."

Anne rarely heard him bitter, but he had been bitter then, and close as they were lying together, their heads on one pillow, he had seen her worry, had lifted himself a little and smiled down at her and said, "But they don't hunt us here in England, my love, because . . ." Had kissed her forehead. ". . . here in England . . ." Had kissed her nose. ". . . there are no Jews . . ." Had lightly kissed her lips. ". . . for them to hunt." Had kissed her then in a way that made all other things cease to matter except that he kiss her more and go on to more than kissing.

Which he had. But afterward, when he was gone and she was left to her thoughts, her thoughts had gone where she did not want them to go. Yes, here in London Daved was safe because here no one looked to find out Jews; but mostly he was elsewhere, and for some of that time when he was not here he gave up his seeming to be Christian. Somewhere he had a Jewish home, a Jewish life. Somewhere between where he was known as a Christian merchant and where he was known as a Jew, he slipped from his Christian-seeming into his Jewish life and then he was open to all the perils that came with being a Jew. And even in the whiles that he seemed Christian, how safe was he, when there were men in other countries whose whole purpose was to find out secret Jews?

Those were thoughts from which she tried to keep; and tried the harder when Daved was away from her. Tried, too, not to think of where he might be, what he might be doing, what might be happening to him. And when he *was* here, she only wanted to think about their happiness and naught else. Most especially did not want to hear some preaching friar threaten damnation to heretics because—another thing she tried not to think on—it could be said *she*, by lying in lust with a Jew, was a heretic and as liable to the Church's wrath as he was.

Brother Michael brought his arm down to sweep the pointing finger at the upturned faces below him. "Lollards could be among you even here! On consecrated ground. Feigning to be Christians even as corruption gnaws at their souls, devouring them to damnation!"

Anne wanted to hear no more. The friar's words had nothing to do with her love, nothing to do with Daved, and while Brother Michael warned, "If you listen to these heretics, you risk your soul being damned to burning Hell along with theirs," she backed from the crowd's rear edge and walked away.

From here, she had choice of going by either Foster Lane or Gutheron's to reach Kerie Lane. She meant to take Foster today, it being nearer, but as she went toward it along Cheapside the shift and flow of the ever-moving crowd was changing to clots of people standing in talk with voices rising. That had to mean some news of something was come, but she saw no one she knew to ask what was toward and then had no need, able to hear enough snatches of talk to understand the rebels out of Kent were come back to Black Heath. To hear more as she went, she passed Foster Lane, going on to Gutheron's, and along with word of the rebels what she heard was open anger against King Henry. "Because if he'd done what he should at the start, we'd be done with them now!" was said one way and another by more than a few, while one man loud among others at the corner of Gutheron's said outright, "It's not with the rebels the fault lies! It's with the king! He's never done good, and by God's teeth he's not likely to start! If he'd kept the upper hand over that ape Suffolk and greedy-handed bastards like Lord Saye from the start there'd be none of this we've had this year!"

On the whole, there was more anger than fear, because there was still the river and London bridge between them and the rebels; and then Anne, turning into Gutheron's Lane, forgot it all because maybe twenty feet ahead of her—his back to her—was Daved, going with his straight, long stride. Partly because they were best not seen so openly together, but mostly because of her sudden pleasure in watching him when he did not know she was, she did not hurry to overtake him.

Losing sight of him when he turned left into Kerie Lane, she hurried then, but when she reached the lane herself, still did not see him. She had left the upper half of her fore-door open to the air when she went out. He would have rapped on the door frame and gone in, calling to Bette, and Bette would have come from the kitchen to say she was gone marketing but would be shortly back. But why was Daved come so earlier than usual? Was something gone wrong that he was come so much before his time? Anne dared not hurry. She did not know how much of his comings and goings her neighbors had noted, and after all he was so rarely here and so often came after dark or at hours when folk were busy at their suppers, and left in darkness, before dawn. No one had yet said anything to her of him, anyway, not even her priest or Mistress Upton, and she'd not draw anyone's heed by haste now when there was no open need of haste. But when she was come to her door, was inside and closing it and setting the latch, Bette's laughter in the kitchen made her smile in relief. If Daved had Bette laughing, then nothing could be too far awry, and she called out, mock-sternly, "Bette, have you a man in there with you?"

"That I have, mistress," Bette called back merrily.

The last of Anne's worry went away as Daved met her in the kitchen doorway, smiling as he took the market basket from her arm, and she said past him to Bette as if she had never had any fears at all, "I found everything you asked for. Has the poulterer's boy brought the chicken?"

"He has," Bette said. "I'm rubbing it with rosemary right now. Then it goes in the pot with a little of this wine Master Weir has brought."

She held up a leather bottle. Daved, setting the basket on the table, protested, "I didn't bring that to please a chicken."

He pretended a snatch at it. Bette laughed at him, kept it out of his reach, then gave it to him, saying, "Nay, I have what I want for the fowl, but since you're both so young and nimble, you can take your wine upstairs yourselves, the pair of you, and leave me to my business. Go on."

Daved paused to plant a kiss on her cheek that made her laugh again, and then he and Anne obeyed her. Up the stairs, the wine set aside, Daved kissed Anne on other than her cheek and for long enough that they were both breathless when they drew apart. Only barely was Anne able to gather her wits enough to say, "You're early. Is everything well?"

"With me, most well. With the rest of the world, not so well. Besides Cade's rebels being back, Hal hasn't shown himself, and Pernell knows it and is not happy."

Anne realized with a pang that she had not given the missing Hal a single thought since Friday, nor Pernell, either, and guiltily she said, "I never thought Hal wouldn't be back by now. I've meant for more than a week to visit her anyway." The more especially since Pernell, nearing her time to bear her second child to Raulyn and kept at home by her wide body, was in need of visitors to divert her. "I'll go tomorrow. But all's well with you?" She had hold of the front of Daved's doublet, unwilling to loose him. "You're not here to tell me you're to sail again this soon?"

"All's well with me," Daved assured her. He began to un-pin her veil from her wimple. "Things have merely fallen out well enough that I was free to come to you now instead of later." He laid pins and veil on the table beside the wine bottle and drew out the pins of her wimple so that its folds fell away from her face and neck, leaving them suddenly cool to the air. "I hope you do not mind seeing more of me than you thought to."

"I never mind seeing *more* of you," Anne said, beginning to unfasten his doublet.

Daved set the wimple aside and slipped her close-fitted cap from her head, put it aside, too, and pulled out the two long wooden pins that held her hair in a coil behind her head, letting her hair fall loose to below her waist. But Anne stepped back, realizing, "I'm dressed work-a-day. I didn't mean for you to see me work-a-day."

Smiling at her, his hands on her shoulders keeping her from drawing more away, Daved said, "But I want to see you work-a-day. I want to see you every way." He drew her near for another kiss as long as the first, and still holding her to him, gathered a handful of her hair, smelled it, and sighed, "Chamomile. Like summer sun."

She would have stayed leaning against him, weak with her happiness, but he set her back from him at his arms' length and said, "Before we go further, I have two favors to ask of you."

"Ask, good sir."

"First, that I be allowed the favor of your company this day despite I came before my time."

"Easily granted. The favor is given."

Daved slipped his hands down to take hold on hers, and his merriment went out of him. "The second thing is some-what more difficult to ask."

Holding to her smile despite her heart sinking a little, Anne said, "Ask."

Daved led her to the bed. Its curtains were still drawn between it and the streetward window so they would not be seen as he sat her on the bed's edge and sat beside her, still holding her hands, his eyes searching her face. Her smile gone, Anne as intently searched his, clinging to the hope that surely he would not have been so happy when he first came if he was come, St. Clare forbid, to tell her something ill.

Carefully he said, "I've kept you apart from my work. I wanted to, and there was never reason to do otherwise. Now I must do that otherwise."

He paused as if trying to find how to go on. Anne waited. She knew he and Master Bocking, his uncle, were merchants, partnered together and dealing in rich cloths and finer goods. He had spoken now and again of Bruges, Antwerp, Rouen, and St. Malo as places they went, but she knew nearly nothing else, not even whether his uncle was Jewish or had turned Christian in truth. She had met Master Bocking sometimes at Raulyn's but hardly spoken with him, and Daved talked mostly of their travels—places seen, people met, inns both good and bad, weather out of the ordinary— things he might share with her easily—but hardly ever of his actual merchanting. Like his Jewish life, his merchanting was a thing that took him elsewhere, away from her, and Anne made effort to think of all that part of his life as little as might be.

With his gaze fixed on her face, Daved said, still carefully, "I do more than only merchant, Anne. There are things I do that must be done . . . less openly."

She did not want to know, she had to know, and in almost a whisper, she asked, "What?"

Daved let go one of her hands and reached inside his doublet to bring out a small leather pouch. He tossed it onto the bed beside them. It landed heavily but without a sound. "That is some of it," he said. "In there is a small fortune in gold coins for the duchess of Suffolk."

Anne drew back the hand she had stretched toward the pouch. She had never seen in all her life as much gold as must be in there, and with a different fear than she had had a moment ago she asked, "Why? Why do you have it?"

"Because I've brought it secretly into England, and it must go, likewise secretly, to her grace."

"*You* brought it into England?"

"I brought it."

"Secretly?"

"Secretly."

He waited for her to ask more, but she did not. Not yet and maybe never. Too much of their time together could be lost in questioning what she did not need to know—too much of their time together, and maybe too much else if she knew more than he wanted her to know—and with a calm that surprised her she asked, "What do you want me to do with it?"

Daved's face lighted with laughter. He kissed her hands quickly, first one and then the other, and exclaimed from Solomon's Song, " 'Behold, you are beautiful, my beloved; behold you are fair,' my woman of valor, *eishet chayil*."

Anne leaned forward and kissed him lingeringly on the mouth, as much to hold at bay what else he would say as for the pleasure of doing it. But though he shared the kiss as thoroughly as she gave it, when they drew apart he asked, "Raulyn has spoken with you about a nun who's to come about the duchess of Suffolk's vestments?"

"A week or more ago, yes," Anne said; and what she would be paid for that work would keep her secure for the year and maybe longer.

"So far as the vestments go, all is as he said. This gold is by the side of it. When the nun comes about the vestments, you need only give her this purse, just as it is. Raulyn has told her of it. You give it to her and it becomes her trouble and not yours or mine. Tell her there will be more . . ."

"More?" More gold than was already there, lying on her bed as casual as if it were not a fortune?

"I would risk only so much at a time, not all the gold at once," Daved said, and Anne tightened her hold on his hands.

She lived with the smothered fear that if aught ever happened to him when he was away, she would never know why he never came back to her, but that was a fear for all those days and nights he was not with her. There shouldn't be fear now, not when he was here with her and safe. But he had said there were "things" he did. There were other secrets, then, not just this gold, and if he had to be this careful of this gold, had to keep it so secret here, then fear was here, too, and . . .

Pleased to hear her voice steady, she asked, "Does Raulyn know of the gold?"

"He knows."

So Raulyn was part of Daved's other secrets. How much more was there about Daved, about Raulyn, that she didn't know? How much more was there for her to fear?

That was probably something she would do better not to ask; and she took the pouch and went away with it to the chest beside the door, slipped it well down inside a back corner, under folded table linens and the small box that held her few documents, closed the chest's lid, fingered its key out from the ledge hidden behind the chest's right front leg, locked the chest, and put the key into her small purse hanging from her belt.

Behind her, Daved had risen to his feet but stayed beside the bed. Anne returned to him, put her hands on his waist and stood looking up at him as he looked down at her, both of them searching into the other's eyes before he asked, "No other questions?"

"No questions," she said quietly. Because, still, what mattered most to her was that he was here.

Chapter 5

By evening Frevisse knew that her own and Master Naylor's alarm over the rebels' return was shared by almost no one else. Even among the nuns in St. Helen's, there was less worry over the rebels than anger at the king and his nobles. As one nun declared, "The king will have to make an end of them now. They'll not be given a second chance."

"They shouldn't have been given a first chance," an older nun snapped. "What ails the king, to let them away the way he did?"

Dame Juliana joined in the talk excitedly, but Frevisse listened with an unease that shifted from worry about the rebels to worry at the deep-set discontent against King Henry. Anger at his present failures was one thing and not good, but that anger looked to be grafted now onto already deeply rooted discontent; and if discontent was this deep inside St. Helen's, how much worse must it be among other people? King Henry VI had come to the throne at nine months old, had been king now for nearly twenty-eight years, ruling in his own right for the last fourteen of those, but the great hope that he would reign as his father, famed Henry V, had reigned had faded over the years as he let too much of his power slide away to a few favored lords.

Mainly the duke of Suffolk.

Unfortunately, Suffolk's willingness to power had not been matched by ability to wield it to anyone's good but his own and that of his near followers. Even before this present uprising, the government had been foundering, deep in debt and with a war in France that Suffolk had seemed determined to lose and a French queen——of Suffolk's choosing—— who had yet to birth an heir to the throne. And now Suffolk was dead, and neither King Henry nor any of the nobles around him had taken up his place and power. As the slack handling of the rebels all too clearly showed.

But Dame Juliana's only worry about it all——said when she and Frevisse were alone in the cloister walk the next morning while St. Helen's nuns held their daily chapter meeting——was that Master Naylor would insist they leave. "Simply because he's afraid of trouble that isn't going to happen," she complained.

Frevisse made a wordless sound that meant nothing, unable to say that, whatever Master Naylor might want, they had to stay until Alice's business was done.

"It would be a shame, too, to leave without seeing more of London than we have," Dame Juliana sighed.

Frevisse sharpened to that and instantly encouraged, "Why not, while I see to this matter of the vestments, see what you can of London?" Making it easier for her to meet alone with this Mistress Blakhall. "I doubt the Tower, the

Thames, or St. Paul's have changed over-much since I saw them years ago. Let me see to the vestments while you see more of London, before Master Naylor decides we should be away."

"We can't go out without each other," Dame Juliana said doubtfully.

"There are surely nuns here would go with us both." And when the time came, a St. Helen's nun would likely be easier to leave aside than Dame Juliana would be. Planning rapidly how to work the day to her own ends, she added, "I'll take Master Naylor with me. That way he won't be grumbling at you about everything." And because he would be less trouble to her than young Dickon, overeager to know everything "Dickon can go with you, along with another nun and some nunnery servant to be your guide and keep all well. Yes?"

"Yes," Dame Juliana agreed happily.

St. Helen's prioress, when asked, agreed to it all as readily, saying, "Dame Ursula can accompany you, Dame Juliana. A day's long walking will do her good. For you, Dame Frevisse, I think Dame Clemens will best satisfy. She has family near St. Paul's. She'll know the way to Kerie Lane and then can visit them while you see to your business."

Even Master Naylor made no great objection to their plan, and when all the morning Offices and midday dinner were done, Dame Juliana set out one way with Dame Ursula and Dickon and an older servingman, while Frevisse went her way with Dame Clemens and Master Naylor. Merry at the chance to visit her family, Dame Clemens led them toward St. Paul's, slanting from Bishopsgate by way of Broad Street to the Stocks Market and across to Poultry and along it into Cheapside, talking happily the while. Frevisse tried to match her good humour at least outwardly and ignore Master Naylor stalking silent behind them. They were not yet to St. Paul's when Dame Clemens said, "Here's Gutheron's Lane," and turned rightward into a street not even a fourth so wide as Cheapside. The sky instantly lessened to a narrow band of blue between the houses overhanging the street with their out-thrust upper floors. In rainy weather they would give shelter to anyone walking there and today gave welcome shade. They were none of them so grand as those along Cheapside but all were well-kept, and people called out ready greeting to Dame Clemens from shop and doorstep as she passed before she stopped beside one house's yellow-painted door and said, "Here's my family's place. That's Kerie Lane just there." She pointed across the way to another, narrower lane. "Mistress Blakhall's house is the blue door on the left side along it. You'll not miss it."

Frevisse had never found being assured she could "not miss it" certainty of anything, but she thanked Dame Clemens, and with Master Naylor still following her crossed to Kerie Lane, where Mistress Blakhall's blue door, with a sign of silver scissors on likewise blue hanging above it, was indeed easy to find. The wide shutter covering the shop window was still closed, but the top half of the door was swung open into the shop's shadows, and at Master Naylor's loud knock an old woman in a brown gown and with a clean, white apron and headkerchief hobbled into sight from somewhere beyond the shop. As she peered out across the door, Frevisse stepped forward and said, "Mistress Blakhall expects me, I think. I'm here about the vestments for Lady Alice."

"My mistress will be pleased to see you," the woman said, bobbing a curtsy and opening the door.

The shop was a single open-beamed room the full width of the narrow building, with a closed aumbry with locked doors against one wall, and a tailor's wide wooden table for the cutting of cloth, although there was no sign there had been any tailoring of late.

Then a woman who must be Mistress Blakhall herself came through the doorway at the shop's rear. She was a moderately made woman, in a quiet blue gown with a simple, rounded neck and plain, straight sleeves, with no flourish to her white veil and wimple; but the gown was of finely woven linen, its skirts falling in full and graceful folds to her feet, and her veil was of starched and crisply pressed white lawn. If what she wore were of her own making, she displayed well both her tailoring skill and quiet good judgment.

Frevisse said, "I'm Dame Frevisse. I've come on the Lady Alice's business."

Understanding beyond the outward meaning of that flickered in Mistress Blakhall's eyes, but she only said, making a deep curtsy, "My lady. You're most welcome here."

"It's my pleasure," Frevisse returned, which was, strictly speaking, untrue.

Looking past Frevisse to Master Naylor still outside, Mistress Blakhall asked, "Will it please you to come in, too?"

Her servant-woman did not give him a choice, beckoning at him briskly, saying, "No need to loiter there in the street. Come you in. You can keep me company in the kitchen the while they're at talk."

"We'll leave you to Bette, sir," Mistress Blakhall said; and added to Frevisse, " If you'll come upstairs, please?"

Frevisse had quick sight of the kitchen beyond the shop— a cleanly kept room with a wide-hearthed fireplace against one wall, a well-scrubbed wooden table, several stools, and a window and back door opening to a garden's greenery— before she gathered her skirts away from her feet and followed Mistress Blakhall up the steep stairs into a pleasant chamber that was plainly where Mistress Blakhall mostly lived.

Frevisse guessed she much worked here, too. An embroidery frame stood near the wide southward window, and while Mistress Blakhall crossed toward a small table set with a pewter pitcher, pewter cups, and a cloth-covered plate, Frevisse went to see what work she had on the frame. Her soft exclaim, though, was for what she saw beyond the window, and Mistress Blakhall, coming with a filled cup in one hand and a plate with sugared borage petals and small ginger cakes in the other, said, "It does startle, doesn't it?"

"It does," Frevisse agreed. She leaned outward to look up and farther up at St. Paul cathedral's central tower and soaring spire, huge and graceful against the sky, with no clutter of buildings between to lessen the power of the sight.

"In winter," Mistress Blakhall said, "when the sun rides low, the spire's shadow slides across the roofs like a sundial's shadow across the hours."

And when the cathedral's bells rang out for any reason, the glory of their ringing must crash down over the rooftops louder than thinking, Frevisse thought.

But today, at this early afternoon hour, they were quiet, and at Mistress Blakhall's gesture, Frevisse sat on the seat below the window, took the offered plate and cup, and then, while Mistress Blakhall returned to the table for her own, leaned over to see the work on the embroidery frame. On the square of heavy linen held flat and taut by a strong cord laced back and forth through its edges and to the frame was lightly drawn St. Mark's winged lion in a ten-inch roundel. The background was complete, done with a stitch that Frevisse knew was quick and easy. But she also knew, from sorry experience the misguided times she had tried to learn needlework, that however quick and easy a stitch might be, whoever plied the needle and thread could still do it badly and this work was done very well. Besides that, the lion was outlined with a thin black backstitch and the first gold thread curved into the flare of its mane, held in place by stitches of linen thread brought through from the underside to catch a small loop of the gold and hold it in place invisibly. Nothing more than the first curl of the mane was done but it was enough, and Frevisse looked up with willing respect at Mistress Blakhall waiting on the other side of the frame and said, "It's beautiful work. Were you taught in France?" Because the *opus anglicanum*—English needlework so beautiful it had for centuries been desired by popes and given as royal gifts among kings—had lessened over the years into barely more than ordinary, and this was not.

Mistress Blakhall's eyes brightened. "You've seen French needlework?"

"I was twice at school in French nunneries, and I've seen Parisian work."

Smiling, Mistress Blakhall sat down beside her. "My teacher was from Paris. She married someone of the duke of Exeter's household and ended here, teaching girls who—" Mistress Blakhall tried for a French way of speaking. "—'have the fingers of pigs and the eyes crossed, they see so poorly what they do so badly.'"

Frevisse laughed, then nodded at St. Mark's lion. "You at least must have pleased her."

"She did finally say she'd not mind admitting I was her student."

"It was praise truly earned." Frevisse looked around the room, and thinking of the little-used shop downstairs, asked, "Do you have your workshop elsewhere? Or do your women work at their homes?"

"Save for another woman I sometimes hire to work plain repeating patterns for borders, I do all my own work."

"You've no apprentices?"

"None at present. When my husband died, he had none because we were still working to establish ourselves as makers of church vestments and altar cloths and banners and such."

"His skill as a tailor joined to yours," Frevisse said.

"Just so." Mistress Blakhall's smile was tender with remembrance. She was young but had lived enough to have lost youth's blandness; her face was the more comely for having years of life and love and memories behind it, and her husband must hold a dear place in those memories because she still smiled as she said, "Matthew always said he was only a plain tailor doing plain work, and I'd laugh at him because his 'plain' work was so far beyond only 'good.' Near the end he even had a commission from as far off as Lincoln, from a canon willing to pay for an excess of gold thread to have what he wanted."

"That he might outshine his fellows when saying Mass," Frevisse suggested.

Mistress Blakhall laughed. "Without doubt. But we loved doing lesser commissions, too, for poorer priests and less wealthy folk. Matthew would tell me to work some gold thread into a halo and not charge. 'It will be our gift to the saint,' he'd say. He was a very good man, was Matthew."

And his wife had loved him dearly. Was that why she had not married again, Frevisse wondered.

But maybe thinking she had gone too far from business, Mistress Blakhall said more crisply, "I was the more able to carry on the work after he died because I was already a femme sole and in the Broiderers Guild." Not one of the great guilds of London nor wielding any power worth mention in the city's government, but giving her place and rights in the city and some warrant of her work, because like other guilds, the Broiderers protected its members by overseeing the quality of work done under their name.

Frevisse nodded, understanding all of that, but asked, "If you work almost alone, this commission from her grace of Suffolk will take a lengthy time, won't it?"

"If done well, yes. But then this is work over which time may be taken."

"There being no great haste, I suppose," Frevisse said. Since his grace the duke was going to be dead for some time to come.

But that brought thought of why else Frevisse was here and she added quietly, "There's the other matter, too."

Mistress Blakhall immediately rose, left her cup and plate on the table, and went to a chest standing against the wall beside the door while taking a key from the small purse hung from her narrow belt. Frevisse rose to her feet, too, went to set down her own cup and plate on the table, then waited there while Mistress Blakhall unlocked the chest, opened the lid, took something out, and came back to the table carrying a leather pouch in a close-fitted net bag hung from a long loop of stout cord. The pouch was not large but large enough that Frevisse wondered with dismay how she was supposed to hide it on herself between now and giving it to Alice. Her dismay deepened when she took the pouch from Mistress Blakhall. It was heavy, and weighing it in her hand, she asked, "Do you know what this is?"

Mistress Blakhall hesitated, then said, "I was told it's gold coins that you're to take secretly to her grace of Suffolk. The rest will be here later. That's all I know."

Sharply, too surprised to hide her surprise, Frevisse said, "What rest?"

"He didn't want to risk bringing all of it at once." Mistress Blakhall sounded as suddenly doubtful as Frevisse was surprised. "You didn't know there was going to be more?"

"I didn't, no."

They stared at each other, and Frevisse sensed that Mistress Blakhall was no happier than she was at the business. They were both being used to other people's purposes, and Frevisse decided that whomever she was angry at, it was not Mistress Blakhall, who now said hesitantly, "I put the pouch in that net bag and added the cord so you could wear it around your neck and hidden down your gown. I thought it would help."

No, she was not angry at Mistress Blakhall at all, Frevisse decided. Her plain, practical help was welcome in the midst of this nonsense of someone else's making; and Frevisse smiled and said, "Will you help me, so I needn't unwimple altogether?"

Between them, they got the cord around Frevisse's neck, under her wimple, and the pouch slipped inside her gowns, hidden by the heavy layers of cloth. Mistress Blakhall stepped back, studied her, and said, "There's no sign of it. No one will wonder anything."

How she would keep it concealed at St. Helen's Frevisse did not know, but sufficient unto the moment was the trouble thereof and she only said, "You have patterns to show me, I think?"

They spent a pleasant while then with a gathering of patterns Mistress Blakhall kept. All were of the expected angels and saints, various beasts and birds, twining vines with leaves and flowers or fruit. Most were usual, but some had a grace the others lacked—a turn of a head, a body's curve, the lift of an angel's wing that just a little more pleased the eye. At Frevisse's question, Mistress Blakhall said those were her own, and Frevisse's opinion of her as a craftswoman rose more.

On the last of the papers were drawings of the duke of Suffolk's heraldic arms—a shield with a bar across its middle, two leopards' heads above and one leopard's head below. On the paper around the shield Mistress Blakhall had been trying variations of the leopards' heads. By the laws of heraldry they could be presented only one way: a neckless head facing straight outward. Although there was no choice about that, she had been planning with pen and ink how to lay the stitches when the time came and trying different shapes for their eyes. There were pairs of eyes narrowed, pairs of eyes wide; pairs of eyes very round; pairs of eyes half-shut; and in a lower corner, eyes very crossed.

"I made a start on the arms," Mistress Blakhall said, "on the chance my lady of Suffolk wants them on the cope."

"She does, but not boldly." Not for humility's sake, Frevisse suspected, but because it would be safer, given the general hatred there was for Suffolk, even dead. "The choice of saints has been left to me, though. I was thinking, in keeping with Suffolk's death, they should maybe be saints who had been beheaded." She had also been thinking how they would look across the great curve of the cope: an array of saints all holding their particular symbol in one hand— St. Paul with the sword that had beheaded him, St. Denis with his stake, St. Winifred with her pastoral staff, St. Urban with a scourge, St. Osyth with her crown and keys . . . while their other hand held their head in the crook of their other arm.

The thought was only a jest and a poor one at that, and before Mistress Blakhall might start to take her seriously, she said, "Perhaps one beheaded saint, anyway. St. Denis, I think, since Suffolk had such ties with France. But since I must needs come see you again, perhaps we'd best not decide everything this time."

"There's still much deciding to do," Mistress Blakhall assured her. "We've hardly made a beginning. Not least will be choosing the cloth, though Master Grene can help with that, if you like. Would you care for something more to eat and drink before you leave? Bette will have something ready in the garden. It's cooler there than here by now in the afternoon."

"Something to drink would be welcome," Frevisse said, and they went downstairs and through the kitchen, into the garden where it was indeed cooler. Like the house, the garden was long and narrow, with a board fence down either side and across the end to give some privacy from its neighbors. Its beds looked to be mostly herbs and vegetables—the peas were in full flourish, ready to be picked—but an iris grew in a blue-glazed pot the other side of the doorway and something boldly yellow was flowering in one corner.

A small roof built out from the house wall beside the kitchen door gave sheltered sitting, and Master Naylor rose to his feet from one of the kitchen stools set in its shade.

Bette was there, too, and the pottery cup in Master Naylor's hand showed he had not been neglected. By the time Frevisse and Mistress Blakhall had sat down on other stools and Frevisse had bade Master Naylor sit again, Bette had hobbled into the kitchen and out again with more cups and a loaf of bread on a cutting board to set on the little table there. The bread surprised Frevisse. Rather than a plain loaf, it was made of several thick strands of dough—four, she counted—braided over and under one another in a complicated way she had only ever seen . . .

She looked across the table at Mistress Blakhall and found her staring at the loaf as if startled to see it. The next moment Mistress Blakhall's look flashed up, first at Frevisse, then to Master Naylor, with worry and question in her eyes. Master Naylor seemed to have no especial thought about it, or if he did, he had it as hidden as Frevisse had hers; and Mistress Blakhall looked to Bette and asked lightly about butter.

Frevisse was still left wondering. In her childhood travels with her wide-wandering parents she had seen such oddly made bread in only one place, a Jew's house where her parents had sheltered during a bad stretch of winter weather. She had been too young to understand much, only that her father had sometime befriended Master Ezra and now was being befriended in return, and that for some reason their stay with him had to be kept almost secret, as if being there were something wrong. Later, when she was older, she had understood that Christians were not supposed to mix with Jews or Jews with Christians, each supposed to look on the other as unclean and damned. But of Master Ezra and his household she had only good memories, and few though those were, they included watching Master Ezra's wife make the Shabbat bread.

Challah. That had been what Master Ezra's wife had called it, and said, "So we have made it for every Shabbat since the days of Moses and maybe longer. Longer than Rome was, or Pharoah in Egypt." Her name was gone from Frevisse's memory, but her words had stayed, along with the opening out of time they had given her. Time as a vast thing longer than Frevisse's life, longer than more lives than she could imagine, back past the stories of Rome her father sometimes told her, back to all the stories from the Bible that she knew had taken hundreds of years to happen.

Because of that she had remembered challah.

But why was it here, on Mistress Blakhall's table? To judge by her startlement, she surely had not meant it to be seen. Which meant it was indeed something more to her than merely bread. But she couldn't be Jewish, not here in England where there were no Jews. Could she?

Chapter 6

Relieved to be rid of the gold, Anne had been enjoying the nun's company until sight of the challah jarred her out of all pleasure. She had forgotten to ask Daved if challah could be treated the same as other bread after the Shabbat; had put it away in a stone crock in a corner of the kitchen only to forget about it yesterday, too, when he was here. What had prompted Bette to remember it and set it out for a guest? But of course it was only bread to Bette, and to Anne's relief neither Dame Frevisse nor her man gave sign it was anything else to them, either. And anyway, how could it be?

Still, keeping up a quiet courtesy was become an effort, and Anne made no demur when Dame Frevisse said, "Pleasant though your garden and company are, I fear we should return to St. Helen's before the day is later. When would be best for me to come back?"

Her man said, displeased, "You didn't finish today?"

"No," Dame Frevisse said calmly, untouched by his displeasure, keeping her questioning look at Anne.

"Tomorrow in the afternoon should do well, if you will," Anne said, because Daved would likely bring more of the gold when he came tonight.

"Tomorrow then," Dame Frevisse agreed and stood up, and Anne willingly saw her through the house to the front door and stayed on the doorstep after their farewells, watching her, followed by her man, to the corner.

Only as she turned to go back inside did she see Mistress Upton waving for her to come join her in a cluster of other women from along the lane. Expecting to be asked who her visitors had been, she went to join them, but Mistress Upton burst out, short-breathed with excitement, "Have you heard? About the bishop of Salisbury?"

"No. What of him?" Anne asked, trying to put a face to the name. Bishop Ayscough of Salisbury was King Henry's confessor, a royal councillor, and among those around the king much disliked for their greed and ill-governing but not someone much seen in London.

"He's been murdered!" Mistress Smith exclaimed almost triumphantly. "Pulled from the altar while saying Mass and murdered by his own people!"

Anne gasped. "In the cathedral? When?"

"This Sunday just past. Not in his cathedral, no. Just off in Wiltshire somewhere." Mistress Upton waved a vague hand at the wide, strange world beyond London. "Brother Michael was preaching in Grey Friars yard today. I was just coming away from there when the word came spreading. It will be to the other end of London by now."

"It's not just some rumor?"

"No! It's certain! It's straight from Westminster. It's put

the cat into the dovecote there, for certain! That's two bishops murdered this year. And the duke of Suffolk. Two bishops and a duke. Has there ever been the like? Where's it to end? You have to wonder."

Anne shook her head, in disbelief more than answer. Angry troops at Portsmouth, tired of being told there was no money for their pay, had killed the much-hated bishop of Chichester in January. Then there had been the duke of Suffolk. And now the bishop of Salisbury. And the rebels were returned to Black Heath. Mistress Upton's question was only too apt. Where *was* it to end?

"You should come again to hear Brother Michael," Mistress Upton was urging. "He's saying it's the Lollards. That it's them profaning against God and not enough being done to stop them that's bringing all this on us."

"I shouldn't wonder it was some of them killed Bishop Ayscough," Mistress Hopton put in.

"At least there'll be no talk of making him a martyr," her daughter laughed. "He was no Becket, the greedy-guts."

"It's what the world is coming to, I have to ask," Mistress Upton insisted. "And why isn't the king doing something to mend it all? That's what I ask."

Anne began to retreat, saying, "I must go help Bette with supper now."

"So who was the nun?" Mistress Smith asked. "More business for you?"

Still retreating, Anne said something about a new commission for vestments from a lady in Oxfordshire, avoiding mention of the duke of Suffolk and smiling as if she felt like smiling, but when her door was shut behind her the smile disappeared, and she went into kitchen where Bette was washing the dishes from their guests and the challah sat cloth-covered on the table. With no word to Bette, whose back was turned, Anne took up the challah, went out into the garden, broke it into small bits, and scattered it along the path between the garden beds. The sparrows were swooping down for it before she turned away.

That done, and leaving Bette to the kitchen, Anne went upstairs, meaning to work on the St. Mark lion while the afternoon light held, hoping the needlework would keep her from other thoughts. From dead bishops and challah and the time to wait until Daved would be here tonight. Surely one of needlework's comforts was that work as fine as for the lion kept her from too much thought, even of Daved. The underside couching she was using needed high skill, while to lay the gold to the lion's shape so the beast did not simply lie flatly on the cloth but seemed about to move out from it with life of its own was another skill all of its own, and both of them requiring care rather than hurry.

She had made good progress, was pleased with her work when time for supper came, and afterwards she and Bette sat together in the garden, talking a little about their day's visitors and the Suffolk vestments and Bishop Ayscough's death, before Bette asked, "What of Mistress Grene's boy? Has he shown himself yet?"

"Not that I've heard, no," Anne said, with the guilty thought that tomorrow she would *have* to go and see Pernell. "But surely he's back by now," she added hopefully.

"Otherwise he's been gone too long, even for a boy's jape," Bette said. "And his mother so near her time, too."

Anne's guilt grew. Too taken up with Daved, she'd given neither Hal nor Pernell enough thought.

"You don't think maybe he's gone to join the rebels, do you?" Bette asked.

"Hal?" Anne laughed. "Not Hal."

"Um," Bette said, unconvinced.

They sat then in silence for a while longer until, with the blue evening shadows deep around them and St. Paul's spire gold against the sky with setting sunlight, Bette said she'd go bedward now. Anne helped her lay out her mattress and blanket on the kitchen floor, undid her headkerchief for her and helped her out of her over-gown and to lie down, Bette grumbling all the way about stiff fingers and stiffer knees. Anne knew the grumbling was to cover the arthritic's pain; knew, too, that Bette feared what would become of her when she could no longer work at all, despite Anne had promised more than once she'd always have a home with her. Bette had been part of Matthew's life, and Anne meant never to dishonor his memory by failing Bette in her need, but she also knew how fears could be stronger than assurances and likewise knew she was failing Bette in a different way by not bringing in a girl to help her—someone young enough for Bette to train but too young to be a threat of soon succeeding her. The trouble was that someone else here would be someone else to know about Daved, and Anne did not want that. Daved. Even his name was like the beating of her own heart. She would never make more chance-ridden the little they had. Not for Bette or anyone.

With the hearthfire covered and Bette still mumble-grumbling, Anne closed and barred the kitchen door and window, shutting the kitchen into night-darkness, and went into the equal darkness of the shut and shuttered shop, needing no light to find her way to the long-legged stool set beside the door where she could wait in quick reach of the latch. She had dressed well for the nun's visit, had no need to change for Daved, and so was left with only the waiting. And thinking. What she most wanted to think on was Daved—to close all else but him out of her thoughts—but instead found herself thinking about the waiting.

Waiting now made up so much of her life. But there had been other waiting, too, and in the way thoughts had of going where they would, she found herself remembering the hours of waiting and praying beside Matthew's bed through his last illness. Praying first that he be healed, and then—when that was past hope—for his easy passing out of pain.

That had not been given, either, and since then prayer had come less easily to her. Not because her faith was less, but because she doubted how much use her prayers were. God's will was God's will, and what good were prayers?

She had not said that to anyone. Most certainly had not said it to her priest. She had bought Masses for Matthew's soul; still went to church on Sundays and holy days and some saints' days; still made confession and Communion at Eastertide; had even confessed her sin of lust, naming no names, and faithfully did penance for it two days a week by fasting. Since her longing for Daved was unabated and she gave way to it whenever he was here, she didn't know how much good that penance did her soul and did not want to know, because knowing would make no difference. She would have Daved while she might and, when she could not, then make what fuller recompense she could.

And, despite herself, she prayed that recompense would be long in coming.

So here she sat in darkness waiting for him. Worried because he wasn't yet here. Afraid, as always, that something had happened to him. Knowing the day would come when he would never come to her again, that time would come when even these little whiles of him would end and she would maybe never know why. Life held so many perils, and more perils for him than for most because he was a merchant and traveled, and more beyond that because of his deadly secret. And there was always illness. And he might decide he loved his wife after all, or at least owed her the duty of faithfulness.

Anne's hands in her lap clutched tightly to each other. Mostly she kept away from thought of Daved's wife. Like her own marriage to Matthew, Daved's marriage had been made for him, but he had been hardly fifteen at the time and not even met his wife before their wedding but, "There's nothing against her," he had said the one time he had talked of her. That had been before he and Anne first came to-gether, when he had been warning her about himself. "She sees well to everything that's ours when I'm gone. When I'm with her, she sees well to me. But for no one's fault, except maybe mine for being gone so often and long, there's never been more than duty between us."

Because she and Daved had both known where their talk was going, what they both intended before they were done, Anne had been able to ask, "Do you . . . bed her?"

Gently, steadily, Daved had answered, "I do all a hus-band's duties. It's her right."

"Will she know about me?"

"I will not tell her, no."

But this woman whose name he had never said would be the one told if anything befell him. She would be the one able to grieve for him as his widow if, God forbid, he died. And Anne—whether she ever learned his fate or he simply never came back to her—would never be able openly to grieve at all. No matter what their love, all she could ever be was one of the secrets in his life. And the secrets in his life were begin-ning to frighten her more, the more she knew of them. This secret shifting of gold for one. He was very at ease with the se-crecy of it. How much of such things did he do? That Raulyn was part of it still a little surprised her but . . .

Sitting there in the dark, able to look at nothing but her thoughts, she looked inward for her surprise that Daved did such a thing and found no surprise at all. Why not? But she knew. Had known from the first that there was more to him than his outward seeming.

Or did she tell herself that to ease the new fears that came with knowing yet more of how deep that other part of his life must run, how much besides "merchant" he was?

How many seemings—how many lies—did Daved live with?

The question came unbidden and unwanted. He seemed

to be only a merchant but he was more. He seemed to be a Christian and he was not. He seemed to love her . . .

Was that another lie among the rest?

With a certainty that went beyond thought, Anne refused that. Their love was no lie. And if it came to lying, what of herself? She seemed a chaste widow and that was a lie as deep as any in which Daved lived. She was anything but chaste, and at that moment she heard his footfall and was on her feet before his first soft knock. She had not barred the door, only needed to lift the latch, slightly open the door, and he was there, slipping past her, briefly a blackness against the light of the lanterns hung at either end of the street, then simply a felt shape behind her while she shut the door and swung the bar down across it.

With all the world and its fears shut out, she turned to him, put her arms around him, drew him to her even as he pressed her back against the door, his body to hers, their mouths finding each other in the darkness. With fiercely matched need, they took each other there against the door; and later, naked then, in her bed; and then again, until finally they lay quiet in each other's arms, satiate and tired at last.

She slept a little, her head on his shoulder, and awakened to his hand slowly stroking down her spine. She shivered with pleasure and lifted her head to smile into his eyes, able to see him in the starlight through the open gardenward window. She had always slept with windows closed until one warm night Daved had said he spent many a night, shipboard and otherwise, without a window to shut and had never suffered for it, so would she risk the night vapors or did he have to smother here? She had laughed and set the shutters wide, and often did now, even when alone. That Daved brought her to dare things and see things in ways she would not have without him were among the reasons she loved him.

Whether, at the last, that would be to the good or bad

she mostly kept from wondering—most carefully kept from wondering it when they were together, because in those brief whiles she wanted no thought of anything but him, no thought of otherwise or afterwards, and now she smiled into his eyes, and he smiled into hers, said softly, "My love," and touched her cheek with the gentleness that always came to them after their desperate need of each other was eased. "My very love."

"*My* very love," Anne softly echoed, kissed him gently, and settled her head into the curve of his shoulder again. They lay content to be with one another; but before long the night's deep silence and their peace was stirred by, first, a bird's twittering under the house eaves and then a cautious bird-trill from the garden. Dawn was nearing and Anne's arm tightened across Daved, both of them knowing he should leave in darkness the way he had come in darkness. But for a little longer . . .

Daved sighed and stirred and Anne let him go. Careful not to touch each other, they slid from the bed and dressed. Hers was the easier. She only slipped on her chemise, and Daved, sitting on the bed-edge to pull on his hosen, glanced at her and whispered, "That's unkind."

"Sir?" Anne asked innocently.

He reached out and cupped a hand over one of her breasts. "To put so little over your loveliness that I want to strip you naked again."

Anne laughed softly and reached toward him in return; but Daved stood abruptly up and away from her, saying, "Oh, no you don't."

Anne laughed again and stayed where she was, admiring his legs while he took his shirt from the floor where it had fallen. With it, he took up the narrow length of soft-woven wool, tasseled at each corner, that he wore under his shirt, wrapped around his waist and always out of sight. She knew the thing had something to do with being a Jew and that was all, and she turned her eyes away until it was hidden under his shirt and he was putting on his doublet. While he buttoned the doublet's front, she picked up his belt and its purse and sheathed dagger from the floor where they had dropped when she had undone the belt from his waist in her eagerness to have him. She held them ready while he tied his hosen to his doublet's lower edge, sat on the bed again, groped for his shoes, and put them on. Standing, he took the belt, buckled it on, settled the purse on one hip, his dagger on the other, and paused, one hand on the purse as if he had remembered something. Not the gold. The one thing they had done between coming upstairs and reaching the bed was he had given her another pouch that she had already locked away. But with apology in his voice, Daved said, "There's one more thing I'd ask of you. I've lacked the chance to do it myself and don't know, now, if I'll have the chance." He brought out a folded, sealed paper from his purse. "This is a letter that needs go to Joanne of Dartmouth in the House of Converts outside Ludgate. Do you know it? Could you take it to her?"

"Of course," Anne said and held out a hand as if her mind had not paused and jerked at his words. What had Daved to do with the House of Converts? The place had been founded, when there were still Jews in England, by a long-gone king as somewhere for Jews to live after they had become Christians. Because by Christian law every Jew in Christendom was the property of one lord or another, with each lord free to make what profit he could from them, and because no lord relished his loss of profit when one of his Jews turned Christian, a Jew who converted forfeited all that he held—land, house, all lesser goods, even his clothing and the tools of his trade—to his lord. The House of Converts had been endowed to shelter and support Jews impoverished by their baptism, and through all the years since Jews were gone from England it had sheltered Jews who came from abroad to its safety. Anne could remember at least twice when prayers were asked in London's churches for the soul of a Jew newly come to Christ and England. But what business did Daved have with anyone there?

"It's a thing my uncle and I sometimes do," he said. "We bring letters that can't come into England any other way."

Letters. Another thing about him she hadn't known, and a small corner of her mind went cold with wondering yet again how much else there was in his life secret from her. But she only said, "Joanne of Dartmouth. Yes. I'll take it to her."

Still with apology, Daved said, "She may not be there anymore. I don't know how long ago it was she converted. Her family disowned her when she did. Or her brother did as head of her family and no one else had a choice. He's lately dead, and there are some who want to know how she does and to tell her how they do. But that's a thing best not done openly, for her good and theirs. If you can find a way to give this to her with no one else the wiser, that would be good. Anne, I'm sorry. I wouldn't ask this if so much else wasn't happening."

She went to him, as if closing the distance between their bodies might close the distance her thoughts were making between him and her. Since she had known from the first the necessity of secrecy in his life, should it make difference there was more secrecy than she had ever guessed at? With a quick, firm kiss she resealed their never-spoken bargain against questions between them, and Daved held her tightly to him, his face pressed against her hair.

But there was ever more birdsong in the garden, and Anne drew back. He had to go while darkness held and they both knew it, and he turned from her, gathered his loose, open-fronted surcoat from the chair, and went down the stairs, Anne following him. In the shop he shrugged into the surcoat while she unbarred the door, and when she turned from doing that, he gathered her to him for a last kiss. Then he was gone, slipped out through the barely opened door and away into London's dawn-darkness.

Silently, with the great care of wanting to think of nothing else, Anne shut the door behind him, barred it again, and stood listening for any outside sound that might mean trouble but heard only Bette's even breathing from the kitchen. Staying where she was, Anne prayed him safely away through the streets. Their small whiles together were all they had—were all they were ever likely to have—and in those whiles she wanted no question in her heart or mind about what had gone before or would come afterward. It was when he was gone from her that questions came. Questions and grief for all they would never have, all she must never hope for.

Pressing her hands flat to the door and leaning her forehead against the wood between them, she let the hot, slow tears slide down her cheeks.

Chapter 7

The clear dawn was slowly blooming into a spread of gold, greens, reds, and blues through the painted glass of St. Helen's church's east window above the choir stalls where the nuns were making their way through the sunrise-welcoming Office of Prime with psalms and prayers of hope for a good and godly day to come.

Frevisse, too wryly aware of how often that hope was unfulfilled, especially doubted today would be either good or godly. Nor were her feelings helped by being in an unfamiliar church among unfamiliar nuns. The Offices of prayer were the same across Christendom, but each nunnery was its own place, and the differences of pace and blended voices through the prayers and psalms might be slight but it was like the slight stubbing of a toe when walking a familiar way—it threw off the stride.

Besides that, the midnight Offices had come, as always, in the middle of the night, with afterward return to bed until time to rise for Prime, and summer nights were shorter than winter ones. This near to midsummer, dawn came far too soon after midnight and last night Frevisse had slept little even in that little time meant for sleep. After Lauds, her thoughts had started up and refused to be quelled, and though she had hoped to weave her worries into Prime's psalms and prayers and leave them there, this morning worry was stronger than intent.

"*. . . in Domino confisus, non vacillavi. Scrutare me, Domine, et proba me . . . Non sedeo cum viris iniquis . . . Odi conventum male agentium et cum impiis non consido.*" . . . in the Lord I trust, I have not wavered. Search me, Lord, and prove me . . . I do not sit with unjust men . . . I hate a gathering of evildoers and with the impious I do not sit down.

Instead of shelter, the words brought up thoughts of the bag of gold weighing twice as heavy on her mind as it presently did around her neck. What wrongs had Suffolk done to gain such wealth? What more wrong was being done in the shifting of it out of England and back again? Was she, by helping at it, "sitting down with unjust men?" And how much more of it would there be? How could she hide it all well enough to keep it secret, now she had committed herself to this deception?

And there was the bishop of Salisbury's murder. Dame Clemens had been exclaiming over it when they rejoined her yesterday, and loud, satisfied talk of it had been in the streets all the way back to St. Helen's, with the general anger at the king added in, one man loud among other loud men along the street declaring, "That Jack Cade has the right hold on things. By the sound of him, he's nobody's fool."

"Not so much a fool as the king is, anyway," someone else said, and they had all broken into rawking laughter.

In St. Helen's the talk had been more hushed, but a nun's slight mention of Salisbury as a martyr had brought surprisingly rude laughter from more nuns than not.

"There was nothing of the martyr about either him or that Chichester," an older nun had said bluntly. "They were greed-ridden bastards, and the worms are welcome to them."

There was talk, too, that King Henry was gone from Westminster and not toward the rebels but north, maybe to Berkhampstead.

"Why there?" a nun had asked.

"Because it's on the road to even farther away from London," another snapped.

It seemed even the nuns had had enough of the king, but Frevisse's own great worry remained the gold. In the dorter here, as in St. Frideswide's, she had a sleeping cell to herself, so at bedtime she had slipped the pouch under her pillow when she had undressed to the undergown in which she slept. Nunnery pillows were thin, though, and the pouch had made such an uncomfortable lump under her head that she almost welcomed slipping the cord around her neck again when she went to the Offices. How much more would there be? Suppose there was finally too much of it for her to carry unseen? What was she supposed to do then? Apparently that problem was to be all hers.

Prime came to its end with the blessing, *"Dies et actus nostros in sua pace disponat Dominus omnipotens."*—May the almighty Lord place in his peace our days and acts.—and she made the response, "Amen," with her whole heart, little though she thought peace was likely to come to her soon. Indeed, she was worrying at the problem of the gold again by the time she and Dame Juliana were following the St. Helen's nuns along the cloister walk to the refectory for their slight breakfast of ale and thickly buttered bread that was supposed to curb their hunger until midday dinner.

Today, though, dinner would be more than ample for her and Dame Juliana. A message had been brought after her return here yesterday, inviting her and Dame Juliana to Master Grene's house to dine. It was for more than courtesy's sake, Frevisse supposed. He likely meant it for chance to show them his best cloth, in hope Frevisse would buy from him what was needed for the Suffolk vestments, and Frevisse thought she very likely would, since he was unlikely to risk the duchess of Suffolk's disfavor by ill-dealing with her. But going there might keep her from Mistress Blakhall's today, and except she had to keep a goodly outward front for why she was in London, she would have been tempted to refuse.

There was still the matter of the cloth for St. Frideswide's, too. She had considered the possibility of hiding at least some of the gold in the cloth; but even if she somehow did, when time came to give Alice the coins how would she go about getting them out again from cloth wrapped and packaged for travel without curiosity if not outright suspicions being awakened? Her better thought—and the one she settled on while breaking her fast among the other nuns—was that the books she was supposed to buy unbound would surely be wrapped in waxed cloth to protect them. If she likewise demanded a box for them, too—a small, lidded chest—and had it with her in her sleeping cell, she would easily be able to spread coins flat in the box's bottom or layer them between pages. With the box then strapped shut, the coins were unlikely to be found by chance, and it was against chance she had to guard, because anyone who knew she had the gold and looked for it would find it, whatever she did. That was the point of all the present secrecy—to keep anyone from even suspicion the gold existed. And if to justify buying the box she had to buy more books than first intended, then she would, and Alice could repay St. Frideswide's for them. And for the box.

With that thought, she suggested to Dame Juliana after breakfast that they forego Nones this morning to go book-buying before dinner at Master Grene's. "Then that much at least will be done and off our minds," she said.

Dame Juliana willingly agreed, a servant was sent to inform Master Naylor, and he and Dickon were waiting at the gatehouse for them after Tierce, Master Naylor looking less than happy and saying, when he and Dickon had straightened from their bows, "You might want to think again about going out today, my ladies."

"Is there new trouble?" Dame Juliana asked.

"Not since yesterday, no. That's not saying more isn't on the way."

"Better we see to our business before it comes, then," Frevisse said and went out the gateway before more could be said by anyone. Both Dame Juliana and Dickon followed readily and Frevisse wished she was more of their mind and less of Master Naylor's; and before they had gone much along Bishopsgate she was even more of his mind. There seemed less buying and selling today than talk even louder and more angry than yesterday's. London seemed like a seething pot on hot coals, ready to roil into full boiling trouble if the fire rose under it even a little.

At the Gilded Quill the handling of books and making choices somewhat eased her mind away from all of that and even from Master Naylor's silent disapproval looming solid as a stone-built wall outside the shop door where he and Dickon waited. Still, in all conscience, she could not buy *Regiment of Princes,* but with an inward defiance—and an outward assurance to Dame Juliana that Lady Alice would pay for most of it—she purchased not only the children's abece and Capgrave's *Life of St. Katherine* but the fables *and* the *Siege of Troy,* then bargained with Master Colop first on a price that satisfied them both, then that the books be delivered to St. Helen's not only wrapped in waxed cloth but with a solid, lidded, wooden box to be provided by Master Colop.

"Because we'll be going so far with them," she said firmly enough to prevent any questions; and added, "Master Naylor," for him to come forward to count out coins into Master Colop's hand.

He did, grimly and silently, and with Master Colop's promise that the books in their box would be at St. Helen's before Vespers today, they left, Frevisse saying when they were in the street again, "We should be away to Master Grene's now. He's at the sign of the Red Swan in St. Swithins Lane off Lombard Street, not much beyond the Stocks Market."

With people drawn homeward to their dinners, the streets were somewhat less crowded; they went easily back to the market place where London's stocks stood and from there along Lombard Street, Master Naylor needing only to ask which corner was St. Swithins Lane. It proved to be a narrow street but with goodly houses on each side, some of them with courtyards closed from the street by gates, most of them with street-facing shops mostly displaying mercers' wares, but there was a jeweler's, too, with gold and silver chains and a few gems laid out on black velvet to show their beauty the better, and a cordwainer's with particularly fine shoes and boots of cordovan leather on show.

Master Grene's place, with its painted sign of a Red Swan hanging out above its door, was one of the larger places, set on the right-hand side of the street with both a shop fronting the street and a wide, red-painted gate into a yard behind it. Master Naylor had been leading, but he slowed, probably uncertain whether to go to gate or shop, until a servant wearing a plain-cut red tabard over his tunic, stepped forward from beside the gate, and asked, "You're here to dine with Master Grene?"

"These ladies are, yes," Master Naylor answered, and the man, moving toward the narrow door cut into one wing of the gate, said, "I'm here to see you in then, if you please." And went on over his shoulder as he opened the door, "Have you heard the latest talk about the rebels? There was a man just come past with the news. They're on the move again."

Master Naylor, about to stand aside for Frevisse and Dame Juliana to go ahead of him, stopped short. "Away, I hope?"

"Nay, not away. Why should they go away, now the king has shown his back to them?" the man said almost gleefully.

Not gleefully at all, Master Naylor said, "You mean they're coming this way."

"That's it," the man said happily. He bowed to Frevisse and Dame Juliana going past him through the door, but went on, "Things are happening, right enough. There's going to be changes finally, whether the lords running the king want it or not."

"Yes," Master Naylor agreed grimly. "There'll be changes, surely." But he did not sound as if he thought they would be good ones.

Chapter 8

nne had gone back to her bed after Daved
was gone, had lain with her arms around
his pillow and her body wanting him, but
had not slept but lain listening to the birdsong thicken
from garden to garden behind the houses and the first rattle
of early carts along Foster Lane until one of St. Paul's boom-
ing bells rang out for Prime and the lesser bells of London's
parish churches followed it. She willingly gave up bed then,
wanting the small flurry of every day's early tasks to fill her
mind.

Over breakfast Bette complained the day was going to be
over-warm before it was done. "But my arthritics are enough
better today, I'll go out to the morning marketing, if you
like."

"What you want is to hear the talk," Anne teased.

"Well, you're not the best at bringing it home," Bette mock-grumbled. "You with your head all full of that Master Weir and not much else." She gave Anne a sly smile. "No need to ask if he was here last night, is there?"

"You just go marketing and don't worry yourself about whether Master Weir was here or not," Anne said. She set to clearing the plate and cups from the table. "I'll see to this."

Bette, chuckling, shuffled away with the market basket, leaving Anne with only herself for very poor company. Unable to settle to her work, she wandered the chamber restlessly, shifting the cushions on the window seat and shaking the bedcurtains to hang straighter from their rings, knowing all the while what she was trying to avoid. She had sent yesterday to see if Pernell would welcome a visit but instead had been invited to dinner by a hastily penned note from Raulyn that ended, "Dame Frevisse will be here, but Pernell is keeping to her chamber. If you could be another woman at the table, it would help."

And very likely Daved would be there, and the letter she had promised to take to Joanne of Dartmouth was lying on the chest, with no reason not to be rid of it this morning. Except she did not want to go to this House of Converts.

She would rather have spent the morning with her needlework and remembering last night with him, but worry about the gold locked into the chest and all the fears and all the questions about him that she tried never to have were circling and circling in her mind. She did not trust herself to sew when she was like this, and because the letter, at least, she could do something about, she made up her mind, put the letter in the bottom of the rush-woven basket lined with linen in which she carried her lesser finished work when delivering it herself to her better customers, and laid over it folded cloth she had already cut to make into a shirt for Daved. If anyone asked why she was there, she would pretend she had heard Joanne of Dartmouth was a sempster and that she hoped to hire her for some slight work.

She had never been wont to find ways around the truth, but so often now she did it easily because of Daved. They loved each other, but that was almost the only truth their love could afford. Beyond their love, everything had to be lies. And fear.

Lies, because that was the only way their love would be allowed to live.

Fear, because of all those lies and the even greater lie in which Daved lived when he was not with her.

Once, when they were lying side by side in the dark, satisfied of each other but unready yet for sleep, she had murmured something of her fear, and he had stroked her hair and told her, "There's hardly more need to fear for me than if I was any other merchant. The only difference is the time when I go from Jew to seeming Christian. And back again. Through the several long days of travel between where I'm known as a Christian and where I'm known as a Jew, I have to take care to be seen by no one who knows me as one or the other. Otherwise I'm safe enough."

Except that a Jew never lived safely. All the time he lived as Jew, Daved lived in danger because any Christian flare of anger against any Jew could lead on almost the instant to a hunting and killing of any Jews that could be found. And when he seemed a Christian there was the danger he would be found out. And now she knew he had even more secrets and so there were more reasons for fear.

But the day was not yet too warm for walking, and doing anything rather than only thinking helped. Anne found her dark humour lifting as she passed out of Ludgate beyond St. Paul's into Fleet Street. The House of Converts was somewhere this way, she knew, and paused at a market stall to buy some apples and ask the way. She need only turn right at Temple Bar into Chancery Lane and it was along there, the market woman told her. That was simple enough, and then Anne asked a young clerk with a bundle of papers under one arm which of the places along the street was the House, and he pointed her to a low, stone-built gateway and went on his way without anything like curiosity at her. At the gateway itself, an elderly man was sitting on a short-backed chair at his ease in the sunshine, talking with another elderly man leaning on a cane. They both looked at her with the open curiosity of men with nothing better to do, but when she asked for Mistress Joanne of Dartmouth, the porter said courteously enough, waving her through the gateway, "That would be Alis you want. She'll be in the garden."

The gateway opened into a small yard surrounded by low buildings. Across it, a passageway looked Anne's best way to go to find a garden, and indeed at its far end it opened into a square garth enclosed by buildings on two sides and by a high, gateless stone wall on its two others. As with her own garden, the way in was the way out, but here the sense of being shut away was heavy, the stone walls high enough there was only sky to see beyond them. In a far corner, beyond the beds of vegetables and herbs, was a wooden bench under an apple tree, with a woman was seated there, and there being no one else in the garden, Anne went toward her. She was older than Anne, well into her late middle years, with a quiet face to which not much had happened except those years. She had been shelling peas from a basket at her side into a wooden bowl on her lap but she set the bowl aside as Anne neared her, and when Anne asked, "Mistress Joanne?", she answered courteously enough, "She's dead, I fear. She died last year."

Anne stared blankly at her with no thought of what to say next.

"She was my mother," the woman offered.

"That's why . . . when I asked for Joanne . . . the porter said Alis."

"The porter?" The woman was momentarily puzzled, then said, "That would be Martin. He's not the porter. He only sits there and watches the world go by."

"He's a Jew?" Anne blurted out.

"A Christian," the woman said calmly. "We're all Christians here."

"Yes," Anne said. "Of course." Unsure whether she had given offense or not.

"We hardly need a porter here," the woman went on, mildly enough. "We're not much visited. The occasional churchman or a royal officer comes to make sure all is well. Or sometimes someone comes who's merely curious to see Jews."

Anne realized she was staring and said quickly, "I've come with a letter for your mother." She fumbled in her basket for it. "I suppose you should have it."

She held it out. Alis looked at it, not taking it. "A letter for my mother?"

"It's from your family, I think. Your mother's family."

The woman still did not take the letter. "After all this time," she said. "And now a year too late." She shifted her look to Anne, her voice and gaze sharpening a little. "How did you come by this?"

"That I can't tell you."

The woman's gaze returned to the letter. "No," she said. "I don't suppose you can." She took it but made no move to open it, just went on looking at it. "Never a word in forty years, and now a letter."

"Forty years?"

The woman lifted one shoulder, as if to shrug the years away. "What else could they do, my mother's family? And what could she have done? She was in England because she thought my father had come here." The woman shook her head. "She didn't find him, but she was found out to be Jewish. What could she do then but become Christian? It was that or die. I was baptized with her." She shrugged. "I was only six. After it, we were brought here. Here we stayed. Here I am."

Here she was. A woman staring at an unopened letter in her hands.

Anne stood up. She did not want to be here any longer. And yet, despite herself, she asked, "You could leave here, couldn't you? If you wanted to?"

The woman looked at her. "Oh, yes. We can leave. If we want to. If we have somewhere to go. I don't. So I stay."

She stayed. And her mother had stayed. For forty years. And then had died.

To what Anne had not asked, the woman said, "We have our life here. We garden and cook and go to prayers. There's a chapel here. And I have my rooms. There are only four of us here now. There are rooms enough."

But not life enough, Anne thought. By whatever chance, this Alis of Dartmouth's soul and her mother's had been saved, and surely there was no greater good than that. But frighteningly, treacherously, Anne found herself wondering at the cost. A woman shut off from the world the whole of her life. A woman who had faded without ever having brightened. All for the sake of saving her soul. But what was her soul worth now? When finally freed from the flesh, how could it go to God with joy, having never known joy in life?

Anne cast that question instantly away, afraid of it. She had not meant to stay this long, and with some murmured farewell, she made to leave; but Alis of Dartmouth put out a hand and asked, "If . . . if I . . ." Faltered. Gathered herself. Tried again. "If I want to make answer to this letter, can you see to it going?"

Anne wanted only to be away and never come back, but found herself promising, "I'll come back, yes. In a few days. To see if you have an answer. Yes." She was retreating even as she said it; started to turn away; then turned back and asked, "In all this time, you've never wanted . . . your mother never wanted to return to . . . your people?"

The woman stared at her as if the question made no sense. And then, for the first time, she smiled. A small, sad, pitying smile, though whether the pity was for herself or for Anne's ignorance, Anne could not tell as the woman said quietly, "If ever my mother had tried to be a Jew again, the Church would have burned her for a heretic. As for me . . ." She looked around where she was without much seeming to see it. "Where else do I know? What else can I do?"

Anne, making her escape, thought those were much the questions everyone lived with. What else do we know, besides what we've been told? What else can we do, besides what we're doing?

Except she knew that she loved Daved and that he loved her—and that by everything she had ever been told, their love was wrong. Wrong beyond redemption of their souls.

And yet it was not in her not to love him. Whatever came of it.

Chapter 9

Through the door in the red gate Frevisse, Dame Juliana, and the Naylors passed into a roofed, wagon-wide passage running perhaps fifteen feet between the blank walls of buildings before opening into a small, roughly square, cobbled courtyard tightly enclosed on three sides, including that of the gate, by half-timbered buildings two storeys tall. The one toward the street was Master Grene's shop. Others were probably storerooms and workrooms, while ahead across the yard wooden stairs led straightly up to a stone-built great hall that would be the heart of Master Grene's house.

The servingman led them to those stairs and up, into the screens passage that separated the hall itself from doorway draughts. On the other side from the wide opening into the

hall were several other doors, probably to kitchen and but-
lery and pantry, and a tight spiral of stairs going upward,
down which was coming a brisk older woman in a fine coral-
red gown and beautifully veiled wimple, saying as she came,
"I saw you from the parlor window, my ladies. Welcome.
I'm Mistress Grene's mother. I fear my daughter is keeping
to her chamber these days. I'm Mistress Hercy. She hopes
you'll spend an hour with her after dinner."

"She's not badly ill, I hope," Dame Juliana said.

"Not ill at all, St. Margaret be praised. She's bearing, is
all, and near her time. The stairs aren't safe for her, now that
she's gone large enough not to see her feet well anymore."

"Is this her first?" Dame Juliana asked with ready interest.

"In faith, it's her fourth, all of them living, God be
thanked. Only her second for Master Grene, though. She's
given him a son already and, God willing, will soon give him
another."

She had waved the servingman to see to the Naylors and
was leading the nuns into the hall while she talked. The
place was not so large as a nobleman's hall but fair enough for
a merchant's London home, with two tall, narrow windows
toward the courtyard, set too high for seeing anything but
sky through them. The white-plastered walls along both
sides were covered from the spring of the rafters to almost
the floor with hangings of bright red cloths printed with
twining patterns of green vines and blue cloths printed with
yellow stars, while behind the long table set on the low dais
at the hall's upper end there was a painted hanging with
round-bottomed ships sailing a wave-tossed blue sea between towered cities on green-cragged shores. Master Grene
was standing at one end of the table on the dais, in talk with
three other men, two of them churchmen—a priest and a
grey-robed Franciscan friar—and a woman whom Frevisse
saw with surprise was Mistress Blakhall.

She had been hoping her promise to visit Mistress Blakhall

today would serve as excuse not to linger here longer than need be. Escape might not be so easy now.

While Frevisse was thinking that, Mistress Hercy's talk had moved on to her daughter's son by her late first husband. "A darling boy. Apprenticed to be a mercer himself. But he's reached 'that age.' He's gone off on some youthful roam these past few days with never a word to anybody. It's never been like him to give his mother to worry, let be at a time like this. When his master has had his say, never fear so will I. But aren't we in good fortune with the weather of late?"

Frevisse wondered how long the boy had been gone while noting that besides the high table, a long, bare-topped one along one side of the hall was set with places for eight lesser members of the household—probably journeymen and apprentices—with a serving woman presently bringing two settings more for the Naylors. Then Master Grene was coming to greet her and Dame Juliana and bring them onto the dais to name them to the others, explaining how and why they were come to London on the duchess of Suffolk's behalf and smoothly including praise for Mistress Blakhall's work with, "Embroidery worthy of a duchess' need."

Mistress Blakhall laughed at him in the way of longtime friends. "Don't fail to add your own part in the matter, sir, and your hope it's from you Dame Frevisse will buy the cloth for these vestments."

Master Grene made a small bow to her and Frevisse together and said with his hand on his heart, laughing, too, "But only out of hope to be of yet more service to her grace of Suffolk. Though I do have on hand a figured black damask just come into England by way of this man's good ship."

He gestured to a black-haired young man in a well-made, dark green doublet and blue surcoat, who bowed to Dame Juliana and Frevisse and said, "I can only hope to have

some share of honor in serving her grace," in a warm voice
with a foreign tinge to it that Frevisse could not quite place as
she matched manners with him and Master Grene, saying,
"We'll be most happy to see the damask when dinner is
done." Because what else, in all courtesy, was she supposed
to say?

Master Grene went on, "This is Master Daved Weir of
Bruges. He and his uncle Master Bocking, who is behind
his time in joining us this noontide . . ." He looked questioningly at Master Weir, who slightly shook his head,
showing he did not know the why of his uncle's absence.
". . . are my two best suppliers of cloth out of Flanders and
northern France."

Frevisse tried to keep her gaze from sharpening on this
Master Weir out of Flanders and France, because it could
well be by way of him that the gold so heavy around her
neck had come into England. Then she reminded herself that
was something of which she was better ignorant, and after a
silent bend of her head to his bow, she turned to the priest
to whom Master Grene was now naming her and Dame Juliana. He was a short, plain-faced man in a black gown of
plain cut and plain cloth, solemn-faced as he slightly bent
his head to her and Dame Juliana as they curtseyed to him
while Master Grene said, "This is Father Tomas of our parish.
He's one of the Mass priests at our St. Swithin church."
Meaning his main duty was to celebrate endowed Masses at
the various altars in the church for whatever benefactor had
paid for them.

"And please you to meet Brother Michael, too," Master
Grene went on, turning to the friar. "He's as new among us
as you are."

The friar had been hanging back and somewhat aside until then, so that only now did Frevisse look full at him—a
man of moderate height, austerely gaunt even in the bulky

grey robe of a Franciscan friar belted thick at his waist with a knotted rope but with no look of ill-health from over-fasting about him. Indeed, he was sun-browned like a man much out of doors, and his eyes were alert with the intent mind behind them, giving Frevisse the instant thought that here was someone who saw what he looked at and thought about what he saw.

"Brother Michael was of late a scholar among scholars in Paris," Master Grene was saying, "but presently he's at Grey Friars here in London. If you've not heard him preach at St. Paul's, you truly should. He draws a goodly crowd."

They had heard him, Frevisse realized. He was the friar at St. Paul's Cross to whom they had not stayed to listen. Since it seemed better not to say that, she said nothing as she and Dame Juliana curtsied and Brother Michael said with a smile, "It was not so goodly a crowd this morning. People are more taken up with these rebels than with Lollards at present."

"It's been years since we heard much about Lollards in Oxfordshire," Dame Juliana said.

"Little heard about them means only that they've learned to lie more low and keep the quieter at their work," Brother Michael said. "Their poison is still here and only the worse for being subtle. I was ordered here from Paris particularly to work against them."

From almost their beginnings, the Franciscan and Do-minican friars' place in the Church had been to wander and preach, to reach the common people in common ways and live by daily charity rather than settled endowments. That latter ideal had much failed over the years; friaries were now often rich enough to rival any monastery, and while some friars still wandered, others were known as fierce scholars defending the Church against heretics of whatever kind, a driving force of the Inquisition.

"The household is in place," Mistress Hercy murmured to her son-in-law, with a small nod toward the servants and Naylors standing along the lower table.

Master Grene immediately said, smiling, "By your leave, my ladies, sirs, we'd best be seated or else risk the cook's ire."

With a reasonably correct eye to precedence, Mistress Hercy saw everyone to their proper places behind the high table, with Master Grene at the center and on his left Brother Michael, then Frevisse, Master Weir, and Mistress Blakhall, while Mistress Hercy had place at Master Grene's right where otherwise her daughter would have sat, with Father Tomas beside her, Dame Juliana beyond him, and an empty place at the end for Master Weir's missing uncle.

Like the hall, the high table displayed Master Grene's prosperity, its tablecloth of spotless white linen, the goblets of silver, the plates of pewter polished to near silver's gleam. As everyone along both tables sat, servants brought the first remove, a green salad and a roasted fish in a sauce that looked to be of onions, wine, and cinnamon, setting the platters on the table between each pair of guests and family, for each man to serve the woman next to him. Frevisse wondered in passing if seating Mistress Blakhall beside the well-favored Master Weir was doing the young widow no favor. How willing to a man's blandishments was she likely to be?

But Brother Michael was politely asking where in Oxfordshire her nunnery was, and she turned her thoughts to him and her food, answering graciously while finding the fish was very good.

"Is it true that there's no overt trouble from Lollards there?" he asked. "No stirrings of heresy heard from . . . it's Banbury you're near?"

"None that I've heard, no," Frevisse said, and took the talk elsewhere with, "Master Grene said you're lately come from Paris. But you're English."

"I did indeed grow up near Ely in the fens, and first went to school in the monastery there. The monks sent me to Cambridge."

"But you became a Franciscan. A friar and not a monk."

"The abbot saw my God-given gifts lay not only in learning but in preaching. The latter gift would have been wasted in a monastery, and he blessed me when we parted."

"It was the Franciscans, then, who sent you to the university in Paris?"

"They did, and there I've been these past ten years."

Cutting a morsel of fish, Frevisse asked, "Your work was with the Inquisition there?"

From the side of her eye, she saw Brother Michael pause with a piece of fish partway to his mouth and give her a sharp look. "Yes," he said. "Is that talked of here?"

"I only reasoned that, given you're a Franciscan blessed with learning and a skill at preaching and that your interest here is plainly in Lollards and their heresy, you were probably continuing work you had done in France. Not against Lollards, certainly." Those being peculiarly English. "But such others as there might be there."

Brother Michael nodded in firm approval. "You have it. Well reasoned. Is your priory of St. Frideswide's particularly given over to learning?"

"By no means. We live a plain life of prayers and work, as we're vowed to do." She made it sound more perfect than any nunnery's life ever was, wanting to keep him from unneeded interest in St. Frideswide's because the less the Inquisition looked at something, the better, to her mind. The Inquisition was to the Church what a surgeon was to a man's body. When disease was found in the body that could not be cured, a surgeon must needs cut it out. When corrupting beliefs were found in the body of the Church, they either had to be removed by curing those who held them or else by removing the diseased persons before they corrupted others. So the Inquisition was a necessary thing. But it could also bring out the worst in men—hatred where there should only have been regret against error, a delight in pain rather than in Christ's love. Brother Michael was probably not one of those but she was glad when he said, as if satisfied, "You lead a goodly life there, then. Prayer and work. Would all were so wise."

Master Grene spoke to him on his other side then, and she was left to her food, Master Weir and Mistress Blakhall being in easy talk together about whether it were better that raw silk be brought into England for spinsters here to turn into thread and then dye for English use, or if the quality of silk thread brought in already made and dyed was too high to challenge. But when the dishes were being cleared at the remove's end, Master Weir turned to Frevisse and said, "I neglect courtesy to you, my lady. I pray your pardon."

"I confess I've listened to your talk with Mistress Blakhall and enjoyed it. I gather you've met before this."

"She does me the favor of buying such thread and sometimes cloth as I offer her now and again."

"Your English is very good."

"Thank you, my lady. I served a time in a mercer's household here in London when I was my uncle's apprentice, both to better my English and learn English ways. With things as they have been these past years we have not come so often as we might, but when we do, my young years spent here serve me well."

The second remove began and Master Weir turned to serve Mistress Blakhall. Brother Michael did the same for Frevisse but over his shoulder continued his talk to Master Grene, saying, "With any heresy, Lollard or otherwise, the less it's seen, the worse it is, like a secret rot in wood, unknown until too late."

"You're saying the more secretly someone is a heretic, the more dangerous he is?" Master Grene asked, serving Mistress Hercy but likewise turned more to his talk than his task.

Brother Michael thumped the spoon dangerously back into the dish of apple tart and custard, declaring, "*Any* heretic is dangerous. Secret or otherwise. Rot is no less dangerous for being known. The Church must be cleansed of any and all! Another crusade against the Hussites is long past due, nor have the Waldenses been hunted as they should be. Like Lollards, they've become subtle, harder to be found out, but found out they must be. And then there are the Jews." Brother Michael tapped a stiff forefinger against the tabletop, his voice rising, food and polite talk forgotten. "Look at them! Openly defiant in their heresy. A beacon and flame for all others who would deny Christ. Until the Church has dealt with *them* . . ."

Frevisse knew this was a fine time to keep her thoughts to herself, but with outward mild demur she said, "Doesn't someone has to have held a faith before they can be heretic to it? Having never been Christian, how can Jews be heretics?"

Brother Michael swung around to her. "They're heretics to their own alleged faith! For centuries they've lived under the Church's protection, allowed to dwell among Christians to serve as dread example of what comes to those who choose to live in darkness. For that reason only have they been allowed to exist among Christians."

"For that," said Master Weir quietly, "and because they're profitable to Christians. Because they traded widely across Europe when few others did, they brought money into the reach of kings, princes, bishops, and lords. Money both to be loaned because Jews were allowed usury when no Christians were, and money to be taxed away into the coffers of those kings, princes, bishops, and lords. At least so I've understood it, and that therefore Jews were allowed to live among Christians. Now, because matters have changed and we Christians can do much of what only Jews did before, they're no longer needed. So—"

"That is *not* where the trouble lies," Brother Michael snapped. "Those are worldly matters. I'm talking of the heresy the Jews have brewed in their secret teachings. Among themselves they've corrupted the faith of their forefathers into something else than what it was. By that they've broken their covenant with the Church that kept them safe in Christ's care and become heretics!"

"But the Christian faith has changed with the centuries," Master Weir said mildly. "Why—"

"The Church has never changed! It is the same now and for all Eternity," Brother Michael interrupted vehemently. "Forever true to—"

"Until St. Gregory the Great declared otherwise, the bishop of Rome was seen only as a bishop among bishops. Not head of all the churches of Christendom," Master Weir said, his voice level. "It was an even later pope that claimed to hold sway over all earthly rulers, and . . ."

"Everything taught by the Church is contained in Christ's teachings." Brother Michael tapped the table again. "Only the working out of time was needed to make them known and clear."

"Can't the same be claimed for the 'changes' you allege the Jews have made in their understanding of God's word?" Master Weir asked. "That in the working out of time, they've come to understand better what was always there for them to know?"

Brother Michael cast that aside with a sharp gesture. "When they clung to the Old Law, refusing the New Law of Christ, Jews forfeited all *right* to change. Having nonetheless changed and been found out in their vile corruption, they've voided their right to the Church's protection and laid themselves open to the same fate as any heretic. They—"

Mistress Hercy, in the clear, calm voice of someone taking control of her guests, broke in with, "Here comes Master Bocking at last. Master Bocking, we pray all is well?"

Master Bocking, striding vigorously up the hall, was a man of hale middle years, his black hair well-greyed. He bowed deeply to both Mistress Hercy and Master Grene at once and said, "All's well enough with me and mine. Not so good otherwise." His English was not so clear as his nephew's but clear enough. "The rebels are into Southwark, and the bridge's gates have been shut against them."

Master Grene thumped a fist onto the table. "Where, by all that's holy, is the king? Or least his lords?"

"What matters," Mistress Hercy said firmly, gesturing Master Bocking toward his place at the table's end, "is that you're here and they're not, nor likely to interrupt our dinner."

"Or our supper, either," Father Tomas said, trying for lightness. "Not with the river still between us and them."

That brought approving laughter along the table, even from Master Bocking, and talk went on around him while he ate, not about the rebels but in complaints against the king's failures, until Father Tomas asked if anyone had heard more about the rumored rebel stirrings, in Essex now, rather than in Kent.

"I hadn't heard of them at all," Mistress Blakhall said.

"It's no more than another of the rumors we've heard a hundred of this year," Master Grene said, dismissing them.

Which was true, Frevisse thought. Except that Essex was very near to London—and on the same side of the Thames. The meal finishing then, Mistress Hercy asked if the ladies would go up with her now to keep her daughter company a while. "Leaving the men to make what they will of the world and all," she said.

There being little choice, Frevisse, with what outward good grace she could, followed the other women from the hall and up the stairs into the expectedly rich parlor of a wealthy London mercer in what looked to be a range of rooms running along the south side of the courtyard. Well-windowed to north and south, it was filled with the afternoon's warm light, with beautifully braided reed matting on the polished wooden floor, bright cushions along the window benches, several backed chairs and carved joint stools and floor cushions. On a square-topped table in the room's middle was a silver bowl holding white roses and blue love-in-a-mist, and on the far wall, beside a door that probably opened into a bedchamber was a woven tapestry showing Dido and Aeneas on the shores of Carthage.

Mistress Grene was seated in one of the chairs, the spread of her yellow loose gown of fine linen over the wide curve of her child-swollen belly leaving no doubt how near to birthing she was. She did not try to rise from her chair, only held out her hand to Mistress Blakhall, who went to take it while a half-grown girl stood up from the nearer window bench and made a deep curtsy to them all.

"Mistress Grene and her daughter Lucie," Mistress Hercy said, smiling on the girl with a grandmother's deep affection. "Show the nuns what you're embroidering for your brother-to-be, Lucie."

Everyone duly praised the small cap Lucie was embroidering with a cross-stitched pattern of tiny flowers, and Frevisse supposed that next they would all sit and fall into talk, and that in a while servants would bring something to drink, and sometime Master Grene would come and wonder if she and Dame Juliana would care to see his damask, and somewhere in the house Master Naylor was fuming because the rebels were in Southwark at the far end of London bridge, and only finally would she and Dame Juliana be able to return to St. Helen's. The best she could hope for was a quiet word with Mistress Blakhall on when they might meet again at her house.

But they had only just sat down when Master Grene came in, all his smiling graciousness gone. Giving no one else any heed, he crossed to kneel in front of his wife, taking both her hands as he said, "Pernell, my love, Father Walter has just sent from St. Swithin's to say there's been a body found in the church. He wants . . ."

Chapter 10

Mistress Grene began struggling to rise, crying, "It's Hal!", but Master Grene sprang to his feet, holding her by the shoulders, saying quickly, "No. Listen."

"I know it's Hal," she cried. "I know."

"We don't know," Master Grene insisted. "That's why Father Walter sent for me. Because they don't know. I didn't want you to hear from a servant that I'd gone, and where, and why. I knew what you'd think. But you mustn't. Not until we know. Hush now. For the baby's sake."

Mistress Grene was clinging to his hands now, desperately wanting to be reassured, but she looked to Mistress Blakhall and said, her voice catching on the words. "Do you go with him. To see for me." And pleaded when Mistress Blakhall drew back in her chair, her eyes widening with refusal, "Please. I can't."

"I'll go," Mistress Hercy said despite she was gone as white as her daughter.

But Mistress Blakhall had overtaken her unwillingness and said firmly, "No, I'll go if you need me to, Pernell."

Mistress Hercy looked about to protest that, but Frevisse, to sort them out the more quickly, said, "Mistress Hercy, you should stay with your daughter. Mistress Blakhall, I'll go with you if you like, so you won't be alone in this. Dame Juliana, will you stay here with them for their better comfort?"

Having held office often enough at St. Frideswide's to value the use of strong decisions quickly made, Dame Juliana nodded ready agreement.

Master Grene quickly kissed his wife's cheek. "I'll send word as soon as I'm sure. It's going to be all right." One of those meaningless promises that served to soothe only those who didn't think about them.

Brother Michael, Master Weir, and Master Bocking were waiting at the stairfoot. They looked their surprise at seeing the women, but Master Grene said, "Master Bocking, would you go up and keep my lady in talk? So she doesn't fret more than need be while I'm gone. Brother Michael, Daved, I'd like you with me, if you would."

Master Bocking said, "But of course," gave a brief bow to Frevisse and Mistress Blakhall and went for the stairs as Master Grene started for the outer door, saying, "Let's make haste and have this done."

Outside, in the yard, Master Naylor and Dickon came from among the household servants gathered staring and talking there. "You're going?" he asked Frevisse.

Without pausing, Frevisse said, "With Mistress Blakhall, yes. Dame Juliana is staying to keep Mistress Grene company."

"We'll come with you, then," Master Naylor said and fell behind her with Dickon.

She let them because there was no reason not to, and after all they had not far to go. St. Swithin church stood where St. Swithin's Lane met wide Candlewick Street, and what neighbors did not provide toward the crowd starting to gather in the churchyard, passersby on the busy street did; but a way cleared readily for Master Grene, who only shook his head and did not answer what questions were asked as he passed. The two men on guard at the church door to keep out the curious stood aside to let him and the others go in, and Frevisse barely saw the statue of St. Swithin with his crozier, closed book, and cloud on the gable above the door before she was inside. It was an older church, with the round columns of Norman times along the narrow nave, but newer aisles added to either side and the roof raised by a new-made clerestory of pale stone and glazed windows that filled the church with sunlight told of the wealth of its parishioners here in London's heart. Despite the guard outside, there were a number of men already here, mostly priests and probably belonging to the church, and from among them Father Tomas came toward Master Grene, saying, "The body is below. In the crypt. The constables and under-crowner have been sent for, but Father Walter thought you should come because . . ." The priest dropped his voice. ". . . he does think it is Hal."

"Thinks?" Mistress Blakhall said with distress. "He can't tell?"

"Anne," Master Grene said gently. "Hal's been missing nearly a week. You'd maybe best not . . ."

Mistress Blakhall lifted her chin. "I told Pernell I'd see."

"You shouldn't," said Master Weir.

"Father Walter," Father Tomas said carefully, "says he died a bad death."

One way and another, Frevisse had seen violently dead bodies before this, and she doubted with the men that

Mistress Blakhall should see this one; but stubbornly Mistress Blakhall said, "I told Pernell I'd see for her. I have to." However little she wanted to hold to her word, now that she had found out what it would mean, Frevisse thought, and thought the better of her for it.

Father Tomas still hesitated, looking to Master Grene, who after a moment nodded for him to lead on.

The way to the crypt was through a door standing open in a west corner of the nave. Stone steps went down into thick shadows, with only the uneven flicker of a single candle on a pricket at the stairfoot to light the way. Father Tomas went first, Master Grene and Brother Michael behind him and then Master Weir, who turned sideways to hold Mistress Blakhall's arm as she descended. Frevisse paused to say to Master Naylor, "It's maybe better you and Dickon wait here. There's going to be people enough in the crypt, as it is."

"It's maybe better you wait here, too," Master Naylor said.

Not deigning to answer that, Frevisse turned from him, cleared her skirts from her feet, and started down. Was halfway down when the gorge-rising smell of rotting flesh reached her. At the stairfoot Mistress Blakhall had started to gag, and Master Weir was saying quickly, "Hold your sleeve over your nose and mouth. Breathe through it."

Fumbling with haste, Mistress Blakhall did. Frevisse noted that he did not. Nor did she, knowing that in a while her mind would refuse the stench and she would cease to note it. Or at least to note it so stomach-churningly.

They moved away toward an unseen lantern's light at the crypt's far end, Master Weir steadying Mistress Blakhall on the uneven earthen floor, Frevisse taking care of her own steps in the darkness between the stairfoot's candle and the lantern-light beyond the piled wooden coffins that half-filled the crypt, set on shelves along the walls and between the two

rows of squat stone columns running the crypt's length—
stunted brothers to the ones in the nave above them.

The body lay on the floor in the gap between the last
piled coffins and the crypt's end wall, hidden by two men already there beside it. Frevisse looked first at them, rather
than trying to see the body, guessing that Father Walter was
the middle-aged priest with a silver-gilt crucifix on a silver
chain around his neck and an appearance of authority, while
the other was simply a plain-dressed young priest, kneeling
beside the body with eyes closed, murmuring in rapid
prayer, his face the whey-color of someone who had just
been—or was going to be—very sick.

Mistress Blakhall, ahead of Frevisse, able to see the body
first past Master Grene and Brother Michael, gave one sickened cry and turned away. An arm around her waist, Master
Weir moved her away into the shadows, and Frevisse edged
forward to look past Father Tomas and the other men.

The body was lying naked on its back, legs straight, arms
outstretched to either side. Rats had been at it, and bloating
had begun. In places the greenish skin had begun to slip
loose from the flesh. The days of decay, even in the cool
crypt, had had their toll but . . .

Hush-voiced, Father Walter said, "It's Hal, isn't it?"

The words flat with his strangled feelings, Master Grene
answered, "It's Hal. Yes."

Father Tomas knelt down and began to pray with the
young priest, their voices low together. ". . . *animam famuli
tui, quam de hoc saeculo migrare iussisti, in pacis ac lucis regione con-
stituas . . .*" . . . the soul of your servant, which from this life
you have ordered to go, into the place of peace and light . . .

Brother Michael, still standing, went on staring at the
body, seemingly intent beyond horror.

"My wife . . ." Master Grene said. "She can't see this. She
can't ever know . . . what . . . how . . ."

"Not while she's bearing," Mistress Blakhall choked, still with her back turned. "It would kill her and the baby both. Or mar the child."

Brother Michael, his voice odd, said, "Those marks on his chest and stomach."

Of them all, he and Frevisse were the only ones still fully looking at the body. The sight sickened her, but a week ago this ruined, decaying body had been alive. Had been a boy with thoughts, feelings, hopes. Had been someone who expected to be alive this day and other days after it, had expected to see summer end and autumn come and winter after that and another spring. Not be a rotting corpse unfound and unmourned for almost a week. He deserved more than her sickened, averted glance, and she looked at what was left of him, trying to see beyond it to the boy there had been, despite how little of his face remained.

But like Brother Michael she was also seeing the shallow wounds all over his chest and stomach. The rats did not account for the score or more of long, blood-blackened gashes into the corpse's chest and belly—thin slices into the flesh, done with the point of a very sharp knife or dagger—except for a single, wider one under his right breast that looked to have been a killing-deep thrust to the lung. She hoped that had been the first one—that he had been dead before the rest were done to him.

"And the wounds in his hands and feet," Brother Michael said.

Frevisse had not seen those until now—the deep cuts driven into both of his hands and both of his feet. She was refusing to understand them when Master Grene said with hush-voiced horror, "He's been crucified."

Father Walter groaned, "I know. God save us. Devils and fiends were here."

"Not devils," Brother Michael said. "Jews."

The young priest broke off praying with a gasp. Father

Tomas went quiet. Somewhat desperately Father Walter said, "There've been no Jews in England for a hundred years and more."

In a voice as dark as the lantern shadows cast upward on his face, Brother Michael said, "Jews are everywhere. Known and unknown. Secretly as rats in walls. Waiting to pollute—"

Heavy footsteps down the stairs and the sudden jump of new lantern light among the crypt's shadows interrupted him. Of the two men who came with the light, the first carried himself in a way that told he was either the under-crowner or else a constable even before Father Walter said with open relief, "Master Crane," and added to Brother Michael, "He's a constable of Walbrook Ward here."

"And Master Lewes, my clerk," Master Crane said. He started to say more, but his gaze had fallen toward the body, and his words and face froze. Then he crossed himself, saying, "Dear God."

Frevisse, stepping back to make room for him, glimpsed Mistress Blakhall and Master Weir where they stood beyond the nearest pillar, safely beyond seeing the body and turned to each other, only shadow-shapes against the distant candleglow but with something in the way they were together—a unexpected nearness that she would, another time, have thought on; but over the boy's body Brother Michael was repeating his assertion against Jews to Master Crane, with, "My work in France was to find them out, so I know . . ."

Seeming not to care what the friar knew, Master Crane asked Master Grene, "This is your stepson? You're sure of it?"

"I'm sure."

"How long has he been missing?"

"Since Thursday last past. In the evening. He's apprenticed to Master Yarford in Rother Lane. He went out after supper and didn't come back."

Master Crane stared grimly at the body. "Looks to have been dead that long, too." He shifted his stare to Father Walter. "You found him? Why wasn't he found before? By the smell, if nothing else."

"It's cool in the crypt," Father Walter answered, firm in his authority. "Corruption comes more slowly here. The floor of the nave is stone, and so there's no smell in the church yet. It was only because I came down here I found . . . smelled . . . found him."

"Why did you come down here today and not before?"

"There was no need before today. But Master Neve died at dawn, and his wife wants him in the crypt. I came to see about a place for him."

"All of which is neither here nor there," Brother Michael broke in almost angrily. "I'm saying it was Jews did this profanation."

"Why are you so set on that?" Master Crane demanded at him. "Yes, I see the hands and feet and the wound in the side. I'm not blind. But those could be done by some half-mad Christian without bringing Jews into it. There've been no Jews in England—"

"Those marks," Brother Michael interrupted. "The Hebrew letters gashed into his flesh. Who else but a Jew would make them? Why else would they be made except for a Jew's purpose? This was no plain killing. This was done by Jews. It was one of their ritual murders!"

Silence deep as the darkness in the crypt's far corners enwrapped them. No one moved and no one spoke, all stares fixed on Brother Michael, whose own look dared anyone to deny his charge. Of all the crimes that could be done against Christendom, ritual murder was among the worst—the killing of a Christian child by Jews in mockery of Christ's crucifixion. England had two boy-saints, St. William of Norwich and Lincoln's little St. Hugh, both said to have suffered that fate generations ago. Throughout Europe, an accusation that a child found dead had died at Jewish hands was all too often all that was needed to bring on a seeking out and killing of Jews—any Jews—men, women, children—in blind revenge. But into the crypt's heavy silence full of that thought Frevisse said slowly, "Pope after pope has decreed there's no such thing as ritual murder by Jews."

"And yet there . . ." Brother Michael pointed at the body. ". . . *there* is proof of it!"

"Those marks," Father Tomas said, his voice small, as if he would smother the words as he said them, "are not Hebrew. They are maybe meant to look so, but they are not."

"You'd know Hebrew to see it?" Brother Michael challenged with an edge of scorn.

Gripping the cross hanging on his breast with a trembling hand, Father Tomas met the friar's stare with his own straight look. "I would know."

Brother Michael's scorn went into something sharper. "How?"

Afraid though Father Tomas openly was, he lifted his head, bracing for an attack he knew would come, and said, "Because I saw my grandfather's Jewish books when I was young."

Chapter 11

Brother Michael's was not the only sharp-drawn breath, but his was the accusation afterward. "You're Jewish!"

"I am Christian." With no going back, Father Tomas seemed to gather strength. "I was baptized at birth. My parents—"

"Where?" Brother Michael demanded.

"Antwerp. Where my parents went after being forced from Portugal."

"Because they were Jewish!"

"Because their parents had been Jewish. In Spain now that is not forgiven even unto the third and fourth generations." Father Tomas' bitterness was undisguised. "*Conversos* and their children and their children's children are watched and hunted by the Inquisition. For the chance to be Christians in peace, my parents left, taking my father's father with them, the last of any family they had left. In Antwerp no one knew they were anything but Christian, so they lived in peace until they died."

"Except your grandfather still had his Hebrew books," Brother Michael accused.

"Because my grandfather was a learned man who valued the learning in those books."

"Tainted beliefs. False beliefs."

"I did not say they were books of religion," Father Tomas said back at him. "More than that can be written in Hebrew."

"He lived as a pretend Christian among honest men . . ."

"He pretended nothing. He lived in a back, upper room of my father's house, never leaving it, never seeing even our servants, through all the last years of his life. He was old and tired and did not want to learn new ways."

"So your father hid him and let him live his Jewish life, false to his baptism."

"He sheltered his aged parent and left him in peace. Does not the commandment say to honor your father and your mother? It does not say 'unless' or 'except,' only 'to honor.'"

"He had Jewish books, and you read them," Brother Michael said.

"I did not. I only followed his finger as he read aloud to me. Read poetry and history, not religion. But I saw the letters while he read, and *those*—" Father Tomas pointed at the slices in the body "—are maybe meant to look like Hebrew, but they are not anything."

Brother Michael drew a deep breath to say more, but Frevisse said from where she stood behind the men, at the edge of the lantern-light, "Nor was the boy crucified."

"What?" Master Grene asked quickly as Brother Michael turned an angry look to her.

The friar's claim was too dangerous to leave unchallenged. "The wounds in his hands and feet are wrong. Look at them."

Master Crane already had. Instead of at the wounds he looked at her and agreed, "They aren't nail-wounds, no. They looked to have been stabbed into him with probably a dagger."

"Whereas for a true ritual killing nails should have been used," Frevisse said. "Nor should he have been dead when it was done. But he was."

"Nails or not," Brother Michael declared, "and whatever is claimed against those letters . . ." his look at Father Tomas was ripe with accusation. ". . . this was a ritual killing of a Christian boy by Jews."

"Likewise the time of year is wrong, isn't it?" Master Weir asked from the deeper shadows. "Isn't part of the purpose said to be to get blood for their Passover rites? That's at Eastertide, not midsummer."

"Could any of those wounds have been used to drain his blood?" Frevisse asked, sure of the answer.

"I'd say no," answered Master Crane. "None of these wounds bled. As you say, everything looks to have been done to him after death."

"Then how did he—" Master Grene started.

"Can we go elsewhere with this talk?" Father Walter asked. "It's unseemly over the poor boy's body." Though he sounded as if it were less the unseemliness that troubled him than his own sickness at it all.

"I've seen what I need to see," Master Crane said. "When Sir Richard has viewed the body . . ."

"I wonder where his clothing is," Frevisse said mildly, as if more to herself than anyone. "He wouldn't have been brought here naked."

From the stairway a man none of them had heard coming declared loudly, "Where in the name of blessed Saint Lucy are your lights?"

"Sir Richard," Master Crane said, raising the lantern he held. "We were waiting for you to illumine us."

"Humph," Sir Richard said in return. He came into what lantern-light there was, a man not so tall as Frevisse, with a thin, weatherworn face and a swordsman's walk that suggested his knighthood was more than an easy courtesy. He was so surely the under-crowner there was no need for anyone to say so, but despite one way and another he must have seen bodies enough, at sight of Hal's he grimaced and swore, then said to Frevisse, "Your pardon, my lady," and added over his shoulder to Mistress Blakhall in the shadows, now standing a little apart from Master Weir, "Yours, too, I pray you," before he glared at Master Crane and demanded, "Should these women be seeing this?"

"They should not, no," Master Weir agreed quickly. "I'll see them out."

He made to take Mistress Blakhall toward the stairs, but Frevisse said to Sir Richard, "We were just wondering where the boy's clothing was."

"Well?" Sir Richard asked at Master Crane, and at his clerk Master Crane said, "Take the lantern and look through the crypt."

As the clerk obeyed, Sir Richard said, "Now tell me what we have here."

By the lantern's bobbing light Frevisse saw Mistress Blakhall and Master Weir were at the stairs waiting for her, but she stayed where she was, listening as Master Crane detailed what had so far been said, with a hard look that silenced Brother Michael when he started to speak. He did tell the friar's assertion, though, and Father Tomas' answer to it, and although Sir Richard listened closely, Frevisse thought he no more leaped at accepting Brother Michael's accusation than Master Crane had.

"I've found them," Lewes said from the farthest corner of the crypt.

"Bring them here," Sir Richard ordered, pointing to the floor near the body. "I'll take your lantern."

He went and took it from him, and Lewes picked up the clothing in its heap and brought to put down beside the body. Standing over him with the lantern, Sir Richard ordered, "Sort through it. See what's there and what isn't."

While everyone watched, the clerk went through the clothing naming each thing as he found it. Everything was there that might be expected—undergarments, hosen, shoes, shirt, an apprentice's plain tunic. The tunic and shirt stayed stiffly wadded together, though, when the clerk handled them, and Sir Richard said, "Unfold them."

As Lewes pulled apart the stiffened folds, a small, gold-gleaming cross on a chain fell to the floor. "Not robbery, then, if that's still here," Master Crane said as Father Tomas bent to pick it up.

"The only robbery was of his life," Brother Michael said sharply. "I tell you this was—"

"We know what you say it was," Sir Richard interrupted. "Father Tomas says otherwise. That leaves the question still open. Master Grene, was that the boy's cross?"

Father Tomas held it out to Master Grene, who only looked at it and said, "Yes. It was his father's."

The clerk held the blood-stiffened tunic up in the lantern-light for them to see, and Sir Richard said, "By that, he looks to have been stabbed in the back. Turn him over."

Master Crane knelt down and eased the body onto its side. In the lantern-light three black-mouthed dagger wounds showed below the shoulder blades, two to the heart-side, one to the other.

"Made sure of him, didn't they?" Sir Richard said. He shifted the lantern and looked at the earthen floor. "Did it here. That's blood darkening the dirt." He pointed with one forefinger, outlining the stained area that spread from beneath the body, unnoticed in the shadowy light until now. "Stabbed him, stripped him, mangled the body while it was lying in its own blood."

Master Crane had bent for a closer look at the back of the head. "He was struck here, too. Clubbed, by the look of it. Hard enough to split the skin but . . ." He felt at the wound. "No, the skull's not caved in. He would likely have been unconscious but not dead. It was the stabbing that finished him." He eased the body down again and stood up. "I'll get more light down here, and we'll finish looking to see if the murderer left aught else, but we can move the body now, can't we?"

"Yes. Best look through the church, too," Sir Richard said. "Unless he came down here of his own will and then was killed, he was most likely struck down in the church, rather than out in the street. Easier to get the body into the crypt unseen from the church than the street." Sir Richard pointed at the bloodied ground beside the corpse. "Who knelt there?" Without waiting for an answer, he bent over and poked with his finger at a slight, rounded hollow indented in the hard earth. "Not done today," he said. "That was done while the dirt was blood-softened, by the murderer kneeling to his work." Standing up, he added mordantly, "All we need do is to find someone who had one of his hosen, or his tunic, or his gown bloodied at the knee five days ago. That shouldn't be hard in London."

As Father Tomas bent and laid the cross gently on the boy's maimed chest, Frevisse turned away, having seen enough, and followed Mistress Blakhall and Master Weir from the crypt, to pause, blinking, at the top of the stairs while her eyes grew used to daylight again. For probably the same reason Master Weir and Mistress Blakhall were stopped, too, standing apart from each other now as Mistress Blakhall said miserably, "What am I going to tell Pernell that won't kill her to hear it?"

"That it is her son," Frevisse said. "That he's been dead several days and looks to have been stabbed. That he died quickly and knew nothing. More than that she doesn't need to hear."

"There'll be talk. If not from us, she'll hear the worst from someone else."

"Use that she has to keep to her rooms from now until her baby's birth," Frevisse returned. "Tell Mistress Hercy enough so that she'll see no one sees her and that the servants don't talk where Mistress Grene can hear them."

"It would be best, too, that Hal be kept here," said Master Weir. "That the body be readied for burial and buried straightaway. The fewer who see him, the better."

Mistress Blakhall closed her eyes and pressed her fingers to her forehead. "There was never harm in him, ever. Why would someone . . ."

"Let it go for now," Master Weir interrupted gently, firmly. "Before anything, Mistress Grene needs to be protected."

Lowering her hands, Mistress Blakhall took a deep breath and said steadily enough that Frevisse believed her, "I'll do what needs doing."

Frevisse looked to Master Weir. "If I see Mistress Blakhall to the Grenes', will you stay to tell Master Grene that we think this is all his wife should hear?"

"I'll tell him now, but do you wait and I'll see you back there. There'll be people wanting to question you."

Frevisse accepted that with a nod, willing to add his help to the Naylors'; and she took the chance as soon as he was gone to say to Mistress Blakhall, "I'll come to your house tomorrow for the gold. Will that do?"

"Tomorrow. Yes. Tomorrow," Mistress Blakhall said, as if unable quite to believe in tomorrow just now.

"In the early afternoon," Frevisse said.

"Yes. Then."

Master Weir returned, Father Tomas with him, and Frevisse was glad of the chance to tell the priest, "That was bravely done, facing down the friar."

"I likely did little good," Father Tomas said doubtingly.

"You did what good you could," Master Weir said. "Not that there's hope of changing that friar's mind," he added dryly. "He too much wants to believe in his Jews. But you gave Master Crane grounds for holding off talk of 'ritual murder' and that's to the good." Smiling, he added to Frevisse, "You joined in boldly, too."

"I don't like the willful use of ignorance as a weapon," she answered.

"I hardly think Brother Michael is ignorant," said Master Weir. "He gives every sign of being very learned."

"I don't doubt he's learned," Frevisse returned, not bothering to keep her anger from her words. "But he's not learned enough to wonder why any Jews secretly here in London would announce they were here, let be by something so ugly as this murder. Besides that, I've never seen any reason why Jews would commit such blasphemous murders in the first place, and this one wasn't even done rightly for the 'ritual murder' it was supposed to be."

Supposed to be.

There was something to wonder. Why would someone have wanted it to seem a murder done by Jews at all?

She thought she saw the same question quicken in Master Weir's face, but before she could say anything, Father Tomas murmured something about satisfying his fellows' curiosity and went away toward the men gathered farther up the nave, and Master Weir started them toward the outer door where a crowd and questions would have to be faced. And then the dead boy's mother.

Chapter 12

The Naylors and Master Weir saw Frevisse and Mistress Blakhall through the people still waiting in the churchyard, Master Naylor clearing the way, looking more grim than usual, Master Weir keeping himself between Mistress Blakhall and everyone, a steadying hand on her elbow, while Dickon shoved people away on Frevisse's other side. Questions were being called at them, and to someone who called her by name Mistress Blakhall answered, "It's Hal, yes. He was stabbed."

Her few words spread through the crowd, turning people to exclaim to one another, and with most of the gawkers choosing to stay at the church, they went faster once out of the churchyard, Frevisse and Mistress Blakhall with their heads down, answering nothing, Master Naylor and Master

Weir merely telling people there was nothing else to tell. At the house, when the servant keeping guard at the gate had let them in and shut the door hard behind them, Master Weir asked, "Wyett, you've let in no one else?"

"None, Master Weir. Is it Hal?"

"It's Hal, yes."

As the man crossed himself, Mistress Blakhall said, "We have to go to Pernell."

But Master Naylor said to Frevisse, "Your pardon, my lady. With the rebels into Southwark, it would be well for you and Dame Juliana to be back in St. Helen's as soon as might be, until we see how things are going to go."

"James and Rafe have been down to Hay Wharf," Wyett said eagerly. "They say there's nothing happening across river. No burning or anything." He was near to sounding disappointed.

Still directly at Frevisse, Master Naylor repeated, "It would be well for you to be back in St. Helen's. Whatever needs doing here, others can do."

And was none of her business anyway, he did not add aloud, but she heard it clearly enough. Heard, too, that he was past arguing over the matter. He *would* have her and Dame Juliana back in St. Helen's or make enough trouble over it she would wish she had gone. But she meant to make no argument—not so much because of the rebels, but because the day had been long and she was tiring and others could better do what would have to be done here.

Besides that, Mistress Blakhall was saying, "You've already done beyond measure, going with me to the church as you did. Wait here, and I'll send Dame Juliana out to you."

More than willing not to see Mistress Grene in her grief, Frevisse thanked her, and when Mistress Blakhall and Master Weir were gone away across the yard beyond hearing him— and not caring that the man Wyett could—Master Naylor turned on Frevisse and said, "The rebels are too close now.

We should be more than at St. Helen's. We should be out of London."

Trying to appease both him and her own worry, she said, "The rebels can't cross the river, and surely the king will have to do something now it's come to this."

"We'll have to wait for time to prove the truth of 'they can't' and 'he will'," Master Naylor snapped. "For myself, I'd rather not be here to see how it plays out."

Neither would she, but the best she could offer was, "I promise you, the instant we can leave, we will."

"Supposing we can when that time comes," Master Naylor said back at her.

The more stiffly because her own feelings so nearly matched his, she answered, "We'll simply have to see how things go this next day and so." And was greatly thankful to see Dame Juliana hurrying from the house.

She joined them at the gate with, "Was it her son? Mistress Blakhall said you were waiting, and I didn't stay to ask anything."

"It was," Frevisse said, and Dame Juliana signed herself with the cross, but Master Naylor was already herding them out the gate. He then set a pace back to St. Helen's that had them nigh to breathless but at the nunnery's gateway as the bells began to ring for Vespers. Dame Juliana thanked Master Naylor, who bade her welcome and good evening with a bow to them both but no look at all at Frevisse. Too wise to go against his father's humour, Dickon had been quiet the while, but as he straightened from his own bow to them, he gave Frevisse a quick smile before turning to follow his father away. For him the rebels were an unlooked-for adventure, and because nothing and no one about the dead boy was known to him, Frevisse did not begrudge him his somewhat lighter heart. She only envied him for it.

She hoped to find refuge in Vespers, but did not. Even in the first psalm her mind was going too many ways other than into quiet. Around her and with her the voices rose: *"Beatus, quicumque times Dominum, qui ambulas in viis ejus . . . beatus eris et bene tibi erit . . ."* Happy, all you that fear the Lord, who walk in his ways . . . Happy will you be and good will be to you . . .

But neither happiness nor good had come to the boy Hal, and surely he had never done anything so far out of the Lord's ways to deserve that death and what came afterward. It did not matter that she knew full well that what came to someone too often seemed to match nothing in their life to earn it. It didn't matter that she knew the psalm's promised happiness and goodness were the happiness and goodness given by God after this world. Knowing a thing and being at peace with it were too often two different things, and to-day most certainly she could not reconcile them. For now, as the Office neared its end and the nuns chanted from one side of the choir, *"Oremus pro fidelibus defunctis"*—We entreat for the faithful dead—and the other side answered, *"Requiem aeternam dona eis, Domine, et lux perpetua luceat eis"*—Give eternal rest to them, Lord, and perpetual light shine on them. Pray for the dead boy's soul was all she could do.

After Vespers and supper came the hour of recreation in the nunnery's garden before Compline. Dame Juliana walked in talk with some of the nuns along the paths between the summer-flourishing beds of flowers and herbs, but Frevisse knew she would better let her thoughts run now than later and went aside to one of the turf-topped benches, to sit with a book laid open on her lap, hoping that if she looked to be reading she'd be left alone. Not that her thoughts did more than circle, she soon found. What bedeviled her was know-ing too much and yet not enough. The questions she wanted to ask were Sir Richard's and Master Crane's to do because the places and people of young Hal's life were all beyond her reach, and she might as well set her mind to accepting the whole matter was over and done for her. She told herself she was willing enough to that. She told herself she would even succeed at letting it go. That she might as well let it go because there was nothing she could do.

And instead found herself thinking about Brother Michael.

There in the garden's peace, she could almost not believe in the ugly fears he had conjured with his talk of secret Jews and ritual murder. Fears not of Jews and what he charged against them, but of what might come if the Inquisition was set strongly going in England. Granted, heresy must not be allowed to thrive, destroying souls, but Frevisse in her childhood spent wandering with her parents had seen a little of the Inquisition's work. Had understood, even as a child, that despite what good the Inquisition might do, there were men among the inquisitors for whom the love of wielding power of life and death over others was stronger than their desire toward the salvation of souls. To save a soul meant less to them than their pleasure in decreeing men's destruction. "And the death-wielders' numbers are growing," her father had said once, when the small band of players with whom he and her mother and she were presently traveling were sheltering through a rainy night in a barn somewhere in France, having left a town by one gateway as the Inquisition in the form of five Dominican friars rode in through another. Frevisse still remembered the firelight on tired faces, the rustle of rain on the roof, the warmth of her mother's arms around her. Remembered what her father had said because the word "death-wielders" had stayed with her.

She did not like how readily Brother Michael had accused Jews of the boy Hal's death. She was willing—barely—to grant there might be Jews secretly living in London, pretending to be Christian. There had been the bread she had seen on Mistress Blakhall's table, for one thing. But a braided breadloaf was too little to build long thoughts on. Worth more thought was Father Tomas. He had very possibly earned the friar's dislike and certainly opened himself to the friar's questions if Brother Michael kept eager to his Jew-hunt. What she had protested in the crypt was true—popes had steadily decreed, one after another, that the accusations of ritual murder by Jews were false—but those repeated decrees had stopped neither the belief nor the butcheries, and Frevisse doubted they would stop Brother Michael. His ambition to find out heretics and Jews looked to be too strong. And whatever the friar did or didn't do, there would be those who saw Father Tomas differently now that his Jewish parentage was known.

She welcomed the small bell ringing to Compline and obeyed it with the hope she would succeed in Compline's prayers where she had failed at Vespers, that she would sink deep enough into their peace to quiet all her thoughts and let her sleep deep tonight and without dreams.

Chapter 13

For Anne, the day's one mercy was that Mistress Hercy had given order that no neighbor was to be let in until certain word came back from the church; and when Anne returned to say it was Hal, Mistress Hercy gave the order anew without Anne told her more. Then the ill news had to be given to Pernell, and after that there was nothing Anne could do but wrap her arms around her and hold her and weep with her as she sat rocking her body back and forth, wringing her hands, crying out through streaming tears, "Why? He never hurt anyone! *Why?*", while Mistress Hercy and Lucie held each other and cried with them.

Only finally did Mistress Hercy force a drugged wine on her daughter, saying, "Drink it. For the baby's sake, if nothing else," and after that at last they got her to bed. When the restless twisting of her head on the pillow quieted at last, they left her, and in the parlor Mistress Hercy, with her own and Lucie's tears worn out for a while, held her granddaughter in a brief, tight embrace, then told her, "Wash your face and afterward fetch my box of herbs from my chamber and some warm water from the kitchen. We'll put lavender in it and bathe your mother's face to ease her if she rouses again and help her back to sleep. There's a good girl." But, when Lucie was gone, she turned to Anne and said, "Tell me the worst about his death. So I'll know from what I have to protect them. Because there is worse, isn't there?"

"There is," Anne said, and told her as briefly as might be—not what Brother Michael had said against Jews and most certainly not how Daved's arms had tightened around her and his face become a rigid mask in the odd-thrown lantern-shadows—but all the rest, sparing nothing. At the end Mistress Hercy signed herself with the cross and said, "Thank you. Now I know and will speak to the servants," with a grimness that boded ill for anyone who let a word of any of that horror slip to Pernell.

"Lucie, too," Anne said. "If it can be kept from her . . ."

"Lucie, too," Mistress Hercy said.

Anne made her escape soon afterward, pausing only to bathe her own face clean of its tears and ashamed of how relieved she was to be away, though she soon lost that relief as she made her way home. Used though she was to London in all its humours, this afternoon there was everywhere a such seethe of loud and angry talk—and even now more against the king and his lords than at Jack Cade and his Kentishmen—that she was thankful beyond measure to reach Kerie Lane and close her own door behind her.

But Bette was brimming over with the same talk if not the anger, exclaiming while Anne was taking off her veil and wimple, baring her head to welcome coolness, "Mistress

Upton is just gone. She's been down at Queenhithe and Vintry wharf with other folk, looking to see what they could across Thames."

Turning to the waiting basin of water, Anne asked, "Was she?" Ready to welcome anything that would take her mind from everything else.

"She didn't see all that much," Bette complained. "Some men staring back from the Southwark side is all, but she made the most of seeing them, swearing they had to be rebels. No sign they're doing any harm to anybody, though. No rioting or burning or anything. It's just as folk have been saying. That Jack Cade is keeping everything right because they're only out to be rid of those around the king as shouldn't be there." Bette dropped her voice. "She said some are saying we should let them into London, let them get on with things."

Anne, who had been washing her face and throat, glad of the cool water, straightened and stared at her. "Let them into London? That would be mad."

"Still, it would make plain we mean to have changes or else," Bette said. "How did your dinner at Master Grene's go? How goes it with Mistress Grene?"

So Anne had to tell the half-truths all over again, but Bette's exclaims were easier to endure than Pernell's tears, and because there was only so much to be said about the pity and wickedness of the murder, over supper Bette's talk went back to the rebels, where Anne willingly kept it until her time for going up to bed.

Unhappily, bed proved to be neither comfort nor shelter. In a darkness made darker by her thoughts, she lay awake a long while, aching to have Daved with her, half-hoping he would somehow know her need and come to her, at the same time knowing she did not want him out in London's streets tonight, able to guess from the number of times the Watch went along the streets warning that all good men should be in their beds that too many men were not. So, no, it was better Daved be safe at Raulyn's.

But how safe was he even there now? She rolled over, pulled the other pillow to her, and wrapped her arms around it, holding it the way she wanted Daved to be holding her. London had been safest of anywhere for him because no one looked to find Jews here. Now Brother Michael would be looking. Would start with Father Tomas and then . . .

Anne sat upright in bed, staring into the darkness, remembering her morning errand. Daved had said he and his uncle sometimes brought letters to London. Other Jewish letters? Until now she had thought only herself and Raulyn knew Daved's secret. But if there were others, he was even less safe.

And how far was Raulyn to be trusted if worse came to worse?

Startled by the question, she reassured herself quickly that of course he could be trusted to the end. Aside from his friendship with them, Daved and Master Bocking brought him profit and he'd not endanger his profit.

Anne lay down slowly, staring at that thought.

Was that where she put Raulyn's friendship? At no higher worth than his own profit? What of his friendship with her then? Until this commission of the Suffolk vestments, their friendship had been more to her profit than to his, so profit wasn't his only reason for friendship.

Or was it a different sort of profit he hoped from her? There was the sometimes half-wantonness in things he said or half-said to her in jest. Or that was what she had always told herself. That he was only jesting . . .

Anne sat up again and threw the pillow across the room, wanting to throw her thought away with it. Raulyn was her friend and there was the end of it. Anything else was only her *own* wantonness speaking. And angry at herself, angry at Raulyn, angry at Daved, angry because she was awake and wanted to be asleep, she flung herself down again, closed her eyes . . . and found herself staring at the thought that among the dangers to Daved was herself.

She had said she would go back to the House of Converts, to see if the woman Alis had a letter for her family. Now she must not, because if Brother Michael turned his heed that way and she was found out, she would be a link to Daved.

Blessed St. Anne. If once Brother Michael began to look for Jews, how many ways were there he could be led to Daved?

But she should not be crying out for comfort to St. Anne, faithful wife and holy mother. Her better hope lay with St. Mary Magdalene. But the Magdalene had repented her sins, and Anne repented not at all her desire for Daved. She wanted him now, here, with her.

But he was not here, and he did not come, and sometime after the passing Watch had cried, "One of the clock"—without the usual "and all's well"—she finally slid into a dream-ridden, restless sleep, to awaken late and unrested in a morning already warm before the sun was fully up. Tired with her thoughts and lack of sleep, she put on her lightest undergown, bound her hair up uncovered, and went downstairs to find Bette and the market basket gone.

Before Anne could begin to worry, Bette shuffled in at the front door, laden market basket over her arm, and Anne hurried to take the basket, chiding, "I'm not that late up that you had to go."

Readily giving up the basket, Bette sank onto her stool beside the hearth but waved aside Anne's protest, saying, "I wanted to hear for myself all that's going on. You never have enough to tell."

Beginning to empty the basket onto the table, Anne asked, "What did you hear?"

"Nothing about Hal's death, for one."

Anne stopped, a breadloaf in her hands. "Nothing?"

"Not with bigger things to take folks' tongues wagging." Bette rubbed at her knees. "There's report there's more rebels coming."

Taking a second loaf from the basket, Anne said, "We've still the bridge between them and us. The king will have to come sometime to deal with them."

"Nay, it's not more Kentishmen. It's men out of Essex and thereabouts. *This* side of the river. They're coming to Mile End it's being said, and there's talk there's more gathering in from the west, and talk that the king is gone from Berkhampstead yesterday because he knew it then, and that now he's gone . . ." She paused, gleaming with her news. ". . . for Kenilworth or Coventry!"

"But they're . . ." Away somewhere. North, but she didn't know how far except it was far. "What good can he do us from Kenilworth or Coventry?"

"None," Bette said. "It's said the mayor and alderman are to meet at the Guildhall on what we're to do, since no one else is going to do aught for us, seems."

Anne realized she was holding a third breadloaf and that there was a large lump of probably cheese wrapped in waxed cloth still in the basket; and holding up the loaf and pointing at the basket, she asked, "What's this? It's more than we usually buy in a week."

Bette straightened, hands resting on her knees and satisfaction on her face. "To see us through if we have to keep inside for a few days. I mean to go out later for more."

"You'll not. You'll be unable to walk for a week if you do. I'll go." Because Bette was right: if bad enough trouble came, they might have to keep to the house.

"You'd best go soon, then. I'm not the only one who thinks things may go worse before they go better. We'll want water, too."

At least it was something to do besides thinking, and

Anne broke her fast with bread and an apple while putting on her outer gown, wimple, and veil. Marketing in her turn, she bought no more bread—it would not keep—but did get another cheese. Kept in a cool crock, it should do. And the last dozen salted herring at the fishmonger's because they would keep, too. With that and the dried beans and peas they already had, they should do well enough for food, and after giving it all over to Bette, she went back and forth a few times to the nearer Cheapside conduit, fetching water to fill everything they had to spare for it in the house, and hearing while she did more about the rebels out of Essex.

"A good few thousand of them," a man was saying to someone else while she waited for her bucket to fill under one of the fountain mouths. "At Mile End outside Aldgate, aye."

"What do they want?" a woman asked.

"Same as Jack Cade's lot, I hear," someone else said; and the woman said happily, "That's all right, then."

From what Anne heard and didn't hear, there seemed no great trouble happening in Southwark—nothing beyond the expected reveling among the taverns and brothels—with people still saying that gave weight to Cade's promise the rebels weren't out to make trouble, only to right wrongs and be rid of the corrupt men around the king. "And that can't happen any too soon," a woman filling a pitcher beside Anne called to some nearby talking men, while another woman shouted at them, "Best hie yourselves to the Guildhall and tell the mayor and all!"

One of the men shouted back, "They couldn't hear us over their own tongue-flailing! Best we just open the gates and let Cade do the talking for us!" And the general laughter at that sounded less at a jest than approving a thought that was gaining ground.

Over their dinner of bean pottage, bread, and apple tart, Anne reported all of it to Bette who muttered about fools and kings and thought she'd go to talk with Mab next door.

Anne, ready to be alone, went upstairs, meaning to work while waiting for Dame Frevisse to come; but the thoughts she had lost in the morning's busyness came back on her in a dark rush, and not about to imperil the gold lion or costly thread with her distraction, she tried to work on a garnet-dyed linen band she was embroidering with a green fretwork in simple cross stitch, but her stitches proved to be as uneven as her thoughts and she soon gave it up and simply sat. She didn't want sewing. She wanted Daved.

She had left the top of the streetward door open for air to move through the house, and he must have let himself in, because she had no warning except his quick footfall on the steps before he *was* there, and she was barely to her feet with a small cry of disbelief, relief, and joy before she was in his arms.

Too soon, though, he drew back a step, not letting her go but telling her without words they would go no further yet. In return, Anne fought herself to steadiness, slipped her hands down to his waist to hold him as he was holding her, and said, smiling, "I hoped and hoped you'd come to me today."

"I hoped I'd be here before now." He took another quick kiss. "And I wish I could stay."

Even expected, her disappointment was sharp. Only barely she kept her voice light as she said, "But you can't."

"I can't. It would leave too much on my uncle. We're moving our goods back to the ship . . ."

"You're leaving?" This time Anne failed to keep raw dismay from her voice.

"Not yet, no, and we may not. This is only against the chance things go to the bad."

His other times in London, they had sometimes had a month and more together. This was barely a week, and Anne said, sounding pitiful and pleading even to herself, "You'd leave? Now?"

"Only if there's no safe other way." Unexpectedly he was

pleading back to her. "There are too many people's lives depend on our returning with what we've gained this journey. We can't risk losing it, my uncle and I."

Almost Anne demanded, What of *our* life? But that was against all the rules she had set herself; she had strangled the words unsaid even before Bette called up the stairs, "Dame Frevisse is here, mistress. Shall she come up?"

Anne gasped, but Daved nodded his head toward the window bench where she'd been sitting and moved away to sit himself in the chair while she called, "Of course. Thank you, Bette," and sat down at the window, so that when Dame Frevisse appeared up the stairs, they were both able to stand up to greet her as if they had been sitting in simple talk until then, Daved saying as he bowed Dame Frevisse to the chair, "You're bold to brave the streets today, my lady."

"I'm hoping to finish my business with Mistress Blakhall and leave London." She made a small smile. "That was the only way my steward was persuaded to let me leave St. Helen's at all. Unhappily, I hear there are rebels rumored to the west now. Please," she added as Daved remained standing. "Won't you sit?"

She gestured toward the long window seat, and with a small bow of thanks Daved sat down a careful distance aside from Anne while saying, "It's possible. The anger against King Henry is running deeper and wider all the time."

With the bitter likelihood of soon losing Daved spilling over into bitterness at the king, Anne said, "The only place we haven't heard of rebels is northward. That must be why he's run that way."

"That report is true, then?" Dame Frevisse asked.

"I gather so, yes," Daved answered. "There were some several boatloads of clerks and documents came down from Westminster to the Tower on the last tide. The guess is that they were bringing things to safer keeping."

"He won't even defend his own," Anne said. "What does he expect from us if he won't do even that?"

"He probably expects London to look to itself," said Daved. "The way he's looking to himself. Isn't it usually the way with great lords to see to themselves first, and if they think of their people at all, it's only to wonder how hard to tax them?"

"Then King Henry should most particularly want to defend London," said Dame Frevisse dryly. "Given the wealth here to be taxed, you wouldn't think he'd want to lose it to rebels."

"He probably supposes London will defend itself for that very reason—its own wealth," Daved answered. "Why trouble himself when they will do it for him?"

"Too fair and likely a supposition," Dame Frevisse granted. "Have you heard anything of what's toward at the Guildhall?"

"Master Grene went himself to hear what he could. He came back to say he couldn't get near. The Guildhall was full to the walls and out the door. The word spread out from there, though, was that the mayor and aldermen are debating the rebels' demands. There's strong talk that Cade and his Kentishmen have the right of it, so why not join in with them since the king is doing nothing to make anything better."

"St. Paul defend us," Anne breathed.

"Mistress," Bette called from the stairfoot. "I've ale ready if someone will fetch it."

Daved immediately made to rise, but Anne was more quickly to her feet, calling, "I'm coming."

Behind her as she went down the stairs, Dame Frevisse said, "Daved is not a common name in France or Flanders, is it? Are you part Welsh?"

Taking the tray with cups and pitcher, Anne's thanks to Bette were short as she listened to Daved answering easily,

"My mother was the daughter of a Scottish man-at-arms who made his fortune in the French war." There was a smile in his voice. "Fighting for the French against the English."

"Helping keep the English busy there, rather than in Scotland," Dame Frevisse acknowledged, an equal smile in her words.

"Just so. He married there, and here I am, trading with the English. A different way of raiding them, I suppose, from what my grandfather used to do."

Dame Frevisse a little laughed at that, and Anne set the tray on the table, smiling with them both, hiding her thought of how easily Daved had given that lie. It was probably one he had given other times before now, and there was no good reason why it should hurt her to hear it, but it did. Not for itself, she thought as she poured ale and handed a cup to Dame Frevisse, but because she was coming to see how so much of his life was a lie, was becoming frightened of how many lies there were.

Her mind was jerked elsewhere by Dame Frevisse asking Daved, "How is it with Mistress Grene?"

Anne knew she should have asked that at first seeing him and was ashamed as Daved answered gravely, "Much as you might expect. Mistress Hercy does what she can, but how much can be done against such a grief?"

"What of Lucie?" Anne asked, bringing a filled cup to him.

"I think she still only half-believes it's true."

"Is anyone doing anything for Mistress Hercy?" Dame Frevisse asked.

"She cares for herself by taking care of others, I think."

Dame Frevisse nodded understanding of that likelihood. Anne sat down with her own drink and a little silence fell among them, Dame Frevisse looking down into the cup in her hands resting on her lap, Anne looking at Daved, Daved looking at Dame Frevisse. Anne knew his face well enough to know he was thinking of something more than just the moment, but she had no guess what before he said quietly, "Dame Frevisse."

She raised her gaze to him, her look as quiet as his voice.

"About the duchess of Suffolk's gold," Daved said.

Anne drew in a sharp breath, but Dame Frevisse only said, "Yes?"

Daved slightly smiled. "You already thought I had something to do with it?"

"Given one thing and another, it seemed likely. And the more likely when I met you here today."

Daved's smile deepened. "All our hope for secrecy seems to have been as undone by Jack Cade as the king has been. I came here today, yes, to give Mistress Blakhall the last of the gold."

Hurt twisted in Anne. She had thought it was for her alone he'd come.

"The trouble is," said Dame Frevisse, "that I haven't even taken the second one. I'm here for it today. And now you say there's a third."

"The last. But I fear you'll have to take both today."

He began to unfasten his doublet. Anne rose and went to the chest beside the door. By the time she returned with the purse from there, Daved had brought out another one and was giving it to Dame Frevisse, who took it without pleasure, looked at the one that Anne laid on her lap beside it, and said, even-voiced, "I'm not happy about this."

"None of us are," Daved answered.

They sounded so alike that Anne suddenly wondered what things the nun, like Daved, kept hidden behind quietness.

Then Dame Frevisse looked up at Daved and surprisingly smiled. "At least you're quit of it. You can be glad of that."

He matched her smile. "I promise you I am." He made a slight bow to both her and Anne. "Now, by your ladies' leave, I must go about my other business."

Despite the sharp cut of her disappointment, Anne said evenly, "I'll see you to the door." Hopeful of another moment alone with him.

"My thanks, but no," he said. "You have your other guest." And he bowed to them again and left, leaving Anne bereft of even a final touch of his hand.

Chapter 14

Frevisse, watching Mistress Blakhall watch Master Weir leave, thought they would do well to be seen together as little as possible. With what she had seen yesterday and Mistress Blakhall's many small betrayals today, her guess was strengthened that they were more familiar with each other than outwardly admitted. How much "familiar" was not her business, she firmly told herself and held up the two purses of gold and asked, "Can you help with this again?"

Mistress Blakhall readily fetched a large scrap of heavy cloth and a length of thick cord from a basket near the window seat and sat down beside her sewing basket to begin cutting a circle from the cloth, asking while she did, "Are you still wearing the other?"

"It's safe in St. Helen's," Frevisse said. Empty, she did not add, and the coins spread under unbound pages of books in the box strapped shut and put under her bed.

"That's to the good. You'd be more than a little burdened otherwise."

"The thought of it all is burden enough."

"True." Mistress Blakhall paused to push a straying wisp of hair from her damp forehead out of sight under her wimple before choosing a needle and threading it.

Watching as she began deftly to stitch along the folded-over edge of the cloth, Frevisse asked, "This Master Weir. "Won't his coming here so often—three visits near together to bring this gold—raise talk among your neighbors?"

Mistress Blakhall's hands did not falter. She went on working her needle quickly in and out while answering easily, "He's been here sometimes before now. It's known I buy Paris-spun gold thread from him. Some kinds of better silk thread, too, at a better price than I'd have from a draper or mercer. It's a kindness he does me because he knew my father. The neighbors talk, but their talk is something I live with anyway, being a woman living alone and working my own way in the world."

"You prefer that to marrying again?" Frevisse asked mildly.

"I do." Mistress Blakhall paused her sewing and looked up. "Another man so good and loving as my husband was would be hard to find, and since God has seen fit to give me such skills that I need not marry from necessity, I've chosen not to. I've come to like my life as a 'woman alone.'" She went back to stitching. "Will you leave London now you have all the gold?"

"If it's at all possible, we'll be away on the next upriver tide."

"Will that be safe if there are rebels to the west, the way rumor is running?"

"We can only wait for better word or else take our chance," Frevisse said calmly. And did not add the question large in her own mind: How safe was London going to stay? Gates and bridges depended on people's willingness to keep them shut, and from what she had heard, London's willingness had begun to waver. Master Naylor had been disappointed to the edge of anger today that Dame Clemens was willing to go out of St. Helen's with her again; had insisted he and Dickon both accompany them and was downstairs now, waiting with undoubted restlessness to be away, both from here *and* London. With that thought, Frevisse said, "Concerning the cloth for the vestments. May I simply give you leave to choose such as you deem best for the work and recommend you have it from Master Grene?"

"That would serve well."

And both she and Master Grene would play straight in the matter, Frevisse thought, because the duchess of Suffolk was a woman only fools would try to cheat, and why do so when her future favor would be worth far more than some present small gain?

Mistress Blakhall had finished her stitching, was beginning to work the cord through the cloth's folded-over edge to become a drawstring.

Frevisse watched in silence, and when Mistress Blakhall gathered the cloth on the cord, completing the bag, Frevisse gave over the two purses. Mistress Blakhall put them into the bag and helped Frevisse put the cord around her neck under the concealing folds of her wimple. The weight was doubled from last time but again, with the purse slipped inside her gown, nothing showed, and Mistress Blakhall gave a sigh of relief much like the one Frevisse supposed she'd give, too, once she was as quit of the gold as Mistress Blakhall now was.

But the woman had taken more trouble to help her than she need have taken, and despite suspicion of her and Master

Weir, Frevisse realized she liked her, both for her kindness and for her willingness to dare life alone. The behest to "Judge not, lest you be judged" was all too often easier said than done, but this was maybe a time for it.

"There's only the matter of the patterns then," she started.

But Raulyn Grene called up the stairs, "Anne, may I come up?" and already was, there even as Mistress Blakhall stood up, saying, "Raulyn. Yes. Come up. Is it Pernell? The baby?"

"Not the baby, no, but could you come to her? My lady," he added with a quick bow to Frevisse. "For her mother's sake as much as hers, could you come, Anne?"

He was red-faced with heat and hurry, the assured merchant gone from him, and Mistress Blakhall said with sharp concern, "Raulyn, sit down." Taking him by the arm and making him sit on the chest beside the door. "Dame Frevisse, bring some ale, please. Raulyn, what's happened?"

Frevisse quickly filled a cup and brought it to him. He had pulled off his hat, was catching his breath, but beyond being hot, he looked a man stretched too many directions at once and confused and in pain with it. He took the cup from Frevisse with a nod of thanks while answering Mistress Blakhall, "It's all that's happening. What has to be done because of Hal. The rebels. And then Pernell. Nothing is as it should be. Mistress Hercy is doing what she can, but between Pernell and Lucie and seeing to the household, it's too much for her alone. Pernell shouldn't be left to herself, but we don't dare let anyone with her who might say too much. Could you come to her? For only a while. It would help."

"Drink," Mistress Blakhall told him. "Of course I'll come."

He drank, but when he lowered the cup he said to Frevisse, "Would you, too? You'd be someone different. Anything to turn her mind even a little aside." He was a man grabbing for any hope. "You could pray with her. Father Tomas has but . . ." He made a helpless gesture.

In all charity Frevisse could hardly refuse his plea, and she bent her head with a slight, accepting murmur. Which was less than Master Naylor would have to say about it, she thought bleakly.

Mistress Blakhall was looking about for what she might need with her but asked, "You've been able to keep much of it from Pernell then?"

"She only knows he was stabbed and left dead in the crypt." Master Grene's breathing and color were evening, letting his face settle to grimness. "Talk has to be rife elsewhere, though. My worst fear is that damned friar is going to make worse trouble of it. He won't let go that Jews did it."

Mistress Blakhall swung around from closing her sewing basket. "Father Tomas denied that!"

"How likely is he to believe Father Tomas?" Master Grene returned. "He wants Jews, and he'll keep at it until he's found them."

"Except there are no Jews in London to find," Frevisse said quietly.

"We'd better hope there aren't," Master Grene said back. He stood up, ready to leave. "But there's Father Tomas for a start."

"He's a Christian priest," Frevisse returned.

"That hasn't been enough to save a man in other places."

"How far has Brother Michael spread this talk?" Mistress Blakhall asked.

"Not far yet, I gather. Mostly he's been pressing Father Tomas on it. Pushing to know more. He—Father Tomas—was warning me of it when he came to see Pernell. What he's said at Grey Friars I don't know. Brother Michael, I mean. What I fear is the hell that'll break loose if he does start up a Jew-hunt."

While he spoke, he stepped aside to let the women go down the stairs ahead of him, but Mistress Blakhall stood rooted in the middle of the room, staring at him. For a long moment he looked straight back at her, and to Frevisse it seemed they were sharing an unsaid thought that neither of them liked. Then Mistress Blakhall dropped her eyes and started forward. Frevisse followed her, and above them as they went down the stairs Master Grene said, "One thing to the good about these rebels is that with all the talk and trouble over them, less heed's been given to Hal's death than would have been. Maybe Brother Michael's troublemaking will go the same way."

It was a backhanded kind of hope, but better than none, Frevisse supposed as she asked, "Have you heard aught from crowner or constable?"

"Nothing. What can they hope to find out after all this time?" Master Grene said.

Told the changed plan, Master Naylor looked sour but only said, "We'll be nearer St. Helen's. That's something."

Getting Dame Clemens from her family, everyone in talk about the rebels and more excited than alarmed, took time but at last they had her away and walking at haste along Cheapside, Master Grene's hurry leaving her too short-breathed to say more than, "Yes, of course," to Frevisse's explanation of where they were going and why. That left Frevisse time to see that in even the while she'd been at Mistress Blakhall's the feel of London had worsened. Where there should have been the flow and busyness of a London midweek day, people were gathered in ever larger and louder clots and clusters, the anger and restless unease there had been changing now to a roiling sense of being done with waiting.

Frevisse felt what she imagined she would feel if standing below a weakening dam with flood waters rising behind it—a great desire to be elsewhere. To find the shops and houses in Swithin's Lane all closed was only the more unsettling, and the servant keeping the gate to the Red Swan's yard was on the inside this time, peering out so carefully in answer to Master Grene's knock and, "We're here, Pers," that Master Grene slapped the flat of his hand against the wood, demanding impatiently, "Open it!"

Pers hastily got the door and himself out of the way. Master Grene let the three women enter ahead of him, then followed them, with Master Naylor and Dickon coming last as Master Grene ordered over his shoulder at Pers, "Bar it again."

At the yard-end of the gateway passage their way was blocked by two young men and a half-grown boy trundling a lurching one-wheeled barrow laden with a large canvas-wrapped bale of something over the cobbles toward the hall. Two other like bales waited there at the foot of the steps, and Mistress Blakhall asked "Raulyn, what's toward here?"

"I'm shifting things from the shop into the hall's cellar for safer keeping. Wyett, is this the last of them, or all that you've done while I was gone?"

Not pausing in wrestling the unwieldy barrow forward, the older of the two men said, "This is the last of it. Everything else is in and down."

"Safer keeping?" Master Naylor challenged. "Why? I thought everyone was saying the rebels can't get into London."

"They can't 'get' in," Master Grene said grimly. "That doesn't mean they won't be 'let' in. So better safe now than sorry afterward."

"Let in?" Master Naylor gestured angrily at Frevisse and Dame Clemens. "What are these women doing here, then, when they should be where they belong?"

"They're safe enough for now," Master Grene said. "Nothing has happened yet, and maybe won't. I'm only—"

Dame Clemens interrupted, her voice rising, "I want to go back to St. Helen's. Now."

"Yes," Master Naylor agreed, moving back toward the gate. "Now, while the going is good. Dame Frevisse—"

"Dame Frevisse, please," Mistress Blakhall said unexpectedly. "Between us, we can reassure Pernell better than I can alone."

Frevisse knew "lie to Pernell" was what she meant, and if London's patience was about to break under the weight of all the angers at the king, she wanted herself and the gold safe into St. Helen's before it happened. But the lives of both Pernell and her unborn child might well depend on how well she was guarded from the truth, and since surely Master Grene said true that Mistress Hercy was wearing out keeping guard for her daughter's sake, Mistress Blakhall's plea was hardly to be denied; and far more steadily than she felt, Frevisse said, "I'll stay."

She met Master Naylor's glare and added, refusing all his furious, silent objections, "Do you and Dickon see Dame Clemens back to St. Helen's. Then return for me. I'll have done what I can here by then. Master Grene, would you send a woman with them, for propriety's sake?"

Dame Clemens, already edging back toward the gateway, said quickly, "There's no need. Things as they are, we'll just go."

Master Naylor stayed where he was and demanded, barely on the right side of courteous, "Dickon stays with you, and I'll be back as soon as I've seen Dame Clemens into St. Helen's. You swear you'll leave then?"

"Yes." Silently blessing him for that way out.

Master Naylor nodded sharply, said to Dickon, "She's your duty then til I return," made her a sharp bow that ignored everyone else, turned on his heel, and followed Dame Clemens' hurry toward the gateway.

To his back, Dickon said gladly, "Yes, sir," openly pleased not to be tucked away into the nunnery again.

As Master Naylor and Dame Clemens went out the gate, Master Grene's men were heaving one of the bales of cloth up the stairs to the hall, and Frevisse said at Dickon, "Help them."

Dickon readily bounded up the steps to add his strength to theirs, and left alone and unable to go forward for the moment, Master Grene said low-voiced to Frevisse, "Do you have it all now?"

"Yes."

He gave a single, satisfied nod and turned to Mistress Blakhall. "I'm trying to get Daved to bring his uncle to sail at their first chance. The sooner they go the better. If you have chance to urge him . . ."

Sounding both bleak and defensive, Mistress Blakhall said, "I will."

All of which told Frevisse that Master Grene knew something of whatever was between Mistress Blakhall and Daved Weir as well as about the gold.

The way now clear, they went on up the stairs and inside, Master Grene saying as they went, "I'll leave you to go up to Pernell. I'm bound for the cellar to see how my men do." He smiled. "I keep my wine down there, too." His smile disappeared. "Anne, do all you can for her, please. Everything's gone so wrong."

"I will," Mistress Blakhall promised.

He left them, and they went up to the parlor where Frevisse had so briefly been before, still a pleasant room but with all pleasure was gone from it. Pernell was standing at the window overlooking the yard, her hands under the great swell of her belly to ease its weight a little. She still wore a loose child-bearing gown but this one was black-dyed, and her fair hair, which had been fastened up and covered by a light veil yesterday, was hanging loose and uncombed down her back. The little girl Lucie, likewise gowned in black, was curled on one end of the other window bench, looking much like a small animal wanting a burrow in which to hide, her eyes red from crying, the rolled cloth of a sampler clutched in her hands but no sign she had been sewing on it.

Pernell's eyes were red and swollen, too, as she turned from the window and held out her hands, saying, "Anne," and Mistress Blakhall went to her as Mistress Hercy came from the bedchamber carrying a goblet. The marks of grief were less on her, probably from the necessity to be strong for her daughter, granddaughter, and unborn grandchild, Frevisse guessed; and she likewise said, "Anne," but briskly; and to Frevisse, "My lady. Lucie, bring wine for our guests, please." Continuing to Pernell while Lucie uncurled and went into the bedchamber, "You promised you'd drink this if I made it, and it's made. Borage and valerian in pale wine," she added to Mistress Blakhall and Frevisse. "To quiet the mind and ease the heart."

Mistress Grene took the goblet but said while she did, "Nothing will ease my heart. There's only grief from now onward."

"There isn't," her mother said, guiding her toward the nearest chair. "I've lost two children in my time, and my husband, too, and despite it all have found pleasure in life again afterward. You did, too, after your Henry died, remember. Not the same pleasure, no, and the sorrow never truly goes away." She made Pernell sit. "But it lessens, because you still have the living. Raulyn and Lucie and little Robert and the baby to come. So you drink your drink. For the baby's sake if not yours. That you've lost much doesn't mean you should set yourself to lose more. The Lord gives, and the Lord takes away." She paused pointedly.

Dully her daughter finished, "Blessed be the Lord's name."

Mistress Hercy patted her shoulder approvingly. "You remember that. Give thanks for what you have and let the rest be as it has to be. Anne is here. You talk with her awhile. Let her tell you what foolishness people are up to in London today."

Mistress Blakhall drew two stools to Pernell, lifted Pernell's feet onto one, sat on the other, and with Pernell's free
hand clasped in hers, began to talk quietly. Mistress Hercy,
released from her daughter's need for maybe the first time
that day, turned away. For just a moment her unguarded face
showed all her own grief and weariness, and Frevisse said,
"Will you sit, too?", moving away to the window seat on the
room's other side.

Mistress Hercy went with her and sank onto the cushioned bench with a slow stiffness as Lucie returned with
three silver goblets instead of only two clutched together in
her hands. Sensible child, she brought them first to her
grandmother and Frevisse before going to Mistress Blakhall,
who took the offered goblet in one hand and put her other
arm around Lucie's waist, drawing the girl to her side affec-
tionately. Pernell began to sip absentmindedly at her own
wine, and Mistress Hercy, watching her, eased a little, saying
softly, "That's better." She smiled wanly at Frevisse. "She's
ordered all her bearing-gowns dyed black. My worry is she'll
bring more grief on us all by a bad birthing."

"How long has it been since her last?"

"Little Robert is nearly three. He's at nurse in Sheen."
Mistress Hercy took a long drink of wine. "She's trying, for
the baby's sake, to hold back from worse grieving, but it's
hard enough to have lost Hal without it was this way. And
it's only made harder because she can't even choose his burial place in the churchyard or go to his funeral. All she's
been able to do is send good linen for his shroud."

And all Mistress Hercy had been able to do was
smother her own grief while tending to her daughter's;
and because letting her talk was the only help Frevisse
could presently give, she asked quietly, "When will the funeral be?"

"Tomorrow. Rebels and all allowing." Mistress Hercy
shook her head, drank some more, recovered a little, and

looked at Frevisse. "What are you going to say if Pernell asks you about Hal?"

"That he didn't die in fear or pain, only suddenly."

It was surprising how harsh with anger a face as soft and round as Mistress Hercy's could go. "If I knew who'd done it to him, I swear I'd kill the bastard cur if ever I had the chance. Do you swear what was done to him was all done after he was dead?"

Steadily, for what small comfort it might be, Frevisse said, "I swear it."

Mistress Hercy regarded her for a long, unmoving moment, then nodded, dropped her eyes, and drank again. In her turn, Frevisse said quietly, "Master Grene says naught's been learned toward who did this thing."

"Nothing that helps anyway. Master Crane was here today and I made Raulyn tell me afterward what he said, but the sum of it was nothing. Hal went out that night, and that was the last that was seen of him."

Keeping her voice carefully level, Frevisse asked, "Who stands to gain by Hal's death?"

Mistress Hercy had begun to take another drink of her wine but stopped, lowered the goblet, and gave Frevisse a sharp, fixed, dry-eyed look before answering, "You're the first to say that aloud, but I've wondered it."

"He had inheritance?"

"A goodly one. So does Lucie. She'll have it all now."

But she surely had not arranged her brother's murder, so, "Who else gains?"

"No one. Raulyn was granted wardship of the children and their property when he married Pernell." A London citizen's orphans coming by law into the London council's care, their wardships were kept or granted as seemed best and usually to their mother's new husband if she married again. "That's unlikely to change, so no one gains there, though Raulyn has lost what he would have made from Hal's marriage." Since money tended to change hands between the buyer and seller of an heir's marriage.

"And if Lucie dies?"

"Then all goes to a cousin of their father. He lives off in Leicester, hasn't been to London in years, and so far as I've heard lately he's prospering in his own right."

Frevisse knew she had no true business asking these questions, took a deep drink of her wine to stop herself, and was saved from discovering whether she would have succeeded by voices sudden and loud in the yard below the window and Pernell immediately crying out in alarm, "What is it?"

Mistress Hercy was already on her feet, making haste across the room to the other window, saying soothingly as she went, "It's just . . ." She reached the window and leaned out the better to see and hear, and her voice sharpened. "It's Master Bocking and Master Weir. They're . . ."

Mistress Blakhall left Lucie and Pernell in a rush, to join her at the window, asking, "What's happened? Are they hurt? Is there fighting?"

"No. They're saying . . ." Mistress Hercy leaned farther out. "No. It's our folk are shouting. They're saying—" She broke off, pulled back from the window, and turned to say with open dismay, "They're saying the rebels are crossing London Bridge. Someone opened the gates. They rebels are crossing into London."

Chapter 15

nne had barely time for her relief at seeing
Daved was safe, never mind the news he
had brought, before she had to turn back to
Pernell struggling up from her chair, crying that she needed
to see for herself what was happening. Mistress Hercy was already away toward the stairs, but Anne and Dame Frevisse,
with Lucie hovering close, helped her to her feet and to the
window. There was little to be seen by then, only two of
Raulyn's men heaving the last bale of cloth up the outer
stairs, and Pernell had sunk down on the window bench, a
hand pressed between her breasts as she tried to catch breath
into her cramped lungs, when footfall too quick for Mistress
Hercy came up the stairs.

Knowing it was Daved even before he was through the doorway, Anne's heart leaped, and she knew her face must betray her, but everyone's heed was on him as he went to Pernell and down on one knee before her, catching her free hand in his own while saying quickly, his own breath short from his hurry, "Raulyn said I should tell you he's set watch at both the front gate and in the rearyard. Has ordered all the lower windows shuttered and barred. Has clubs for all the men. There's no need for you to be afraid. Everything here is safe."

Pernell gripped his hands tightly and said desperately, "But if they burn everything, if they burn London . . ."

"There'll be no burning. They want London on their side, not destroyed." Daved had his breath now, and his face lightened almost to laughter as he added, "But if need be, I shall sweep you into my arms and carry you to safety, fair lady."

Pernell was surprised into a half-tearful laugh at thought of anyone sweeping her ungainly body into their arms.

From where she stood, a few paces aside, Dame Frevisse asked, "Master Weir, what's truly happening? What have you seen?"

Standing up, still smiling, Daved answered lightly, "Not much. My uncle and I were readying to row out to our ship from Botoph Wharf just below the bridge. With the bridge so full of houses, we couldn't see much of what was toward there but heard the roar of shouting from its far end well enough. While we stood trying to guess what was happening, the shouting started to cross the bridge. If there was fighting, it was done almost before it started, but there were surely a great many men on the move, and by the sound of it they were being welcomed. That told us someone must have lowered the drawbridge and opened the gates."

"St. Paul bless us," Pernell breathed. "St. Paul bless *you* for coming to warn us."

Dame Frevisse asked, "Then they're fully into London by now?"

"As we crossed Fish Street past St. Magnus church, Cade's banner-bearer was just riding off the bridge. If we hadn't been running, we'd never have been ahead of them."

"But what will they do now?" Pernell asked, all her fright naked in her face and voice and rigid back.

"That we'll have to wait for," Daved said easily. "But we're safely tucked in here."

Raulyn hurried in then and Pernell held out her hands to him with a sharp, glad cry. Daved moved aside and Raulyn in his turn clasped one of her hands and, sitting down beside her, asked, "He's told you? That there's no need for worry?" while holding out his other hand to Lucie, who took it quickly. Sagging gratefully against him, Pernell half-sobbed something into his shoulder that only he could hear.

While he quietly answered her, Dame Frevisse moved away to the other window, leaving them private together; and for seemingly the same reason Daved came the few steps aside to Anne, as if to assure her, too, that all was well. That was as alone as they were likely to be here, and Anne snatched the chance to say, low-voiced, "You should have gone to your ship. You'd be safe if you'd gone on."

"Safe is so tedious," Daved said, his voice low but still light. "Besides, Raulyn said he meant to bring you to Pernell today. On the chance he had, here I am." As if that had made his choice simple; but he added letting go a little of his lightness, "Now promise me you'll stay here until we're more certain what's happening."

"Bette is alone at home."

"You could do naught to make her safer by being with her. You can be of better use here with Mistress Grene in her need."

"Will you be staying?"

Daved searched her face, maybe reading how half-ready she was to forego his warning. "If you do, yes. For tonight at least. Until we know more how things will be."

She ached to touch him, to have him touch her in return, but they must not. It had to be enough that he was there, and she said, "I'll stay at least tonight."

Dame Frevisse turned from the window and made a small beckon at Daved and her. They joined her, and she asked, "Is that what you heard?" toward the window.

Daved listened for a moment, then said quietly, "Yes."

"What is it?" Raulyn asked sharply.

"We can hear them," Anne answered. "Not fighting," she added quickly. "Just shouting, just as Master Weir said."

From apprentices' sometime holiday-brawls in Cheapside, she knew the scruff-sounds of fighting in the streets. This high-hearted shouting was nothing like that. Was more like what there had been three weeks ago, when King Henry had ridden toward Black Heath to deal with these same rebels now being shouted for.

Raulyn gave Pernell a quick kiss on the cheek and left her, asking as he crossed to join them at the window, "Can you tell where they are?"

Daved leaned out the window. "By the sound of it . . ." He paused, listening. "They're coming along Candlewick." The street that St. Swithin's Lane met beside the church.

"This way?" Pernell cried. "They're coming this way?"

Daved moved away from the window. "I'm going out to see what's happening."

"I'll come with you," said Raulyn. Pernell began to protest, and he went to her, took hold on her hands so she could not grasp at his clothing and kissed her quickly but drew back almost as he did, saying as he let her go, "By the sound of it, it's safe enough. We have to find out what's happening, that's all."

Pernell cried out, "Raulyn!" But he and Daved were both gone, and for one bitter moment Anne flared in anger at them—that they could come and go so easily, so readily, while she had to stay. And Pernell, even trapped by her body as she was, at least could cry out to Raulyn and hold to him when he was here and be held *by* him, while Anne could hold and cry out to no one. And her anger faded into a sadder, darker humour. All she had was her love for Daved, without right to cry out to him or dare to have him hold her. And her love could keep him with her no more than Pernell's love had held back Raulyn.

But Pernell was struggling to her feet again, Lucie trying to help her, and Anne went to steady her just as Mistress Hercy returned, bringing a pitcher of probably more wine. Pernell cried out to her, "Raulyn is going out! He mustn't!" But Mistress Hercy said briskly, setting the pitcher on the table, "He must. It's what men do. Don't fear. Master Weir will see to him. Come away to your chair again."

Pernell let herself be guided back to the chair and sat down heavily, saying on a half-sob, "And there's Hal lying there in the church alone, with no one praying over him."

"We've paid Father Tomas good coin to pray beside him," her mother said.

"Paid prayers!" Pernell snapped, suddenly angry. She lurched to her feet again and away from both her mother and Anne, awkward with the straddled walk of a bearing woman, her hands clasped under the weight of her belly and angry tears running down her cheeks. "He needs more than paid prayers! He's lying there alone. He's . . ."

Out of the way and silent until then, Dame Frevisse said, "He isn't there."

Pernell paused her pacing. "What?"

"Your son has long since gone free. It's not your Hal there, only his body." She went to Pernell, took her by the arm, started her walking again but slowly now, saying with steadying calm, "Grieve for him being gone, but let go worry for his body. Whether it's buried or lying in the church, he's done with it. Until the Last Judgment and the Resurrection, it matters not at all. Whatever comes to it, Hal is gone from it. Only your love for him still matters, and nothing can hurt or touch that, can it?"

"No." However much bewildered she might be by all the rest Dame Frevisse had said, Pernell was sure of that.

But shouting more near than before jerked everyone's head around to the window, and on a sob of fear, Pernell said, "Oh, please," though for what was unclear. God's help? Strength? Safety? Dame Frevisse turned her in a gentle curve toward the southward window, saying, still quietly, "Listen. Those are glad shouts, not angry ones."

Anne, Lucie, and Mistress Hercy joined them at the window. The nun was right, and Mistress Hercy added firmly, "They're going past, staying on Candlewick. 'Strike your sword on Londonstone. Claim the city for your own.' That's what Cade's doing."

The large, rough stone sat in the middle of Candlewick Street, no one certain from when or why, but yes, there was a rhyme that went that way, and as a greater shouting burst up beyond the houses hiding view of Candlewick, Dame Frevisse said, "He's done it, I'd guess. Struck Londonstone and claimed the city for his own."

"Seems he's welcome to it so far the king cares," Mistress Hercy said bitterly. "Now you'd best sit again, Pernell. Remember you've a babe that needs you careful of him."

Dame Frevisse began to ease Pernell toward the chair again, and Pernell let her, seeming calmer, as if finally willing to be comforted. Mistress Hercy—with a wary eye on her daughter—put an arm around Lucie still standing beside her straight-backed and wide-eyed, maybe afraid to move or cry for fear of making something worse, and said,

"Come, Lucie-dear. Whatever else is afoot, everyone is going to want their supper. Let's go be sure the servants are seeing to their work, not thinking to go out to see the sport."

Even as she lightly said it, a look of understanding and agreement passed between her and Dame Frevisse. She would see to Lucie and the servants. Dame Frevisse would see to Pernell; and while Mistress Hercy bustled out with Lucie, Dame Frevisse sat Pernell down, sat down beside her, and Anne copied them, sitting on the window bench with wary care, half-fearing a sudden movement would unsettle the little peace. In that moment she envied Mistress Hercy and Dame Frevisse, both of them so ready and certain at decisions not only for themselves but for others, both of them— being widow and nun and much of an age—free of the burdens of childbearing and the body's passions. Just now Anne would have given much to be free of her body's passions—fear, for one, but also her ache to be in Daved's arms and alone with him again.

Mistress Hercy's round sewing basket sat in the bench's corner, its lid shoved aside, a baby's unfinished yellow gown partly hanging over the edge. Anne took up the gown, found the needle and thread where Mistress Hercy had left off gathering the cloth into a narrow neckband, and began to sew. Dame Frevisse seemed to be praying with Pernell, and Anne, making even in-and-out stitches, thought how sewing was for her much what prayer must be for the nun— giving her mind comfort and sanctuary, somewhere to be besides in worry.

But not from hearing the rabble-noise as it rose momentarily louder through the window. Pernell's head jerked up and around, and Anne said, deliberately going on with her sewing, "They sound farther off, don't they? They're headed up Walbrook, I'd say. Toward the Stocks Market. They'll be making for St. Paul's. Or the Guildhall, I'd guess. It sounds like holiday-making, doesn't it?"

"Not like riot or fighting, certainly," Dame Frevisse said, and Pernell murmured agreement and bowed her head to the nun's praying again.

Done with stitching the small gown into its neckband, Anne took up Lucie's sampler. A strip of fine-threaded linen cloth with each and fastened to a wooden rod so it could be rolled up at one end while being unrolled at the other, the sampler was Lucie's guide to all the stitches she learned and record of patterns she might some day use. Unrolling it to the beginning, then rolling her way forward, Anne smiled at the evidence of Lucie's growing skill these few past years, trying by that small satisfaction to turn her thoughts from her body's need, her heart's longing, her mind's fear. Trying, but not much succeeding.

Chapter 16

Frevisse had long ago found that she was better at watching than at being part of what went on around her. She had passions, she knew, and they ran deep and strong; but their running was toward God rather than into the passing happenstances of every day, and sometimes, even now, she wondered whether, if she had chosen marriage and motherhood, her passions would have turned as fully to husband and children or whether, instead, she would have failed both husband and children, drawn as she was so fully another way. She would never know. She had followed where her heart and mind had led her and never regretted her choice. Her only—and only sometimes—regret was that, living her half-step aside from other people as she did, she sometimes saw more than she was happy to see.

Living that little aside from the thick swirl of desires and
fears by which most people let themselves be governed, she
was able, even here and now while comforting Pernell and
listening for any change to the street-shouting, to be thinking how steadily less happy she was with what she saw between Anne Blakhall and Daved Weir. Their awareness of
each other was sharp enough to cut; beyond doubting there
was more between them than should be between a virtuous
widow and any man.

But outwardly Frevisse went on comforting Pernell as
best she could, leading her in the Kyrie, saying with her,
"Kyrie eleison. Christe eleison. Kyrie eleison."—Lord have mercy.
Christ have mercy. Lord have mercy.—over and over because
words said over and over until the mind was given up to
them could serve to loosen the mind's tight moorings to
the world, letting it float free toward what lay beyond the
body's fears and needs, away from the Lesser and toward the
Greater. If Pernell was to have any deep comfort at all, it
would be there, in the Greater. So, *"Kyrie eleison. Christe eleison. Kyrie eleison."* Lord have mercy. On the living, and on the
souls of the dead.

But even while doing that she was listening to the shouting going more northward than westward, and judged it was
not toward St. Paul's then but still with no sounds of fighting. With no threat seeming near to hand, a quiet scratching
at the stairward door frame was too slight a thing to fright
even Pernell, who simply broke off praying to say, "Yes?" and
Dickon sidled warily into the room, maybe afraid he would
find frantic women.

Quietingly Frevisse said to Pernell, "He's mine." And to
Dickon, "Yes?"

He bowed in a general way to all of them and said to her,
"My father hasn't come back. I was wondering . . ."

"We'll stay here until we know better what's toward,"
Frevisse said. And added, knowing full well how tempted

he must be to see for himself what was happening in the streets, "You and I will *both* stay here."

Although his face was younger and less formed than his father's, it matched Master Naylor's in giving nothing away. Only the faint underlay of disgust in his voice betrayed him as he said, "Yes, my lady."

"Meantime," she said, "help as you may with whatever watch and guard is being kept here."

He bowed again and left. Pernell, gazing after him, said, "My Hal would have grown to be much like him," and bent her head, her tears falling into her lap; but they were quiet tears, not rending ones, and Frevisse let her cry in silence, and she was done before Mistress Hercy returned with Lucie and quick, diverting talk about having kept the cook and kitchen servants to their business of readying supper. Frevisse moved away, leaving Pernell to Mistress Hercy. Because Lucie had gone to sit beside Anne, Frevisse went to the other window, that overlooked the yard, with Mistress Hercy, behind her, asking Pernell's help in planning coming meals. "Because it's best to make what we have on hand last. I don't want to pay what the market-rascals will be asking if this goes on."

She did not add that there had to be the worry, too, that if alarm spread too greatly into the countryside, the daily inward flow of food to London could stop, leaving bakers soon out of flour for bread, greengrocers of fresh produce, the flesh markets of meat. But while they talked and Anne occupied Lucie with some new stitch for her sampler, Frevisse was left with nothing but the waiting, hoping for Master Naylor's return. Wherever the rebels and loud Londoners were, she could no longer hear them. Were they too far off for any harsh sounds of fighting or the thicker noise of pillaging to reach here? At least there was no black-clouded smoke from burning buildings that she could see, but the quiet now settled onto London was, in its own way, disquieting. She had grown used to the constant undersound of London busy about its business and pleasures, and she admitted to herself that, much like Dickon, she would rather find out for herself what was happening, not have to wait here to be told.

Nor did it help that by supper's time Master Naylor still had not come back, nor Daved nor Master Grene. The women ate the scant meal of fried eggs in a green sauce of peas and scallions in the parlor, joined by Master Bocking, who told how guard would be kept in watches through the night at the house's foregate and rearyard; and at the meal's end, when Pernell began to fret openly for her husband's return, Master Bocking fell into talk about his travels. Listening to him, she was somewhat eased, with Lucie leaning against her to listen, too; and by no spoken agreement, Anne and Frevisse drifted to the windows, Anne to the south, Frevisse at the north; and watching and listening, Frevisse slowly began to hear . . . not shouting but . . . many men on the move. Anne rose in no haste and crossed the room to her, to ask low-voiced and looking out the window, "What is it? Where?"

"East of us." Maybe a street or so away, but it was hard to tell.

Anne leaned suddenly forward, looking down. The pale twilight sky was clear and full of light, but thickening shadows filled the yard; only barely Frevisse saw two men crossing it toward the hall. Master Grene and Daved Weir, she guessed, since there had been no challenge from the gate guard. Neither she nor Anne said anything, but something in their watching must have caught Pernell's eye because she called out, "Are they back?"

"I think so," Anne granted carefully.

"Master Bocking, would you——" Pernell started, but he was already going.

And was back mercifully soon, bringing Master Grene and Daved with him, followed by a household man carrying a lighted candle. Pernell cried out, "Raulyn!", holding out her hands to him, and while he went to her and quickly kissed her and assured her he was well and all was well, the man lighted the pricket-held candles along the walls, and Daved closed the shutters across first one window and then the other, and maybe only Frevisse noted how Anne's eyes followed his every move in the warm, growing light.

Master Grene was still assuring Pernell, "I'm here. I'm well. Everything's well. Look, love, I've brought James to hear what I've to say, so he can tell the rest of the household how well it is. We're unscathed, and so is London." He gave a sudden, sharp laugh. "Except for Philip Malpas. *He's* scathed and no mistake."

Ready to be alarmed out of her relief, Pernell said, "They've killed him. He's so hated, someone has killed him."

Frevisse whispered to Anne beside her, "Who's Philip Malpas?"

"A very hated alderman," Anne whispered back while Master Grene answered Pernell with a shake of his head and half-mocking regret. "No, he wasn't fool enough to stay where they could get their hands on him. He couldn't take his house with him, though. They've ransacked it. The rebels and a good few Londoners."

Pernell gasped, but Mistress Hercy asked crisply, "Only Malpas' place? None other?"

"None other," Master Grene said.

"What would Cade have against him in particular?" Frevisse whispered, but Anne only lifted her shoulders to show she did not know.

"What else has happened?" Master Bocking asked.

"Cade has been speech-making," Master Grene answered. "We heard the end of one at St. Magnus church and went with the crowd along to the Londonstone—you heard that surely—and on around to Leadenhall market where he said it all again. He's got himself a white horse from somewhere and a couple of banners, and is making a good show of it. He had maybe a thousand of his men with him."

"Five hundred or so," Daved put in quietly.

"Enough, anyway," Master Grene said. "He's saying what he's said all along. That the rebels mean no harm to London. They're not against the people. It's the corrupt bastards around the king they want to bring down."

Probably understanding full well the difference there could be between the thing said, the thing meant, and the thing actually done, Mistress Hercy asked, "What else did they do besides have speeches and attack Malpas when he wasn't there?"

Master Grene shrugged. "Not much."

"He went out to meet with the Essex rebels," Daved said, "but we don't know what was said there. Now he's on his way back to Southwark with his men for the night."

"So we came back to tell you all's well." Master Grene kissed his wife's hand. "As you can see."

"This Jack Cade. What's he like?" Anne asked. "To see, I mean."

Gravely, Daved answered, "He's a large man. Tall, well-set, well-featured. Rough-mannered, but that may be for the sake of keeping hold over his followers. To over-awe them. Surely those with him today did nothing he did not order."

"You think then they're not simply men looking to make trouble?" Frevisse asked.

Daved bent his head in grave agreement to that. "Those with him today, anyway. They looked mostly like ordinary lesser folk of otherwise honest life who've had too many wrongs and want them righted."

"There looked to be soldiers among them, too," Master Grene said. "From Normandy would be my guess."

"From Normandy," Daved agreed. "They'll be thinking their wrongs the worse of anyone's." And well they might,

Frevisse thought. Many of them would be men given land there over the years when England was winning; men who had probably had French homes and families and hopes and plans—and now had nothing, not for themselves or for their families. Reason enough to set them in rebellion against the government that had betrayed them.

"What about the rebels still reveling in Southwark?" Mistress Hercy asked. "The ones Cade didn't bring with him. There must be several thousands of them."

"They're Southwark's trouble," Master Grene said. "It's the place to be if you want to revel, after all."

"They may be London's trouble in a while," Daved said. "Cade had the ropes to the drawbridge cut as he crossed it. It can't be raised again."

And since Cade had given no sign yet of being an outright fool, Frevisse had to suppose his men were now the gate-guards there, too. The Thames, which had seemed London's best safeguard, no longer made a difference.

Master Grene loosed himself from Pernell and went to the table to see if there was any wine left in the pitcher there. "Cade has sent word he wants to meet with the mayor tomorrow, and he's proclaimed there'll be no pillaging by his followers, on pain of death."

"They ransacked Malpas' place," Mistress Hercy pointed out.

"Only on his orders and for good reason." Master Grene's smile widened as he poured himself some wine. "No one will hold that against him. Malpas is hated all over London, the usurying bastard."

"Cade had thought through the business against Malpas," Daved said. "He made his second speech at the Leadenhall, hardly a stone's throw from Malpas' door."

"When he had a door," Master Grene laughed.

"They didn't burn his place, did they?" Pernell asked in alarm.

"No," Daved quickly assured her. "Cade wants London for him, not against him. There was no burning, only the ransacking of Malpas' place. He's gone back with his men to Southwark for the night to show his good intent toward the city."

Carrying his goblet of wine, Master Grene returned to Pernell and took her hand comfortingly again. "So, see, love, you can give over your fears. Cade has all well in hand and means no harm to folk like us. James, you can tell the household all of this and send them to bed."

"Except the guard should be kept anyway," Daved said lightly. "Not against any rebels, but against Londoners who might think 'rebelling' suddenly looks good."

"Just see that none of our folk go out to join them," Master Grene added, matching his lightness.

James bowed agreement and left, and Master Grene said, smiling on Pernell, "See, love? All is well in hand."

Pernell smiled back, finally ready to believe it, and Mistress Hercy took that advantage to say, "Then it's time to persuade her to bed, Raulyn. It's where she should be. And the rest of us, too. Lucie-love, you and Anne are to share my chamber, remember. Dame Frevisse, you said you'd sleep here, yes? I've ordered bedding brought. Raulyn, you'll be with Master Bocking and Master Weir again tonight?" And Mistress Hercy would spend the night in Pernell's chamber, Frevisse knew.

On the lift and bustle of her words, Master Grene helped Pernell to her feet, and guided her toward the bed-chamber with an arm around her to steady her. Her mother and Lucie went with her, and Frevisse, Anne, Daved, and Master Bocking were left looking at one another. Frevisse could only guess what would have been said if she had not been there, but she took the chance to ask Daved, "This Cade. Will he keep his word about no trouble in London?"

Daved paused as if deciding how much truth was safe with her, then said, "He may mean to. Whether he will . . . that will depend on whether he can keep his followers as well in hand as he did today. If once they start to riot, one man's will won't stop them, whatever his word. The business at Malpas' place, he kept that in his control because today he brought in men he knew would obey him."

Keeping watch on Daved's face to be sure he understood she wanted truth rather than soothing, Frevisse asked, "What if he brings the rest of his followers into London? Will he be able to keep them as much in hand as he kept these?"

"That," said Daved, steadily meeting her gaze, "we will have to see."

Anne now asked him and his uncle together, "Do you mean to go back to your ship tomorrow?"

It was Master Bocking who answered, with a glance at Daved, "It's come to me there are very likely frighted merchants here in London who may be presently willing to sell what they have cheaply against possibly losing it to the rebels if things go badly. Coin is easier to hide than bales of goods, you see."

"And so," Daved said, mockingly earnest and with laughter behind the words, "to ease their minds, my uncle would like to buy what they have to sell. To ease their worry. An act of Christian charity on his part."

All unexepectedly, Anne laughed.

Daved bowed his head to her. "My lady," he said mock-solemnly.

"Good sir," she returned in kind and with a bow of her own head.

For a single, unguarded moment they were looking at one another with no one and nothing else mattering; and in that small, unguarded moment, Frevisse saw that there was also more than only lust between them, more than simply their bodies' craving. There was an understanding of spirit that was maybe even love; and if it was, God and St. Mary Magdalene help them, Frevisse thought, because how much did Anne truly know about him? He was more than a merchant. The Suffolk gold proved that. But how much more?

Chapter 17

That night passed well enough—no alarums, no outcries, no clash of weapons, no stench of burning buildings—and from the quiet in the bedchamber Frevisse supposed Mistress Hercy had given Pernell a sleeping-draught. For herself, the straw-stuffed pallet on the parlor floor made for as good sleeping as a nunnery bed ever did, though from long usage she awoke sometime in the middle of the night for the Offices of Matins and Lauds. She said their prayers and psalms silently, without rising, and then slept again, to awaken near dawn to say Prime before the day began. She was sitting at the parlor's southward window, watching the first full sunlight spill over London's housetops, when an indeterminate sound of many men moving told something was happening toward London bridge again; and when shortly a maidservant came to say she was wanted in the hall, she went readily, hardly holding back from outward haste, and was relieved to find Master Naylor there, in talk with Master Grene, Master Bocking, and Daved, with Dickon hovering nearby.

She heard, ". . . not so mannerly as yesterday's lot, either," before Master Naylor saw her, turned to her and said, more his grim self than usual, "Cade's back into London. He's brought a good many more men with him this time. They—"

"You saw him?" she asked.

"He was riding up Gracechurch Street as I was coming here, his men behind him, but some of them already breaking off down other streets. My guess is they've been too long in Southwark and will be hoping for like sport here. I wanted to have you back to St. Helen's this morning, but I'm not minded to chance the streets now."

Frevisse started to answer that, but he turned back to Master Grene. "If by your leave she can stay on here, we'll stay, too, Dickon and I, and help your men stand the guard."

"The more the merrier, as the saying goes," Master Grene said readily. "She's welcomed to stay and so are you."

Frevisse could not tell whether he was almost enjoying all the uncertainty or only putting a good front to it for his household to see. What she did know was her irk at Master Naylor for not asking her what she chose to do. That he was right—she probably should not dare the streets—kept her from challenging him, but her voice was crisp as she asked, "How does Dame Juliana?"

"She's safe enough in St. Helen's," Master Naylor answered. "It's you I feared would venture out when you shouldn't."

Goaded, Frevisse said sharply, "I'm not a fool."

"You're not," Master Naylor agreed sharply back. "But sometimes you're over-bold."

Master Grene showed fleeting surprise at the bluntness between them, but it was silent laughter that briefly crossed Daved Weir's face.

Paying neither of them heed, she asked Master Naylor, "How many men would you guess Cade's brought in today?"

"Some several thousand, I'd say."

"Lord God of Hosts," Master Grene breathed. "He'll not have those in hand as readily as he had yesterday's." Then, grimly, "I'm going to Guildhall. That's where talk will be thickest, the news most straight." He turned to Frevisse. "You'll have to keep it from Pernell that I've gone out."

"I'll go with you," Daved said, moving with Master Grene toward the outer door. "Uncle, you'll stay here?"

Master Bocking acknowledged he would, while Master Grene said to one of his men standing nearby, hearing everything, "Wyett, you're to see to things here."

Then they were gone, and Master Bocking, sharing a look with Master Naylor, said, "Ach, young men." To which Master Naylor nodded dourly.

Frevisse, wondering how she was to keep from Pernell that her husband was gone out again, returned upstairs to find Pernell already knew it. From a window Lucie had seen the men leaving and exclaimed at it, and Frevisse was left with the task of making little of their going and much of how good it would be to have true news of what was happening.

But the morning passed in a weariness of waiting. Once a great shouting passed through the Stocks Market and away eastward, sounding like a great many men enjoying themselves, but that was the most that happened, and Pernell sank into a numb endurance while Frevisse read aloud to her from a book of saints' stories in verse, and Anne occupied herself and Lucie with sewing. To Frevisse's mind, Mistress Hercy had the best of it, busy with seeing to the household.

The morning was almost gone and they had slightly dined on fish in a mint sauce when Raulyn was suddenly there in the parlor, so openly unharmed that Pernell could only cry out in joy as he came to kiss her cheek. It was Anne who asked, "Where's Daved?"

"Telling his uncle, the nun's man, and the household what we've seen," Master Grene said; and to Pernell, "My heart, we've been to the church and agreed with Father Tomas that Hal should be buried today, come what may."

She looking instantly to her mother and Anne. "You must go since I can't!"

"No, love," Master Grene said gently and quickly. "They mustn't go. The streets aren't that safe. There's talk of putting barriers up to close off streets to the rebels, but right now I'd not answer for anyone's safe-going even to the church."

"The streets are that unsafe?" Anne asked quietly.

Master Grene paused as if searching out the right words, finally saying, "Unsteady rather than unsafe. No rioting, but there are outbreaks."

"We heard shouting once," Frevisse said.

"That would have been the rebels hauling Crowmer to Aldgate," Master Grene said, pulling a stool close to Pernell and sitting down, taking her hands and saying to her while he did, "Remember Crowmer was one of the king's men the rebels have been against? He and his father-in-law Lord Saye?"

"The king arrested him and Lord Saye into the Tower," Anne said. "How could the rebels have him?"

"Crowmer wasn't in the Tower today when Cade went after him. He was in Newgate prison."

"Newgate? How did he come to be there?" Mistress Hercy demanded.

"No one seems to know. Or how Cade knew he was. No, let me start at the beginning, with what went on at Guildhall with the mayor and Cade and all."

He told it well. It seemed that by the time Cade came back into London, the mayor and aldermen had already been

in session at the Guildhall with some of the few justices
who'd not gone scarce with the king. "Daved and I were well
out on the edges of the crowd, but we heard enough. They
set to indicting everyone on the rebels' list of men they want
removed from around the king."

"Most of whom are gone with the king," Frevisse said.

"And fortunate for them they are," Master Grene said.
"But there was Crowmer right to hand and easily got. Cade
had him and some clerk dragged out and through the city to
the Essex rebels at Mile End, then had them beheaded."

"What?"

"Merciful Christ!"

"He *didn't!*"

The women's cries burst out together in alarm and disbelief, but Master Grene only said, "He did. That much Daved
and I saw on our way back here. Their heads on tall poles being carried through the streets, being—"

"Oh, don't!" protested Pernell, and from Mistress Hercy,
"That's enough, Raulyn."

He looked immediately ashamed. "I'm sorry, yes, enough
and too much. I'm sorry, my heart."

"Where's Cade now?" Frevisse asked.

"Come back in to London. He looks something, let me
tell you. He's wearing some nobleman's blue velvet coat with
sable trim and is carrying a drawn sword in his hand but has
a straw hat on his head."

"What else is happening?" Anne asked. "Are his men still
in hand?"

"Tolerably well. A few spots of trouble. Nothing much."
He gave his wife's hands an affectionate shake. "Nothing
enough to be a worry anyway."

Except to the people suffering it, Frevisse thought. Thankfully that was a thought Pernell did not have. As Master
Grene surely intended, she smiled and eased and was willingly distracted by Daved coming in, to add his assurances to

Master Grene's that all was reasonably well through London.

"Your Master Naylor is not a trusting man, though," Daved said to Frevisse. "He's still not willing to risk a return to St. Helen's."

Frevisse bent her head in silent acceptance of that and kept her thoughts to herself. The men stayed only a while before leaving the women to each other again, and then Pernell, holding Lucie to her, wanted the comfort of Frevisse praying with them for Hal's soul. Frevisse did what she could, but what little peace came with the prayers was again and again broken by noise from the streets, some distant, some too near, thankfully none in St. Swithin's Lane itself.

At last, probably more from the weariness than because she was truly comforted, Pernell slept where she sat, and Frevisse took the chance to escape from the parlor. Downstairs, by asking a servant, she learned Master Naylor was taking a turn at watching the rearyard gate and was told the way—by one of two doors at the far end of the screens passage and down stairs that split to go either into the kitchen or to a heavy, wooden, ironbound door. She found the way easily enough and went outside into a small and cobbled yard, enclosed by the hall on one side and by a head-high wooden wall on the other three. This late in the afternoon, sunlight from the westering sun filled it pleasantly, but other than a large, open-sided shed full of firewood at one end, there were only a midden pile of household waste and rubbish beside the gate and a wooden bench beside the door where Master Naylor, Dickon and, surprisingly, Master Bocking were sitting together, each of them with a thick, two-foot-long, wooden club laid across their laps.

They rose and bowed to her, and she asked, looking around, "This is all there is? No garden?"

Master Naylor bent his head toward the gate. "Out there's a common garden shared by most of the houses along here and the next street over."

"With no direct way into it from any street?"

"There are alleyways," Master Naylor said. "Two of them. The one that runs along here, just the fence's other side, opens out by the church, whatever that street is there."

"So watch is needed here."

"It is. Though I'm the only one properly on guard. These two are only keeping me company."

"With these," Dickon said, hefting his club. "Master Grene said most houses keep some of these to hand on chance there's trouble in the streets and they're needed. Apprentices rioting or lords fighting or suchlike." He was openly finding this much better than quiet country life.

"Master Grene says there's not much trouble in the streets today," Frevisse said, with a hard look at Master Naylor to tell him she wanted true answers,

"That's what he says for his wife to hear," Master Naylor answered tersely. "Master Weir tells it differently for the rest of us to know. There are outbreaks of trouble all over the city. Whether it's Londoners as well as rebels is hard to sort out, but what's certain is that there's hundreds of trouble-makers spread out through London."

"My nephew thinks Cade still has some governing of his men," Master Bocking said gravely, "but doubts it will last long when they've seen more how rich London is."

"Between that and Londoners joining in, either for the 'sport' or with scores to settle, it's likely going to get worse instead of better," Master Naylor said. "The only question is when."

"My nephew says things are such that all could turn to ugly on an instant and with no warning," added Master Bocking.

"With you all too easily in the wrong place at the wrong time when it comes, my lady," Master Naylor said. "Given that, you'll do best to stay here."

The words were respectful but with a stubbornness behind them that said she *was* staying here. More mildly than she felt, Frevisse said, "As you think best." But only because he was probably right and she should not chance the streets.

Taking her thoughts with her, she went inside. Over her years as a nun she had become patient with many things but not with being kept ignorant where knowledge would serve her better, so she was grateful to Master Naylor and Master Bocking for telling her so much, however unhappy she was to know it. Was thinking, too, as she made no haste along the screens passage toward the parlor stairs, how the already slight chance that Hal's murderer would ever be found was now lessened to nearly nothing, the boy's "small" death lost under all this greater trouble.

Though given the trouble Brother Michael had wanted to make of it, that might be for the best.

Her foot was on the first step when Daved came in the outer door in haste and demanded at her, "Is Raulyn here? Has he come back?"

"Come back? He didn't go out again?"

"We both did, but I lost him in the press of people after Lord Saye was killed. Could you—"

"Lord Saye? How could—" But that question could wait. "Doesn't the foregate guard know if Master Grene is here or not?"

"They've just changed men, and the man there now doesn't know anything before the past handful of minutes. Could you call Mistress Blakhall down to you here?"

"Of course." Going partway up the stairs and pitching her voice to careful lightness, she called to Anne, who came with finger to her lips, saying, "Pernell is still sleeping."

"Master Weir wants to see you," Frevisse said, and Anne went quickly past her and down the stairs. With no hesitation whatsoever, Frevisse followed her.

"Raulyn isn't here, no," she answered Daved's question. "What's happened? How did you come to lose him?"

"It happened in the crowds this morning, too, but he found me then. But this time we were separated in the shove and push of people while Saye was being killed, and things are ugly in the——"

Anne gasped. "Killed? He was in the Tower in Lord Scales' keeping. How . . ."

"Lord Scales handed him over."

"To Cade?" Frevisse demanded. That was beyond belief.

"He might as well have. That inquest at Guildhall this morning, with the mayor and all, that found Lord Saye guilty along with the rest? Lord Scales gave him over this afternoon to be arraigned."

"But he had to know that once Lord Saye was out of the Tower . . ." Frevisse began.

"Of course he knew," Daved said darkly. "The wonder is that Lord Saye made it as far as the Guildhall. He was standing before the judges demanding trial by his peers when Cade's men seized him, took him away to the Standard in Cheapside, and on Cade's order cut off his head while a priest was trying to shrive him."

Frevisse and Anne both crossed themselves in horror.

"The last I saw, the rebels had his head on a pole and were carrying it with Crowmer's through the streets, with his stripped body being dragged away behind a horse to do God knows what with it."

"But why?" Anne cried.

"Because he could," Daved answered. "Cade is finding out just how much he can do, and he's doing it." Daved shook his head and turned away, settling his belt-hung dagger closer to his hip. "I'd best see if I can find Raulyn."

"Daved, no," Anne said, taking a step after him, reaching toward him. "Don't go out again."

He stopped, turned, took her hands, said, "I have to."

Frevisse wondered if they knew how much they both betrayed in that moment.

Then Daved went without looking back. Anne made a single, protesting step after him, but Frevisse took her by the arm, not certain whether Anne was simply past shame or too fearful for her lover to think of anything else. Whichever way it was, she was not fit to return to Pernell yet, and Frevisse drew her into the hall and sat her down on one of the benches there with no word between them, because what was there to say?

Through the hall's two tall windows Frevisse could see the afternoon was slipping away. Westward the sky would soon be full of sunset colors. Here, with the windows facing east, it would soon be lamp-lighting time, and the gathering shadows were maybe a kind of hiding for Anne. Though her hands clenched her lap finally eased and lay open, she made no move to leave and did not speak. Nor did Frevisse, and the quiet drew out between them until a sudden, savage yelling somewhere in the lane beyond the foregate brought them both to their feet.

Anne cried out "Daved!", and started away. Frevisse might have stopped her but didn't, instead went with her into the screens passage and toward the outer door, only to be pushed aside by Master Naylor, probably just come off guard, and Master Bocking in a rush to be ahead of them, with Dickon only slightly behind. By the time Frevisse and Anne were at the head of the stairs to the yard, the men were down them and running toward the gate, joined by Master Grene's men Wyett and James running from another doorway in the yard, carrying clubs, too.

At the gate the man Pers was standing on a barrel to look over the fence and shouted from there, "It's Master Grene! They're attacking him!"

Frevisse tried to catch Anne's arm but failed. Anne went down the steps behind Dickon, and Frevisse followed her.

Ahead, one of the men yelled, "Open the gate!" and Pers leaped from the barrel and grabbed for the bar. James, reaching him, shoved him aside, exclaiming, "We're ordered not to open!"

Wyett, catching up to him, shoved him aside in turn, yelling back, "If he's out there, we—"

"What if they get in?"

"—can't leave him!"

"They—"

Master Naylor broke their beginning struggle for the bar, pushing them both away, ordering at them, "Be ready," as he threw the bar aside one-handed, his club ready in the other. Pers sprang forward to pull one side of the double gate open while Master Bocking, with club in one hand and drawn dagger in the other, ordered the others, "Follow us!" sharply enough that they left off quarreling and obeyed as he and Master Naylor charged out the gate toward the wide scuffle of men in the street.

Frevisse saw, before Master Naylor and the others piled into it, that the fight looked to be eight men at the most, with Master Grene and Daved Weir against six others, so that it might have been going worse than it was except Daved Weir had a dagger in either hand and the look of someone who knew how to use them. It was his foot, though, that he planted hard into a man's groin, sending the fellow reeling back into one of the others, and only then did Frevisse see that Father Tomas was there, too, stooped over and dragging someone out from among the fighters' feet that Frevisse did not clearly see as she caught Anne by the arm at last, stopping her in the gateway passage, saying at her, "Leave them to it! We'll be in the way!" as two more servants from the house raced past them and out the gate, clubs in their hands.

Anne understood well enough that she held where she was. And with Master Naylor and the rest into the fight, everything was breaking apart into a wilder flurry until suddenly some of the men were breaking clear, starting to run up the lane, one of them bent over, more shuffling than running, another clutching his upper leg and limping. Master Naylor's barked order stopped the several household men ready to pursue them, while all along the street other men with clubs and daggers were bursting from doors and other gateways, too late for the fight but one of them calling, "Grene, are you all right?" and another, "Raulyn?"

Master Grene, short of breath and disheveled, waved a hand at them all. "Done," he called between panted breaths. "All over. They're gone."

"Though I doubt I want to be out here if they come back with more of their kind!" Daved called, backing away through the gateway with Master Grene and the others.

Enough people agreed with that, that there was a general withdrawing behind all the other doors and gates while Master Grene ordered, "Close it," at Pers, who readily slammed the gate shut, with Wyett swinging the bar into place across it at the same moment Master Grene turned on Daved and raged, "What in hell's teeth were you thinking of, throwing yourself into that fight like that? You near as damn-all got us killed!"

Of the two of them, Daved Weir looked the worse. Though he was without apparent wound save for a red mark on his jaw that would probably be a bruise before it was done, his doublet was torn open and his shirt ripped to almost his waist as if he had grappled close with someone; but still high-blooded with the joy of battle, he laughed and said, "There are worse ways to die than suddenly, Raulyn."

"Maybe for you!" Master Grene stormed back at him. "But I'd rather not!"

Somewhat aside, Dickon and Father Tomas were helping Brother Michael to his feet from the cobbles. The friar was the worst battered of anyone—with no blood on him but short of breath and partly bent over in pain, one hand pressed to his ribs as if he hurt there. Past Master Grene, Daved asked, "How is he?"

Brother Michael answered for himself, leaning on the priest but straightening a little as he said, "Beaten. But otherwise unmarred. They were using feet and fists, not weapons."

"I was coming from the church," Father Tomas said. "To see Mistress Grene. I saw him ahead of me. They came from the other way, those men, and attacked him. Went for him for no reason."

"They didn't say anything?" Master Naylor asked.

Brother Michael straightened a little more, still holding his ribs but his breathing more steady. "Asked if I was the friar that was preaching at St. Paul's. I said I was, and they—" He stopped—not from a stab of pain, as Frevisse first thought, but staring at Daved before then jerking fully straight and snatching at the front of Daved's doublet, crying out, *"You! This!"* in both oath and accusation; and Frevisse saw he had hold not on Daved's doublet or shirt but the end of a narrow length of pale cloth showing through the shirt's tear. In the yard's shadows Frevisse thought there was a fringed knot at one corner but that was all she clearly saw before Daved clamped a hand around the friar's wrist and ordered, cold and low-voiced, "Let it go."

Brother Michael pulled, both at the cloth and to be free, and Daved must have done something because the next moment the friar let go the cloth with a gasp of pain and snatched back his hand. But with unabated fierceness, glaring at Daved, he started again, *"You—"*

Master Grene stepped between them, saying in loud interruption as he gripped the friar by the arm and turned him toward the hall, "Better we take this inside, Brother Michael. Wyett, keep guard here with Pers for a time. Nicol, shouldn't you be gone to the kitchen? The rest of you go on,

too. You did well, all of you. My thanks. Anne, Dame, go tell
Pernell all's well."

He was drawing the friar hallward with more force than
courtesy while scattering his household men with orders;
but Brother Michael broke free, spun around to point fiercely
at Master Naylor and Dickon, nearest to Daved, and ordered,
"You two! Take hold on him." He swung his pointing finger
to Master Bocking. "On both of them. On your souls' peril,
seize them both!"

Master Bocking said something in a language Frevisse
did not understand, and together he and Daved moved for
the gate. Master Grene's two men were there but not ready
for trouble. Daved shoved one of them one way, his uncle
shoved the other the other way, and Daved had his daggers
drawn again to hold them at bay, while Master Bocking
swung the bar clear and began to pull open one side of the
gate.

"*Stop them!*" roared Brother Michael, and the man Wyett
had wit enough to swing his club not at Daved who was beyond his reach but at the opening side of the gate, driving it
shut just as Master Bocking slipped through the gap, not
catching him in it but leaving Daved shut in and without
time to open it again before Wyett, Pers, Master Naylor, and
Dickon closed on him. For an indrawn, frightened breath
Frevisse thought he would fight them. But the intent went
out of him and instead he dropped his daggers, yelled something upward over his shoulder—again in a language she did
not know; meant for his uncle, surely—then stood with his
empty hands held out to either side of him.

Chapter 18

Uncertain what came next, no one moved except Brother Michael, drawing himself up as straightly as Daved was standing, to say with assured authority, "By right of my place in the Church's holy Inquisition I order you to seize this enemy of Christ!"

Anne's small sound in her throat cut off as Dame Frevisse took harder hold on her arm, warning her silent as Pers and Wyett, still not understanding what was happening, moved toward Daved uncertainly.

"Seize him!" Brother Michael ordered again. "On your souls' peril! He has to be brought to the bishop! Open the gate—"

Quickly Raulyn said, "You can't trust yourself to the streets again, Brother Michael! Not now and with dark coming on. You've seen yourself the Kentishmen have slipped Cade's leash. By now I wouldn't dare the streets outside even my own gate, let be between here and anywhere else."

Brother Michael had stopped, was listening to him. With Dame Frevisse's fingers digging into her arm, Anne kept silent the sobs trying to rise in her throat as Raulyn urged, "Keep here for now anyway. You risk losing him otherwise. His uncle is out there, remember, and who knows who else, ready to help him."

Brother Michael looked toward the gate. With his hurts still fresh on him, he couldn't doubt Raulyn's warning, but he hesitated half a moment longer before finally granting harshly, "Here then, yes. We'll stay here with him under guard while we wait it out." He suddenly pointed at Father Tomas. "And you'll wait with us. What your part in this has been we've still to learn. The abomination didn't happen in your church by chance. And you," he added at Raulyn. "You'll have to prove you knew nothing of what they are, or you'll have both the bishop and the king's officers to answer to." He started toward the hall, ordering at Raulyn's men, "Bring him."

"I need my men on gate-guard here," Raulyn said.

Brother Michael pointed at Dame Frevisse's men. "You two, then."

Both men looked to Dame Frevisse, who nodded for them to obey, and with no eagerness, they closed on Daved from either side. Anne willed him to fight them off—or run—or do whatever he needed to win clear and away. But rather than that, he suddenly threw up his head and laughed in a way Anne had never heard from him—laughter bitter and bright and barren of joy unless it was the joy of a man refusing to fear a fight he knew he could not win; and like a man flinging himself open to a dagger-blow, he let the Naylors take hold on his arms and start him toward the hall.

Anne began to twist against Dame Frevisse's grip, meaning to go to him; but Daved caught her eyes and gave the slightest refusing twitch of his head, telling her no. Then he was past her, and Brother Michael was herding Father Tomas toward the hall, and Raulyn, having stopped to pick up Daved's daggers—where had the second one come from?—came aside to say, "Anne, go back to Pernell now, please."

His words came from some hollow distance beyond having any meaning. Anne gave them no heed, not taking her gaze from Daved's back going away from her between his guards. She had to be at least near him, and she forced her legs to steady, gathering herself to follow them. Raulyn, seeing her intent, said, "No, Anne." Laying a quick hand on her shoulder. "Don't. I'll do all I can. Anything you do will only make it go the worse for him."

Worse than burned at the stake? Anne thought; but Raulyn had not waited for her answer, was gone after the men now going up the steps into the hall. Anne would have followed him, not caring what he had said, but Dame Frevisse still held her arm, still held her where she was, and said, "We'll follow in a moment. But one thing. What was it set the friar off against him? That cloth. What was it?"

Started to pull against her hold, Anne paused, repeated blankly, "What?" Among her fear-scattered thoughts, her only clear one was that she had to go to Daved, and instead of the denial she should have made she blurted out, "It's something he wears. It's for prayer or . . . it's because he's Jewish. I don't know . . ."

The nun's grip on her arm became suddenly painful, pulling Anne around to face her. "He's *Jewish?* He's Jewish and you *knew* it? You took a Jewish paramour?"

That the nun had known Daved was her lover jarred as much as the depth of accusation in the words, and Anne said

sharply back, "I didn't know he was Jewish when I fell in love
with him."

"But you had to know afterwards. If nothing else, he
must be circumcised!"

"He told me. Before ever we became lovers, he told me.
So I knew, yes!"

"And you . . ."

"I *love* him." What else could she say? She knew what
was said of coupling between Christian and Jew—that it
was a bestiality that only the harshest penance could
cleanse, that the soul was supposed to be as polluted by it
as the body was. But she had been in love with Daved before she knew he was Jewish, and her love had burned past
all else. Including caring what anyone thought of her love.
And now the Inquisition had him, and every nightmare she
had ever had about him might be going to come true, and
with a twist that hurt her arm she wrenched free of Dame
Frevisse, gathered up her skirts, and ran after the men,
leaving the nun to think what she would and follow as she
might.

Inside, Mistress Hercy had met the men in the screens
passage, but the Naylors were standing behind Daved, not
holding onto him, and she seemed not to know there was
trouble that way but was demanding at Raulyn, "What do
you mean, he was attacked? By whom? Why?"

"We don't know who. Just some louts. Someone who's
against friars, that's all. He's safe and staying here a time.
What of Pernell?"

"The noise wakened her, but it was over before she knew
what it was, thank blessed St. Mary. Father Tomas, come up
and give her some comfort about Hal."

"I will." Father Thomas answered unsteadily, drawing
away toward Brother Michael waiting impatiently just inside the hall. "I'll be there—"

"Later," Raulyn interrupted. "We must needs talk first. By your leave." He started forward, past Mistress Hercy, with the Naylors crowding Daved to go ahead, too.

"Anne," Mistress Hercy said. "Come help me tell Pernell all's well."

Anne brushed past Mistress Hercy, following the men into the hall, saying in echo of Raulyn, "Later. I'll be up later."

Behind her, she heard Mistress Hercy say to Dame Frevisse with quiet-voiced worry, "There's something more, isn't there?," and Dame Frevisse answer, "Yes." At the far end of the hall's near side, the men were going through the doorway to the old solar, save for Raulyn stopped in the middle of the hall, saying to a maidservant there, "No. What I want just now is no one in the hall at all until I say differently."

The maid curtseyed and left as Raulyn put out a hand to stop Anne going past him, saying, "Anne, no."

Avoiding his hand, Anne said only, "Yes," and went on, into the solar.

Until the new wing of rooms had been built along the yard, this had been where the family withdrew from the household's general life to the privacy they now had in the parlor upstairs. It was become Raulyn's office, used for such business as might not be done in the shop and to keep his records and "For somewhere he gets away from an over-womaned household," Pernell had once said, smiling. With twilight deepening outside the single window, the men were only shapes in the room's gathering shadows, with Brother Michael nearest the door, his back to her, making certain no one left. Daved, still flanked by the Naylors, was across the room, facing his foe, while Father Tomas stood alone to one side, looking shrunken and huddled.

Anne eased sideways from the doorway, keeping behind the friar, letting Raulyn go past her. He did, going to lay Daved's daggers on his desk beside several account rolls, some pens, and a silver inkpot. Brother Michael started to say something to him but broke off as Dame Frevisse entered with a lighted candle, throwing sudden brightness across the room, and saying as she came, "I took the candle from the servant bringing it. I thought you'd want no one else here."

"Nor do we want you," Brother Michael snapped.

But Dame Frevisse was already going to light the fat candles waiting on a wrought-iron stand beside the desk. The growing golden light shone on the polished wood of the desk, the chair there, the several heavily locked chests against the walls. Underfoot, the carpet's crimson, green, and yellow pattern was mostly left to shadows, but the woven tapestry of St. Nicholas, patron saint of merchants, sailors, and children, on one wall was caught into brightness and so were the men's faces: Daved's set and hard, all look of a merchant gone from him but something of harsh laughter still glinting there; Father Tomas' with fear as openly on him as his priest's gown; the Naylors' wary, watchful, uncertain yet about what any of this was.

"You." Brother Michael pointed at the younger of Dame Frevisse's two men. "Get between him and the window. And you," at Master Naylor. "Have your dagger out. If he tries anything sudden, kill him."

Anne pressed her hands over her mouth to stop an outcry, her gaze desperately on Daved, willing him to find escape from this as Raulyn protested angrily, "Sir!"

Done with the candles, Dame Frevisse blew out and laid down the one she had carried and drew aside, against the wall and, like Anne, mostly behind Brother Michael in undoubted hope he would forget she was there, which he well might, his gaze fixed on Daved like a hawk on its prey. But Daved looked less like prey than a hawk in his own right, head raised, the candlelight catching deep on the scorn and anger in his dark eyes. He had hidden the fringed cloth under his shirt again, but that was all he had hidden. The courage that had let him dare his game against Christians all these years was bared and shining, and with it the deep-set certainty and pride of who he was. Whatever Christians thought of him, he had no shame that he was Jewish. He had not hidden the cloth again because of shame. He had hidden it to keep it from profane eyes.

From Christian eyes, Anne thought with a pain under her heart almost worse than her aching fear for him.

In the desolation of knowing more clearly than ever how much there was about him she did not know and had no hope of understanding, she pressed back against the wall, arms wrapped around herself, as Brother Michael said, first at Raulyn, "What we need is rope. Or, better, chains." And at Father Tomas, "Stand over there with him."

Father Tomas, his voice fear-thinned and shaking, said back, "I am not Jewish. I will not be tried by you as a Jew."

"This is no trial," Daved said, laughter harsh under the words. "This is an ass of friar pretending to rights he doesn't have."

"I have rights over you, heretic," Brother Michael said back at him. "I have the right to hold and question you, to find out the depth of your treachery and heresy, your—"

"To be a heretic," Daved said, "I would have to have been a Christian first. I have never been baptized, never been Christian. Therefore you have no claim on me as heretic."

"What you are," Brother Michael said with cold anger, "you and all your kind, is a disease in the body of Christendom, to be cleansed by baptism or cut away by force if you refuse to change from your diseased ways."

"*That* is straight against what your own popes have said, one after another, for generations," Daved returned. And Anne realized he was fighting in the only way left to him. With words. If not with hope. "By your popes' orders, that you claim to obey, Jews should be left to live in peace. But the dog Dominicans and you Franciscans have decided otherwise, have set to hunting us to the death against the word of your own popes."

"You were allowed to live among us out of pity for you, blindly clinging to the Old Law, unable to see the light of Christ, yet owed some debt of gratitude because it was from your ways the way of Christ came."

"*That* is not answer to what I said," Daved shot back at him with scorching cold. "We're allowed to live among you because we make money for Christian princes."

"By usury," Brother Michael said with cold scorn back at him. "Bleeding Christians of their wealth to your own foul ends."

"By loaning money," Daved agreed with matching scorn. "A thing unallowed to Christians, but a thing that Christians need. For how many hundreds of years were we invited—even paid with privileges—to move into kingdoms, princedoms, cities, towns by kings, bishops, and lords? Not out of 'Christian charity' or anything like it, no, but so we could make money in ways forbidden to Christians. Money that those kings, bishops, and lords then taxed from us without stint, leaving us hated by those around us and struggling to survive ourselves."

"You had but to turn Christian to live as cleanly as anyone else," Brother Michael said coldly.

"Yes," Daved agreed again. "Save for the small point that by Christian law there are no free Jews. Every Jew is some Christian lord's property, to be used or even 'given' away as a lord's gift to someone, the way a hound or a field might be handed over for their use and profit. A Jew who turns

Christian deprives his lord of a piece of property, and so a Jew who turns Christian forfeits to his lord everything he owns in recompense, to begin his Christian life with nothing. Such is Christian 'mercy' and 'charity.' He loses all and gains nothing."

"He gains his soul's salvation!" Brother Michael returned sharply.

"He gains poverty, desolation, and the unending suspicion of any Christian who knows his past." Daved jerked a nod at Father Tomas. "Look how readily you want to believe the worst of him for no better reason than that he had a Jewish grandfather."

"The Jewish taint remains in the blood, generation unto generation. That is proved and known."

"I thought that your rite of baptism was supposed to cleanse and make anew the soul of Man."

"It does, but as a dog returns to its vomit—"

"And an ass to its braying," Daved snapped.

Anne had seen him angered in small ways a few times. What she had never seen was him *in* anger—anger around him like a dark and burning cloak, still in his control but—like fire—no less dangerous for that. But what she also saw was the gathered horror in the stares the nun's two men now had on him, as if somehow, now that they understood what Daved was, he was turned into something hideous. But he wasn't. He was still Daved, and Brother Michael would give him over to men who would kill him for it, would torture him to break his will and body, then burn him alive, chained to a stake, helpless while flames leaped up around him through high-piled wood, with no hope except that his executioner might strangle him before the fire reached his flesh, and if that mercy weren't given, then the agony as the flames took him from the feet upward, his flesh scorching, blackening, burning. His screams until finally the flames finished with him, and there was nothing left but ashes and charred bones. All of his beauty, his laughter, his kindness and strength and clever mind gone in screaming agony to nothing.

That was the death he had played against every time he had taken on the seeming of a Christian. And he was still playing against it, Anne realized. Goading the friar. Keeping him at word-war. Holding off the moment he would be bound, chained, locked away until taken to the bishop's prison. Maybe hoping—Anne's heart lifted with the desperate thought—hoping that the trouble in the streets would spread into enough confusion that somehow he'd have chance at escape. Or that his uncle would come back with, somehow, rescue. Or fighting because it was not in him simply to give up.

But Brother Michael's urge to battle looked to be no less than his, and past Daved's words he was saying on, ". . . even so man returns to his old sins and, worse, finds new sins in which to wallow. Look you at the Church's mercy, leaving Jews through all these centuries past to follow your faith, such as it was, because it was the faith of Abraham, Isaac, and Jacob, the faith of the Prophets, the faith given to mankind to ready us for Christ's coming. Despite your blindness to the Light of Christ, despite your persevering in darkness, the Church sheltered you as one shelters a cripple. And yet treacherously, under that protection, you have corrupted the very faith you professed, that very faith of Abraham, Isaac, and Jacob that was the Church's reason for mercy to you."

Daved laughed shortly, bitterly. "For that, and because we made money your Christian princes could leech from us by bushelfuls."

Brother Michael raised his voice. "You were allowed to dwell among us in hope the Light would finally end your blindness, despite you've lived by usury and other foulnesses, preying on Christian weaknesses."

"We've lived by whatever ways Christians leave to us," Daved said sharply back at him. "And those ways become fewer every year. Whenever we have something that a Christian covets, it's taken from us, sooner more usually than later. Does a Jew hold land and make it prosper? A Christian finds a lord to give it to him instead. Let Jews have lands or vineyards or trades that prosper, laws are passed that take away the lands, the vineyards, forbid us those trades. We used to practice every craft in Christendom, but steadily, steadily, we've been forced back and back into lesser and lesser lives. And then you scorn us for how we live, for what we do to stay alive with the less and less you, in your Christian 'charity,' leave to us."

"As hope lessens that you as a people will accept the Light, so should your place in the world grow less," Brother Michael said, his words edged with anger for the first time. "And even such mercy as you've had, you no longer deserve. Your treachery is found out, and an end must be made. Justice—"

"Do you mean my particular treachery or my people's at large?" Daved asked mockingly.

"Both," Brother Michael said back, judge-stern and certain. "You'll die both for your own treachery in seeming Christian and for your treacherous heresy as a Jew, faithless as you Jews are become to even your own poor faith, the covenant broken that let you live safe in the Church's grace and care . . ."

" 'Safe' except for whenever a pack of Christians felt like killing Jews," Daved said, rude and bitter together.

" . . . so that by right of your treacherous heresy, you will all be brought down, death no more than you deserve, who refuse the light of Christ!"

"The charge of heresy against us is a lie," Daved said quietly, his quietness as dangerous as his open anger had been.

As if he were lecturing a slow student, he said, "We have not corrupted our faith. We are not heretics, nor lawfully within the compass of your Christian 'justice,' except as you've corrupted that 'justice' to your own ends."

"Our ends are to cleanse the world of the Devil's works. For long and long you hid behind your false language, your false hearts, but that ended when at last we ceased to take you at your word and read for ourselves your perverted, and perverting, writings."

"What you mean," said Daved with cold scorn, "is that some Christian scholars finally bestirred themselves—after how many hundreds of years?—to learn the language in which their holy book was first written."

"And thereby," Brother Michael said, his voice rising, "found out that rather than living only by your Torah, as you claimed and for which the Church gave you leave to live, you had given way to the shifts and subtleties of foul corrupters, taking their twisting of truth to your hearts in place of God's clean word. Rashi. Maimonides. Ibn Ezra—"

"Whose names should not even be in your mouth, befouled by your ignorance," Daved said.

"They are the befoulers! Corrupting your Jewish faith so far astray from God's given word as to leave you no going back. Dark with ignorance though your forefathers were, in their darkness they at least followed a once-hallowed way and were therefore tolerated in the body of Christendom. By heeding these others, you've forsaken the way where you trod safely in your error, have broken the covenant between Church and Jew, are heretics and must be pursued as such, lest your corruption spread, destroying others with you!"

"Those scholars you condemn," Daved said, "have no more 'corrupted' our faith than your own vaunted scholars have 'corrupted' yours. Your Augustine, Bernard, Aquinas, Anselm, and how many dozens others whose words you study over and over. If to talk of and interpret God's word is the same as corrupting that word, then your Christian faith is corrupted at its very roots, from the time of your Paul, who never saw or heard your Jesus but went on at length about what was meant by and could be drawn from what he *heard* your Christ had said."

"He followed the light of Christ, not the darkness of unbelief. There isn't even ground to stand on for debate between us. Your guilt and heresy are set and certain." He turned his hawk-gaze on Father Tomas. "You are Jews, and therefore—"

"I am *not* a Jew," Father Tomas declared, sounding both angry and desperate.

Brother Michael swung full around on him. "The full truth of *that* remains to be found out. But you . . ." Turning fiercely on Daved again. ". . . you are beyond denial a Jew. Look you, Master Grene, with him or them surely lies the answer to your stepson's murder."

"He never harmed Hal," Raulyn protested. "I won't believe that."

"A Jew did it. I saw and said that from the first, despite no Jews were known in London. Now we know of three, and unless the two we have can tell us of others here, they are the only Jews we have."

"Father Tomas said the marks—" Raulyn started.

"Do you think 'Father' Tomas wouldn't lie to—"

"I am a baptized Christian and a priest," Father Tomas cried out.

"Your guilt or innocence will be found out." Brother Michael's threat in that was open and did not change as he shifted his hard look to Raulyn. "Just as yours will be, Master Grene. The layers of crimes and guilt look to be many here and will be found out, I promise you. Whether you knew this man and his uncle were Jews and how much else you know—all that will be found out."

If Raulyn had answer to that, he had no chance to make

it as a short, hard-knuckled rap came at the door, and Mistress Hercy entered.

"Madam—" Brother Michael began at her, but she swept a look as sharp and hard as his own at everyone and said at Raulyn, "Your wife needs you. Now."

Chapter 19

istress Hercy turned her demand from Raulyn
and toward Anne. "You, too, Anne. Please."
And while Master Grene said, "I can't come
now. Anne, would—", Frevisse answered for her, "Of course,"
and had her by the arm and toward the door before Anne
could answer, Mistress Hercy barely able to step from their
way. Anne tried to twist free of her hold and look back, but
Frevisse's grip and haste kept her from it.

Did Anne have any thought at all of how much her face
betrayed? Frevisse thought fiercely. If the friar had looked
her way even once, he would had her into his net of suspicions on the instant. However wrong she was to have taken
a lover, let be a Jewish one, Frevisse saw no help in letting
the Inquisition have her and did not slow their fast walk

down the hall, Mistress Hercy hurrying to catch them up. She knew it was probably her own anger at the men driving her as much as anything. Among the many things she had not perfected in her nun's life was patience at debate that was not debate. Brother Michael had declared his accusations and shoved aside, half-heard at best, whatever Daved Weir said back at him, no matter how to the point, well-taken, and well-reasoned Daved's answers had been. Brother Michael was of a kind she found least easy to bear—so certain of his answers to everything that anyone who questioned against his certainty was not only wrong but to be scorned. To be that certain of anything besides the love of God seemed to her a cowardice, a wish to hide from any thought but those in which you felt safe. Whatever else could be said against Daved Weir, he was not a man who hid from thoughts. Trapped though he was and surely doomed, he'd held his own against Brother Michael with cool boldness.

All else aside, Anne Blakhall had taken a brave man for her lover.

But how, as a merchant, had Daved Weir become so learned that he could meet a friar of the Inquisition blow for blow? Not that his learning would save him. He was too far in the wrong, being in England at all and seeming Christian. Nothing except truly turning Christian and a lifetime of penance would keep him alive, and Frevisse did not think fear or force or any persuasion would bring him to that. Unless he loved Anne enough . . .

Mistress Hercy overtook them at the foot of the stairs where they all had to pause to gather their skirts for going up, asking as she did, "Why can't Raulyn come now? What was the matter in the solar just now? Something was the matter. More than the friar having been knocked about."

Anne drew a harsh breath to make probably a harsh answer, but Frevisse raised a silencing finger and ordered,

"Not a word. Not one. Would you make everything worse for him?"

Anne snapped her mouth closed on whatever she might have said, but Mistress Hercy demanded, "What worse? What are you talking of? What's toward in there?"

Keeping one hand for her skirts, Frevisse took hold on Anne's arm again and started up the stairs, taking Anne with her and answering as she went, "It's been found out Master Weir and his uncle are secretly Jews. Brother Michael—"

"Jews?" Mistress Hercy gasped and not for the stairs' steepness. "*Jews?*" She caught at Frevisse's skirts from behind, stopping her. "They're never. Are you certain?"

"Brother Michael is," Frevisse said. "Master Bocking has escaped, but he's questioning Master Weir for it even now."

Alarm and questions of her own crossed Mistress Hercy's face, but before she could ask them, Frevisse said, "What's amiss with Mistress Grene?"

Instantly turned to what mattered more to her than Jews, Mistress Hercy answered, "Fret and worry and grief." She let Frevisse go and went past her and Anne, leading now up the stairs, saying as she went, "We're hearing more from the streets all the time. Why hasn't Cade taken his men back to Southwark? He did last night."

"I don't know. Maybe he's losing his hold on them."

"Well, that's no surprise to anyone but maybe Cade," Mistress Hercy said tartly. Now at the parlor door, she paused. "Best say nothing about Jews. I don't believe it. It's nonsense. You can tell Jews from Christians, can't you? They look different. And there's the smell. Of sulphur, from being the Devil's servants. Master Bocking couldn't be—" She broke off, shaking her head. "That friar is loose-witted is all." She lifted and lightened her voice, saying as she went into the parlor, "Pernell, my darling, here's Anne and Dame Frevisse anyway. Raulyn is at man-talk with the others and will come soon."

Frevisse paused to let Anne go ahead of her, judging by a quick look at her face in the lamplight through the opened doorway that she had steadied, was better-hiding her raw feelings. That was something, anyway.

The child Lucie was sitting on a joint stool near the table, sewing by the lamplight, but Pernell stood at the southward window, turned from it toward the door, her hands spread over the swell of her belly, her face creased with worry that made her look like an uncertain, frightened child as she said, "I can hear shouting. There's fighting started, isn't there?"

"It's nothing but high-heartedness," her mother said bracingly, crossing to the table to take up a goblet waiting there. "You need to finish this, sweetling."

"Raulyn has gone out again, hasn't he?" Pernell said, her voice thin with fear.

Anne, going toward her, said with what could pass for light ease, "I promise you he's here. But you know what men are when they get to talking."

Pernell turned away from the goblet her mother was now offering her, back to the window. "I woke up to what sounded like fighting just outside."

Anne put an arm around Pernell and gentled her away toward her chair, saying with just enough laughter to make it the more real, "It's nothing more than we hear when things go out of hand at a holiday time. It's our worry makes everything sound worse, that's all, and we shouldn't be worried. Master Bocking and Master Weir were out for a while and came back to say it's only the rebels reveling a bit to make up for those nights they spent on Black Heath."

"So there," Mistress Hercy said, following them with the goblet. "Whatever is happening, it can't be too stirring, or Master Weir at least would have stayed for the sport instead of coming back."

Pernell gave a shakey laugh at that and let Anne set her in the chair.

"Besides that," Anne said, "Raulyn has set good guard. We're as safe as anywhere in the city, save maybe the Tower."

"Trust Raulyn to see to his own best interests," Mistress Hercy said, pressing the goblet into her daughter's hand. "No, sweetling, everything is locked and shuttered and barred, and besides our own folk and Master Bocking and Master Weir, we have Dame Frevisse's two men here, too. The only way someone can get in here is over the rooftops, and I doubt there's a drunken rebel going to take that much trouble. Not with all London's alehouses and taverns to be gone through."

That won another laugh from Pernell, and she took the goblet and drank whatever was in it—something to make her sleep again, Frevisse supposed.

"And here's Lucie," Mistress Hercy said. "Still up at this hour. Let's to bed with you, young woman."

"I want her with me tonight," Pernell said.

"Best you come along together," Mistress Hercy said cheerfully. "You'll go to sleep better if your mother is with you, won't you, Lucie dear?"

That succeeded in getting Pernell to bed, though as she let her mother take her toward the bedchamber she asked Anne, "You'll send Raulyn in when he comes, won't you?"

"I will," Anne promised, smiling. She held the smile until the bedchamber door was shut. Then all her forced brightness vanished and she sank into Pernell's chair.

"Can you keep up the pretense if this goes on?" Frevisse asked.

Wearily, Anne answered, "I've hidden more than this from more people than Pernell."

"You mean what's between you and Daved Weir," Frevisse said; and when Anne did not answer that, asked, "Does anyone else know of it?"

"My servant. And Raulyn. Others may know. Or suspect. I don't know." Anne covered her face with both hands and said, in pain, "Oh, God, they can't kill him. What am I going to do? Oh, my God, what?"

"There's nothing you can do," Frevisse said, unable to give comfort where none was to be had. "Not now he's been found out."

Anne dropped her hands into fists in her lap and said fiercely, "It's the friar. Without him there'd be no trouble. No one would have known. Daved should have let those men kill him. They were probably Lollards." Fear wrenched into her voice again. "And he's accused Daved of killing Hal!"

Frevisse make a shushing gesture at her, warning against going any louder because besides Pernell in the bedchamber, someone was coming up the stairs. Anne, hearing that, too, sprang to her feet and went quickly, saying at Master Grene as he came in, "Where's Daved? What's he done with him?"

"He's still in the solar. He's bound now . . ."

Anne moaned and covered her face again. Master Grene put an arm around her shoulders and guided her back to the chair, much as she had done with Pernell. "No, listen," he said. "It was the solar or the cellar. I refused the cellar. And I refused to have Father Tomas held prisoner. He——"

"The solar," Anne said with sudden hope. "He could escape from there. You can help him, Raulyn."

Master Grene took her by both arms, bringing her around to face him while he said carefully, to be sure she understood, "Anne, he's tied hands and feet and to a chair, and Brother Michael means to stay the night there for better measure."

"With the Naylors keeping guard, too," Frevisse said, to discourage whatever foolishness Anne might desperately think to try.

"No, not the Naylors," Master Grene said. "They have to rest, to be ready for their turn on watch."

Anne took hold on his doublet and pulled demandingly. "It has to be tonight you help him. Before he's taken to the bishop."

Master Grene loosened her hands from him but kept hold on them. "Anne, there's nothing I can do. Brother Michael isn't going to drop his guard, and I'm near to being in trouble right along with Daved. If Daved escapes, by any means whatsoever, I'll be the one to answer for it, no matter what my innocence else. Anne, I have Pernell and the children to remember. I don't dare do more than I have."

Anne gave a sob dry with a grief and hopelessness past tears and leaned her forehead against him. He put his arms around her and pleaded, "Forgive me."

Anne straightened and said wearily, "There's nothing to forgive. I know how it is. But, please, isn't there some way I can see Daved again, talk with him for a moment? Half a moment." Her need was giving her strength again. "I *have* to see him."

Master Grene took her by both shoulders and said steadily, as if willing her to understand, "Anne, for now Brother Michael has no reason to look at you. For everyone's sake, keep it that way. Give no sign Daved is anything to you. It will only go the worse for him, let alone you, if you're found out. There's nothing you can do. Father Tomas is already lost. Don't you be, too."

"Father Tomas is a priest," Anne said wearily. "Nothing will happen to him."

"Anne," Master Grene said very gently, "there's Hal's death."

Anne wrenched free of his hold and stepped back, staring at him. Half-strangled on sudden anger, she said furiously, "That's not something even to be thought! Father Tomas had nothing to do with that!"

"Somebody did," Master Grene said, sounding too weighed under his own weariness and grief to meet her anger. "Anne, somebody did, and it's Father Tomas' word against the friar's that those aren't Jewish marks cut into Hal's body."

He looked to Frevisse for help, and she went to lay hands on Anne's shoulders and draw her away, saying, "Master Grene should go in to Pernell now. Best you come sit and recover yourself."

Anne let Frevisse seat her while Master Grene went into the bedchamber. A goblet and a pitcher stood on the table, and Frevisse poured wine and gave it to Anne, who was drinking it as Mistress Hercy came from the bedchamber. In the unguarded moment when she turned from closing the door, deep-worn lines of weariness showed in her face before she gathered herself, shoved away her weariness, and bustled toward Frevisse and Anne with, "Bed for the rest of us, too, I should think. Anne-dear, why don't I see you to yours before I settle down with Lucie on the truckle beside Pernell?"

Anne emptied the goblet in a long gulp, set it down ungently on the table, and came abruptly to her feet. "Yes," she said. "Bed. Thank you. Yes." And left. All so suddenly that Frevisse and Mistress Hercy were left staring after her, wordless, until Mistress Hercy shook her head, said, "Well. I was going to say you could share the bed with her tonight, since Lucie won't be, but . . ."

"Here still suits me very well," Frevisse said.

Master Grene came from the bedchamber, shutting the door with silent carefulness before he looked around to ask, "Where's Anne?"

"Gone to bed," Mistress Hercy answered. "And Dame Frevisse is about to, I think. Is Pernell asleep?"

"She and Lucie both," Master Grene said, going to the southward window to look out. "No sign of anything burning," he said after a moment and began to close the shutters across the window. "I've shuttered the window in the bedchamber and am going to close these, so if trouble does break out in the night, maybe Pernell won't hear it."

"Well thought," agreed Mistress Hercy, and she went to close the shutters across the window overlooking the yard. "Now, Raulyn, what's this with that friar and Jews? There's nothing in it, is there?"

While Raulyn told her there was something in it but tonight wasn't the time to talk about it, Frevisse drew her last night's bedding from the corner where it had been left all day. Mistress Hercy insisted on more from Raulyn and when she had it, tersely though he told it, she veered between dismay that it could be true and declaration that she did not believe such treacherous pretense of either Master Bocking or Master Weir.

"It's what Brother Michael believes that calls the dance," Master Grene answered. "I'm going to see to the watch now. Father Tomas and I will be where we were last night if you need me—or us—later."

Mistress Hercy let him go, stood silent in apparent thought for a moment after he was gone, then asked Frevisse, who now had the mattress unrolled and blankets spread, "Will you do well enough tonight, my lady? Do you need aught?"

"I need nothing," Frevisse assured her. "See to yourself for a while."

Mistress Hercy's smile was small, all her weariness openly upon her. "If everyone will just stay asleep until dawn, I'll do well enough. By your leave, I'll bid you goodnight, then." And she went into the bedchamber, silently closing the door behind her.

Frevisse, at last blessedly alone, blew out the lamp and knelt to Compline's prayers, but they did not come, only an ongoing churn of worries and, she realized, anger. At what? she wondered; and the answer came easily. At Brother

Michael and his *eagerness* to bring Daved Weir and Father Tomas to destruction.

Knowing that lying down to sleep would be no use, she rose and went to partly open one of the shutters at the southward window and sat down on the seat there, looking out. She had never seen London so dark. The law might be that householders were supposed to have a lantern lighted outside their door through the night, but very few folk tonight were willing to chance drawing unwanted notice their way. Such glows as she could see looked to be torches on the move in the darkened streets; but she still heard no screams of fear or anger, only what sounded like loud tavern-reveling. Out-of-the-ordinary loud and from too many places, though, and she doubted the likelihood of Brother Michael getting Daved Weir to the bishop tomorrow through streets full of roving rebels.

That, in its way, was to the bad, because the sooner Daved Weir was away the better, before Anne Blakhall betrayed herself too openly. For her to confess to her own priest and be given deep penance for her sin was one thing and necessary. It was another matter altogether to think of her put to Brother Michael's mercy. Heresy was a treachery of the mind, not a sin of the body. Whatever Anne's wrong in taking Daved Weir for her lover, Frevisse had no doubt she was misled by her body's passion, not by any thought of heresy.

Frevisse also had no doubt that the Inquisition would see it otherwise.

She understood the guard that had to be kept against the corrupting danger of heretics. It was the charge of heresy against the Jews that she didn't accept. As Daved had said, scholars considering, explaining, amplifying the Bible's teachings had been part of Christianity from the beginning and many of them had been saints. No one charged that their studies had corrupted or changed Christianity, nor had Brother Michael in his furious exchange with Daved explained why it should be otherwise for Jewish scholars, why their learned men discussing and interpreting God's word turned their faith to heresy. Until someone brought her to understand that, she would not accept it. Or that Daved Weir was a heretic.

Besides that, she fiercely liked the way he had held his own against the friar. One of the things that made the friars of the Inquisition so terrible was their skillful use of their great learning as a weapon against all foes; but watching Brother Michael and Daved Weir had been like watching two equally armed men. Learning for learning, certainty for certainty, Daved had wielded words and knowledge as readily as Brother Michael had. There had been nothing of the merchant in his dealing with Brother Michael. No bargaining. No seeking to make things better. That was probably because he knew there was no "better" for him now. Even should he turn Christian and so save his life, he would be expected to betray a great many people. She did not doubt it would take torture to bring him to that betrayal, and tortured he would be, because although torture was against civil law in England, it was not against the Church's.

And if he broke to the torturer, Anne Blakhall was among those he would betray.

Frevisse closed the shutter and readied for bed in the darkness, taking off only her veil and wimple. Like last night, she would otherwise sleep clothed, not only for seemliness' sake but because there was nowhere to put the gold hanging heavy from her neck except where it was. She lay down and took the first prayer that came to mind—*Noctem quietam, et finem perfectum concedat nobis Dominus omnipotens.*— A quiet night and a perfect end grant to us, almighty Lord.—steadily repeating it until it carried her into sleep. A sleep from which she was jerked by fast-thudding footsteps up the stairs. With effort so sudden it hurt, she sat up as a maidservant burst into the parlor, hand up to shield the flame of the candle she carried from the haste of her going as she crossed the room, ignoring Frevisse and calling as she went, "Mistress Hercy! Master Grene says come quickly! The friar's been killed, he says!"

Chapter 20

As the maidservant obeyed Mistress Hercy's call to come in, Frevisse struggled to her feet, groping for her wimple and veil in the uneven candle-shadows, putting them on by feel, used to that in the nunnery dorter's darkness, while the maid's voice and Pernell's shrilled together in the bedchamber. By the time Mistress Hercy had commanded and soothed both maid and Pernell to quiet, Frevisse had her veil pinned into place; and when Mistress Hercy came from the bedchamber, bedrobe wrapped around her and saying over her shoulder, "No, Pernell, just keep in bed. I'll see what this is about. Stay with her, Lucie," Frevisse followed in her and the maidservant's wake out of the parlor and down the stairs.

Jumping candle-shadows and lamp-flare ragged with people moving in the screens passage made the stairs treacherous in the dark and only the worse for having skirts to handle. Mistress Hercy stumbled once. The maid caught her arm to steady her off the bottom step and into the passage, and here Mistress Hercy shoved into a clutter of servants, men and women together, demanding, "Where is he? The friar and Master Grene. Where are they? What is this, Wyett? James, aren't you supposed to be at the rear gate?"

James immediately began to fade backward among his fellows while Wyett pointed toward the outer door, saying, "They're out there. Master Grene sent us inside. Pers found him. He was outside the gate. He . . ."

Already going for the outer door, Mistress Hercy snapped over her shoulder, "You, stay here," at the maidservant, who instantly stopped where she was. Frevisse might have been included in that order but chose to think she was not—nor would have obeyed anyway—and followed out the door to find she had slept more than she had supposed. A fading to the darkness over the eastern rooftops would soon be dawn. But more by the clear night's starlight than otherwise, she and Mistress Hercy made their way down to the yard and toward the black shapes of a few men gathered around the yellow glow of a lantern set on the cobbles just inside the foregate.

Reaching the edge of the lantern light and men, Frevisse saw Master Naylor and Dickon were among them, standing with a household servant beyond Master Grene and Father Tomas kneeling to either side of Brother Michael laid out on his back on the cobbles. The friar's face was hidden by Father Tomas' shadow, but the grey friar's gown twisted around his body made certain who he was. Unless, somehow, it was another Franciscan friar, Frevisse thought. Or someone else in Brother Michael's robe. Or . . .

Before she could go further through that scattering of thoughts, Father Tomas sat back on his heels, away from the body, and the lantern light showed not only his own face, tired and stricken, but Brother Michael's, slack-jawed with death, eyes emptily staring.

Heavy-voiced, Father Tomas said, "He's gone," and reached a hand to close the eyes.

The men and both women crossed themselves even as Mistress Hercy asked, "He wasn't dead yet? Emme said he was."

Master Grene stood up. "Pers found him in the street and dragged him in the gateway, then ran for help. I think he was dead. Father Tomas . . ." He moved a hand vaguely at the priest.

Hand still on the eyes to be certain they would stay closed, the priest said slowly, "I said the words. I had no oil or anything, but I did that much." He dropped his hand back into his lap. "I'll swear his intent was there. His soul is safe."

"But he said nothing?" Frevisse asked.

Father Tomas shook his head as if too tired for words. It was Master Grene who answered, "Nothing."

"But what happened to him?" Mistress Hercy persisted. "How's he dead?" Because nothing showed in the lantern light of any wound.

"He looks to have been stabbed," Master Grene said. "In the back. At least that's where all the blood is."

"He wasn't beaten? There wasn't an attack on him like yesterday?" Frevisse asked.

"Nobody heard any, no."

"But how did he come to be outside the gate?" Frevisse persisted.

"My lady," Master Naylor said, "should you be out in the night air?"

Frevisse knew when she was being quelled, and Master Naylor was maybe right that questions here and now over the friar's newly dead body were unseemly. But what was more seemly than trying to find out how he had come to be so suddenly dead? Mistress Hercy, disregarding seemly or unseemly, demanded at the household man standing there, "Pers, it's all well to say you found him, but why did you let him out the gate at all? And why did you hear nothing of something happening?"

The man gave a rather desperate look at Master Grene while answering, "I didn't let him out. I wasn't here. Master Grene was."

"I was here a while," Master Grene said. "When I was going the rounds to be sure all was well, I found Pers here more asleep than awake."

"Not full asleep," Pers defended.

"It's all right," Master Grene said. "I told you so then. You'd been at it for the most of two nights. The fault was mine for not setting matters better."

Father Tomas began to climb to his feet, stiffly like a far older man than he was. Master Grene put a hand under his elbow, steadying him while going on, "I sent him to have a sleep for a while in the back of the shop, saying I'd keep the watch myself. But I never saw Brother Michael, either."

"We can't leave him lying here," Father Tomas said. "We need to get him at least to the church."

"We can't risk that," Master Grene said sharply. "Listen. They're still at it." And that was true enough. The sounds of merry-making in surrounding streets were much lessened, men finally wearing out with the night, but there was still too much of it. "I'm letting no one out this gate, and not in the dark, surely."

"Why did you let Brother Michael out?" Frevisse asked. "And how didn't you hear the attack on him?"

"I *didn't* let him out! That's the trouble. I didn't, nor Pers, either, from what he says."

"Then how——" Master Naylor began impatiently.

Master Grene said sharply, "I had to go once to ease myself. There's a closestool in the rear of the shop. So if someone is tending the board alone, he doesn't have to leave it. It's not fifteen feet away." He pointed toward the shop's back door. "It took no time at all, but that's when he had to have let himself out."

"He surely opened the gate's door, rather than the gate itself," Frevisse said. "You didn't hear it open?"

"It's kept well-oiled," Master Grene answered.

"But it's kept barred, like the gates. Didn't you see it wasn't barred anymore?" Master Naylor asked.

"We aren't keeping guard with a great light blazing. Why draw anyone's heed to here? So, no, in the dark of the passage here I didn't see the gate was unbarred. Nor did I check it," he said, forestalling the next question. "Why should I?" he added, irritated, as well he might be. A dead friar at his gate was going to bring questions down on him from Church as well as constable, crowner, and sheriffs before this was done.

"But you heard nothing else, either? Not here or in the street?" Frevisse insisted.

"Nothing."

"How was Pers back at the gate after you sent him off?" Mistress Hercy asked.

Master Grene made a short, unhappy sound. "I started to turn sleepy myself. I fetched him out with hope he'd had enough sleep to take over until at least dawn." He looked around and said, surprised, "Now it *is* dawn."

The passage was still in darkness, but beyond it the yard was indeed grown grey with dawn's coming. There would soon be no need for lantern light.

"We can't leave him lying here," Father Tomas said again, his hands clutched together, more to keep from wringing them than in prayer. "We have to move him."

"To the cellar," Master Grene said. "He can be laid out decently there without setting people to worse worry by seeing him the way they will if we put him in the hall. We can set candles around him if you like. Pers," he ordered, "fetch someone and see to it."

Pers shot away as if glad of any task that took him elsewhere.

"But why would he have gone out the gate at all?" Frevisse asked again. "And why was he stabbed instead of beaten, like before?"

"Because someone would have heard a beating or any outcry. Even Pers," said Master Grene. "This was done by someone who simply wanted him dead and quickly."

A momentary silence among them then was broken by Master Naylor saying, "Master Bocking."

"Where's Daved Weir?" asked Frevisse.

Not sounding certain, Master Grene said, "He's still in the solar."

Master Naylor started toward the house. "We'd best see, hadn't we?"

"But Brother Michael . . ." Father Tomas protested.

"Stay with him," Master Grene ordered, starting after Master Naylor. "Pers and someone will be here."

Dickon was already at his father's heels, and Mistress Hercy and Frevisse followed, hurrying to keep up to the men's long stride. In the screens passage Mistress Hercy gave curt order in passing to the servants there to be about their business, that breakfast would be wanted soon, whatever else was happening. Her pause let Frevisse go ahead of her so that she was close behind the men when Master Grene opened the door into the lamp-lit solar; and she saw over their shoulders Daved standing in the middle of the room, his arms around Anne and hers around him and, "Damn all!" Master Grene burst out. "In hell's teeth, what are you doing free, Daved?"

"Raulyn, let him escape. Please," Anne pleaded, holding tighter to Daved. "Before Brother Michael comes back."

"Brother Michael is dead." Master Grene crossed to his desk and leaned on it, head hanging. "He's dead, and you're loosed, and so it can be said you did it."

"No!" Anne said fiercely. "I freed Daved and only now!"

Gently loosening Anne from him but keeping her close with an arm around her, Daved asked, "How is he dead?"

"Stabbed from behind," Master Grene answered bluntly. "Not here. Outside the gate. In the street."

"What was he doing there?" Daved asked with apparent surprise.

"Leaving, I suppose. Hoping to slip through the streets and darkness back to Grey Friars. Or to find some of the bishop's officers and bring them here to take you under guard. I don't know."

Master Naylor asked at Daved, "He left you here unwatched?"

"Where was I going to go, bound hand and foot there?" Daved jerked his head toward a heavy wooden chair to one side of the room, a sprawl of ropes on the floor beside it. "He thought he could safely leave me for a time, I suppose."

The ropes had been cut, Frevisse noted, and going forward past Master Naylor, she asked, "Where did you get the knife to cut the ropes, Mistress Blakhall?"

Anne, still with one arm around Daved, said defiantly, "His daggers are there." She pointed to the desk where they did still lay from yesterday. "I used one."

Master Naylor picked up one, then the other, taking a long look at both in the sinking lamplight before saying at the second one, "There's blood on the blade."

"I cut a man in the fight yesterday," Daved said. And added dryly, "I've not had chance to clean it yet."

As Master Naylor set the dagger down, Frevisse asked, "How long ago did Brother Michael leave? And why?"

"Someone came to the door," Daved answered. "They didn't come in, and I didn't see them."

That was possible, Frevisse thought. The door opened inward, would have been between anyone who stayed outside the room and Daved where he had sat bound.

"How long ago?" Frevisse repeated.

Daved stretched and twisted his neck as if it were stiff. "There was nothing to tell the time by. A fair while, but I couldn't say certainly how long."

She could not tell if he were lying much or little—or at all. Could it have been Anne at the door? Could she have somehow lured Brother Michael outside the gateway and then stabbed him? With one of Daved's daggers, taken up from the desk without Brother Michael seeing it? Then slipped back into the house and freed Daved? All in the two little gaps of time Master Grene had been away from the gate?

That was too chance-ridden to be likely.

Unless Master Grene was part of it.

Or else Master Grene had done it all, and Anne had no part in it. Brother Michael might well have gone out of the room to talk with him. But out of the gateway?

Frevisse raced her thoughts through possibilities and, yes, Master Grene might have sent Pers to rest, then come to lure out Brother Michael—maybe by telling him the streets were quiet enough he should take the chance to slip away to bring men back for Daved.

Except she could not see Brother Michael leaving his prey behind him. Not for an unneeded skulking through dangerous streets in the dark when he only need wait for a more sure time. Nor would he have left Daved in Master Grene's keeping, not when he had already said outright he distrusted him.

Or was it because of that distrust Brother Michael had meant to slip away unknown to anyone, counting on being back with help before Master Grene dared do anything? That did not set easily with her, either. But if Master Grene had killed the friar, then why hadn't he freed Daved and seen him away?

Or, if Daved had freed himself and killed the friar, why would he stay here, feigning he was just freed? Why not straightforward flight once the friar was dead? And why bother to put his body outside the gate?

But if Brother Michael *had* gone out the gate on his own and secretly, had he been chance-killed by someone passing by, or was Master Naylor's guess at Master Bocking right? Yet how likely was it Master Bocking had lingered—or come back—to the place least safe for him to be, on a very narrow chance of somehow helping Daved, and chanced instead on the friar?

All of those might-have-beens were too full of chance and unlikelihood, and while she tried and failed to settle even one of them into her mind, Master Grene pushed himself upright from his desk with his braced hands and said at Daved, "Leave now. While you can. No one here will stop you."

Master Naylor shifted, ready to protest that. Frevisse lifted a hand to hold him silent. Both Daved and Master Grene saw it; and Master Grene said—for whose benefit she was not sure—"After all, until yesterday I didn't know you and your uncle were Jews. All I'll be guilty of is ignorance and letting you leave here after I did know it, but in times like these, how great would my blame be for that?"

"Slight, I should think," Daved said easily.

That was probably true enough, but that Master Grene had not known they were Jews . . . that was a lie. He had been appalled yesterday, yes, but at them being found out, not at finding they were Jews. The only exclamation at that had come from Mistress Hercy, who presently was standing in the doorway here, staring from Daved and Anne to her son-in-law and back again.

"The trouble is," said Daved, "that I've maybe nowhere to run. If my uncle has any sense, he sailed on the tide."

"He wouldn't leave you," Anne protested.

"We agreed long since that neither of us would play the fool and risk everything in pointless effort to save the other. Things being otherwise, I would have sailed and left him. And even if, for some reason, he hasn't and I make it to one of the landings, there are likely no boatmen there to take me out to my ship or any other. They'll have shoved off to keep clear of trouble. That's one thing to the good of being a boatman," he added thoughtfully. "You can cast off from trouble."

"At least leave here," Master Grene said impatiently. He looked at Master Naylor. "Where you're known."

"Where's he to go? There's nowhere safe in London just now," Anne protested.

"There have to be places safer than here," Master Grene returned.

"Master Naylor is my man," Frevisse said. "He'll do as I bid." She hoped. "Our present need is to keep safe here against any rioting there may come. For that, it's better to have Master Weir with us. Yes?" she added directly at Master Naylor.

"Yes," he granted, though his teeth were maybe gritted on the word.

"So you and Master Bocking *are* Jews," Mistress Hercy said from the doorway.

Daved made her a courteous bow. "We are," he said.

"Then I've heard much nonsense over the years," she said briskly and came forward into the room, saying to everyone, "Now see, there's trouble enough outside we need make none in here. No one here had aught to do with the friar going out the gate and getting killed. That's what matters. That, and that there's nothing we can do about it for now. So Raulyn, go you to Pernell. She needs to hear from you what's happened and see that you're unharmed."

"In a while," he said. "Not just now."

"Just now is when she needs you," Mistress Hercy said. "And all of us need to break our fast. We'll all be the better for food. Going hungry won't make anything better."

Master Grene gave a shaken laugh and stood up. "Food and something strong to drink. You're in the right. That will help all of us." He started toward the door.

Past him to Daved, Mistress Hercy said, "Best you stay in here, though. There's no one in the household knows certainly what this business between you and the friar was . . ."

She broke off with a questioning look at Master Naylor, who said, "We've answered all questions by saying we couldn't say."

"Good," Mistress Hercy approved. "So better you stay here, Master Weir, away from questions. Anne, best you come with us. Pernell will need you."

"No," Anne said.

Daved made to step away from her, saying gently, "The farther you keep from me now . . ."

"No," Anne repeated flatly.

Master Grene turned in the doorway. "Anne, he's right. You're better away from him for now." The stubborn set of Anne's look at him told her answer without she need say anything, and Master Grene shifted his own look to Daved and said, deliberate at it, "Do you know that she fasts two days a week as penance for what she does with you?"

He waited long enough to see by the sudden blankness of Daved's face that he had not known. Then he left, and Mistress Hercy, after a quick frowning look at both Anne and Daved, followed him. And Anne spun immediately to Daved and cried out, "You have to get away from here. Now! What if Brother Michael was *coming back* when he was killed, and someone else knows now?"

Frevisse felt an instant fool for not having thought of that possibility but said before Daved made any answer,

"You'd have him go with no one knowing whether he'd murdered Brother Michael or not?"

Anne turned on her. "He couldn't have done anything until I cut him loose, and the friar was dead by then."

"The question has to be," Daved said quietly, "*when* did you cut me loose, my love."

"They came in just . . . "Anne caught up to where Daved already was. Her voice went flat. "There's only our word."

"And our word is suspect, my heart," Daved told her.

"Therefore, you have more than one reason to stay until some manner of answer is found," Frevisse said.

"Or until you can give up pretense and surrender me to the Church?" Daved asked.

That was a fair challenge, fairly given, and Frevisse answered straightly back, "I have no quarrel with you that you're a Jew." But was surprised to hear herself saying so, not having known it for certain until then. "Nor do I intend to tell anyone that you are. I likewise order my men to keep silent on it." She looked at Master Naylor, daring him to refuse her; but he gave her a curt nod of acceptance, and she returned her look to Daved. "But murder is another matter altogether. If you leave before we learn who killed Brother Michael—or determine that it was no one here—you would have to be hunted."

Daved regarded her steadily for a long moment, then said, "I reserve the right to run if it comes down to that or being taken prisoner."

Frevisse thought he was a little laughing at her but bent her head slightly in agreement. "You'll run if need be," she said. And thought how little she would like finding out he was, after all, Brother Michael's murderer.

Chapter 21

ame Frevisse left, her two men with her, closing the door behind them, and Anne spun on Daved, demanding again, "Never give mind to what she said. Leave London. Hire a horse and go to some other port and sail from there. Leave!"

Daved laid his hands on her shoulders. "Is it true about the penance?"

Meeting his deep look, Anne forced herself to answer straightly, "Yes."

"You confessed to a priest about us, and he laid this penance on you?"

She lifted her chin. "I couldn't confess what I fully mean to go on doing."

"Then why . . ." His voice was very gentle. ". . . do you do this penance?"

Very gently in return, she said, "Because it's sin, what we do between us." She gave herself suddenly to sad laughter and took his face between her hands and drew him down to her. "But I'd rather do the penance than cease the sin."

She kissed him lingeringly, a kiss that he returned; but as he drew back from her, he said, "Anne, my heart, this penance, it . . ."

"It's nothing. I never meant for you to know of it." It was not nothing. Except when constrained by being in company and wanting to keep her secret, she had only bread and ale to eat and drink on her penance days; or in bitter winter weather, hot broth. She was not trying to break her health, only admit to God that she knew there was wrong in her loving with both heart and body where she should not love at all, and it was with that love she now said desperately, "Daved, never mind. Or what you told the nun. Leave before you lose the chance to. None of Raulyn's men will stop you. Please, go! You'll be safer in the streets than here."

"Oh, my heart, I might well be, but what of you? How safe will you be? If I didn't kill the friar, then almost surely someone else here did."

If that was true, she might have been frightened but, "He wasn't killed here. He was killed in the street, trying to leave."

"And so you'd have me try to leave, too?"

He was silently laughing at her, and she knew it and slapped his arm, impatient at his lightness. His courage was among the things about him that she loved, but this was not when and where she wanted it. She wanted him away from here and out of England. Daved caught her hand and kissed it.

"Think," he said, still easily. "How likely does it seem that Brother Michael would leave me unguarded or decide to go back to the friary or anywhere in the middle of the night? How likely is it he had no more than stepped outside the gate than someone came up behind him and stabbed him dead without so much as word or struggle?"

Anne tried, "It could have happened," and heard her own lack of certainty even as she said it. She tried again, more strongly. "Master Bocking could have been waiting for him, could have been lying in wait."

"And the thought my uncle stabbed him in the back doesn't bother you?"

"He meant to do worse to you," she said fiercely.

"I swear my uncle will have sailed by now."

"The attack on Brother Michael yesterday," she said, trying again. "That was surely Lollards meaning to be rid of him, and some of them could have been waiting for whenever he would come out again."

Daved laughed aloud. "Anne!" he protested.

Stubbornly, she insisted, "They could have been. Or even just one." Because that would be by far the best of answers.

Daved granted, still near laughter. "It could have been Lollards, yes." Then the laughter was gone and there was steel behind his words as he went on, "But against that I have to ask who came to the door here? Who did he go away with? Because almost surely that's who killed him."

He was right, and only slowly Anne said, "It could have been me."

"It could have been," Daved agreed. "I know if I had been the friar, *I* would have let you lure me from the room. Even gone out the gate with you and maybe put my back to you." He drew her to him. "Though it's not my back to you I want." He took his time over another kiss that left her wanting to cling to him with her body as well as her lips; but he set her back from him and said, "But would Brother Michael?"

Anne looked up at him, silent for a moment. In that while they had clung together, she had felt in him more than only his passion for her. He was taut with the pleasure of the fight he was in, and she was left as shaken at understanding that as by his kiss; but she gathered her wits, lifted her chin, and answered his question, "He might have done, yes."

"It is somewhat more likely than lurking Lollards," Daved granted. "So. Was it you who did for him?"

Anne knew he was jesting and—determined to show as brave as he was, however much she wasn't—she jested back at him, "If I did, I'd not admit it."

Daved laughed, and she was happy to have made him, but in her fearful need to have him safe she went on, fighting and failing to keep her voice steady, "It doesn't matter who was at the door. What matters is for you to be away."

"What matters, among other things, is that I don't leave you here where there's a murderer." He laid gentle hands on her shoulders. "Nor leave you with no certainty in your mind that I am not. After all, you and no one else knows that you found me with the ropes already cut when you came in here. Nor can you know how long I had been unbound. It might have been long enough to kill that friar and dump his body in the street."

"If you'd done that, why not just go on? Why move his body at all? Why not kill him here and escape and be done with it?"

"I'll do what I can to think of reasons, if you like," Daved offered. "It won't be easy. In the meanwhile, I want to see the friar's body."

"Daved!" she exclaimed, but he had already started away from her, and without any quick reason that would stop him, she followed him. In the hall two maidservants were setting out bread and cheese for breakfast on a trestle table. They looked a little confused at seeing him and one of them even a little frightened, which meant something was being said through the household over what had happened yesterday, but when Daved paused to ask them, "Do you know where they've put the dead friar?", one of the women answered readily enough, "In the cellar, master."

As Daved went on, the other said, protesting, "Master Grene said you were staying in the solar."

Daved threw her a smile over his shoulder, said cheerily, "But as you see, I'm not," and was out of the hall.

Avoiding their eyes and any question they might have asked her, Anne kept after him. There were two sets of stairs at the rear end of the screens passage. One led down to the kitchen and the rearyard, the other to the cellar under the hall. Because goods of his own were sometimes stored in the cellar, Daved did not need to ask the way, or even to pause at the heavy door since it stood open to the wide, deeply shadowed cellar stairs. Daved took them without hesitation, but Anne had never been this way and went more slowly, holding to the rope strung along the wall for railing, until she turned the stairs' corner and found herself nearly at their bottom, with enough candlelight ahead of her to show her way better despite the sweep of Daved's shadow back at her, large among the close-set stone pillars holding up the beams of the hall floor too near above her head. Crowded farther off in the shadows were thicker darknesses that would be the stacked bales of cloth and chests of other goods stored here for safety, but the candlelight was straight ahead, spread out from several fat tallow candles set on prickets thrust out from stone pillars, lighting a square between four of the pillars where Brother Michael's body must be.

Father Tomas' shadow met Daved's as the priest hurried toward Daved from the candlelight. Anne saw him take hold of Daved's arm as they met just beyond the stairfoot but missed whatever Father Tomas first said and what Daved answered him, only reaching the bottom of the stairs in time to hear the priest say, his voice low and shaking, "No. Now. Get away while you can. You have to flee *now*. Brother Michael is not the only one who saw too much. All one of Grene's men has to do is talk of your tallit, not even knowing what it is, with the wrong ears to hear it . . ."

"It will be as God wills," Daved said steadily.

"If you're taken, you'll be tortured. The Church can do it. They'll have everything from you." Father Tomas' fear was painful to see and all too nakedly as much for himself as Daved. "Everything. And then . . ."

"What of you?" Daved asked. "More people heard what you told Brother Michael about yourself than ever heard his accusation of me."

Father Tomas stopped short, staring, before he said, his voice still low but suddenly steady, "I'm a Christian priest. I will not be otherwise. Here is where I belong."

"And here is where *I* must presently be," said Daved and went on.

Anne followed him past Father Tomas, briefly touching the priest's arm in sympathy but felt him trembling and moved the more quickly after Daved, afraid Father Tomas' fear would only make her own fear stronger.

A piece of rough canvas had been laid on the stone floor for Brother Michael's body, but he was laid out on it as if on a proper bier, his robe straight around him, his wooden cross on his chest with his hands resting on it. His mouth was closed now, as well as his eyes. Closed once and for all but not soon enough, Anne thought viciously. And was appalled at herself an instant later and crossed herself but was forestalled from any prayer by surprise at seeing Dame Frevisse there, standing beyond the corpse, nearly invisible against the darkness behind her until she lifted her head and her white wimple and pale face showed in the candlelight.

Her long-faced Master Naylor was there, too, a few paces aside and looking no happier than he had in the solar. Anne was uncertain how much danger to Daved he might be, but she trusted him less than she did the nun. And did not trust her very much.

Now fully into the candlelight, Daved stopped, and over the corpse he and Dame Frevisse regarded each other a moment, before she said, "Have you come to pray for his soul?"

"My faith does not require me to love my enemies," Daved answered. "I'm willing to leave to God where his soul should go."

"This man's soul went before its time."

"Can someone die before God wills it?"

"Does God will murder?"

Daved spread out his hands, palms upward. "Who understands the will of God?"

The smallest of possible smiles touched the corners of Dame Frevisse's mouth. "A point well made. Though I believe the Commandment says 'You shall not slay wrongfully.' It would seem that makes clear enough God's will in the matter."

"Therefore, let us hope he also wills that we learn soon who this particular murderer is."

Dame Frevisse went suddenly still, looking at Daved as if he and she had become the only people there, until finally she said, quite quietly, "Is that something you truly want?"

"Why shouldn't I?" Daved returned.

"Why should you? He would have brought about your death. Instead, he's dead. That could easily be enough for you. What does it matter to you who killed him?"

"He would have brought about my death, yes." Black, unexpected laughter glinted in Daved's voice. "Wrongfully, to my way of seeing it. Instead, he's dead, but also wrongfully. Therefore, if I thought ill of myself being wrongfully killed, must I not, by the bonds of logic and despite whatever else I thought or felt toward him, also think ill of his death, it being likewise wrongful?"

"By the bonds of logic, yes," Dame Frevisse granted.

"There, then. All your questions are answered."

The wry set of the nun's mouth suggested they were not, even before she said, "Let us say *some* of my questions are answered. But to go back to where we began, if you've not come to pray for his soul, why are you here?"

"To find out his murderer," Daved said. "Lest I live under the suspicion of his death hereafter."

Anne, from where she stood slightly behind him, saw Dame Frevisse's gaze slide sideways to her in a brief, assessing look that made Anne want to grab Daved by the arm and tell him this wasn't something he had to do for her, that she would rather he hazard escape than chance staying here to prove something of which she was already sure.

Only the certainty that her words would make no difference held her silent, as with again that flickering of black laughter Daved went on, "At least the corpse is not bleeding in my presence. That's to the good, isn't it?"

"Only if you believe dead bodies are so obliging as to bleed anew in the presence of their murderer," Dame Frevisse returned.

"You don't?"

"I've never seen it happen."

"You've had much to do with murdered bodies?"

"Yes."

The flatness of her answer stopped Daved. Then he asked seriously, "Have you?"

"Yes," she said again; and then, matching his challenge, "Have you?"

Quietly Daved said, "Yes."

The nun seemed unsurprised by that. "Then what do you make of this?" she said and knelt down. Daved went to kneel beside her. Unlike Father Tomas who had come silently to kneel at Brother Michael's feet with his head bent in prayer, there was no sign of prayer in Daved and Dame

Frevisse's kneeling. Instead, Dame Frevisse took Brother Michael's head between her hands and lifted it, saying, "Feel the back of it."

Anne, able neither to pray nor look away, watched Daved do so, his face set. When he withdrew his hand, Dame Frevisse gently lowered the head to the cloth and asked, "Well?"

"He was struck there," Daved said slowly. "He was clubbed from behind." And even more slowly, "As Hal was."

"Yes," Dame Frevisse said. "Struck down and afterward stabbed to death. Like the boy."

And Anne was suddenly aware of how much this was how it had been in St. Swithin's crypt—the crowding darkness, the body laid out . . .

"Then maybe, as we think with Hal," said Daved, "he was struck down somewhere else and carried outside the gate and then stabbed. But the gate was guarded."

"Which could mean either Raulyn or Pers had been part in it," Dame Frevisse said.

Anne put in hurriedly, "Raulyn was twice away from the gate. Once of necessity, once to rouse Pers back to his post. Pers could have been away, too. For necessity. Like Raulyn."

"How was that?" Daved asked.

Dame Frevisse made explanation, ending, "But it's trusting heavily to happenstance for the murderer to have happened on any such time to reach the gate."

"Not if he had seen Raulyn take Pers' place," Daved said. "He could within reason assume Raulyn would sometime go to fetch Pers back to duty, leaving the gate unguarded for that while."

"And in readiness for that, lured the friar from the solar, struck him unconscious . . ."

"So there would be no blood in the house to show it was done there."

"Then waited, hidden somewhere with the unconscious

body, until Master Grene left the gate, carried the friar to the gate and out, laid him down, stabbed him, slipped back inside the yard and to the house, all without being seen, in the time it took Master Grene to waken Pers and come into the yard again." Dame Frevisse's voice was gone dry with her deep doubt of all that.

"And he would maybe have had to set the body down to open the gate, too," Daved said, matching her doubt. "One thing, though—we're only supposing it was someone already here who did it, rather than someone from outside."

"You think someone came in? How? Over the rooftops?"

"Or over the wall. It's not beyond possibility for someone moving carefully and keeping low to come over a wall in darkness unseen and move silently through shadows."

"You speak as someone who knows," Dame Frevisse said.

Daved did not answer except to meet her sharp look and slightly smile. After a moment she gave him a narrow smile back, and with a start, Anne saw they were both enjoying their sharp trade of thoughts. And likewise saw that however far apart their lives were in most ways, here in this quest they were met on ground they both knew.

"So," Dame Frevisse said, "you're saying we now have to think that maybe someone came from outside, wanting the friar dead and knowing the house well enough to find him." She did not sound as if she thought that very likely.

"Finding him would be none so hard," Daved said. "He could likely be heard talking by anyone who chose to hear, either through the window or the door. And, yes, I see my uncle is to be suspected here."

"I take it, though," Dame Frevisse said, "from what you didn't say upstairs, that Brother Michael made no exclamation of surprise when he saw whoever was at the solar's door. Which means that whoever was there was someone he could reasonably expect to be there."

"One other thing," Daved said. "We've supposed that whoever put him outside the gate came back inside. They may not have. Is someone missing from here today? But," he added before she could answer that, "if they were going to leave anyway and thereby announce their guilt, why bother with killing him outside when they could have done it with less trouble inside? Thus, his murderer is most likely still here."

"Except we've also been supposing that Brother Michael was carried out the gate," Dame Frevisse said. "He could have been persuaded to go out, then struck down, then stabbed."

"Again, though," Daved said, "we come up against it having to be done when no one was be at the gate."

"That, yes."

They both fell silent. Overhead, feet were passing—people going back and forth as breakfast happened. Somewhere was daylight, the beginning of another day of near-siege and worry, and Anne wished she were there, with things no worse than they had been yesterday, instead of here in the shadows with new death in front of her and fear for Daved wrapping ever more closely around her.

"I'd like," said Daved, "to see the wound that killed him."

"It's in his back," Dame Frevisse answered, raising a hand to gesture Master Naylor forward.

Father Tomas raised his head. "You aren't going to strip him, are you? Not here, like this."

"No," Daved said quietingly. "I only want to see where the wound is placed. Has anyone done that?"

"Not yet," Dame Frevisse said. She had slipped the cross from under Brother Michael's hands and now stepped back to give Master Naylor and Daved space to ease Brother Michael's body over. Anne took one of the candles from its pricket and brought it where the light would fall better on the friar's back, taking care to keep from looking straight at him herself. Daved crouched down to him, though, and Dame Frevisse bent forward readily, and Daved said, "He was stabbed more than once." And after pause, "Four times. You see?"

"Four times," Dame Frevisse agreed. "Yes."

"None straight to the heart," Daved said. "But together enough to do the work."

"Master Naylor," Dame Frevisse said, looking up at him. "Would you, now that there's light enough and hopefully before too many people have passed, go see how much blood there is on the paving outside the gate? Let's be more certain that's where he was actually killed."

"Because if it was not," Daved said, "then somewhere there is likely a quantity of blood besides what's soaked into his robe, and that might tell us something."

Master Naylor gave a slight, curt bow and left. Daved started to roll the body onto its back again, but Dame Frevisse caught at the dead right hand, said, "Wait," and held it into the candlelight to see it better.

"What?" Daved asked. Both he and Father Tomas shifted to look, too.

"His fingers," Dame Frevisse said. "There's blood on them."

"Blood?" Daved said, puzzled. "His own?"

"Lay him on his back again," Father Tomas said, suddenly firm with command. Daved did, and the priest took the candle from Anne and held it so the light fell full on Brother Michael's face. "There," said Father Tomas. "On his forehead. He signed himself with the cross there."

Even Anne leaned nearer to see. Because the body should not be washed until the crowner or at least a constable had seen it, there was still street-dirt on the friar's face and so the cross was not readily seen, but it was there on his brow, small and uneven and undeniably in blood, darkened though it was by now.

Very softly Dame Frevisse said, "He came enough to his senses to grope at the pain in his back. Enough to know he was dying."

"But why didn't he cry out?" Father Tomas said. "Even dying, why didn't he cry out for help?"

"He was stabbed at least twice into his lungs," Daved said grimly. "They were probably filling with blood. He could make no cry that would be heard."

"All he could do," Dame Frevisse said, "struggling to breathe and guessing he was dying, was sign himself with the cross. In hope of his soul's salvation."

Father Tomas turned to put the candle back on its pricket. In the shifting light, Dame Frevisse laid Brother Michael's wooden cross on his chest again, was laying his hands over it when Daved said quietly, "It was not a skilled killing."

Dame Frevisse paused, then lifted her head to meet his gaze and said as quietly, "No more than was Hal's."

In the deeper quiet that followed, they went on looking at each other, nothing alike in any outward seeming, but at that moment looking very alike in the way their thoughts were running fast behind their eyes.

Never had Anne felt further from Daved. How did he come to know so much of stealth and wounds and killing? She'd known she knew only a little of his life. Was maybe what she knew not merely little but the very least part? And was she the least part of the least part? How very, very little part was she in his life at all?

Chapter 22

ore aware of the cellar's darkness all around her than she had been, Frevisse lowered her gaze from Daved's, back to the friar's body. She had learned all she was likely to learn from it. It was only another darkness now, like the darkness of the cellar, the life put out the way the candles' light would, in a while, be put out. With the difference that the candles could be relighted when they were next needed, but there was no use left to Brother Michael's body. It was only dross and waste, to be buried before its decay became an offense.

Against that thought, though, had to be set the knowing that when the candles were burned out, they were utterly gone, vanished as if they had never been, but in the Last

Days, when God's final Judgment came, all of mankind's bodies would be called forth, the souls returned to them for their eternity in Heaven or in Hell.

She wondered sometimes why, since the body was such an undesirable thing—unceasingly demanding, treacherous in its desires, a constant barrier between the soul and freedom—souls had to return to them at Judgment Day. She had never presumed to ask that of a priest, had settled for supposing it was because when God created bodies and souls at the beginning of all, he had meant them to be one, and at the Last Judgment their unity—lost by Eve's and Adam's fall from grace—would be restored.

Except for those damned to Hell forever. Their bodies restored to them would never be a blessing, only eternal torment, and that was a thought with which she was never easy, save at moments like this when her anger burned deep at whoever would make such cold and willful deaths as these of the friar and the boy Hal.

Except that neither murder had been cold. Their bodies had been stabbed and stabbed again as if for the pleasure of it, for the pleasure in the power to do it. And that someone had killed with pleasure—had maybe even killed *for* pleasure—and with no care for what pain he brought to anyone else was a fearful thought.

Someone like that might well deserve Hell's torments for all of eternity.

And that these two murders were so much the same fairly ended the possibility that the boy's murder and the friar's were by chance or different people. Instead, even not knowing the why behind the murders, she had to think the murderer was likely someone here among them, and she stood up with a fierce desire to be away from the cellar's crowding shadows, into clean air and light. "I'm done here," she said and started toward the stairs.

"What if I choose simply to leave here after all?" Daved asked, staying where he was. "You're the only one likely to give order to stop me. Would you?"

"I thought you were determined to stay."

"Would you order your men to stop me? I'm after all a Jew and maybe a murderer twice over."

"Daved," Anne said in distress.

Frevisse, understanding his challenge, met it straight on. "Even if I believed in ritual killings of Christian children by Jews, I doubt you're fool enough to do it here in London, nor have I heard any reason why you'd want Hal dead. Therefore, I have no reason to lay his murder on you. You might well have killed Brother Michael. He was your deadly foe. But the manner of his killing does not set well with you having done it. And you were bound and helpless when he died and therefore are clear of it that way, too."

"Which settles the likelihood of my being a murderer. What of my being a Jew?"

"I've told you I've no quarrel with you because of that, whatever the Inquisition claims to the contrary. That you're here at all is flat against England's law, and that is another matter, but given the misguidance and corruption of England's laws these past years and the chaos into which London is presently fallen because of it, I do not find myself at all moved toward denouncing you on that front, either."

"And the matter between Mistress Blakhall and myself?"

Frevisse held silent, considering her answer before finally saying, "It's not for me to judge. Lest I be judged."

Something in her answers must have satisfied him, because he said, "It wasn't Mistress Blakhall who cut me loose."

"Daved!" Anne protested.

He slipped a small knife from the inside of his left sleeve and held it out for Frevisse to take. It was small, hardly

more than the length of a man's finger and some of that was
the bone hilt, but the blade looked to be sharp enough.

"I set to work to win free as soon as the friar left me,"
Daved said. "I'd only just finished when Mistress Blakhall
came in."

Frevisse gave back the knife. "Those ropes weren't thin.
It would have taken a lengthy time with a blade that small
to cut yourself free, supposing you could reach the knife or
ropes at all."

"There are ways to keep from being tied too tightly,"
Daved answered evenly. "Also a skill to tying men so they
can't move at all. I have the first skill. Your Master Naylor
does not have the second. So the business was not so hard as
it might have been."

"Show me your wrists."

Daved pushed his doublet and shirt sleeve up one arm,
then the other, and held them out. On his left forearm was
strapped a small sheath, the knife in it again—Frevisse had
not seen him return it—and both his wrists were the
scraped-raw of someone who had twisted hard against binding ropes. Anne gave a low gasp, but Frevisse only nodded
acceptance of what she saw. She did not think he was a man
who would struggle without purpose. If he had fought the
ropes that hard, it was because he had a chance of freeing
himself just as he had said. But, "Why tell me?"

Pulling down his sleeves, Daved said readily, "Because
if we are able to learn better when the friar was killed,
then maybe we can learn who was not where they should
have been then and therefore could have done it." He
looked at Father Tomas. "Father, where did you spend the
night?"

The priest looked startled to be suddenly included in
their talk. "I slept," he said. "All the night."

"Where?" Frevisse pressed.

"In the chamber above the screens passage."

"There's a small room there behind the minstrel gallery," Daved said. "It's where my uncle and I have slept since Mistress Hercy has the guest chamber. We shared it with Raulyn two nights ago. I suppose he was there last night, too."

"He settled to bed when I did," Father Tomas said.

"Did Brother Michael come there at all last night, Father?" Frevisse asked.

"No. Unless so quietly I never woke, and I think I would have. I did not sleep that well. I knew when Master Grene went out and came back."

"When was that?" asked Daved.

"I do not know the times, only that I was asleep between them."

"He went more than once?" Daved prompted.

"Twice, yes. I doubt he slept much at all."

"Was he gone long?" Frevisse asked.

"I slept and half-slept the while. I could not truly say for how long he went."

"You couldn't guess at what times he left?" Frevisse prodded. "Or when he came back?"

"The watch has not called the hours for two nights now," Father Tomas pointed out.

"And the chamber's one window is small and faces west," Daved said. "So there's not even much help of star-shift or moonlight."

"That is the way of it, yes," Father Tomas said, sounding grateful for the help. "I know he was there when someone came to tell him Brother Michael had been found."

"Can we go somewhere other than here?" Anne asked suddenly.

Daved put an arm around her and drew her to his side, saying, "We can go up, yes. There's no more we need do here."

But as Daved led Anne away, Father Tomas did not move from where he stood beyond Brother Michael's body; and when Frevisse looked questioningly at him, he said, "Someone should be here with him. To pray for him."

Something under his words said he thought Frevisse should stay, too, but she only gave him a short nod before following Anne and Daved away to the stairs. The lesser shadows of the screens passage were welcome after the cellar, but Frevisse found Daved alone there and asked, "Where's Mistress Blakhall gone?"

He bent his head toward the other stairs. "To find something to put on my wrists."

Watching his face, she said, "She cares most deeply for you."

"As I care for her," he answered steadily back.

"She can't go with you when you leave."

"It would be her death to do so, yes."

"So when all is done, you'll go free and clear, back to whatever else is your life, and she'll be left to her shame."

"You mis-guess," Daved said, his gaze and voice level. "Whatever comes, I'll never be 'free and clear' of our love. No more than I would be clear of an inward wound that never heals."

"You see love as a wound?"

"Where the joys of it are brief and rare, and the pain often and long, yes. Love then is a wound. But rather that wound than that our love had never been."

"You'll not dare return to England after this. She'll be left alone with both her inward pain *and* shame."

Daved's own pain showed then in the tightened twist of his mouth, as if Anne's pain added to his was more than he could hide; but he met Frevisse's challenge with his own, saying, "Have you never had in your life an outward shame worth the cost of holding to an inward truth? Haven't you ever chosen the pain and cost of holding to that truth because to deny it would have corrupted your very soul?"

Silent, Frevisse held his gaze with her own for a long moment, letting him read there what he could, then said, "You're far more than a merchant, aren't you?"

His face lighted with one of his sudden smiles. "Aren't we all far more than only our outward seeming? You are, aren't you?"

That was another question she would not directly answer but said instead, "Show me the stairs to this upper chamber where you and your uncle slept."

He pointed past her right shoulder. "It's there."

She turned and saw a narrow gap in the wall easily missed in the passage's half-light. Closer look showed it gave onto a steep upward stairs so narrow a man would have to twist a little sideways to clear the walls as he went up or down. Frevisse did not favor trying them herself and settled for asking, "There's no other way from the chamber than this?"

"Only the window that only a child could use."

"Is a light kept along here at night?"

"No."

"In the hall itself?"

"Not last night. Master Grene thought a darkened house less likely to draw unwanted eyes. The shutters were left open, though, for what light might come in."

That meant that someone at the foot of these stairs would have been almost certain of going unseen while waiting to be sure the way was clear to the parlor or wherever else he might want to go unnoted.

"Where was the household sleeping if no one was in the hall?"

"They've been all together in the kitchen these past two nights. To keep each other's courage up, and because shifting the guards is easier if everyone is in the same place."

At the passage's far end the outer door opened, letting in morning light and Master Naylor with Dickon and the man

Pers close behind him. Frevisse went toward them, meeting them at the doorway into the hall where sight of the table being cleared by two maidservants awoke her to her own hunger, and with a small sign to Master Naylor to follow she went that way. There was only bread and cheese and ale, and the portions the maids gave her and Master Naylor and Daved were small, with one of the maids giving a laughing shake of her head at Dickon when he put out a hopeful hand.

"You've had yours," she said.

Frevisse's own thought, watching her set down the bread knife, was that it was a pity there was no way to compare the dagger-thrusts into Brother Michael with those that had killed Hal, to tell if they had maybe been made by the same weapon.

One of the maids, handing a cut of cheese to Daved, asked him, "So why was the friar angry at you, and where's Master Bocking gone?"

That she could ask those questions was some assurance the household still mostly did not know exactly what had passed or why. And Daved smiled warmly and said easily, "Goodly questions to which, alas, I cannot make goodly answers. My uncle is gone his own way, the friar is beyond answering for himself, and I cannot."

Before the maid could take it further, Frevisse, with her hunger a little quieted by a few bites of food, said, "Pers, how did you come to find Brother Michael outside the gate? Did you hear him? Did he make a sound or was it something else?"

"It wasn't anything, my lady," Pers said. "It was just it was come light enough I saw the door in the gate wasn't barred anymore. That's not right, I thought."

"Then he went and opened it, like a dullard," one of the maids said. "There could have been anybody out there."

"I listened first, didn't I?" Pers returned hotly. "I didn't hear anything. If someone had been wanting to come in, they would have by then, the door already being unbarred. Right?" he demanded of Master Naylor.

Master Naylor granted that with a small nod, less from certainty, Frevisse guessed, than to keep Pers talking. Which Pers did, going on, "So I looked out and saw the friar lying there. I didn't know it was the friar right off. There wasn't that much light yet. But I could see it was someone and in a long gown, so I guessed it wasn't one of the rebels." He was warming to the chance to talk about it and be listened to. "I couldn't hear any trouble nearby, so I went out, and that's when I saw it was the friar, and I thought he was dead, but I couldn't leave him there, see. That's why I dragged the body in before I went for Master Grene."

"Closing and barring the door first, I hope," the other maid said scathingly.

"Aye, I did that. I'm not a fool!" Pers shot back.

To the maid Frevisse said, "It was you came to fetch Mistress Hercy. Where did Master Grene find you, to send you to her?"

"It was Pers, my lady. After he woke Master Grene and told him, he was sent to tell the rest of us and that someone was to bring Mistress Hercy."

"Where were you?" Frevisse asked. "Where were the rest of you?"

"The kitchen. All of us that weren't on watch, like. We've done that the past two nights."

"Cook snores like nobody's business," Pers said. "No one gets good sleep around him. That's why I was sleepy when Master Grene—"

"Outright sleeping is more like it," the other maid said.

"I was *sleepy*," Pers said hotly, "when Master Grene found me. Can I go?" he added at Master Naylor.

"If she's done with you," Master Naylor said, looking at Frevisse. She saw he and Daved had finished eating, while she still held her hardly tasted bread and cheese, and one of the maids was holding out a pottery cup of ale to her.

"Yes. I'm done. Thank you," she said, taking the cup.

Pers gave her a bow, started to reach for a piece of bread as he made to leave, and had his hand heartily slapped by the nearest maid. The other woman had begun to clear the table, and Frevisse ate hurriedly, thinking. With the household folk all in the kitchen except for those on guard, anyone could have come and gone as they pleased through the rest of the house without being noted if they went silently. Certainly no one seemed to have heard whoever came to the solar for Brother Michael, or the friar go through the hall with him, as he must have done.

Supposing she believed someone had come to the solar for him. There was the possibility that Brother Michael had simply fallen asleep there and Daved had cut himself free and struck him with something while he slept, then taken him out of the gate and killed him . . . But that raised the problem of why Daved would then have come back inside. Those dark hours before dawn were when he could have passed through the streets with least trouble. Was there something here he needed?

And still there was the problem of getting past whoever held guard at the gate, whatever time it was done. And it could have been done before Pers' watch, come to that. How long had it taken Daved to cut himself free?

Or what if Master Grene *was* part of it, his whole business of relieving Pers on watch simply to aid Daved in getting Brother Michael into the street. But having done that, why not take the friar farther, leave him dead somewhere other than just outside the gate here?

She was back to needing to know who had come to the solar's door. *If* someone had come to the door there. And she wanted to hear what Master Naylor had found. And . . . She found she had finished the bread and cheese without knowing it and was staring into her cup of untouched ale. She drank it hurriedly, put it down, and said to Master Naylor and Daved, "We should go to the solar, I think." And to the maids, "Where is Master Grene? Do you know?"

"With his wife, my lady."

"Someone has been sent for the constable or crowner or sheriff or someone?"

"Rafe went, my lady. He was to see what there was to buy at the market, too, and find out what he can about what's happening with the rebels. He's not come back yet, nor anybody he went to fetch."

"They're likely over-busy with the living," Daved said.

That was true, and it was not a comfort-laden thought. Frevisse did not suppose she was the only one here to think the troubles in London had yet to reach their worst.

As she made to go toward the solar with Master Naylor, Dickon, and Daved, Anne came into the hall carrying a deep, apparently heavy bowl covered by a linen towel in both hands, with an open-topped pottery pot clamped against her under one arm. Daved immediately turned back to take the bowl from her.

"Have you eaten?" he asked.

"In the kitchen. While I made this." She had the pot safely in her hands now. "For a poultice for your wrists."

They went on to the solar, but as they went in, following Master Naylor, Frevisse paused to look back the hall's length, trying in her mind to see how it had been here in the night. Dark save for whatever light came through the two tall, narrow windows, and that would have only barely thinned the darkness. Dark and empty. If Brother Michael had not been struck down in the solar itself, then it was here someone had felled him with that blow to the back of his head. With what was only too easily answered: the wooden clubs kept beside the outer door were all too readily at hand. Nor had he been a large man. Carrying his body rather than dragging it would have been possible for another man, who "only" needed then to cross the yard into the darkness of the gateway passage and go out the gate unseen. It needed great daring to have chanced that.

Unless Master Grene was the murderer.

Or Pers. Maybe he was secretly a Lollard and had seen Brother Michael a foe to be rid of. But would Brother Michael have left the solar for him, with him?

If it was choice between Pers and Master Grene, she had to favor Master Grene. He, after all, had a sure, clear way to the gate once he sent Pers to sleep. And he had reason to want Brother Michael dead. But if he had done it, had he done it alone? There could have been Daved. Or Father Tomas. Or both of them, both with reason to want the friar dead.

And still chance could not be ruled out altogether. Maybe Brother Michael *had* chosen to try leaving secretly and been killed in the street by someone. Master Bocking? Or Master Bocking had come into the house secretly and . . . But Brother Michael would have exclaimed at seeing him at the door. But she had only Daved's word that he had not. But why leave Daved still tied once Brother Michael was down?

And how did the boy Hal's death tie to it all, if it did?

The circle of possiblities and likelihoods were small, but they tangled back and forth and in and out on one another, and it was with a flare of impatience that Frevisse went into the solar, glad she did not have to face Master Grene at that moment and wishing Daved Weir *had* escaped in the night. It would have made all this so much the simpler.

Chapter 23

Anne pointed Daved toward a flat-topped chest near the window, where the light was best and they could sit with the bowl between them while she tended to his hurt wrists and Dame Frevisse went on with all these questions of hers. Anne had expected prayers from her, or that she would see to helping Mistress Hercy soothe Pernell. What was she doing with all these questions? Did she think she was going to find out the friar's murderer?

At least she was better toward Daved than Anne would have thought she would be. But the quick working of her mind and Daved's together was unquieting, and Anne took the chance as Daved set down the bowl and her back and his were to the room to say to him, low-voiced, "You should have gone on letting it seem I'd freed you."

As quietly, Daved said, "We won't come to find out the friar's murderer by lies."

"Do we care who killed him?"

"We have to care. Else we may become as careless of others' lives as he was. Besides, with all the lies I live in, I like to dare the truth sometimes."

He had begun to take off his doublet, but the scraped-raw wounds on his wrists had crusted and stiffened by now. He winced with the pain of them, and Anne put his hands aside and moved behind him to slip his doublet off him herself, then set it aside before they sat down on either side of the bowl, with Daved holding out first one arm and then the other for her to loosen his somewhat bloodied sleeves and fold them up his arms.

In the middle of the room, Master Naylor was answering Dame Frevisse's crisp questions about what he had found in the street with, "Very little. There was only a slight smearing of blood on the paving there, probably from when Pers rolled him over. That's how it would be if he was lying face down, with his thick friar's robe to soak up most of what flowed."

"He was maybe bleeding inside more than outwardly, too," Dame Frevisse said. "Do you think he was stabbed there? Or is it more likely he was stabbed elsewhere and carried there?"

Anne took the towel from the bowl, uncovering the barely steaming water; laid the towel across her lap; took one of Daved's hands and eased it into the water that was deep enough to mostly cover his wrist. He drew in his breath with a teeth-gritted hiss of pain.

Slowly, as if grudging to give his mind, Master Naylor was saying, "Anyone who carried him after he was stabbed would almost surely have blood on them afterward. Blood is hard to be rid of. If whoever killed him had any sense, they killed him there."

"It would help to know with whom he left this room," Dame Frevisse said. "Do you know—or you, Dickon—if anyone among the servants came here during the night?"

"Not that I know of," Master Naylor said. And, "No," from Dickon, before Master Naylor added, "Given the friar is dead, you'll not likely get anyone to admit they were here, whether they killed him or not."

"Has anyone said they saw anyone where they shouldn't have been last night? Or did you see anyone?"

"Nothing and no one," Master Naylor answered.

"Nor me," said Dickon.

Anne went on gently cleaning the crusted blood from Daved's wrist, aware he was listening as Master Naylor went on, "I'd say, though, they're not looking uneasily among themselves. Not even at Pers. No one has said anything about anyone not being where they were expected to be in the night—all asleep or else standing guard."

"I'd swear the cook slept all night," Dickon said with feeling. "I could hear his snores even while on watch in the rearyard."

"When was that?"

"From midnight until as near to three of the clock as I could guess."

"Who took your place?"

"Wyett."

"You heard and saw nothing and no one in your while?"

"I heard men shouting and laughter and suchlike from a street or so away a few times early on, less later. All I saw were a couple of cats passing by along the fence tops."

"Nothing from inside the house here?"

"Just the cook's snoring sometimes."

Finished washing Daved's right wrist, Anne lifted it to her lap to dry it, nodding he should put the other one to soak.

"Master Naylor?" Dame Frevisse asked.

"My night went the same as Dickon's, except I had the early watch on the front gate and heard far more shouts, laughter, all the rest. Only a few clots of idiots came right past, though."

"On their way between Lombard Street and Candlewick," Daved said. "There being no tavern on St. Swithin's to keep them here."

Anne spread the herb poultice on a strip of clean cloth and wrapped it firmly over the rope-cuts. Dame Frevisse went on asking the Naylors more about the night and what they had since heard and seen among the household, and Anne began to clean Daved's other wrist. The wound there was deeper; he winced and made a small, unwilling sound of pain. She couldn't spare him pain, though, and went on; and he leaned forward and kissed the top of her bowed head, then whispered in her ear, laughter in his voice, "You see? I'm being Christian. Returning good for evil."

Anne lifted her head enough to smile at him, heart-warmed as always by the laughter in his voice. But the warmth was small this time, crushed in the cold grip of her great fear, and she ducked her head down again lest he see the too quickly starting tears.

Still leaning close, still low-voiced, Daved asked, "This penance of yours. Do you truly think of our love as sin?"

Busy being gentle with his wound, Anne could do nothing to stop the tear that brimmed over and fell, its splash small in the basin; but her voice held steady as she answered, eyes still down, "Love is never a sin."

"Yet you do penance."

"What we do . . ." Anne faltered over a way to say what she had always felt more clearly than thought. "What we *do* together is where the sin is, unmarried to each other as we are. It's for that I do penance. *Not* for our love." Then she straightened, lifted her dripping hands to take hold of his face on

either side, and not caring who was there to see it, not caring
if he saw her tears, drew him to her and kissed him, fierce with
both her passion and her fear. And when she had done, she
drew back from him and said, looking straight into his eyes,
"Rather our sin and my penance than the worse sin of denying
our love or our need for each other." Then she returned to
cleansing his wound, aware that across the room all talk had
stopped and that they were being stared at. She refused to care
and did not look up as Dame Frevisse came toward them.

But Daved said, "My lady," and Dame Frevisse, beside
them now, said back, "Your hurts are worse than they seemed
in the cellar. You didn't win free easily."

"No," Daved agreed evenly. "I did not."

"Nor quickly."

"No, nor quickly."

"Had you succeeded just before we found you?"

"Yes."

"Do you think it had taken you a whole watch, or had
Brother Michael been gone less than that?"

"I'd say less than that."

"Why wasn't there anyone else here?"

"Once I was bound, there was no need. Master Grene
asked Master Naylor to take the early watch and said your
other man would do better sleeping, to be ready for his turn
on watch."

"But Brother Michael stayed with you the whole time."

"The whole time, and a great weariness he was. A very
learned man too willing to share his learning at length and
long."

"Was it all theology he talked?" Dame Frevisse asked.
"Or other things? Such as any enemies he might have."

"All theology. I had little liking for your Bernard of
Clairvaux before this. Now I like him even less. But your
Thomas of Aquinas—would that he had run out of pens and
ink before he ever started, that one."

"But nothing about himself?"

"Nothing. I think his learning was all his life."

"His faith," Dame Frevisse corrected. "His faith was his life and the reason for his learning."

Daved gave her an odd, considering look. "Was the reason for his learning his faith or his fear?"

"His fear?"

"Of life. Or of death. Or of both. Most of us live by refusing to look at those common fears. He was a brave man, in his way. Having looked, he maybe then refuged in learning, setting other men's words around him for a wall against his fears, his doubts, and any questionings. Therefore his need to be so certain of everything, and his need to find out and be rid of anyone who doubted the faith that was his hiding place."

It a little frightened Anne when Daved went so far into thoughts she had never had. She was drying his wrist, taking great care over it so she would not have to look up while waiting for Dame Frevisse's answer that was slow in coming. And then it did not come at all, the nun asking instead, "Where did you sleep last night, Mistress Blakhall?"

Beginning to spread the poultice on another strip of cloth, Anne still did not look up as she answered, "In Mistress Hercy's chamber."

"Where is that?"

"Above here." She glanced at the ceiling, then met Dame Frevisse's look. "So I'm as suspect in Brother Michael's death as anyone else."

"More suspect," Dame Frevisse said evenly. "It being your lover the friar held prisoner."

"She could have struck him down," Daved said quickly. "But she could not have moved his body."

"She could have struck him down," Dame Frevisse returned as quickly, "then freed you, for you to move his body, and then you both waited here to be found in seeming innocence."

"Does that seem likely to you?" Daved challenged.

"No. Had that been the way of it, more likely you'd have had her go back to her bed and pretend ignorance of everything, including that you were free. Mistress Blakhall, did you hear aught?"

Beginning to wrap the poultice around Daved's wrist, Anne said, "Sounds from the streets of course and Brother Michael talking on and on. I couldn't hear what he was saying, only his voice and sometimes Daved's."

"Did you sleep any of the night?"

"No."

"So you were awake when someone knocked at the door. You heard the knock."

"I heard it, but nothing else. Not anyone speak to Brother Michael."

"How soon after it did you come downstairs?"

"I . . . don't know. I was pacing. I'd been pacing for hours, I think. In the dark."

"You probably looked out the window sometimes. Did you ever see anyone in the yard? Before then or later?"

"No one. The man at the gate once when he walked out into the yard from the passageway. But he went back into the shadows there again."

"Did you come down soon after the knock, or long?"

Anne was now binding the poulticed cloth around Daved's wrist. Without looking up, she answered, "Long. I didn't understand Brother Michael was gone away. I knew the talking had stopped, but only after a while, because of the knock, I thought he might have gone away and came down in hope I might see—just see—Daved."

"And found Brother Michael gone and Daved free," Dame Frevisse said.

"Yes." When was the nun going to give it up and leave them in peace? Anne finished tying the cloth in place but kept her eyes down and hold of Daved's hand. "I wish I'd come sooner and saved you this," she said.

Daved leaned forward to place a kiss gently on Anne's brow before he took his hand from her, stood up, and asked of Frevisse, "May I talk aside with you a little while?"

Anne started to say something, but Daved silenced her with a small movement of his hand while Frevisse from her eye's corner saw Master Naylor stiffen, disapproving; but she said evenly, "Surely," and let Daved lead her aside to the room's far corner. There, the better to keep their words to themselves, they stood with their backs to everyone, looking more to the wall than each other as Daved said, keeping his voice low, "You've asked near to all the questions there are to ask, haven't you?"

Frevisse held to tight-lipped silence a moment, then unwillingly admitted, "Yes."

"Without yet a set answer to who killed the friar."

Again Frevisse held silent, weighing whether she wanted this talk with him or not, then said, "No. As it stands now, the only things of which I'm sure are that Brother Michael was struck down somewhere, and that he was stabbed to death. Probably in the street outside the gate. Beyond that, nothing I've yet learned lets me sort the lies from the truths in what I've been told."

"Lies. Truths. They're sometimes hard to tell apart even at the best of times." Daved smiled his warm and sudden smile. "And both can be unpleasant to live with."

Frevisse was in no humour for either philosophy or his smile and snapped, "As for lies, you should know more about them than most, given how much you live in one."

He made a small bow of his head to her, his smile deepening. "But don't all of us live with lies? Some of us with small lies and few. Others of us with large lies and many. Or few and large. Or many and small. Or—"

"*You* don't live simply with a lie," Frevisse said. "You live *in* a lie. A lie far larger than the lies most people live with. So far as I've learned, your life is almost entirely a lie."

Daved's gaze held steady on her but his smile faded to no more than a slight bitterness turning up the corners of his mouth, and very softly he said, "There is presently a German bishop who has decreed 'his' Jews are to be expelled from all his lands. Their properties, their businesses, their homes are all to be left behind, and they are to go elsewhere unless they pay him a very great sum of money. He is, in other words, holding them to ransom. He's one of many who play this 'game,' sometimes with only a Jew or two, sometimes with many. A few years ago it was a duke holding a Jew's wife and daughter hostage, threatening to forcibly baptize the girl if the Jew did not pay what the duke demanded. What I do in my lie of a life is gather money—by such services as this to your cousin— to satisfy such Christians as this bishop and that duke. I live lies to keep my people alive a little longer." Daved's bitter smile had lingered until then. Now it altogether disappeared, and he said very quietly but with steel edging his voice and no smile at all, "Which would be better—for me to live in 'truth' and watch these people be destroyed, or live in this 'lie' and, God willing, save them for a few years more?"

Frevisse held back her answer despite she knew it, but finally gave way and said, knowing how many would have condemned her for it, "It's better that you save them."

"I will," Daved assured her, that glint of bitter steel still under his voice.

The silence drew out between them as they looked straight at each other, each of them reading in the other what neither of them would say, until into the silence Frevisse said quietly, "The trouble here is how to sort out the truths and the lies from what I've been told."

And how had she come to this, she wondered: to be seeking out the murderer of a Christian with the help of a Jew whom that Christian would have brought to his death if he had not died instead? But she believed the reasons Daved had given her for staying when he could have fled and believed he wanted the friar's murderer found; and since Christ had said he was "the way, the truth, and the life," was Daved in his search for the truth maybe less Christ's enemy than Brother Michael had been with his readiness to hatred and willingness to destroy?

God help her, but if ever it had come to choice of which of the two men was better, her choice would have been Daved Weir.

Very quietly Daved said, "You know where your questions have brought you."

She knew. And by the way he said it, Daved knew, too.

"If not you," she said, "then Father Tomas or Master Grene."

Daved's slow nod agreed with her.

"The trouble," Frevisse said, "is that we have nothing like proof for either one."

"We have another murder," Daved said quietly.

"Whoever killed Brother Michael might only have copied what we think was done to the boy." First the luring out, the striking down, the moving of the unconscious body, then the killing.

"Copied it but not been Hal's murderer, only the friar's. Possible, yes," Daved granted. "But how many here know that well what was done to Hal? You. I. Anne. Raulyn. Father Tomas."

Slowly Frevisse said, "All of whom, save me, might have reason for Brother Michael's death. But for Hal's?"

"But if the boy, then surely the friar, too."

"*Almost* surely." Though she was sure.

"Almost surely. So. We have to find out who profited from Hal's death, because profit is the most likely reason for it."

"I don't see how Father Tomas . . ."

Frevisse stopped.

Daved finished the thought for her. ". . . how Father Tomas would profit from the boy's death. No. Unless you believe his Christian priesthood is only covering a desire to kill Christian boys in Jewish rituals of murder."

Frevisse gave him the dismissing look that suggestion deserved.

"But if not Father Tomas, then Raulyn," Daved said. "He is, for the friar's murder, very likely. Who could move more freely through the house last night than he could? Who could be more certain of the gate when he needed it? Who had to depend less on chance in everything last night?"

No one else. That was so certain Frevisse did not need to say it. "But why . . ." She stopped, trying to shape the question clearly in her own mind. Daved cocked his head at her, willingly waiting, bright question in his eyes, until she finally said, "But why would he think he could get away with the same kind of murder twice, and so near together?"

Daved gave a smooth shrug. "Why does someone think they can get away with murder at all? Planned murders, anyway, rather than ones done on the instant and in anger. To plan to be a murderer, someone has to think others are too stupid to see through their cleverness. Raulyn has always had great belief in his own cleverness."

"I thought he was your friend," Frevisse said. "He's known what you are and kept your secret for years here in London. If he killed Brother Michael, even that's to your good. Why be so ready to think him a murderer?"

For answer, Daved turned his head to look over his right shoulder at Anne, still seated on the chest but leaned back against the wall now, her eyes closed. The grey shadowing under her eyes argued she had told the truth about not sleeping at all last night; or if she had, it had been little and lightly; and Daved said, gentle-voiced, "When I leave her this time, I may never be able to come back to her. Therefore I'd leave her as safe as might be. If Raulyn has killed twice, whatever his reasons, there's nothing to say he won't kill again if he finds reason to." He returned his gaze to Frevisse. "He desires her. I don't think she knows it, but he does. I've seen his look at her sometimes, and there have been things he's said. If I am gone for good and all, then maybe he thinks he has hope of her. He . . ."

Daved stopped with a sickened look, as if he had bitten down on something foul. Frevisse took only a bare second to see where his thought went next, and with that same sickened feeling that showed on his face, she said, "Then he could have cut those marks on Hal's body deliberately to . . ."

". . . to set people thinking about secret Jews in London, not only to confuse who had done the murder but to make me wary about returning any time soon. Thinking that if Anne despaired of me, she might be willing to him." Anger, not there before, darkened Daved's voice. "If Brother Michael hadn't been there, Raulyn would have named the cuts as Hebrew himself. What he didn't know was Father Tomas' secret. That Father Tomas would say they were false."

"But how would Raulyn know anything of Hebrew letters at all? Even enough to make false ones." But she answered her own question before Daved could. "Books. A picture of Moses with the tablets of the law with a few marks on them meant to be Hebrew. Or Melchisedek with a scroll. I've seen such. But if he wants Anne, why not simply kill you?"

Daved's laugh was brief and bitter. "And lose the profits that come his way through me? I think not. Even if I no longer came myself because of what's passed, I'm his way to others who would come in my stead, and he knows it. He wouldn't want me dead, only out of his way."

"But Hal's death," Frevisse said slowly, thinking as she went. "It didn't have to be the boy he killed and then marked. It could have been anyone. No." She found the objection to that. "It had to be someone he would be called to see, so he could point out the marks were Jewish, lest no one else did. That Brother Michael happened to be there saved him the trouble. But one of his own servants dead would have done as well. Would have been better, given what Hal's death has done to Pernell." She paused, thinking it further, then said more slowly, "Maybe we should suppose the marks were merely a 'benefit' added to another purpose altogether."

"With any secretly done death the question always is who profits from it. The question here, then, is how would Raulyn profit from Hal's death if there was more to it than being rid of me? From all I know, only Lucie profits from Hal's death. The inheritance that was split between them will now be all hers."

"Does Raulyn profit from that? No," she answered for herself. "Mistress Hercy has already told me how that stands. Hal's death hasn't gained Raulyn anything, and it cost him the profit he would have had from selling Hal's marriage."

"Come to it," Daved said slowly, "seen from one way, Brother Michael stood likely to have the most profit from Hal's death. Hunting down Jews was far more to his pleasure than pursuing only Lollards."

With distaste and disbelief, Frevisse said stiffly, "You don't truly think he killed and mutilated the boy."

"No. If we're going to so far afield for possibilities, we might as well consider if there's a Lollard in the household here took this chance to be rid of him."

That being a thought she had already had, Frevisse granted unwillingly, "That's possible."

"But again, there's the matter of the gate. Of being sure of it."

"Unless it was one of the men during his turn at guard there. There was at least one besides Pers, after Master Naylor."

"But he couldn't have been sure of anything here in the house," Daved said. "All his hazard would lie this way instead of the other and still be large. We're brought back to the only one who could be sure both ways."

To Raulyn Grene.

Chapter 24

e're back to gain," Frevisse said. "What does Raulyn gain by Brother Michael's death?"

"First, chance for me to escape," Daved said readily. "He gets rid of me. Second, safety from any stir of trouble over Jews because who is there left to raise it?"

"Myself. The Naylors. We know."

"But Raulyn can count on your silence because you have a secret to keep, too."

Barely, Frevisse held back from raising a hand to the hidden gold. He was right—she would not dare draw attention to herself that might bring on questions about why she was in London.

"For the same reason, you'll order your men to silence," Daved said. "But even if they made report to the bishop despite of you, how interested—with all else that's happening—is he likely to be over alleged Jews no longer here? Raulyn would claim he knew nothing of what we were and might, at most, be fined for his ignorance. The friar would never have settled for so little, would have raised far more trouble. Now he won't."

"Daved," Anne said from just behind them. With their backs mostly to the room and intent in their talk, they had not noted her rise and cross to them, Daved's doublet folded over her arm. They turned to her, and worriedly she said, "You're near to dropping. You need to sleep. Go to bed. I'll mend your doublet the while."

Frevisse was a little ashamed she had been so in talk she had not noted how near to dropping he looked, and she said, "Mistress Blakhall says aright. You should rest a time. The questions we need next answered I think are for me to do."

Before Daved could begin an answer, Raulyn flung into the room exclaiming, "We've got the barriers up at either end of the lane and at the alley end, and there's word Cade's not getting yesterday's welcome at the Guildhall. Sure as sinning, there's going to be trouble." He sat on the edge of his desk, catching his breath and grinning. "Come to it, it looks to be trouble breaking out all over London. I'm for the streets to see what's happening. Who's with me?"

"Raulyn, you can't!" Anne said. "What of Pernell?"

"You'll keep her better company than I can. Daved, you'll come?"

Before Anne could protest that, Daved said evenly, "I'll stay here and see to things."

Raulyn looked to Master Naylor. "What about you?"

"My charge is here," Master Naylor replied as evenly as Daved had; and added at Dickon, "Nor you're not going anywhere, either."

"You're a dull lot!" Raulyn laughed. "I'm away then." And was gone.

For one long, blank moment no one did more than stare after him, Frevisse trying to match what he outward seemed to what she feared he inward was, before Anne said wonderingly, "He's eager for it."

"His blood-lust is up," Daved said grimly. "A liking for sight of other men's blood. Crowmer and Lord Saye provided it yesterday. Raulyn is hoping for more today." Ignoring Anne's stare at him, he said to Master Naylor, "With Master Grene gone, it will be his senior journeyman Wyett who should take over the household and watch. If we—"

"You're not fit to be doing aught," Master Naylor said bluntly. "All you look good for is to fall over. Better you do it on a bed. Wyett and I have been dealing together these two nights and a day past. We'll see to things, both here and with the household's share at the street barriers."

"Good then," Daved said. "I'll go fall onto a bed, since everyone wishes it." And because he probably could not keep to his feet much longer anyway.

He and Master Naylor were much of a kind, Frevisse thought with surprise. Two well-witted men who might have come to friendship if things were otherwise, but because of their faiths' necessities they would deal only distantly with one another and never with full trust and surety between them. A waste and loss it seemed to her.

But then see what waste and loss were come to Anne and Daved *because* they had put aside all the bars there should have been between them.

Frevisse had a sharp, bitter longing never to have been part of any of this. There was too much hopelessly wrong to it all.

But Master Naylor and Daved were trading curt nods of agreement; and saying, "Come," at Dickon, Master Naylor started to go, except Frevisse said quickly, "I'd have Dickon with me, ready to hand if I need send to you about anything. He can keep watch at the parlor windows meanwhile."

"Good enough, my lady," Master Naylor said with a bow and left.

Beside her, Daved said to Anne with a smile and very low, for Dickon not to hear, "Best you go with Dame Frevisse for now. I would not sleep the better having you with me." He shifted his look, less smiling, to Frevisse. "If you mean to do more, take care."

"I mean to talk to Mistress Hercy, maybe others. That's all." Because they needed to know more to be sure of Raulyn's guilt or innocence, and Mistress Hercy was somewhere to start.

"Take care at even that," Daved said.

"I will. May you rest well."

He bowed his thanks

They all went from the solar together, Dickon following, and parted company in the screens passage. Anne's gaze followed Daved as he went away toward the narrow stairs at the passage's far end until Frevisse said, "Come, Mistress Blakhall," and led the way up the parlor stairs, Dickon behind them, enough rebellion in his footfall to tell how little he wanted to be with them, but that was his ill fortune.

No one was in the parlor, but someone had put away Frevisse's bedding and the bedchamber's door stood open, and Anne said, "I'll go to Pernell. Both Mistress Hercy and Lucie surely need respite."

"So do you," Frevisse said, because Anne's face was as marred by grey weariness as Daved Weir's, however much outwardly she was again the calmly capable woman Frevisse had first met.

"I mean to fall on Pernell's pity and let her tend to me for a time. It will serve to turn her mind from other things," Anne said with a wan smile and went away.

Frevisse valued that calm the more, knowing what it cost her. That she was holding so steady through this dark and fear-ridden while told much about her courage and good sense. And deepened Frevisse's pity that she and Daved Weir should be forbidden to each another and that their love had brought their bodies and souls into danger of death and damnation. Though set against the darkness of heart and mind of whoever had killed the boy Hal and savaged his body and then struck down and killed Brother Michael, Anne and Daved's love seemed far less worthy of damnation, no matter that Daved was Jew. Better a man of courage and honest heart than—

Frevisse stopped that thought short. Those were matters for priests and scholars to determine and debate. Murder was what she must needs have in mind, and she said to Dickon, already gone to the southward window in what she knew was a vain hope of seeing more than rooftops and sky, "You'd be away into the streets if you could, wouldn't you?"

His voice heavy with the burden of youth and obedience, he said glumly, "I would. Everything is happening, and I'm seeing none of it."

She forbore to say that with Cade's promise to keep order in London looking to be gone like smoke in a high wind, sideways and away, he still had good chance of seeing trouble. Those barricades in St. Swithin's Lane would do little if true pillage and fighting broke out through the city.

Mistress Hercy came from the bedchamber, shooing Lucie ahead of her with an alacrity that bespoke her readiness to be out of there, and said when the door was closed behind her, "You've been a very good girl. I couldn't take care of your mother so well without you. Now go sit at the window in the sunshine for a while. You're looking wan."

As her grandmother said, Lucie was pale; nor did she smile as her grandmother patted her on her way, only went toward the southward window and Dickon while Mistress

Hercy went toward the other window, beckoning Frevisse to join her, saying brightly, "Do come sit with me. Anne says all is well, there's no news different than there has been." But she was wan-faced herself; and when they were sat down together, she said, her voice dropped to keep her question for only Frevisse to hear, "*Is* all well?"

Her voice equally low, Frevisse said, "No," and told what Raulyn had reported.

"Well," Mistress Hercy sighed. "There's naught we can do, is there? Only wait while the men sort it out. Though why Raulyn had to go out, I don't know. It's just foolishness. Men. This Jack Cade. No one was going to mind he robbed Philip Malpas clean from floor to rafters and did for those men yesterday. None of them were liked. But London won't take general thievery or much killing going on for long, no. Why he was ever let over the bridge anyway . . ." And again, with deeper annoyance, "*Men*." Her indignation seemed to have used up the last of her strength, though. She sank back into the corner of bench and window, closed her eyes, and murmured, "I am so tired." But her hands knotted tightly together in her lap told how little eased she was, and before Frevisse found anything to say, she had opened her eyes again, to look at Lucie.

Dickon had brought out a long string, was playing cat's cradle games for the girl, and Mistress Hercy smiled. "There's a good young man. Poor Lucie. It's all going so hard with her. I gave her some of her mother's sleeping draught last night to help her sleep." Mistress Hercy closed her eyes again. "I wish I could do as much for myself."

"Why don't you?" Frevisse encouraged.

"Because that would be when Pernell started birthing, wouldn't it be?"

"Is it likely to be a bad birthing?"

"No worse than most, save she's so frighted this time. St. Margaret defend us from the worst that could come, but if it did, what could she do, big-bellied as she is and hardly able to stand? Not flee or fight or help herself or Lucie or anyone. It would fright me, too, to be so helpless." Mistress Hercy rubbed at her cheekbones with her fingertips. "I think the world has gone mad." She looked, abruptly sharp, at Frevisse. "With the friar dead, that talk that Master Bocking and Master Weir are Jews will stop, won't it?"

"What? Stop?" Frevisse repeated blankly, left behind by the shift of thought.

"There's no talk among the servants. I've pried. Asked if *they* knew what the trouble was. As if I hadn't been told. So if there's no talk among them, and if you say nothing, or your men either . . ."

"I won't and neither have nor will they."

"And Anne won't say anything. For her own sake as well as Master Weir's." Mistress Hercy slid a quick look toward the bedchamber. "Though what's to be done about her and this . . ."

"Is for her and her priest to determine," Frevisse said quickly.

Mistress Hercy, covering a yawn, granted that with a small nod, and closed her eyes again, murmuring, "True. True."

Her voice trailed so gently to silence that Frevisse hoped she was slipping into sleep. Even a few minutes oblivion would be a blessing. But eyes still closed, Mistress Hercy said darkly, "What I'd truly like to do is get my hands on the villain that lured Hal out to his death. *That* would give me some pleasure."

Frevisse caught on one of her words. "Lured?" No one had said anything about the boy having been lured.

"Lured," Mistress Hercy repeated darkly. Dragged back from however near sleep she had been, she sat up and glared out the window. "Some villain came to Master Yarford's door, asked to speak to Hal, told him he was wanted at home, his mother was in a bad way, and that's the last was ever seen of him. Until he was found."

"I thought he just went out," Frevisse ventured. "The way boys do. And didn't come back."

Mistress Hercy shook her head, firm against that. "This fellow came for him. Hal didn't even stop for his hat, just said over his shoulder to one of the other apprentices that he had to go and went, and that fellow must have killed him." Her glare out the window failed to hide the tears filling her eyes. "God only knows why. There was never a better boy."

Despite it would have been kindness either to offer comfort or else lead her thoughts a different way, Frevisse asked, "You're sure that's what happened?"

Mistress Hercy dashed an angry hand at her tears. "It's what Hal's master said when he came the next day to see how things were with Pernell. I heard him myself. Raulyn made light of it, and we didn't tell Pernell. But after the second day of him being gone and Raulyn still making nothing of it, I knew we couldn't keep it longer from Pernell and went myself to ask questions. Master Yarford hadn't been there that night, see, only the other apprentices, but they said the same about how he'd come to leave."

"They didn't see who was at the door?"

"The boy who answered the door didn't know him. Some rough-looking man like you see being idle in the streets. The kind in riot with the rebels now and likely attacked Brother Michael outside our gate for the sport of it. Unless they were Lollards."

A new thought jarred into Frevisse's mind. She had never questioned that the attack on Brother Michael had been other than by chance—by men who would have attacked any friar they happened on. Or by Lollards. But what if it hadn't been? If his death had been Raulyn's doing, what if the attack had been, too? Had Raulyn hired men to do it? They'd not been using weapons, so maybe Brother Michael

wasn't to be killed, only made to think it was Lollards
so he'd turn his heed back to them. Or maybe he was to be
hurt enough he'd leave matters be a while, until Daved and
his uncle could be gone, hopefully not to come back for a
long while. Raulyn had probably expected only ripples of
talk about Jews after Hal's body was found—enough unease
and talk to drive Daved Weir and his uncle out of London,
nothing more. He hadn't counted on someone like Brother
Michael seeing the body. Nor had he known Father Tomas'
secret. Or that Brother Michael would find out Daved's secret. Or that the rebels would keep Daved in London when
he might have been gone.

By way of all that, everything had become far more dangerous than Raulyn had ever intended it to be. And he'd
surely never meant those men—if indeed he'd hired them—
to attack Brother Michael outside his own gate. Or for himself and Daved to see it. Or Daved to go to the friar's aid.
After that, everything was far worse than before, and Raulyn
had desperately needed to have the friar dead.

If she was right that the friar's death was Raulyn's doing.

She paused, reminding herself she must not take such
tight hold on believing him guilty that she missed anything
leading another way. Everything so far was all so much
guessing.

But she was momentarily out of questions; and Mistress
Hercy, her eyes shut again, looked by her shallow, even
breathing to be lightly sleeping; and Frevisse folded her
hands into her lap and bowed her head, looking for a prayer
that might comfort. Rather than something from one of the
missed Offices, what came into her mind was the prophet
Micah's question, "For what does the Lord your God require
of you but to do justice, love kindness, and walk humbly in
his ways?" And when all was said and done, what else *did*
God require? Christ had said everything was summed up in
"Do to others as you would have them do to you, and love

your neighbor as yourself." If that was all that was asked of mankind—to love, to be kind, to do justice, and to live humbly—why did mankind live instead in angers, hatreds, fears, and greeds? Why were there men like Raulyn Grene—and God guide her right and forgive her if she were wrong about him—who ruined lives without care for anyone but themselves?

The answer was supposed to be Eve's and Adam's sin in the Garden of Eden—the Original Sin from which all others came. But Christ's death was said to have redeemed mankind from that Sin, so if the Great Sin was paid for with Christ's death, what were sins since then? Were all sins no longer part of the great Sin but only petty sins, with men more petty with every one they did, lessening themselves sin by sin until they dwindled away into hell, their souls too shriveled to reach toward heaven anymore?

And why should Daved with his love and his courage be damned forever, while someone like Raulyn Grene could save his soul if on his deathbed he declared he repented of all his sins?

She knew it was not as simple as that. Theologians wrote their thick volumes of arguments and declarations, all followed by thick volumes of church law to enforce those declarations, so it could not be as simple as she saw it.

Or it *was* that simple, and Mankind's sin was crowned in its folly by teaching by way of endless arguments and tangled laws that salvation was more difficult to have than ever God had meant it to be.

She was thankful to be saved from thinking those thoughts further by the maidservant Emme hurrying into the parlor. At the other window Lucie's soft laughter at Dickon's cat's cradle games had not disturbed Mistress Hercy, but at Emme's footfall she immediately lifted her head and asked, "What is it?"

"Cook wants some ginger from the spice chest, please you," Emme said with a quick curtsy.

With a weary sigh, Mistress Hercy pushed herself to her feet. "First, let me see how Mistress Grene does. Wait while I do, on chance you need to fetch anything. No, dearling," she added to Lucie who had stood up, ready to go with her. "You stay there. Your mother doesn't need you yet."

Lucie willingly turned back to Dickon, and as Mistress Hercy left them, Frevisse said to Emme, gesturing to the bench, "Sit down while you can."

Emme did, saying, "Bless you." She was a plain-faced, plain-mannered woman, past her young days but not old, looking to be of settled ways, and making a guess Frevisse asked, "You've been with Mistress Grene a long while?"

"Since before she was Mistress Grene," Emme said readily. "She was Mistress Depham when I first came to her and not even a mother yet. I've seen all her children born and helped to raise them. I remember when Hal . . ." She wiped her eyes with a corner of her apron. "Poor lamb. At least he had a mostly happy life, and that's more than many can say." She gave a chuckle a little choked by her tears. "The worst that ever came to him was he and Master Grene were chalk and cheese together."

"They didn't get on well?" Frevisse asked, keeping her voice level.

"Oh, they didn't quarrel, no, but they couldn't find two things together to say to each other most of the time. Master Grene, he's all sharp wits and doing things. Hal, he let life be easy. Wasn't given to hurrying things. He and Master Grene were both the happier when he went off to Master Yarford."

She was dry-eyed now and even a little smiling. Talking seemed to comfort her, and Frevisse said, to keep her talking, "Well, it's a blessing Mistress Hercy is here for all this. Master Grene must be most grateful."

"If he is, it's the first time he's been," Emme said, just short of a snort.

"Chalk and cheese again?" Frevisse asked lightly.

"More knife and whetstone. One's always sharpening the other, if you see what I mean."

"They don't get on?"

"They do, and they don't." She shrugged. "Not of one mind about most things, and neither of them behindhand in telling the other. Except they both agree he was a good marriage for my mistress."

"Still, they're together in keeping Mistress Grene from the worst of all this," Frevisse ventured.

"They are that. Even though it's not as if any of us would say aught to Mistress Grene would make her hurt worse."

"My guess is that Hal's death has taken Mistress Hercy far harder than she shows."

"Oh, by the Virgin's mercy, yes," Emme said. "It's all for her daughter's sake she keeps such a good front. Hal was her dear and no mistake. The spit of her late husband she used to say. It's been cruel hard on her, for certain."

"Is there any thought at all among the household about who could have done it? Has there been anyone around here of late that shouldn't have been, taking more interest in things than they should have? Any strangers?"

"Oh, we were asking ourselves that before anyone else was," Emme assured her. "But it wouldn't be around here they'd be looking but at Master Yarford's, wouldn't they?"

Frevisse hadn't hoped for better answer to her question. She was merely going blindly, hoping to blunder into something.

A servant carrying a wide, well-laden tray came from the stairs. "Mistress Grene's dinner," he said with a glower at Emme. "Cook gave up waiting for the ginger.

Emme stood up, saying, "I'll be blamed for that, sure," and would have gone to open the bedchamber door ahead of him, but Dickon with a young man's interest in food was quicker, and Emme stayed where she was, going on to Frevisse, "No, the only thing strange of late is that pair of hosen gone missing, and I was blamed for that, too, and it was no more my fault than the ginger. As if I'd lose a pair of hosen between here and the laundry basket and not see them on my way back."

Quickly Frevisse said, "That's just the sort of thing a servant gets blamed for when it's not her fault at all. When was this?"

Willing to have someone sorry for her wrongs, Emme sat down again. "Last week. No, I tell a lie. Monday it would have been when Mistress Hercy was counting out the household laundry before it went to the laundress in Birchin Lane. That's like her, you know." Emme was openly a-grieved. "Mistress Grene has always left the counting to me, and I've never lost anything. But Mistress Hercy must see to everything herself, and there's this pair of hosen gone missing. 'Shouldn't there be more than one pair of Master Grene's hosen here?' she asks and sends me off to search the bedchamber for them. I didn't find them and had to hear about it afterward, and what I wanted to tell her was that if they aren't in the bedchamber and aren't in the dirties, then they aren't anywhere, and it's not my doing!" Emme's indignation had brought color into her cheeks. "That's the truth of it, no matter what she thinks! But it's me that's blamed, and Cook will blame me for the ginger, too," she added bitterly, "which is no more my fault than that was."

Chapter 25

After Emme left her, Frevisse stayed at the window with her suddenly sharpened thoughts, knowing her own dinner would be brought to her in good time. Servants were in a household to serve, but they also saw and listened to all they could of things done and said. She had had no secrets out of Emme, merely what anyone in the household was likely to know, and that Emme's view of matters was probably not that of either Mistress Hercy or Raulyn Grene did not lessen its worth. Briefly, Frevisse wondered what the servants in St. Frideswide's said among themselves about her and decided she did not want to know. The line between humility and humiliation could sometimes be too thin.

Lucie had followed Emme into the bedchamber, and Frevisse called Dickon to her and ordered, "When you go down to your dinner, don't tarry over it. Eat and come straight back. I need you for something."

Dickon brightened. "You know something, don't you? You're going to find out who killed the friar, aren't you?"

Frevisse said quellingly, "What I know is that there are more things I want to know. Eat and come back, and don't say anything to anyone about me while you're at it."

"Not a word. Does Father know what you're doing?"

"Your father knows." Whether he approved or not was another matter. "Go on." As afterthought, she added, "You could bring my dinner when you return, to save someone else the steps."

Dickon bowed and left with eagerness for more than the bread and cheese and cold meat that were likely waiting for him.

The servant came out of the bedroom. Frevisse told him that her man would be bringing her meal, then asked, "Has Master Grene come back yet?"

"Not when I'd come up" the man said, bowed, and left Frevisse to her continuing uncomfortable thoughts. If what she suspicioned against Raulyn were even half true—if he were guilty only of Brother Michael's death—Pernell's life was going to be torn to unmendable shreds; and if the rest of what Frevisse feared was true—if Hal's death were his doing, too—Pernell's pain would be hardly bearable. As great as her grief now was, what would it be then? And her anger. Because anger would surely come, later if not sooner, maybe made the worse because she had borne Raulyn a child and was carrying another for him at the very time he killed her first-born. Would she see her children by him as tainted with Hal's blood because they were Raulyn's, and come to loathe them, even hate them? All that should be set, too, to

Raulyn's account in Heaven's reckoning against his soul, Frevisse thought. The sin of Pernell's hatred should lie as heavily against him as against her, because he was the wanton, willing cause of it all.

Frevisse had found before now how narrowly most murderers saw the world. For most people their own needs and desires were what mattered most to them, but most people also granted the worth of other people's needs, accepted other peoples' right to their own desires, their own lives. Murderers like Raulyn Grene were otherwise—not simply first in their own regard but only. Others were worthless unless of use to them; and if someone else's death might be of worth, then murdering them was reasonable. Only fear of being caught could stop such a man—or woman. Other things than a blind heed of only the self could bring a person to murder, Frevisse knew, but she did not think it was so with Raulyn Grene. But if he had killed Hal, what she didn't see was *why* he had. There had to be more gain from it than being rid of Daved Weir, but what?

Someone was coming up the stairs too heavily and slow to be Dickon, even if he were carrying her dinner, and she was not surprised when Father Tomas entered. She rose to her feet and curtseyed to him, and he made a small sign of blessing at her, but when he would have gone onward to the closed bedchamber door, she said, "I pray you, Father, come sit a while. If you've been praying all this while beside Brother Michael, you've more than earned the right to rest." And added with a nod toward the bedchamber, when he still hesitated, "They're at dinner in there just now. Have you eaten?" Because he was so pale and bow-shouldered with weariness, she doubted he had yet broken fast today.

"Just now I have eaten, yes," but accepted her offer of rest, sitting down on a nearby chair as if his back and knees hurt, which well they might if he had been kneeling on the cellar floor most of this while. "I have done what I could for the dead," he said. He nodded toward the bedchamber. "How does she?"

"I haven't seen her. Her mother and Lucie and Mistress Blakhall are with her."

Hands on his knees, rubbing them, Father Tomas nodded. "Good. Good."

Not knowing how much time or other chance she might have, Frevisse said, "A question, if I may, Father. About Hal."

"Poor Hal," Father Tomas said with a sad nodding.

Frevisse was abruptly irked. She had not gathered Hal had been "poor Hal" while he was alive. Why should he be rendered "poor Hal" forever afterward by his death? Death, in whatever guise, did not cancel out the good days there had been in a life nor the uncounted ordinary days, blessed by their ordinariness. Let him be Hal who came to a wrongful death, not "poor Hal" as if his death was all there had been to his life. And a little more sharply than she might have, she asked, "Was he much given to brotheling?"

Father Tomas' eyes flew open. "What? Mercy of Mary, no!"

"Would you have known?"

"I was his priest. I would have known. Of his own choice he had even made a vow to me that he would stay chaste until his marriage. His last confession—" Father Tomas stopped, his burst of indignation run out, then said wearily, "No. I do not see him brotheling." And a little sharply, "Why?"

"Mistress Blakhall said someone had told her that was why Hal went out that night."

"No." Father Tomas shook his head firmly against that. "No." He shook his head as if understanding none of it and said, sounding bewildered with grief and weariness, "From what is said, he was lured out deliberately to be killed. But why? That is what I do not see."

"And why try to make it seem Jews had done it and in your church? Have you enemies?"

"Enemies?" Father Tomas sounded only the more bewildered. "No, I have no enemies. Nor did anyone know of my family. Only Daved Weir."

"Did he?" she asked carefully, covering her surprise. "How?"

"He brings letters from my sister and takes mine to her."

"And from the rest of your family, too?"

"Such as still live, they do not write," Father Tomas said. "They live as Christians, but in the heart they are not. When I took on the heart as well as the seeming and wished to be a priest, they cast me out. They do not know my sister writes to me or me to her." Father Tomas' tired face firmed and he straightened, made the sign of the cross in the air between them, and said in the set and certain voice of a priest, "What I have told you, I enjoin you to keep secret forever." He made the sign of the cross again. "I bind you to silence on it now and forevermore."

Frevisse opened her mouth in what would have been resentful protest but stopped herself. Both as a priest and as a man protecting himself Father Tomas had the right to enjoin that silence on her. Whether he had the right to keep his family's grievous secret was another matter, but by enjoining silence on her, he kept it his problem and not hers, and she willingly gave up need to think about it in favor of strict obedience to his priestly command, saying quietly with bowed head, "As you will, Father."

That did not mean she was done with questions, though, and as she raised her head, she asked, "Do you know why Brother Michael was in St. Swithin's Lane yesterday when he was attacked?"

"He had been at the church again with his questions."

"Of you? Or about you?"

"Of everyone. And much about me, I think, yes." Sadness as well as weariness showed in the priest now. "There are people not pleased now they know about me."

And Brother Michael's prodding and questioning would have only made that worse. That was beyond her help, though, and she asked, "Did he say he was coming here? Or was he maybe going somewhere else?"

"I do not know whether he was coming here or simply taking this way back to the friary." Father Tomas frowned. "Though if he were bound for Grey Friars, it would have made better sense to go by way of Candlewick to Budge Row than this way."

"Was there anyone else in the street besides the men who attacked him?"

"A few people." Father Tomas frowned more deeply. "But those men went only at him."

Frevisse remembered Brother Michael had said they asked if he was the friar who had been preaching at St. Paul's.

"They were likely Lollards," Father Tomas was going on. "They looked more London roughs than rebels, so I think." His voice went sadder. "My shame is that when they attacked him, I only stood there, staring. It was Master Weir and Master Grene, come from the other way, who went to him. God forgive me, but I do not know if it was fear held me back or my dislike of him."

Nor could anyone answer that truly except himself; but for what comfort it might be, Frevisse said, "You were pulling him from among their feet when I saw you. That's more than many would have done."

"But was it for shame or for love of God?" he asked sadly.

Another question only he could answer, and a little silence fell between them, until a flurry of voices in the yard bought him to join her at the window to see Raulyn crossing toward the house, talking excitedly to two of his household men. One of them laughed to whatever he was saying and turned back to the gate. Raulyn and the other, still talking, went up the outside stairs and into the house.

"Not ill news, anyway," Father Tomas said, drawing back. From the bedchamber Pernell's voice rose, querulous and frightened. Father Tomas turned that way. "I should go to her. By your leave."

He bent his head to Frevisse. She curtseyed in return, and he went to rap slightly at the bedchamber door and go in, leaving Frevisse with the hope that he was as he seemed: a caring priest whose deepest desire in life was serving God.

Raulyn came so quickly up the stairs and into the room that she barely had time to blank her face before he was saying merrily, "Cade has them where it hurts! He's made that fawning Stockwood an alderman, God save us, and is forcing I don't know how many others to open their purses to him because he'll let his men loose on them if they don't!"

Pulling out the one good thing she heard in all of that, she asked, "He still has that much hold over his men?"

"More hold than I thought he'd have by now," Raulyn said. "The city's own curs, they're another matter. He's had a few of those chopped for thieving he didn't order. He's had Hawardan out of sanctuary and dead, and that's as much to the good as anything he's done!"

Frevisse did not know who Hawardan was—or Stockwood, come to that—but Raulyn's pleasure in all of it repelled her, and she was glad Mistress Hercy came from the bedchamber to say at him, "Come in and tell Pernell that all's well. She needs to see you."

Raulyn laughed and went, pecking a kiss onto Mistress Hercy's cheek as he passed. Rubbing at the spot, Mistress Hercy headed toward the stairs, saying to Frevisse as she went, "I'd best see how things are with the household. Are you doing well enough? Do you need aught?"

Frevisse assured her that she needed nothing. Except answers, she silently added.

Dickon must have been about to come up as Mistress Hercy went down; he was in the room almost as soon as she was gone, carrying a tray that he brought to set on the seat beside Frevisse, saying as he did, "It's day-old bread, and the ale isn't new either. The cook is sorry for that. But the chicken is today's chicken. It's good, even without the ginger. Have you heard Master Grene's news?"

"I've heard. Dickon, there's something I need you to do."

"Go back to St. Helen's for something?" he asked hopefully.

"Something here. There's a midden heap by the rearyard gate. I want you to find out when it's cleared away, find out if it's been done this week at all, and . . ."

"The scavagers come around on Wednesdays," Dickon said. "But they haven't this week. Cook was complaining of it this morning."

"Then what I want you to do is go through the midden and find me something if it's there. One or both of a pair of a man's hose. If they're there, they'll be nearer the bottom than the top. At almost the very bottom, probably."

"In the midden?" Dickon asked as if in hope he had misheard her.

"In the midden."

His wrinkled nose and wryed mouth told what he thought, but he backed a step and started to bow but paused to ask, low-voiced and leaning toward her, "Is this to do with the friar's murder?"

Frevisse hesitated, then leaned toward him and answered in an equally low voice, "It has to do with murder, yes. So be careful."

Looking somewhat more ready to the task if still nothing like glad, Dickon finished his bow and left, and Frevisse ate, finding the chicken savory with young onions and garlic, but mostly her thoughts were away to Father Tomas and what he had said about Brother Michael's attackers. They had looked like London roughs to him, and Hal's fellow apprentice had said that about the man who had fetched Hal away. The city's curs, Raulyn had just called them. The kind of men easy to hire for some passing work.

Not for murder, though. Some would be willing to it, yes, but whoever hired them would be open to extortion afterward. She didn't see Raulyn doing more than hiring such a man to take the message to Hal and bring him somewhere Raulyn was waiting with some ready reason why he was there. Hal, set on reaching his mother, would have accepted whatever he said. Then, with the messenger paid and gone his way with no questions, Raulyn need only have had Hal to somewhere he could be struck down—not so very easy, with the city laws that kept the streets well-lighted by lanterns outside householders' doors and people about and no reason to take some back-alley way. Maybe tell Hal they should pause at the church to make quick prayer for Pernell's safety. And somewhere in the shadows strike him down. A dark corner of the churchyard would have given a place to wait, too, until he was sure of carrying Hal inside and to the crypt in safety. Once in the crypt, he would have been free to do all the rest—kill Hal, strip him, mutilate him—with small likelihood of being found at it. Then he need only leave the church unheeded, no great matter at that hour, and go home to Pernell and Lucie as if nothing had happened.

It would mean Raulyn had been bold to the point of foolishness and cold-hearted almost beyond imagining.

And the fact still held that Raulyn had lost rather than gained by Hal's death. That made no sense. And there were two other things she wanted to know: Who had told Anne that Hal went out brotheling that night, and where had Raulyn been when Hal was being murdered?

She was ashamed that latter question came to her only now, when it should have been one of the first. If he had been here, then he had not been out in the night killing his stepson. Was she so set on his guilt that she was failing to think of the plainest questions? What else might she be failing to ask?

Her anger at herself brought her to her feet and started her pacing the room. Come to it, why *was* she so set on finding Raulyn guilty of Hal's murder?

To that at least she found she had immediate answer. If he was guilty of both Hal's murder and Brother Michael's, then all was settled. If he was not guilty of both, then likely Hal's murderer would never be known, and she hated that thought.

Raulyn came from the bedchamber. Frevisse's pacing had her almost in his way to the stairs, and she moved farther aside, dropping her eyes lest her look at him betray too much. He passed her with only, "My lady," and was gone, leaving Frevisse looking after him. A prosperous merchant with a goodly home and a settled place in London's life, in fine health, loved by his wife, father of a son, and soon father of maybe another.

Why would he have killed his stepson?

Father Tomas and Lucie came out of the bedchamber, followed by Anne still carrying Daved's doublet. She closed the door with great and silent care, and only when she had followed them well away from it did she say softly, "Thank you, Father," and to Frevisse, "Pernell finally fell to sleep while Father Tomas prayed and Raulyn held her hand." She looked around as if in hope he was somehow still there. "I wish he would have stayed with her. You're going to leave, too, Father?"

"It's time I returned to St. Swithin. I may be needed there. Or at least missed."

She, Lucie, and Frevisse all curtsied to him, and he blessed them, signing the cross in the air toward them, before he left. When he was gone, Anne turned to Lucie and said, "I still need to mend Master Weir's doublet. Will you find me thread in your mother's sewing basket to close-match it?"

She held out the doublet and Lucie took it and went with outward willingness to sit on the floor beside the sewing basket beside her mother's chair while Frevisse said, "Mistress Blakhall, might I talk with you?" and went away to the far end of the room before Anne answered her. Anne followed her, and because they were likely to have little time Frevisse said immediately, low enough to keep her words from Lucie, "About the night Hal was killed."

Anne flinched. "Please, no. I'd just like not to think about—"

"One question. You said he had gone out to a brothel. Who told you that?"

"Raulyn." Anne's voice fell even lower than it was, and she looked sideways at Lucie to be sure she did not hear. "When Hal was first missing. He thought Hal had gone over the river and not got home before the gates closed."

"Was that something you thought likely?"

"Of Hal? No. Even if he was nigh to old enough by some reckoning, he was young for his age."

"It's not what Mistress Hercy says Master Yarford says happened either."

Anne frowned. "I know. It's odd."

"Why would Raulyn say the other, do you think?"

"Rather than be worried, he was making light of it, I suppose." Anne paused, then said slowly, as if seeing something she had not seen before, "He was greatly merry that day, I remember. Not at all ready to be bothered over Hal gone missing. He'd been gone such a little while, after all. But he knew by then that . . ." Her words trailed off but Frevisse followed her thought easily enough. Raulyn had been told by then that a man had told a lie to have Hal, and yet he had been merry.

Lucie came with the doublet and several twists of thread of different greens. Together she and Anne went to the nearer window to see them better, but something in the yard drew Anne's sudden heed, and she leaned over the sill for a better look. Lucie knelt on the window seat to see, too, and Frevisse, drawn by their suddeness, joined them. There were only Daved and Raulyn going down the stairs to the yard in talk together, but Anne said, aloud but more to herself than anyone, "I hope he doesn't let Raulyn draw him into going out, if that's what Raulyn means to do again."

With sharp fear Frevisse clamped a hand onto Anne's arm and said with all the force she could, "Stop him. Say whatever you have to say, but *don't* let Daved go out of here with Raulyn."

Chapter 26

N ot understanding Dame Frevisse's alarm, only
that it was for Daved, Anne sprang to her
feet, grabbed her skirts out of her way, and
went out of the parlor and down the stairs as near to running as she could, and came from the screens passage to the
head of the outside stairs to see him and Raulyn crossing
the yard toward the gate, still in close talk. She paused to
gather herself and her breath, then called, "Master Weir!"
And when both men stopped and turned toward her with
matching question on their faces, she smiled to let them
know it was nothing desperate and beckoned, hoping Daved
would come back to her. But if he did not, she fully meant
to go after him and take hold on him to keep him here if she
had to.

There was no need. He said something more to Raulyn, and as Raulyn went on toward James and Pers waiting at the gate, came back to her. Anne watched him come and longed to be in his arms and everything as it was a week ago, when everything had been right and she had still held hope he might, some day, for her—

She stopped that thought. She had long forbidden herself hope that Daved might some day become Christian for her. Had told herself that whatever would come from her love for Daved, would come, and she would treasure what she had while she had it. Though it was less than what she wanted, it was more than she had right to, and when the time came to pay the price of it, she would. And still, despite herself, she had hoped. Until yesterday. Until she watched him against the friar and known he would never turn Christian for her sake or any other reason. Had known, too, that the price of her love was come due, and soon she would have to pay it.

And despite she had tried to make her summons to him light and kept her smile, Daved asked intently as he started up the stairs toward her, "Is there trouble?"

Anne felt her mask of a smile fall away and said, "Dame Frevisse says you're not to go out with Raulyn. You're not going, are you?"

"I'm not going with him, no. James is. What is it?"

Anne surprised herself by giving a sob on her half-caught breath and fought herself to steadiness, not understanding why had she been so frighted. "I don't know. She just said I should stop you from going out with Raulyn."

Daved looked back across the yard to where Raulyn and James were gone out and Pers was barring the door in the gate again, then guided Anne back inside, saying as they went, "Tell her I'm not so foolish, and that I'm still asking questions."

No one was in the screens passage, but she held back from even touching to him, only looked up into his face, said, "I'll tell her," and started to turn away.

"Anne," he said; and when she turned back to him, "Anne, I love you."

She smiled with all her heart behind it. "And I love you," she said and left him, taking her pain with her. Only when she was alone again on the parlor stairs did she falter, stop, and lean against the wall, struggling against her tears. She loved him, but their love was not enough to keep him here or safe, and this time when he went away . . .

But grief to come did not lessen present necessity, and she forced herself steady and went on, to find Dame Frevisse still at the window and that Mistress Hercy was returned, was sitting in Pernell's chair with Lucie standing beside her, both of them looking at Daved's doublet. Anne went to Dame Frevisse and quietly gave her Daved's message, to which the nun only nodded. Then Anne drew a joint stool near to Mistress Hercy, holding out a hand for the doublet, saying, "Now I'll show you how to mend that manner of rend, Lucie," and for a simple time gave Lucie a small lesson in mending, starting the mend herself to show Lucie how to needle-catch the torn threads and thread-weave them into the good, then let Lucie try it for herself, Mistress Hercy watching closely and finally saying, "Our Lucie has a way with a needle, doesn't she?"

Anne stroked a gentle hand down Lucie's fair hair. "She's becoming a skilled sempster, yes."

"It's something Raulyn can add to his bargaining for her betrothal," Mistress Hercy said with satisfaction, and lifted her voice a little to include Dame Frevisse with, "I don't suppose you favor marriage, being a nun?"

"I do favor it," Dame Frevisse answered easily. "It keeps a great many women from becoming nuns who shouldn't."

"Myself," Mistress Hercy said, "I've always thought better a bad monk than a bad husband."

"However true that may be," Dame Frevisse returned, "I'll not grant you 'better a bad nun than a bad wife' because I might have to live with that bad nun."

Mistress Hercy and Anne both a little laughed at that, and Mistress Hercy said, "Well, it'll be a few years yet before our Lucie's a wife, but we're hoping for her betrothal before long. Raulyn has lately been talking with a Master Basse in Hertfordshire who looks possible. High gentry he is, so she'd be marrying up. Has several good manors to his name, property here in London, no children yet with any claim on what he has, and a not-too-distant kinship to Lord Warrenne that could lead to something at court and business sent Raulyn's way. The trouble is he knows his own worth, and I gather he wants something more in the way of dowry than Lucie has, but . . ." Mistress Hercy's momentary brightness at talking of ordinary things faded. She broke off with a small cough and a sniff and said, "Lucie dearling, go fetch some wine from the kitchen for us, there's a good girl."

Lucie handed the doublet to Anne without looking up— to hide her own sudden tears, Anne feared—and obediently went away. Mistress Hercy took an handkerchief from her sleeve and wiped her eyes, murmuring, "I didn't want for her to see me crying."

Gently Dame Frevisse said, "It's possible to be too strong for your own good."

Mistress Hercy sighed on her tears. "I know. But just now . . . well, we can't all be crying at once, can we?"

Still gently, Dame Frevise asked, "How much does Master Grene want this marriage for Lucie?"

"Oh, very much." Mistress Hercy wiped her nose. "It's something he and Pernell both want. To marry her better, not just to another merchant, but into the gentry."

"He'll likely have less trouble closing on it now," Dame Frevisse said quietly. "Now Hal is gone and Lucie's inheritance is doubled."

Mistress Hercy tucked her handkerchief away. "Little trouble at all, I suppose. That may be our only comfort in all of this—to have our Lucie married to someone who's near kin to a lord. Raulyn is trying to do well for her, I'll grant him that." Her voice went suddenly bitter, her tiredness and grief lowering her guard, Anne thought, as she said on, "Mind you, it's as much for himself as anyone. A foot in the gentry door with Lucie could open it wider for his sons. Never one to miss his chance, is Raulyn Grene, if you see my meaning."

"I see it," Dame Frevisse said quietly.

Young Dickon came into the parlor, carrying a small, cloth-wrapped bundle in his hands, and Dame Frevisse asked, the words sharp-edged, "You found them?"

"Where you said, my lady. I had one of the maids give me this oiled cloth to wrap them in. They're—"

Dame Frevisse sprang to her feet and went toward him. "Lay it on the floor and open it."

Behind her, Mistress Hercy rose, too, following her, asking, "What's this?"

"We'll see," Dame Frevisse said, and ordered Dickon, "Unwrap them."

He obeyed—knelt, laid the bundle on the floor, and began to fold back the wrapping at an arm's length that Anne understood as a mingled smell of rot and rubbish reached her.

Now standing beside Frevisse, Mistress Hercy demanded more strongly, "What *is* it?"

"Wait," Dame Frevisse said.

Anne stayed where she was, Daved's doublet forgotten on her lap, watching with them as Dickon opened the last fold to show a shapeless wet lump of dark blue cloth. Gathering her skirts carefully back from it, Dame Frevisse knelt at the other side of the bundle from Dickon and with unwilling fingertips began to pick at the filthy thing, saying, "It's from the midden in your rearyard. As for what it is . . ." She separated the thing into two filthy things. "It's a pair of hosen, I think."

"They were where you said they would be," Dickon said. "Right at the bottom."

"Why?" Mistress Hercy asked, with enough demand to leave no doubt she meant to have full answer to it.

But Dame Frevisse made no immediate answer. Instead, she uncrumpled and looked at first one hose and then the other, so intent that Mistress Hercy let her question hang, watching over the nun's shoulder, until at last Dame Frevisse said, "They're neither of them damaged and look to be of good quality cloth. Why would they be thrown out as rubbish?"

"You must have some thought about that," Mistress Hercy said. "Else you'd not have sent your man to look for them."

"Dickon, bring me some water in the bowl there," Dame Frevisse ordered, nodding toward the laving bowl and water pitcher sitting on a shelf beside the stairward door, ready for anyone's handwashing before going down to meals; and while Dickon rose and went to pour water into the bowl, she said, seeming to feel her way through the words, "One of your women complained she was blamed for a pair of Master Grene's hosen gone missing. My guess is that these are those."

"I'd guess so, too," Mistress Hercy said. "The cloth looks good enough." She didn't offer to feel it. "And who else's good hosen would likely be in our rubbish? What I'm wondering . . ." She was demanding an answer now. ". . . is *why*."

Dickon set the bowl beside Dame Frevisse. Still with her fingertips, she handled one of the hose enough to find by the shape of the cloth where the wearer's knee had been and put that part into the water, saying, "If the cloth has kept damp enough in the midden that the blood hasn't set . . ."

"Blood?" Mistress Hercy said sharply.

". . . or if it isn't too mixed with rubbish ooze . . ." Dame Frevisse was scrubbing the cloth against itself while she spoke, but her words trailed off as the water turned faintly pink. Dame Frevisse sighed and sat back, leaving the hose still partly in the water.

Mistress Hercy asked again, quietly now, "Blood?"

Just as quietly Dame Frevisse answered, "Probably." She prodded the hose with a forefinger, and a small swirl of pink spread outward from it through the water. She looked around and up at Mistress Hercy and said, still quietly, "In the crypt, beside Hal's body, I saw where someone had knelt in the blood-softened dirt. Now here are discarded hosen, at least one of them apparently bloodied at the knee."

Anne understood what she was saying and surely so did Mistress Hercy, but the silence drew out and out, and Dame Frevisse and Mistress Hercy looked at one another in it, and Anne and Dickon watched them until finally, quietly, Mistress Hercy said, "No."

Dame Frevisse stood up and held out her hand. Dickon hurriedly brought her the towel hanging beside the water pitcher, and while she dried her hands, she bade him, "Wrap those up again. Then pour that water out the southward window. You'll tell no one about any of this."

Steadily, Dickon asked, "My father?"

"Not even him. No one. But when you've finished with the water, go find Master Weir and ask him to come here. No. Find Lucie first and tell her she's to walk in the yard with you for a while rather than come back here. Then find Master Weir."

"Yes, my lady." He wrapped the hose again, poured the water out the window, bowed to her and all of them, and left.

None of them moved or spoke until he was gone, but then Mistress Hercy went forward, took up the oiled-cloth bundle, and said, "This is mine to see to."

Dame Frevisse did not argue that, only asked, "Was Master Grene here the night Hal disappeared?"

"He was out and hadn't come home when I went to bed. For him to come home late was usual enough, though, and he was here in the morning. Anne, was he with you?"

Taken aback, Anne said, "With me? No! Why ever should he be?"

"I've seen he has an eye for you. I've sometimes thought you must have a lover. I thought it might be him," Mistress Hercy said without apology.

"No," Anne said hotly. "Raulyn has never been my lover."

"Wise of you," Mistress Hercy said and returned to Dame Frevisse with, "He could have been with friends that night, or at some guild meeting. They're forever having guild meetings." She looked at the bundle she held. "That doesn't answer this, though."

"He buried them in the midden," Dame Frevisse said. "thinking they would be taken away, with no one the wiser. He'd probably taken care to keep his shirt clear, and washing his hands clean of blood would have been no great matter, but he had no way to wash these out and had to be rid of them. It was only his bad fortune that everything's been set awry by the rebels and the scavagers didn't come when they should have."

"His bad fortune and God's will," Mistress Hercy said. "Otherwise, how would we ever have known?"

"What you're saying," Anne said faintly, with a sickening mix of disbelief and certainty, "is that Raulyn killed Hal."

The sound of someone coming up the stairs turned them quickly that way, Anne maybe not the only one afraid it was

Raulyn. But it was Daved, and he made his bow to them all, and said, "My ladies."

Mistress Hercy looked at the nun. "What . . ." she began.

"Master Weir and I have already determined that almost surely Raulyn killed Brother Michael." Even said flatly as that, the words were like a blow, but Dame Frevisse went on, "Now I can tell him we've found what makes it likely Raulyn likewise killed Hal."

Mistress Hercy, having caught breath for words, said, "Killed Brother Michael?", at the same time Daved demanded, "Hal, too? You're certain?"

"Certain enough," Dame Frevisse said.

Mistress Hercy turned away, her need to sink down somewhere so plain that Anne sprang up to put an arm around her waist and take her to the window seat. Around all her swirl of thoughts, Anne grasped that this must have been of what Daved and the nun had talked in that while they spent aside from everyone in the solar, because he seemed not surprised, only far from happy.

Clinging to Anne's arm even after she was seated, Mistress Hercy asked, the words strangled, "What are we going to do?"

Daved turned to her. "Little, while London is still taken up with the rebels."

"Hal and the friar both," Mistress Hercy said hoarsely. "My God. Why?" She suddenly looked at Daved, and her voice strengthened. "Because of you. He killed the friar to save you . . ." Her voice flattened again. "No, not you. Himself."

"We think so, yes," Dame Frevisse said, and level-voiced, Daved told what they had determined and why. Mistress Hercy stared at the floor and nodded as he went on; and when he stopped, she raised her eyes to him and asked, weak with hopelessness, "But why Hal?"

"For gain," Dame Frevisse answered. "You just told me . . ."

With widening horror Anne broke her frozen silence, exclaimed, "Lucie's marriage. He did it to add Hal's share to hers."

"Lucie's marriage?" Daved asked sharply.

Dame Frevisse told him briefly of that, and then of the hosen that Mistress Hercy still held in their bundle.

"Something has to be done with that," Daved said with a nod toward it. "Raulyn should not know we have it."

"*Raulyn,*" Mistress Hercy said in a horror-fraught whisper. " How do I keep him from them when he comes back?" Her voice began to rise with alarm. "From Pernell, from Lucie. If he . . ."

"They're safe from him," Daved said. "They're both of use to him and not a danger. They're safe. The only danger lies in any of us—you and I and Mistress Blakhall and Dame Frevisse—betraying that we know about him. Can you keep a fair seeming toward him? Toward everyone? As if nothing had changed?"

"I have to," Mistress Hercy said faintly. "I can. Yes." But a new appalling thought took her, and she said more sharply and with new pain, "Pernell! This will tear her heart out. He's ruined her and her heart will break and she'll have nothing left. Between the crown's claim against him as a murderer and the Church's for sacrilege, everything will be gone. Pernell . . ." She choked on tears and stopped.

Daved went to her, took the bundle from her hands and set it on the floor, then took her hands in his own and said steadily, "The law can't take her dower. She'll still have that and everything she brought to the marriage. Nor there'll be no one who blames her, and she'll still have Lucie and little Robert and the new baby and you."

Mistress Hercy gasped, "The baby. And Robert. They're his. Raulyn's. Blessed St. Anne, what if she hates them for that? For being his. What if . . ."

Daved gently shook her hands. "Heed me in this," he said. "Don't look so far ahead or think her such a fool. Look only at these next days. They're the ones we must get through, until London is itself again."

"What if it's never itself again?" Mistress Hercy demanded on a rising tone of fear and misery. "What if . . ."

"Your merchants and men of power won't hold tolerant of Cade's ways and robberies for long. They're likely already turning against him. We have only to wait it out. But we have to wait it out without Raulyn knowing what we know. You *must* seem as if nothing is changed."

Mistress Hercy lifted her head, straightened her back. Her mouth firmed and her eyes narrowed and she said from far inside her strength, "He'll know nothing from me."

Daved smiled on her, gave her hands a firm, approving shake, and stood up, picking up the bundled hosen as he did. "Good, then. This I'll put somewhere for safekeeping." He looked aside to Anne. "And you, Mistress Blakhall, can you keep countenance through this?"

Anne met his gaze and said evenly, "I can feign whatever I need to." Why not, when so much else of her life, like his, was feigned? Right now she was feigning against a desperate, despairing longing to beg him to go with her anywhere away from here, to go somewhere there would only be each other and no one else and nothing but their love. But all she very quietly said was, "For as long as need be."

Her reward was Daved's smile and a warmth deep in his eyes that told her he understood everything she had not said.

Chapter 27

The afternoon passed in dread-filled waiting. Anne sat at the southward window for the sake of the light and went on mending Daved's doublet. Dame Frevisse kept to the other window, looking outward. There seemed nothing to say between them nor with Mistress Hercy, who came and went, busy with Pernell and the household, her first sharp, open anguish and dismay gone behind an outward seeming that nothing had changed. But once, coming from Pernell in the bedchamber on her way to somewhere else in the house, she said as she passed through the parlor "I wish she'd begin her birthing. It would take her mind from things."

And Mistress Hercy's mind, too, Anne thought. Where Daved was and what he was doing, she didn't know. She only hoped he was not gone out, because through the afternoon there was a constant churn of broken noise coming and going along close-by streets, large gatherings of men passing with shouts and loud laughter. None of it came along St. Swithin's, and though several times she thought she heard shouting at the barriers, no fighting ever seemed to break out.

She had finished mending the doublet and was moving its bottom button to replace the one that was gone when Lucie joined her from wherever her grandmother had been keeping her busy. Anne welcomed her company and settled her to sewing on her sampler beside her, but soon Pernell came from the bedchamber, a bedgown wrapped around her, saying as she went awkwardly to her chair, "I can't bear it in there anymore. Lucie, come show me your work. Anne, talk to me about anything at all. My lady," she added to Dame Frevisse with a small nod of greeting, probably having forgotten her name. Dame Frevisse nodded back.

Anne and Lucie gave Pernell what distraction they could, but she startled at every outburst of noise, until finally to cover outside sounds Anne began a chanting, clapping game with Lucie, insisting Pernell take her turn, and when Mistress Hercy returned from whatever she had been seeing to elsewhere in the house, they drew her into it, too. Their cold suppers brought on trays ended it, startling Pernell with how late the day was gone, but as she began a worry over Raulyn, Emme came in, exclaiming, "The master's back! He's in talk with the men but said I should come tell you!"

"He's unhurt?" Pernell cried.

"Unhurt as ever can be," Emme said as if it were by her own doing he was here and unscathed.

Anne's unbidden thought was how much better it would have been if he had fallen in some wayward violence in the streets and never come home again. But Pernell gasped, "Praise to all the saints." And when Raulyn bounded up the stairs and into the parlor, exclaiming as he crossed to Pernell, "Here! I'm back! Safe, sound, not a hair on my head harmed," Anne's mind faltered away from the certainty Daved and the nun had built in her. Raulyn couldn't be what they said he was.

He kissed Pernell and swung around to the rest of them, saying grandly, "My ladies."

Daved appeared quietly through the doorway. Raulyn gestured to him with a laugh. "He's come to see I don't alarm you with wild tales but all I have is the truth. The tide is turning against Cade in London!"

"Has turned," said Daved far more calmly, "But isn't near to full flood yet."

"It's Cade's own doing," Raulyn said with unabated eagerness. "John Geste—you know, he has the house by Tower Street—had him to dinner today, trying to keep to Cade's good side, the fool. After his goodly dinner, Cade had his men strip the place to the walls!"

"Merciful Mary!" Mistress Hercy cried, and Anne and Pernell, "He didn't!" and "Oh, no!"

Carried by his own excitement, Raulyn went on eagerly, "There's only the beginning. He has his men searching the city for men he's named, taking their goods and them, and holding them to ransom. Though how they're to buy themselves free when he's taken everything of theirs he can lay his hands on . . ." Raulyn laughed. He seemed not to note that no one else did. "He's had another man beheaded, too. Not a Londoner. Someone the Essex rebels handed over to him. But he had Lord Saye's body cut into pieces and—"

"Enough," said Mistress Hercy.

With immediate contrition, Raulyn quickly kissed Pernell. "No more of that, my love, no. The thing is, though, that such of his men as Cade still controls are doing as much hurt as the ones he doesn't, and London isn't half-liking it." Pernell began a small whimper, but Raulyn snatched hold of her hands and said, "Not to fear. He's so far only interested in the richest of the rich, not middling sorts like us. Besides, we're safe as in a castle here. With the lane guarded and our own gates . . . Daved, tell her," he said as Pernell went on shaking her head from side to side, wide-eyed with her fears.

Daved, smiling, came to kneel beside her, took one of her hands from Raulyn and kissed it like a knight to his fair lady before he said, "Good mistress, I promise you there is no lady in London more safely kept than you are here."

Too frightened to be readily comforted, Pernell started to ask, "But what if they—"

"There was a man hanged himself for fear of all the 'what ifs' he thought of," Daved said, kind and solemn together. "We've done better than merely worry over 'what ifs.' We are barred and guarded and armed and ready for anything. No one will come near you or yours, we promise you. Nor will you have to endure much longer. A day maybe, but no more. London's lords will endure much but not being robbed of their earthly goods. There's where Cade has lost them. London will be making common cause with Lord Scales in the Tower before we know it."

"And this will all be done, and we'll be rid of Cade and his rebels," Raulyn said. "In the meantime we're well-guarded here, I promise you with all my heart."

"And with that promise," Mistress Hercy said to Pernell, "let you go back to bed and have your supper there. Raulyn will come with you. You, too, Lucie. Keep your mother company."

Daved stood up and aside, and Raulyn and Mistress Hercy helped Pernell to her feet and away into the bedchamber, Lucie drifting in their wake. From the window seat Dame Frevisse asked quietly, "Master Weir, do you believe what you've said about London and Lord Scales?

"I do indeed. I was out for a time, and matters are much as Raulyn said. Jack Cade will likely be unpleasantly surprised and soon."

"How bad will it be, do you think? When it comes to fighting."

"There's no way to truly say. We'll have to take it as it comes. Hopefully it will not come here. Now by your leave . . ." He bowed to her and Anne together and began to move toward the stairs.

Anne took a step after him, saying a little desperately, "Daved."

He turned again and she held out his doublet to him. "Mended," she said.

He returned and took it from her with thanks and nothing more, except everything she wanted to see was in his eyes, and she hid nothing in her look at him. Then he was gone, leaving her to yet more waiting. To waiting and fear and longing. Nor could she escape into the bedchamber to cope with Pernell's fears instead of her own, not while Raulyn was there. Daved, Mistress Hercy, and Dame Frevisse were so certain of his guilt, and their reasoning and proofs had brought her to believe it, too; but it was still so hard. Raulyn. And what if their proofs were not enough and there were no way, after all, to make Raulyn's guilt sure to jury and judges? What would they all do then, if Raulyn was accused and then acquitted?

Raulyn came from the bed chamber, passing through the parlor with a word and a smile that Anne returned before going to join Mistress Hercy and Lucie in keeping Pernell company. Twilight was well along. Night would be soon. Pernell wanted them all to stay with her tonight, and Mistress Hercy said firmly they would, promising for Anne without asking her, so that Pernell finally drank the wine her mother had mixed with valerian and a little poppy powder, Mistress Hercy saying, "There's nothing there will hurt the baby. Not so much as his mother grieving and worrying herself to death would do."

She even gave a little to Lucie, and soon both she and Pernell were sleeping. Anne wished she had a like escape, but Mistress Hercy did not offer it, only soon went away to her other business, leaving Anne to the night and her thoughts. It was plain weariness after last night that brought her, undressed to her undergown, to lie down beside Lucie on the truckle bed. She even slept awhile, but where two nights ago the darkness had been taut with silence and uncertainties, and last night been now and again broken with noises, tonight London seethed and stirred, and she was awakened time and again to listen as loud groups of shouting, laughing, or quarreling men passed on one street or another. Twice, shouted exchanges with the men keeping St. Swithins' barriers roused her sharply out of sleep, and although no fighting followed, the effort to sleep finally became too much and she gave it up and went to sit at the chamber's window, opening the shutter a little to the night. There was nothing to see but the black line of London rooftops against the blue-black sky and sometimes the trailing glow of torches carried along nearby streets.

She was still sitting there when Mistress Hercy came in, still fully clothed in her gown and wimple and veil, going silently by the small light of a carried candle to see how Pernell and Lucie did. She said nothing and neither did Anne, and she went away again, leaving the door a little ajar and Anne envying her that she had something to do besides wait. Unable to sit longer Anne stood up and moved silently to the door. Not wanting to waken Dame Frevisse if she were sleeping, Anne opened the door wider with great care but saw the nun sitting at the southward window, straightbacked and unmoving, looking outward. Like Mistress Hercy she was still fully clothed, a black shape in the shadows in her black Benedictine gown and veil, with only the strong line of her profile pale against the lesser darkness of the night sky. Anne stood still, watching her, wondering about her. What had brought her to be a nun? Had it been her choice or someone else's? Had there been a lost love? Or never a love? Or was love of God all and enough for her, the way it was supposed to be for a nun?

If the latter, then love of God hadn't been enough to keep her from prying where she had not needed to, Anne thought with an unexpected flare of anger at her. It was her questions and well-wittedness more than anything that had pulled apart the strands of seeming from the strands of truth, to find an ugliness so deep that Anne had a sharp half-wish it had never been found out. She accepted Raulyn's guilt because Daved did, but it was still only words to her, not something in which she fully believed, so that setting the cost of never having known it against the cost in deeper heartbreak and loss there would be now, where was the gain in having the truth?

Or would not knowing have cost more in the longer run?

There was no way to know, and wanting away from that unwanted wondering, Anne altogether opened the door and went into the parlor. Dame Frevisse turned toward her, became only a faceless shape in the darkness. Anne, hoping she was as faceless, sat down beside her. They neither of them spoke. The night was still just then, nothing to be heard but a distant scruff of sound that might have been almost anything. Dame Frevisse seemed willing to stay silent, went back to looking out the window again, but Anne, without knowing she was going to, asked in an anguished whisper, "These murders. How could Raulyn bring himself to them? If he did."

Readily enough that she must have already been this way in her own mind, Dame Frevisse answered, "My guess is that he's so narrow a man he sees only how he wants a thing to be and never why it *shouldn't* be that way. He sees only himself clearly. Everyone else's worth depends on how well they serve his ends. If it's their death best serves him, then they should be dead."

"But how could he bring himself to kill Hal? The friar, yes. But Hal."

"I doubt he had to 'bring' himself to kill Hal. Once he decided Hal dead was worth more to him than Hal alive, he simply made his plan and did it. Probably his only qualm was for his own safety. A blind belief in the rightness of his own greed probably made it easy." She paused, then added, "He very likely enjoyed it, too."

"Enjoyed it?" Anne echoed. "Killing Hal, you mean?"

"Killing him, yes. The power of life and death. Or of death, anyway. Having so much of what he desires in life, Raulyn may very possibly have now discovered the pleasures of death. There was an arrogance in the way he killed Brother Michael, as if he thought that having done murder that way once and been unfound, he could kill the same way again and be as safe. That people would be too blind to see how alike the murders were. He'll be in a fury at being found out. At the wrong we've done him by finding him out."

"The wrong done him?"

"As he sees it, the wrong in this won't be his but ours, for daring to ruin his plans," Dame Frevisse said evenly.

"And you have no doubt of him?"

"None."

Anne had wanted comfort of some sort and been given none. "It's going to be terrible," she whispered.

"It is," Dame Frevisse agreed, still gazing out the window. "That's how it too often is when lies can no longer be lived in."

Anne stiffened.

"The only thing worse," Dame Frevisse went quietly on, still not looking at her, "is living in the lies themselves."

Anne drew a short, hissed breath, then fiercely whispered, "I won't give up Daved. No matter what is said or what happens, I won't."

"And when the time comes," Dame Frevisse said with a quietness worse than any open challenge, "that it isn't a matter of choice but of necessity—what then?"

Frevisse waited, but Anne Blakhall made her no answer, only sat staring at her through a long and wordless moment before standing abruptly up and disappearing into the bedchamber again.

Frevisse was not happy to be left to her own thoughts. They were not the best of companions. She had kept night-vigils before now and knew how the hours passed at their own pace whether she was impatient with them or not. So she had learned patience and that prayer was the best way to pass them; but tonight thoughts came, not prayers, and while some were of London's danger and many were of the gold still hung from her neck in unceasing remembrance of how many troubles besides present ones there were, mostly her thoughts were of the crowded misery and fears all around her tonight, both in this house and beyond it.

She was trying yet again to pray, though the only words that came were *"Dies amara valde calamitatis et miseriae . . ."* —Very bitter day of calamity and misery . . . —when the parlor's darkness moved, and her heart lurched with unbidden fear that it was Raulyn come up the stairs so silently she had not heard him. Then she knew the shadow-shape was Daved Weir, and as he came toward her, one hand raised, warning her to silence, her heart found its pace again. Until he leaned close to her and said, hardly above a whisper, "Come with me. Raulyn is dead."

Chapter 28

ater, Frevisse would think that to have gone so trustingly with Daved Weir could have been foolishness, but at the time she did not question him until they were at the foot of the parlor stairs and then only asked, "What's happened?"

"Mistress Hercy," Daved said, and his grimness was enough that Frevisse asked nothing else, simply followed him into the hall and toward the solar and then up a stairway near it to the bedchamber where Anne must have been last night. Upon a time, it had likely been the house's best, and by day when full of sunlight was probably still a pleasant room, but tonight, in darkness and with the jerking light of a single candle with untrimmed wick juttering black shadows of bed and chest and chair among the roof beams and in and out of corners, it was a darksome place; and on the chair in almost the room's middle Mistress Hercy was sitting staring at nothing on the floor in front of her.

Frevisse stopped at the candlelight's edge, unwilling to go nearer until she understood more. Daved, a little farther into the room, said, "He's there. On the bed."

There was indeed a still shape among the bedcurtains' shadows, and still unwillingly Frevisse went forward to see him better. Fully clothed save for his shoes, he was lying in a tangle of bedcover and sheet, and there was no mistaking his quietness for sleep. Even aside from the eyes' empty stare and the gaping mouth, there was a sprawl and twist and slackness to him that had nothing to do with sleep, and Frevisse had the odd sideways thought that he had seemed goodly featured when alive but he was ugly now and empty—as if showing himself more truly in death than he had in life. She knew she was deliberately keeping her wild, sickened rush of feelings at bay behind carefully chosen thoughts as she said, "He was stabbed once. To the heart."

"To the heart," Daved agreed. "And only the once."

She turned to Mistress Hercy and found the woman had lifted her eyes and was looking at her, the candlelight harsh on her stoney face.

"You killed him?" Frevisse asked.

Mistress Hercy drew a slow, deep breath, straightened her back, lifted her head, and said firmly, "I killed him. Yes."

"In his sleep," Frevisse said, not asking.

But Mistress Hercy answered, her voice hard, "No. I wanted him to know he was going to die."

"He didn't lie there and let you kill him," Frevisse said.

"No," Mistress Hercy agreed, and that seemed the end of what she meant to say. She returned to staring at the floor, and the terrible quiet of death closed over the room again, until she suddenly went on, "I waited for him. When he came off his turn at street-watch, I was in the screens passage as if by chance. I told him how tired he looked and that he should go to my chamber to sleep, that he could sleep undisturbed here and the bed was better. I said I'd bring him some wine. He liked his comforts. He came here, and I waited a little, then brought the wine I'd readied for him. With Pernell's sleeping draught." She frowned a little. "There's not much left for Pernell now."

"We can get more from an apothecary," Daved said gently.

Mistress Hercy made a slight nod, but her gaze did not shift from the floor and again there was the silence before she went on, "I feared he'd taste something was amiss, but he didn't. He drank it all at almost a gulp. Swilled it so quickly he probably didn't taste even the wine. He thanked me." Mistress Hercy's lips twisted with a bitterness that had nothing to do with smiling. "I said he was welcome. Then I waited outside the door. When I heard he was asleep I came in and shoved at his shoulder. If I'd waited longer for the draught to work, I'd not been able to wake him at all, but he woke up enough. I stood there with the knife held over him so he could see it in the candlelight. When he understood . . . when he started to move a hand to stop me . . . I . . ." She gave up words on a shuddered breath and from her lap lifted a broad-bladed kitchen knife—clean of blood as any careful housewife would keep a blade after use, Frevisse thought, still trying to hold at bay the ugliness of it all.

"Like this," Mistress Hercy said, took hold of the knife's plain wooden handle with both hands, and drove the blade downward, only into air this time but with much the force she must have driven it into Raulyn's body. Then she sat back, folded her hands still holding the knife into her lap again, and said, "That way." But now she shuddered, and for the first time nightmare came into her voice. "I thought he'd just be dead, but he wasn't. He jerked. He kicked and he twisted. He . . ." She drew and let out a deep, shuddering breath. "Then he died. He's dead."

Evenly Daved said, "Death sometimes takes a man that way. But you made a clean kill of it. As sure a stroke as any I've seen."

"Too clean," Mistress Hercy said coldly. "He should have hurt for longer."

"That would have been good," Daved agreed. "But not wise. Now we have to do something with his body. It can't be found here."

For a moment Mistress Hercy made no answer or move. Then she raised her head and looked at him. "What?"

"We can't leave him here to be found," Daved said patiently. "We have to decide what to do about him."

"Is that why you fetched me here?" Frevisse asked, hearing her words scale upward with disbelief.

"Do you want Mistress Hercy to die for doing this?" Daved asked.

A wide array of things she could say back at him rushed into Frevisse's mind. Out of them she chose, "Raulyn was never found guilty under law. He was never given chance to answer any accusation against him. Now you want to hide his death."

"With all we learned and found, do you doubt his guilt?" Daved asked.

"No."

"Nor do I. So." As if that settled all questions about the matter.

It did not, and Frevisse demanded at him, "How do you come to be here at all? Mistress Hercy didn't come for you, surely."

"When I came off my watch in the rearyard, I met Mistress Hercy in the screens passage. We spoke. She seemed not herself, but none of us presently are, and I went up to my bed. A little later I heard her speaking to Raulyn below me and thought he would soon come up. He didn't. I slept a little, not deeply, and came full awake wondering what was wrong. You know how it can be? How a thought can work along below outright thinking, then be there suddenly, full and certain? There had been something in the way Mistress Hercy had been, and then Raulyn had not come to bed. Something felt wrong. I went looking for one or the other of them and found this. Now we need to conceal it."

Frevisse tucked her hands firmly into her opposite sleeves and lifted her chin. "What you want is that Mistress Hercy be kept from the law that would have to deal with her according to her crime for the crime it is, in despite of what Raulyn's crimes were."

Daved gave a small, single nod.

"You'd claim," Frevisse said, "that we should do it for the sake of keeping the wrongs Raulyn did from going further and to spare Pernell worse pain than Raulyn's plain death will be."

Still Daved said nothing. He did not have to. She had said it for him, and she turned on Mistress Hercy and demanded, "What did you mean to do after you killed him? Did you have any thought on that at all?"

"I meant to sit here until someone found me," Mistress Hercy said simply. "Then say I killed him, yes, but that I don't know why."

"They'd hang you then," Frevisse said harshly. "Or find you mad and put you into Bethlam hospital with other mad people."

"Yes." Mistress Hercy had already accepted that.

"And Pernell?" Frevisse snapped.

"Better she grieve for us both than know what he did. Better she lose us than lose everything and maybe come to hate her children because they're his."

And Daved wanted . . . what? Not to make everything right, surely, Frevisse thought with fierce impatience. Everything was gone too far past any hope of "right." To make it less bad, then, and God help her, she understood why. There was law and there was justice. If either of those was well-served here, the innocent would suffer the worst. And she turned a look that was mostly a glare on Daved and asked, "She's supposing, too, that you and I and Anne will say nothing about Raulyn's murders."

"She is, yes."

"You won't, will you?" Mistress Hercy asked, alarmed.

Frevisse shifted her glare to her. "What would be the point of it now?"

There had to be law—to keep the world from the kind of chaos Cade and his rebels had brought into London—but giving Mistress Hercy to the law would leave Pernell—who was guilty of nothing—with naught but grief and three orphans. Knowing what she was going to choose, Frevisse tried to believe she made her choice out of Pernell's need, not from her own deep dislike of Raulyn, who deserved to be dead, because no one deserved to be dead this way, with no hope of the soul's salvation. For that wrong against him Mistress Hercy would have to answer; but let it be to her priest in confession, not to the law, Frevisse thought; and said, "It will have to be you, Master Weir, who sees to having his body out of here."

"I'll find a way to that," Daved said. "What we need first to do—"

He broke off and moved with a suddeness to the bed, pulling the near curtain across it and swinging around to face the doorway all in a single movement, so that he was standing as if he had not moved at all, with one hand raised to hold Frevisse and Mistress Hercy silent as he asked, "Who's there on the stairs?"

Anne had slept a little and awoken uncertain of the hour and restless enough she had not dared stay with still deeply sleeping Lucie and Pernell. Finding Dame Frevisse gone from the parlor, she had gone restlessly downstairs into the silence there, hesitated, then come in search of Mistress Hercy. For comfort? For company? Simply for some place else to be, rather than parlor or bedchamber? She didn't know but had hardly started up the stairs when Daved demanded who was there and now she stood on the threshold, startled to find him, Mistress Hercy, and Dame Frevisse all there together, all looking at her as if she should not be.

Then Daved crossed to her as Mistress Hercy stood up, asking sharply, "Is it Pernell? Has her birthing started?"

Letting Daved, his hold too tight on her arm, draw her farther into the room, Anne said, "She's sleeping. She and Lucie both. I only thought, when I found Dame Frevisse gone . . ." She did not clearly know what she had thought, but looking at all their faces she asked, "What's amiss? What's happened?"

With no effort to ease it, Daved answered, "Mistress Hercy has killed Raulyn."

Anne gasped. But even as she made to deny it, she knew by Daved's grip on her and the look on his face that there was no time for the indulgence of refusing to believe him, and she forced herself to steady, so that Daved, seeing she had, let her go and said, "We're deciding now how to be rid of his body and hide what she's done. For now, I say we wrap it in a sheet and stow it under the bed here. By your leave, of course, Mistress Hercy."

"Of course," she said. "Yes, of course." The frozen resignation of despair was leaving her. Daved had given her hope, thin though it was, and beginning to shiver, she gave the bed a sudden, frightened look. "Blood. If he's bled through to the mattress, we'll never . . ."

"I'll see," said Daved. "Anne, see to her while I do."

More than willing to be told what to do, Anne took a cloak hanging from a wall-pole and laid it around Mistress

Hercy's shivering shoulders. Mistress Hercy grabbed one of her hands and held on, while at the bed Daved straightened Raulyn's body and partly rolled it over, then said, "All's well. The blade didn't go through him."

Mistress Hercy began to retch, and Anne hurriedly threw the cloak aside, helped her to her feet and to the basin on a table beside the door, keeping a steadying arm around her while she lost whatever of supper had been still in her stomach. Afterward, while Mistress Hercy washed her face, all the while saying under her breath, over and over, "God have mercy, Christ have mercy," Anne looked over her shoulder to where Daved and Dame Frevisse were finishing wrapping Raulyn's body in one of the bed's sheets.

Raulyn's body.

In some part of herself she did not believe that was Raulyn there—laughing, gallant, jest-laden Raulyn—a dead body wrapped into a sheet, with Daved now lifting it to the floor and thrusting it with no particular care out of sight under the bed. It wasn't Raulyn and none of this was happening. It was all nightmare. Everything for two days past was nightmare. When was she going to awake from it?

Plainly not yet. As she led Mistress Hercy back to the chair, Dame Frevisse and Daved finished straightening the bedcover over the bed, with Dame Frevisse asking him when they were done, "You have some thought of how to have him out of here with no one knowing?"

"London is going to rise against Cade and his rebels within a day, I would guess," Daved answered. "If we can keep Raulyn's body hidden until then, and when the trouble starts send most of the household men out to the fight and gather the women upstairs to the parlor . . ." He paused with that a question to Mistress Hercy. She nodded it could be done. ". . . that gives me a clear way to shift Raulyn's body away, out of the house." He looked to Dame Frevisse. "Perhaps with your men's help?"

"No," she said flatly.

Daved accepted that without question and went on, "We'll set them to guard the front gate then, leaving the rearyard to me. Some guard has to be kept, and the fight isn't ours. That's reason enough to explain why we don't join in. I'll take Raulyn's body out, away somewhere, and leave it in a street or alley as if he was killed there. There'll be bodies enough no one is likely to ask close questions about his."

Mistress Hercy had been regathering both her wits and her strength while he talked. Now she nodded and said, "That could work. Yes. We'll make it work."

"Understand," Daved said, his voice hard. "All of today you will have to seem as if nothing has happened or is going to happen. All of you. If we're found out, if Pernell ever knows, all of this is for naught."

"We'll do what has to be done," Mistress Hercy said. With hope, her will had come back. "All of us."

"Then do you and Dame Frevisse go away now to your beds. Sleep if you can. At least lie down and rest or you'll be no use to Pernell or even yourselves this day."

Mistress Hercy stood up, this time without Anne's help, but said suddenly, "The knife." She looked around to where it had fallen. "It has to go back to the kitchen."

"I'll see to it," Daved answered, taking it up and putting it through his belt at his back before he started for the stairs, saying, "Put out the candle." Dame Frevisse did, and in the instant darkness Daved ordered, "Give your eyes a moment to be used to it, then come."

They did, Anne standing aside to let Mistress Hercy and Dame Frevisse feel their way from the room and down the stairs ahead of her. Behind her, Daved closed the door with a small snick of the latch. In the hall the starlight through the unshuttered windows lessened the darkness enough for her to see the two women going away from her, but she stayed where she was, no word needed between her and Daved as he drew her into the solar.

With the door shut, they were as alone as they could hope to be, and still with no word between them, he guided her to the room's middle, turned her toward him, and took her in his arms. Wordless, they held to each other for a long, long moment, until Anne lifted her face to him and they kissed with a hunger not simply for each other but for comfort and some promise of safety that neither of them could give, until Anne pulled back a very little, drew a long, trembling breath, and said, hushed as if there were someone else there to hear her, "He's truly dead and she truly did it? This isn't a bad dream in a bad night's sleep?"

"He's truly dead and she truly did it," Daved said quietly. "Nor are we sleeping."

"Pernell . . ."

But the mere thought of Pernell kept Anne from going on. It was for Daved to say gently, "It's better she have this grief than the grief of knowing what Raulyn had done. He could not be left to go free, knowing what we know about him. But how could Pernell have lived with knowing her children had been fathered on her by the man who murdered her son? Mistress Hercy saw it clearly enough. There was no other way than this."

"I know," Anne whispered. "But Raulyn . . . I can't make it hold true in my mind that he killed the friars and Hal, too."

"I know," Daved said, the words hard and bitten. "I've had to work at holding to it. I thought he was my friend. I've trusted my life to him here."

Anne wished she could see his face, the better to guess how deeply his pain went, but all she could offer was, "He never meant for Brother Michael to know of you. He never meant."

Harshly, tightening his hold on her, Daved said, "He never meant that, no. What he meant was to have me gone so he could have his chance at you. What he meant was to open his way to greater wealth through Lucie's marriage. What he meant was to keep himself safe by way of the friar's death. Everything he did was for himself. At least when Mistress Hercy killed, it was for someone else."

Anne nodded, understanding all that, and leaned her head against him. Gently against her hair he said, "Pernell will have grief but never know all the worst. For that, your silence as well as Mistress Hercy's and the nun's will be needed. Can you do it?"

"Along with all else I keep silent about?" Anne gave a single, broken laugh. "Oh, surely." But the tears of her fear and misery were too close behind that laugh, and Daved gathered her more closely to him and for a long moment that was enough, simply to have him holding her.

But it was not enough when so much else was still unspoken, and against her hair he said softly, "You know that when this is done—as soon as I've done this thing—I'll leave London. Make my way to the coast, probably, and take ship from there. Away from England."

Holding more tightly to him, Anne whispered, "Yes."

"Let be whatever questions there will be about Raulyn's death, all that the friar found out against me may come out. I do not count on Master Naylor to keep silent on it, once other danger is past. I must not be here if he tells."

"I know," she whispered.

"You know that I'll not . . ." There was a break in Daved's voice that matched whatever was breaking inside of her; but despite her silent willing of him to say nothing more, he went on, "You know that when I leave, I'll not be back soon."

For a long moment Anne held off from answering that, then said quietly against his chest, "If ever."

A longer silence passed between them then before Daved agreed as quietly, "If ever. Yes."

Chapter 29

There was upset in the morning when Raulyn was nowhere to be found and those who had kept the gates swore he had come in and not gone out. Mistress Hercy fixed a hard look on Pers and declared someone had not been looking when he had. Pers protested loudly he'd kept *good* watch last night, which seemed to fix in everyone's mind that he had not and that their master had gone out for reasons of his own and would come back when he would, it was none of their business.

What Mistress Hercy told Pernell to keep her from worry, Frevisse did not know, nor did she see Pernell at all, which made the day somewhat easier than it might have been. But it was a long day, as days perforce were at midsummer, and made the longer with waiting for even one of all the things that might go wrong to go wrong. Frevisse spent it mostly at the parlor's southward window, pretending to read and trying to pray when the hours for the Offices came but mostly thinking around and around where her thoughts had already gone too many times. Now and again shouting surged from one place and another along London's streets, and there were shouting matches more than a few times at the barriers either end of St. Swithin's Lane, but still nothing came to fighting that she heard and that far, at least, her prayers were answered.

Anne, too, kept to herself except when with Pernell, sometimes pacing the parlor, sometimes sitting at the other window, twice sitting to sew with Lucie, taking both their minds from other things by teaching her a new stitch for her sampler; but never once did any word pass between her and Frevisse the whole day.

Father Tomas came in the late morning and spent a time with Pernell and Mistress Hercy, but he no more than sketched a blessing in the air at Frevisse and Anne as he passed through the parlor. Emme, when she brought dinner upstairs, said he had brought men who had carried Brother Michael's body away to the church, to lie there for the crowner to see and until the streets were safe to return it to Grey Friars. "Whenever that may be," Emme gloomed as she went away.

Frevisse expected Daved Weir to bring some word of what more was happening, if only to have the chance to speak again with Anne, but he did not. Master Naylor came in early afternoon during one of the whiles she was alone to say that all was much as yesterday in the streets. Keeping impatience from her voice—if only barely—Frevisse said, "That much I've been able to hear for myself." Then brought herself to ask, "Has Master Grene returned?"

"Not sign of him nor any word. Master Weir has been up and down the street asking after him." Master Naylor paused. Frevisse could almost see the question he was chewing over before, not sounding much as if he wanted to, he asked, "What do you mean to do about this Master Weir and his uncle being Jews? Since I doubt Master Grene will do aught, now the friar is dead."

"I mean to do nothing."

"Nothing?"

"Now they've been found out, they'll leave and not come back, surely."

"It could have been the uncle who killed the friar."

"Do you think it was?"

Master Naylor gave her one of his long-faced looks. "If he had, my thought is he'd have finished the matter by coming in after his nephew and had him out of here, one way or another."

"That's my thought, too."

"So we do nothing about them? Despite they're Jews?"

"We welcome Master Weir's help while he sees Master Grene through this trouble. Then he goes and doesn't come back. That will be enough."

Master Naylor considered that before saying, "Aye. That would be my choice. There's trouble enough without making more."

"Is there any talk of Cade being forced out of London?"

"There's been some word running that way, yes."

"Will London do it, do you think?"

"Who knows with Londoners?" Master Naylor said and went away.

And the waiting went on, into the beginning of the long summer evening, with the clear sky colored rose and cream by the westering sun and fear beginning to twist inside of Frevisse that after all London would not rise against Cade. Not today anyway.

And then the waiting was done.

Anne, in the parlor with her then, knew it was Daved on the stairs and was on her feet and going to him, her hands out, as he came into the parlor. He met her as readily, clasping her outstretched hands, pulling her to him, wrapping his arms around her in an embrace she returned as fully as she returned his kiss.

Frevisse waited where she was, and when they had done, he set Anne back from him and ordered with edged excitement, "Best bring Mistress Hercy to hear, too."

Anne went immediately into the bedchamber, leaving Frevisse and Daved to each other, neither of them saying anything because there was nothing to be said in the few moments before Anne returned with Mistress Hercy, who went straight to Daved, looking ten years older than she had yesterday but asking firmly as she came, "Is it time?"

"Lord Scales is out of the Tower with his men, headed for the bridge, and the mayor and aldermen have called up the wards and are moving to join him against Cade."

"God save us all," Mistress Hercy breathed, signing herself with the cross.

Frevisse and Anne copied her. Daved did not, only went on, "Cade heard something was afoot and spent the afternoon drawing his men out of London, back into Southwark. He probably hoped that if he showed good faith that way, he could go back to dealing with the mayor and all again, but London means to take back the bridge and gates. That's where the fight will be, at the far end of the bridge."

"Will that be enough to let you do . . . this thing?" Mistress Hercy asked.

"There's still trouble enough scattered through the streets, with straggles of rebels and London troublemakers in plenty and likely more at it once night falls."

"When will you do it?" Mistress Hercy asked.

"As soon as it's full dark."

A burst of rabbled noise, muffled by buildings rather than distance, swung all their heads toward the southward window. It might have been anything, but as the sound rose into a clamor that could only be of men meeting with weapons and in anger, Daved said, "It's started. What I need from you now, Mistress Hercy, is to come with me to tell your household men they can go out to the fight. They're jumping out of their skins with wanting to. They won't pause. The street barriers are still manned, so they're not needed here. I've already spoken to the Naylors and agreed they'll keep the foregate, and me the back. Once you have the women up here, it's only a matter of waiting until I judge it's dark enough to go."

Unexpectedly Anne said, "I'll come be watch for you in the house and at the gate."

Daved paused, then gave a single, sharp nod. "When the first star shows, come."

Mistress Hercy pressed a hand over her mouth, her breathing suddenly gone rapid and shallow. She had maybe been looking aside all day from what they meant to do and now was seeing it clearly for the ugly thing it was—a man's body taken out and left somewhere like a dead, unwanted dog's. Even Raulyn's and despite he was dead because of her. But Frevisse had never looked aside, and when she met Daved's level gaze, their understanding measured and matched each other's, both of them knowing the only thing worse than doing the thing would be not to do it.

No, worse would be to attempt it and fail.

And hiding her own other thoughts, Frevisse asked, "We're ready, then?"

Mistress Hercy drew a long breath, steadied, and said, "Yes."

Anne only nodded, wordless.

Daved, with a warm certainty that both lifted them and carried them forward, said, "Good then. Remember, my ladies, what's done is done. Let's do the rest and be done with all. Mistress Hercy, I told the household men I'd come to plead your leave to let them go. Pray, come now and give it."

Mistress Hercy gave a crisp, assenting nod and sailed past him toward the stairs as if she had never faltered. Daved followed her, and Anne watched him go before turning away to the window overlooking the yard again. Frevisse joined her there, and in silence they watched the household's men, clubs in hand, stream down from the hall and away across the yard and out the gateway. "Done," Anne said; and added without looking around, "You'll have to be the one who sees to Pernell."

"And now, I think," Frevisse said, because the women were already chattering up the stairs, and even if all else had escaped Pernell, that would want explanation. But she found that all else had not escaped Pernell. She and Lucie were together at the bedchamber window, worried over what they were hearing from the bridge without being certain what it was.

When Frevisse told her, though, Pernell was more pleased than alarmed, saying, "Thanks be to God it's going to end," and with a hand on her belly and the other braced on the seat, lowered herself to sit there at the window. "That's where Raulyn has been all the day, then. Helping to ready the ward for this. He might have sent me word. Why are men so single-witted?"

She seemed not to expect an answer, and Frevisse, her choice either a lie or silence, chose silence.

From here nothing of the bridge was to be seen, and the distant clash and formless shouting of the fighting told little of what was going on, except it came no nearer, sign that thus far the Londoners must be holding their own. In the parlor the women talked, but in the bedchamber there was little to say and less to do, and finally Lucie curled up on the bed in all her clothing and went to sleep. Pernell soon lay down, too, saying, "I'll only rest a while," but shortly her breathing likewise evened into sleep, and Frevisse, still at the window, was alone with her own thoughts. Full dark was come. More stars than only the first were out. By now Daved must have Raulyn's body out of the house, was likely even quit of it. And then he'd be away, soon to be quit of England, too, and back to his true life.

But which was his true life? He lived in lies so many-layered, did he even know anymore which of his lives was true, which one a lie? She had known people who had come to think the lies they lived in were their truth. Did Daved live so deeply in his lies, they were become his truth?

She laid her hand over the pouch still hung about her neck under her gowns. So many lies. And some of them hers.

So many lies. So many deaths. So many deceptions and treacheries. So much greed and fear. And love.

Frevisse folded her hands into her lap and bowed her head and prayed for the love there was between Anne Blakhall and Daved, for the men fighting on London bridge—those still alive and those already dead—and for Raulyn's doomed, damned soul.

She did not know how much later it was that an outcry among the women in the other room made her raise her head, first looking around to the bed to be sure Pernell and Lucie, for a mercy, still slept; then out the window where she saw the orange glow of fire off a black roil of smoke blotting out the sky above London bridge. The bridge was on fire. In the other room, after their first outcry, the other women's voices went on, hushed and strained. Mistress Hercy came briefly into the bedchamber to be sure of the sleepers, then came to Frevisse and said in a whisper, "He must be away by now."

"Long since," Frevisse agreed.

Mistress Hercy stood a little longer, looking out at the fire-stained smoke, then went away, leaving Frevisse to her thoughts and watching. To her relief in a while it was clear that the fire was not spreading; and by the time the eastern sky was well-paled toward dawn, the battle-clamor had lessened; and by the time full daylight was come there was nothing left to hear but a few distant shouts and nothing to see but a drift of grey smoke thinning across the sky. The rebels had not won their way back into London.

By then Pernell and Lucie were awake and Mistress Hercy had brought in their breakfast tray and the news that all the household's men were come lag-footed home, tired and dirty but no wounds among them, and all the women were in the kitchen with them, feeding them and demanding to hear about everything. The last Frevisse heard as she slipped out to the parlor was Mistress Hercy saying, "No, not Raulyn yet, dear. Give him time."

Eating without much interest the dry bread and cheese waiting for her in the parlor, Frevisse found herself fervently hoping Master Naylor would soon say the streets were safe enough for her to return to St. Helen's. Cowardly though it might be, she wanted to be away from here before Raulyn's body was found.

She had done eating when Anne came slow-footed into the room. Like Mistress Hercy, she looked older. Frevisse had meant to say nothing to her, but with her discretion weighed down under her tiredness she said, "You didn't go with him."

Going slowly to the window seat where she had sat so much of these few days, Anne sat again and only then, as if she had just heard Frevisse's words, said softly, "No, I didn't go with him."

Not able to ask if she understood how small was the likelihood he would ever come back to her, Frevisse found herself saying, meaning it, "I am most sorry things are as they are."

Anne raised her head and looked out the window. Tears

shimmered in her eyes, and her gaze was inward-turned to some place deep inside herself; but calmly and with a pride that came from that far inward place she said, "Whatever else, I am his *eishet chayil*. That will have to do." And took up the embroidery lying there unfinished and began to sew.

Author's Note

To begin at the very beginning, let me say the title was the most ongoing of troubles with the book. It was to be called *The Seamstress' Tale*—until I learned that *seamstress* was a word first made in the 1600s, when older, non-gender-specific words began to be given new endings to differentiate women doing something from men doing the same thing. The older, common words for anyone who sewed were *semster* and *sempster,* and fearing that neither of those would be clear to a potential reader, I wavered back and forth and among other possibilities, but such things as *broiderer* and *brawdster* didn't look likely to ease the problem. But neither could I quite bring myself to the unperiod *seamstress,* and I wish to express my thanks to members of the CrimeThruTime list who took time to tell me what they thought, and my admiration and appreciation of my editor Gail Fortune's patience with me while I made up my mind. Not to mention her patience and sustaining help in general!

My particular thanks go to Susan Weintrob, not only for the first suggestion that I do a story with Jews ("How?" I remember protesting. "There hadn't been any Jews in England since 1290!") but also for keeping me from errors. Such as may be have come from my failure to ask her something that I should have.

Thanks must also go to Chris Laining who has not only made a wonderful rosary for Frevisse but helped Anne Blakhall at her work by guiding me toward such works as *The Conservation of Tapestries and Embroideries* with its inspiring close-ups of medieval embroidery rich with gold thread and pearls, and the invaluable *Medieval Craftsmen: Embroiderers* by Kay Staniland, besides advising me at length on what was period in sewing and what was not. If there are errors, it's because I didn't listen to her well enough.

My research to understand Daved Weir and his double life ranged from children's books about Jewish religious life as a starting point through to such studies as (but not only) Dean Philip Bell's *Sacred Communities*, Jeremy Cohen's *The Friars and the Jews: The Evolution of Medieval Anti-Judaism*, Mark R. Cohen's *Under Crescent and Cross*, John Edwards' *The Jews in Christian Europe 1400–1700*, Menahem Mansor's *Jewish History and Thought*, James Parkes' *The Jew in the Medieval Community*, K. R. Stow's *Alienated Minority*, and Erwin I.J. Rosenthal's "Anti-Christian Polemic in Medieval Bible Commentaries" in *The Journal of Jewish Studies*.

Much told here is true. Among other things, there was a German bishop in 1450 who ordered all Jews out of his territory, and forced baptism was a frequent threat—and practice—against Jews. Oddly, the House of Converts—*Domus Conversorum*—founded by King Edward I not long before expelling all Jews from England, meant for the support of Jews impoverished by turning Christian, survived in almost steady use more than 300 years longer. A list of its inmates through those centuries and speculation on where they came from can be found in *Jews in Medieval England* by Michael Adler. There, you will find Joan of Dartmouth and her daughter Alis named among the inmates from 1409 to 1449 and 1454 respectively.

As for the persistent insistence through the late Middle Ages that Jews ritually murdered Christian children, pope after pope ruled and decreed that no such murders were taking place or had ever taken place. Pope after pope forbade anyone to act on such false rumors, and pope after pope was ignored. In the same way, mob violence against Jews broke out again and again despite the Church's orders to the contrary, including the Council of Bourges ruling in 1236 that "Faith must be kept with the Jews and no one may use violence towards them . . ."

This same ignoring of orders held true of papal opposition to the inquisitorial activities of the Dominican and Franciscan friars. Originally given a brief to work against Christian heretics, many of them made grounds to extend their power to include Jews, exactly as detailed in the debate between Daved and Brother Michael. In despite of repeated papal orders to desist and a papal bull in the 1420s attempting to restrict their claimed authority over Jews, they built up a centuries' long reign of terror against Jews and anyone suspected of being Jewish, mainly in Spain and Portugal but sometimes raising its ugly head in other parts of Europe. For some friars it was probably seen as a holy crusade: for others—well, a convicted heretic's property went to the Church.

I came across no outright evidence of such secret Jewish efforts as Daved's in the 1400s, but there is no doubt of such activities hardly one hundred years later in London, as discussed in Cecil Roth's "Jews in Elizabethan England" in *Transactions of the Jewish Historical Society of England,* and I've no reason *not* to suppose like activities had happened earlier.

For coming to understand bills of exchange and something of international banking well enough to use them in the story, I am grateful to Raymond de Roover's works, especially *Business, Banking, and Economic Thought in Late Medieval and Early Modern Europe.* Of course there is the small bother that the word "smuggling" is from the 1600s, and therefore Daved could not smuggle the gold into England. Hence the need for "illegal conveyance." Nor could Cade's rebels "loot" in London, that being a Hindu word unavailable in England in the 1400s. They couldn't even be a "mob," according to the *Oxford English Dictionary.*

The English uprising in the summer of 1450 did follow the course of events detailed here—or something *like* the course of events given here. The several contemporary and near-contemporary chronicles agree on what happened but not always on which day or in which order things occurred. My reconstruction of the course of events derives from what seems to me most likely—that the London government could put up with Lord Saye's and Crowmer's deaths, brutal though they were, but turned on Cade when he began wholesale seizures of property and money. That this ordering differs from I. M. W. Harvey's conclusions in *Jack Cade's Rebellion of 1450* does not lessen in the slightest my great indebtedness to that very fine coverage of the revolt and its aftermath.

Concerning London itself, some readers will find my description of it at variance with the cliché of filth-ridden streets stinking of garbage and ankle-deep in mud too prevalent in some presentations of medieval London. Whatever may have happened during the breakdown in society that came with the Renaissance and Reformation, the plethora of medieval civic laws concerning streets—paving, repair, and cleaning as well as lighting—would seem to indicate an active effort in all those areas. Certainly John Stow in his later *Survey of London,* when talking about officials in the city's wards, includes scavagers (*non sic*) whose job was to keep a ward clean. Regular, frequent removal of waste was expected and failure fined. London probably smelled in ways we would now find unfamiliar, but have you choked on the exhaust of a passing bus lately?

The biblical quotations are translated from John Wycliff's Middle English version of the Bible.

Enjoy the rich historical mysteries from Berkley Prime Crime

Margaret Frazer:
Dame Frevisse Medieval Mysteries
Joliffe Mysteries

Bruce Alexander:
Sir John Fielding Mysteries

Kate Kingsbury:
The Manor House Mysteries

Robin Paige:
Victorian and Edwardian Mysteries

Lou Jane Temple:
The Spice Box Mysteries

Victoria Thompson:
The Gaslight Mysteries

Solving crimes through time.

penguin.com

GET CLUED IN

Ever wonder how to find out about all the latest Berkley Prime Crime and Signet mysteries?

berkleysignetmysteries.com

- *See what's new*
- *Find author appearances*
- *Win fantastic prizes*
- *Get reading recommendations*
- *Sign up for the mystery newsletter*
- *Chat with authors and other fans*
- *Read interviews with authors you love*

MYSTERY SOLVED.

berkleysignetmysteries.com

Penguin Group (USA) Online

What will you be reading tomorrow?

Tom Clancy, Patricia Cornwell, W.E.B. Griffin,
Nora Roberts, William Gibson, Robin Cook,
Brian Jacques, Catherine Coulter, Stephen King,
Dean Koontz, Ken Follett, Clive Cussler,
Eric Jerome Dickey, John Sandford,
Terry McMillan, Sue Monk Kidd, Amy Tan,
John Berendt…

You'll find them all at
penguin.com

Read excerpts and newsletters,
find tour schedules and reading group guides,
and enter contests.

Subscribe to Penguin Group (USA) newsletters
and get an exclusive inside look
at exciting new titles and the authors you love
long before everyone else does.

PENGUIN GROUP (USA)
us.penguingroup.com

3 1170 00803 7883